I0670274

The Kelton Cases:
The Lost Princess

—

By K. A. Bledsoe

Brick Cave Media
brickcavebooks.com

The Kelton Cases:
The Lost Princess

Cover Illustration Artist: Christian Bentulan

Brick Cave Media
brickcavebooks.com
2025

Dedication

For Dad.
Sorry I didn't get this out in time.
You would have loved it.

The Kelton Cases:
The Lost Princess

By K. A. Bledsoe

Chapter One

Lenore Kelton felt the vibration and consulted the screen on her wristcomp.

Neg 3 lvl. Q.

Lenore was so used to the codes that she translated it without conscious thought: *Nothing to report on the third floor. Quinn.*

She acknowledged her son and sent her own message back. *-1 neg. Main, u 4th* which meant there was nothing unusual in the basement, and she would inspect the main floor next while Quinn checked out the fourth level.

A single pulse indicated his reception, and she climbed the stairs to the main floor of the academy. Three schools in this city had been attacked by a lone gunman who opened fire then disappeared before any security was enabled. Eleven people had been killed so far. Her information indicated that this school was next, so she and her son Quinn were scouting ahead. There was a reward that had been posted privately for anyone who could give information on the killer.

Despite being only fifteen years old, it was easy for Quinn to use his talent at disguise to become a transfer student and was on his second day of studies. She had simply signed on as a substitute teacher, since the usual staff had been calling in sick, to nobody's surprise.

There was plenty of time left in the lunch period to check in with the ship. She tucked her long, light brown hair behind her ear as she tapped her hearing implant twice and gave the subvocal command to call the ship.

"Hey, Mom. What's up?"

Lenore smiled at her daughter Allison's cheerful voice. "Things are looking pretty peaceful here. Are you sure this academy is next?"

"Yes. As I already pointed out," she said with one of her dramatic sighs, "with the previous attacks as a baseline, a sociopath, as I am sure this guy is, has a distinct pattern even though it seems random. Whether an intentional or subconscious pattern is irrelevant. The next attack will be at that school, I am certain."

Lenore could even hear the smug smile, well-earned since she had seen Allison's "certain" correct ninety-nine percent of the time. "Ok, I trust your instincts. I will check in again tonight."

"Sure, Mom."

Lenore tapped her implant twice again to close the communication and then pressed and held it for a few seconds to activate enhanced hearing. As she resumed her walk toward the main hall, she tried not to be concerned. Allison was talented at figuring out criminal minds, but Lenore worried that by repeatedly doing so, her daughter might become a bit like a sociopath herself.

As Lenore entered the lunchroom, her eyes flicked around as she automatically analyzed and memorized the position of students and teachers. She suppressed a snort of derision at the security guards, weapons holstered and the safety probably on. The precaution was no doubt required in a setting with children but useless in any planned attack. Her gaze landed on a janitor entering the hall pushing a mop in a rolling bucket ahead of him. His worn coveralls and heavy work boots fit in, but her gut and past experiences told her something wasn't quite right. Her tension rose as instinct kicked in.

It would be here, now.

The janitor reached into the bucket, and Lenore's earpiece picked up the distinct *click* of an automatic weapon's safety being disengaged. She dropped her bag of books on the floor and primed her defenses in a single heartbeat, touching each like a ritual:

Right palm—needle dart with paralyzing drug

Left wrist—gravitic grapple

Necklace—personal body force field

Right foot—electric dampening field

All these mechanical wonders were courtesy of her husband Diarmin, a mastermind at creating machinery that enhanced her natural skills and were camouflaged well, matching her light skin perfectly.

The "janitor" raised a weapon that she recognized as an expensive laser repeater capable of firing at least thirty shots per second.

"All bow to the Enforcer!" he yelled as he aimed into the crowd of students and teachers eating lunch.

The expected shots never came. As people dove under tables, Lenore pulled back her right foot and threw her left wrist forward. The tiny grapple snatched the gun out of his hand and flew it to hers as her right palm shot out. The gunman grabbed his neck and perceptibly stiffened in reaction to the paralytic dart. Lenore's right hand returned to hover over her hidden stunner even though she knew it was unnecessary. The electrical field she had activated with her foot kept him from sending or receiving any signals so that he was basically helpless.

But before he fell to the ground, lasers hit him from two different sides, vaporizing over half his body. Lenore cursed under her breath and just barely stopped her reflex of retaliating against the security guards.

Well, there goes my interrogation. Amateurs.

Chapter Two

Diarmin pulled himself along the weightless ship, frustrated.

"Drat that girl," he muttered to himself. "There's only so much room on this ship. Where is she?" Not on the bridge where she was supposed to be, nor in her room, or even the bathroom. Diarmin had come from the cargo bay below deck, so the lounge was the last place to look other than the crawl spaces. He heard vague sounds coming from the room ahead.

"Finally," he muttered to himself.

A shout made him pick up the pace. He pulled himself through the doorway in time to see his daughter on the large viewscreen, a huge club swinging toward her head. Before he could call out, she dodged and fired arrows into the monster, an ogre large enough to tower over Diarmin's six-foot frame.

"Allison, what are you doing?"

The eleven-year-old started at her father's voice then pulled off the VR helmet and cursed. "I was winning until you distracted me." In the weightlessness, her dark springy curls surrounded her head like a corona. That was why Diarmin kept his own black curls cropped short.

"You left the viewscreen on."

"Oh, oops." She turned toward the screen, the game tether keeping her in place. With a twitch of her wrist, she used her controller to change from bow and arrows to a sword. The image of Allison, now in full armor, was seen from behind with the ogre staring menacingly as if he could see into the lounge. Allison wielded the control as if it were the sword on the screen and engaged the monster.

"Why are you playing instead of working on the bridge?" Diarmin pushed off and floated across the lounge to grab the VR helmet before it drifted away.

"Mom already checked in," she said, attention still on the game. "And you know how Mom is. No matter what happens, it will be exactly four hours before she checks in again." Duck, jab, block.

"And if there is an emergency?"

"You're here, aren't you?" She swung her arm and the ogre roared. Blood spattered across the screen and background, but both were still fighting. "Besides you know the systems are designed"—stab—"to override"—parry—"oof...and inform of emergencies."

"Alli." Diarmin sighed, losing patience, but didn't speak as he saw the ogre bring his club down heavily. Diarmin winced as the image of his daughter crumpled. He knew it wasn't real, but it still was difficult to see.

"Well, that'll do it," said Allison as the character on the screen let out a roar, shaking the club over its head. "Game over. I am getting closer to defeating that ogre, though."

"Back to the bridge. You are on duty."

"You said Mom and Quinn wouldn't be home until tomorrow." She answered as she stripped off all the gaming equipment, stowing it in a large container before she shut down the game.

"Yes, but I expected you to actually start looking for a new job, so we can have it ready when she gets back." A quick jerk of his head indicated to his daughter that they should return to the bridge.

Allison rolled her eyes. "That only took me fifteen minutes." She undid the tether that held her in place while playing in zero gravity and grabbed her personal pad from between the cushions of the couch, stuffed there so it wouldn't float away. He glanced back as she pulled herself along the corridor behind him and noticed her open a file while absently flitting from handhold to handhold. Diarmin took the pad from her and gave a single, practiced yank on the ladder, letting physics do the work of propelling him to the level of the bridge. Not taking his eyes off the pad's screen, he used his foot to stop his upward motion, then pushed away enough to give Allison room.

A large ad was prominent on the screen. "REWARD FOR ANY INFORMATION LEADING TO THE MISSING PRINCESS OF THE PLANET SULOUS." A brief report with details followed the dramatic headline.

"Not sure if this is a case, Alli. Let's see the date... Allison, this ad is over seventeen years old! Its original posting was a year before that."

"Yes, but look." She bobbed up beside him, grabbed a handhold and pointed at the top of the report. "It was updated five days ago with a new contact and even a bonus if delivered within the time indicated right there." Her finger moved to the relevant phrase. "The reward money would cover what we need to repair or even replace our grav plates with plenty to spare." She retrieved the pad and floated to her personal console next to the navigation board, both stations closest to the viewscreen.

"But someone missing for eighteen years? What are the chances there's any sort of trail left for us to pick up?" Another push of his foot and Diarmin was at the command console in the center of the bridge. The command chair was named so because it had complicated boards built into it as well as on both sides of the chair. A person seated there could access any system. One tap by Diarmin indicated their yacht, a remodeled cargo ship, was still in the same spot as it had been for the past three days, in a stationary orbit of a moon of one of the outer planets of the Gruis system. Close enough for communication with his wife and son currently on the planet Carmal, but far enough from detection by planetary security.

"Hey, I thought we were the best. You wanted 'not dangerous and pays well,' so there you go." Allison shrugged. "Besides, I already downloaded the original files from the local law enforcement and can pick out several places to start digging." She grinned as she rapidly rubbed her hands together.

Diarmin shook his head. "What have I told you about breaking into systems?"

Allison put on her most innocent face. "Don't get caught?" She laughed and turned back to her console, fingers already madly typing. Diarmin smiled and felt extremely proud of his young, genius daughter. He didn't want to think about what shenanigans she would get up to when she hit puberty.

Chapter Three

"Would you mind explaining yourself?" Lenore demanded of the principal after what was left of the body had been carted off. The students and teachers had been sent home, so the principal had insisted they return to his office for privacy. She was now seated facing him across his desk. In the other two chairs were the hired security guards who had committed the wasteful act.

"I think you need to explain a few things first," he responded as two additional local police officers entered to stand behind her.

Lenore ignored the show of force and raised her chin slightly, deciding to take the offensive. "You were informed by your superiors to stand down, that someone would be undercover and handle any situation, were you not?"

"Well, yes, but…"

"And by ignoring those instructions, you ruined the operation."

"Now see here…" The principal was turning red, but Lenore didn't care. "I didn't want my students in danger, young lady."

"They were not in danger." Lenore gritted her teeth to keep her temper in check, especially after the "young lady" remark. "I have been hired by a private service to bring in the shooter." A lie since Lenore only worked for herself, but it never hurt to pretend someone else was giving the orders.

"Security handled it just fine," said the principal.

"You aren't listening. I was supposed to bring in the man. Your people made that impossible."

"But now that the crazy loner is dead, the threat is neutralized. The case is solved, and schools can rest easy."

"On the contrary, the academies need to be even more afraid now," said Lenore, taking little pleasure in the principal's look of total confusion. She sighed and continued. "I am not at liberty to discuss details, but that shooter was just a pawn, a front for another, more dangerous, organization."

"Who?" asked one of the security guards, the woman who had fired first. Lenore turned her head to look at her with clear disdain.

"We will never know now, will we? Because someone had an itchy trigger finger."

The woman's face darkened, and she opened her mouth to retort, but the principal waved his hand to cut her off.

"What makes you think there is an organization behind this and not just one lunatic who had a grudge against schools?"

Is this oaf worth my time and patient explanations of all the legwork my family and I have put in? Lenore considered for all of half a second. "That is privileged information, and I am not required to share any of it with you or these people." She flicked her wrist to indicate security guards and law enforcers alike.

"On what authority?"

"On my authority as a Xa'ti'al."

Silence fell over the group, with one gurgle which might have been a laugh forced back.

Lenore smiled inwardly. There were always some who wanted to laugh but didn't dare. For fear of reprisal or out of respect for the mercenary group, it didn't matter. She sat quietly, waiting for the others to speak first. Her bet was on the principal. The officers behind her shuffled their feet and, in doing so, backed away a little.

"That's...ahem."

I win, she thought as the principal cleared his throat of a squeak.

"That's impossible. The Xa'ti'al are just a myth."

"Perhaps, or perhaps not. Regardless, you are in my way and keeping me from doing my job." Everyone else visibly paled at that. "And have made it a lot harder." Lenore stood, taking advantage of the paralysis that seemed to afflict people whenever the Xa'ti'al was mentioned. "If you are finished spouting nonsense, I need to finish the job." She spun and exited without looking back.

Five steps down the hall her wrist vibrated. She glanced at the message which was fully printed out now that they were not in alert status.

Nice, Mom. Why didn't you just pull out a gun? Probably would have scared them less.

Lenore grinned. She should have known Quinn would have an ear in the room. She sent a quick note back.

Get the info?

Of course. Also, extraction completed. See you at the hotel.

Lenore double tapped an acknowledgment and continued. The mission at this school was finished, and Quinn had taken care of clearing documents and any other indication that they had been there, including recording devices or photos. He was exceptional at nonexistence.

Ten yards from the door, her heightened hearing caught footsteps behind her. From the sound, she guessed it was the female security guard hurrying to catch her before she left. She was tempted to ignore her and quicken her pace to leave before she caught up. She hated this part of being a Xa'ti'al more than the fear and disbelief. But she should play the role.

Lenore heard an intake of breath, so she turned and stood with her hands clasped behind her back, trying to appear harmless as she waited for the young woman. The guard slowed her pace and closed her mouth; evidently, she had been about to call out to ask Lenore to stop.

"You have a question for me?" she asked, tired of waiting for the girl to overcome her shyness. "Eithne, isn't it?"

"Yes," said the guard on an exhale. "How did you know my name?"

Lenore shrugged and didn't bother to mention she had memorized all the information about every member of the faculty and most of the students. "There are always some who aren't afraid to ask questions."

As expected, Eithne's eyes sparkled with excitement as words began tumbling out. "How did you become a Xa'ti'al? I thought I saw the shooter paralyzed. Was that you? And did you really grab his gun with the powers of your mind? I remember it flying to your hand. How is that possible? And what..."

Lenore held up her hand to stop the barrage. Eithne blinked and visibly struggled to be quiet.

"I cannot give away my secrets." She smiled gently. "But I am amazed at how accurate some guesses are." She watched Eithne's chest swell with pride. It never hurt to perpetuate the myths that the Xa'ti'al had certain supernatural abilities when, in reality, it was simply amazing technology. "And you don't ask to become a Xa'ti'al, they will find you if you are worthy." She always wanted to laugh at that line, but this girl had no chance to ever join the elite ranks. Lenore could tell; she'd seen it countless times. She nodded a farewell and turned to leave.

"Wait! Is...is there any advice you can give me?"

Lenore bit her tongue on the sharp retort and instead looked back at the expectant guard. Might as well try to help her, do something good with the idiotic mythos for a change.

"Think before you shoot."

Chapter Four

"Ok what did you pull from the corpse? It better be good or our trip home will be delayed," said Lenore as she entered their room. She carefully deactivated the various devices hidden about her person and stripped her gear off, packing them in their respective storage cases lined up on the bed.

"Hello to you, too," Quinn said sarcastically.

Lenore didn't bother to comment since Quinn always tried to impose manners on the family and they equally tried to ignore him.

He sighed. "I got three clear prints and remnants of identification in the pocket that wasn't disintegrated. Fake, of course, so Allison will have to run a trace for the manufacturer. That should lead us to the organization."

"Excellent. Wait, how did you know the ID was fake?"

"I did a retina scan."

"The head was vaporized, how..."

"I managed to pull a scan before he was so dramatically interrupted."

"You did?" Lenore searched back through her memory, rather surprised that she didn't notice her own son in the room. "The blond student with the green striped shirt?" In answer, he flourished the wig he'd had tucked in an inner jacket pocket. "That's a new one. Impressive. Except..." His grin at her praise disappeared as she continued. "Why weren't you on the fourth floor like you were supposed to be?"

He turned away, packing his own bags. "The top floor was completely deserted. I had nearly finished when you contacted me, and I knew everyone was down at lunch." He shrugged, trying to appear nonchalant yet wouldn't look directly at her. "I was hungry, too, so I figured it would be less out of place if I were in the lunchroom."

Now he looked up, and Lenore could see a slight challenge in his stare.

"Good thing I was," he said.

"No, the good thing was that I was there. If I hadn't

been, you might have been killed."

"Aw, Mom. I know how to duck. And besides," he gave her a lopsided grin. "You're always there, so I knew I was safe."

Though Lenore didn't feel this subject was over, she let it drop as she grabbed a pile of clothes and headed for the bathroom. "I'm going to shower. Send what you pulled to your father and sister. With the information gathered from the body and fake ID, we should wrap this up on time."

"Already done." Quinn bowed with a smile and indicated the pad on the table. "Just waiting for a response."

Lenore nodded, trying not to look too approving. Quinn went back to whatever he had been doing when she came in, probably sorting his various disguises.

As Lenore showered, she tried to decide how she felt about her fifteen-year-old son now able to create his own covers that were good enough to fool her. Granted, he was gifted with the perfect features for camouflage. His skin was an exact mix of her white and his father's dark brown, very easy for makeup to alter. Straight, sandy-colored hair about finger length that took dye and/or curling almost too easily and hid under a wig with no effort. A subtle lens or choice of clothing easily changed the color of his gray eyes. On one hand, she was proud of his burgeoning abilities. But on the other, she knew he would want more difficult duties, and she didn't want any of her family in that kind of position. Safer cases meant less money, but it was worth it to keep her family out of harm's way. She was grateful that her daughter preferred computers, and her husband preferred tinkering with his inventions, so that they were safe and sound back on the ship.

Chapter Five

"They are nearly in range," yelled Diarmin as the ship rocked. "That one was too close. What's wrong with the shields? They won't activate."

Her father didn't look away from the screen as he was too busy attempting to escape their attacker, but Allison knew that he trusted her to find the problem.

"The computer worm is chewing away at the shield program as fast as I can build it back up," she replied. "I told you that last site I hacked into might cause problems."

"Yes, but we got the information your mother needed, didn't we?"

"But finding that drug lord's hideout is what downloaded the worm into our systems. It gave our ship's location to them and is also eating away all the other safety protocols as well."

"Tell me something I don't know."

"Ok, how about this? In about two minutes our reactor will..."

"Hold that thought," Diarmin said as he punched at the controls, taking the ship into a wild spin. Allison braced herself as the ship arced around and jolted as he launched two concussion missiles in rapid succession. The screen lit up with a fiery blaze near the rear of the craft and the attacking ship spun on its axis, engines sputtering out.

"Ha, that'll help," Diarmin said and punched in some more commands "Back to the original course. Now what were you saying, Allison?"

"I was going to say our reactor would go critical unless you stopped them. Now, I can focus on the shields aaaaaaaand...there, back up. Worm vanquished, and the Grand Master Allison Kelton defeats the enemy again." She pumped her fist into the air and then snickered.

"What did you do?" asked her father.

Allison turned wide eyes his way.

"What? Nothing?"

"Alli, what?"

"I just thought I'd give as good as we got."

"What?"

"Only a little something to remember me by."

"Tell me Alli or I swear..."

"I introduced my own worm. One that collapsed their shields and will also destroy all their own worms and viruses. Their firewalls are gone, and anybody can see their files. *All* their files." She hit a key and turned the computer screen, so her father could see it. The picture was of a nude butt with the caption "I'm an ass! Free info about this ass courtesy of the Pirate Peri!"

Diarmin shook his head. "Allison Catherine Kelton, how many times have I told you..."

"I cut the link, Dad, and wiped the origin data. There is no way this can be traced back to us."

"But you use that Pirate avatar way too often. That will eventually be recognized."

Allison felt an excited rush as she smiled. "I hope so. That's how hackers become famous!"

"And get caught. No more avatar viruses."

"Yes, Father," she said as she crossed her fingers behind her back.

Chapter Six

"Well, that was a bit anticlimactic," said Quinn.

"Hm. Can't argue with that." Lenore and her son were watching the local authorities cuffing the few people that had escaped the burning building. The information Allison had found led Lenore to this place, which housed a drug lord who had used the school terrorists as a distraction to keep the authorities focused on the shooters, allowing for easier illicit activities. Lenore had reconnoitered, planted several bugs, and had planned the best way to take them down when all hell broke loose.

People, random citizens as far as Lenore could tell, had gathered outside the building, yelling obscenities. As she mused on how to get past them to avoid detection, a few of the mob started throwing Molotov cocktails through the windows, and within moments the entire building was afire. Authorities pulled up far too quickly to be called for a fire and, instead of arresting the drug lord and his cronies, they were forced to rescue them from a massive blaze. She and Quinn watched from a safe distance as the group was dismantled and the bosses taken into custody.

"Destroy the bugs, please," Lenore said to her son.

"Already done. Well, the ones outside. The fire obviously took care of the rest."

Lenore gave a grunt in approval, but she was baffled.

"What went wrong?" she muttered. Nobody she had met in this city, much less on this simple planet, had the knowledge or abilities to crack this case. Yet someone else had figured it out and given up the criminals.

"Maybe this." Quinn held up his personal comp pad which displayed a local broadcast explaining that the criminal organization had been betrayed from within. Someone had leaked all the private information about their illegal activities to the public on both WorldNet and IntergalacticNet, or IGNet as it was commonly known. Her best guess was that the outraged people attacking the building were the victims of said criminal activities.

"It doesn't look like anyone has claimed a reward,"

commented Lenore as they both scanned the news stories. "Not even the school for killing the patsy shooter."

"Maybe we can still...um never mind." Quinn turned up the volume on the reader as another story aired, this one about a rumor of Xa'ti'al involvement.

"This just in: We have an anonymous source who can confirm the rumor and claims to have met the legendary Xa. Thank you, noble soldier, whoever you are, and that the only reward you seek is justice."

Lenore clenched her teeth on a groan as she felt her stomach turn. She should have known that mentioning the Xa would come back to haunt her, most likely thanks to the principal or security guard at the school. Anyone who truly knew the Xa'ti'al knew that they never did anything for free. But the damage was done.

So, no reward money for her and her family. That was annoying but not as much as someone beating her to the punch, whoever this "source" was. She longed to find out who it had been, but it would change nothing and only waste their time. Quinn nudged her out of her reflections. He seemed to know her thoughts.

"At least we will get home when we originally promised."

***

In less than twelve hours, the shuttle docked with the family yacht in a new orbit around the planet nearest to Carmal. Lenore gave her husband a hug, and then touched middle finger and thumb to Allison's, her daughter's preferred method of greeting.

Quinn bounced up and down on his toes. "Hey, you fixed the grav plates, Dad."

"Rigged up an alternate, but I have no idea how long it will last this time," replied Diarmin. "Don't leave anything sharp lying around."

"I hope you have another job," said Lenore, as they headed down the ladder toward the cabins. "This one did not end up as planned."

"Really?" asked Diarmin, eyeing Allison. "Why is that?"

Quinn answered. "For some reason, the authorities and random citizens got to them before we could. Someone publicly broadcast their identities and crimes. Everyone saw them and reacted as any mob would."

"Hm. Wonder how that happened?" Diarmin looked significantly at his daughter.

Allison blushed, not easy to tell with her dark complexion unless you knew her well. Which her family did.

"What did you do?" Quinn and Lenore asked in unison.

"All I did was recode their worm program and reintroduce it into their system to destroy their security," answered Allison. "Only on the ship's computers, but it must have been linked to the planetary base as well."

"So, someone noticed and went hacking, broadcasting the files for everyone to see?" asked Quinn.

"Well, I...um...wish I could say that but..." Allison hung her head and began to shift her weight from foot to foot, worrying at imaginary dirt under her fingernails.

"Explain, Allison," said Lenore, noticing her daughter wince at the curt tone.

"The parameters indicated an automata-based program, so when I refactored the code—"

"Don't try to confuse us with tech-talk. In laymen's terms please," said Diarmin.

Allison sighed. "I didn't realize part of the program was a unifying link to all connected systems. It's how they gave our location to the ship that attacked us, so when I reversed it, it did the same with the files, sending to anyone who had a system within receiving distance."

"Ship? Attack?" Lenore now looked at Diarmin and by the sheepish look on his face, it was something he hadn't planned on revealing. "Let's circle back to *that* later, shall we?"

"You cost us a job. We needed that money," Quinn said to his sister.

"Not to mention it could have cost us our lives," said Lenore.

"No way," Allison vigorously shook her head. "There was absolutely no possible way to trace that program back to the ship or to you two. It was a completely different class, not even a sub—"

"But what if we had been in that building when the mob attacked?"

Allison's head jerked up, eyes wide in surprise. "I didn't know. I'm sorry. It was an accident...I thought...I..." She didn't finish.

Quinn threw up his hands, swung his bag over his shoulder and disappeared down the ladder toward his cabin.

Lenore just stared at her daughter until she squirmed

and turned even a darker red. "A week's resources, gone."

Allison bowed her head again. Her hair drooped, no mean feat for such long spiraled locks. After a few moments she gained her voice. "I did find another job. Pays twice as much."

Lenore looked at Diarmin, but apparently, he was letting her take the lead. Lenore sighed. She wasn't good at this sort of thing. Facing down terrorist shooters and obstinate people was simpler than trying to get through to children. "Well, Allison, I know you didn't mean any harm, but in the future, consider all the possibilities."

Allison looked up and nodded, hope in her eyes.

"I will consider various punishments, which we will discuss later."

Allison's face fell again, and Lenore finally relented enough to put out a hand in a beckoning motion. "Well, let's have that new job."

"I'll get the reader. It's at my station." Allison raced down the corridor toward the bridge.

Before following, Lenore headed down the same ladder as Quinn to carefully place her storage case in the cabin closet and toss the clothes duffel on her and Diarmin's bed. She eyed the duffel with envy, wishing she could toss herself on the bed beside it.

Can't rest yet, she thought. She left the bedroom, continued down the corridor and ascended the other ladder to the bridge.

Allison's fingers flashed on the keyboard, downloading data into the personal reader. She handed the tablet to Lenore then returned to her computer. Lenore eyed her as she joined Diarmin at the command console, knowing her apparent contriteness wouldn't last long.

"The original report is years old. How are we supposed to pick up such an old trail?" Lenore shook her head.

"Now, you've done more with a lot less, dear," said Diarmin. "Remember that family heirloom that had been lost for three generations?"

"And a princess? Surely such an important person would have meant the most extensive searches and investigations."

"Well, then those will be well documented, and you can find out where they went wrong like you always do," he replied.

"Mmm," she said, pursing her lips and giving him a sour look. "Don't think your attempt at flattery is going to distract me from our little discussion." He reddened, but she wasn't sure if the embarrassment was because she caught on to his ploy or that he hadn't mentioned the attacking ship. "I suppose you have already read this," she said, still somewhat irritated.

Diarmin answered in a soft voice. "Of course. And done a bit of investigating as well."

She didn't know which annoyed her more, him using that tone to calm her down, or the fact that it was working.

"And are there one or two missing girls? These reports say two, but most focus on only the princess."

"Alli and I were confused about that as well." Diarmin rubbed the side of his nose. "We even researched stories from the planet, both news and whatever passes for folklore these days. Some mention only the missing princess, some that she had a companion with her. Almost nothing is known about the other girl, so we assume it was a random friend who happened to be with the princess that day."

"The princess is the one with the reward anyway. Okay, let's contact this person, um..." she scanned the reader again. "Beltan. Set up a meeting."

"Ok...done," Allison piped up from behind her screen.

"What?"

"I had a message written and ready to go, so I sent it out like you said."

"Did it occur to you that maybe we should read it first?" asked Lenore.

"Well, here it is, but I just copied the basics from all your previous first contact messages and wrote a similar one with the new information. Easy enough."

"And how did you get all my previous contact messages? From my protected files?"

Allison shrugged. "It wasn't that hard. I used my hacker program number five and simply..." She trailed off when she saw their faces. "Sorry, I only wanted to help."

Lenore rubbed her forehead. "It's a good thing your intentions are honorable. Well, mostly anyway. First of all, don't do it again and second, you can apologize by writing a hacker-proof security wall for my files."

"No such thing as 'hacker-proof,' Mom. But I can get close." Allison grinned as she grabbed her stuff and disappeared down the stairs to her cabin.

"How many eleven-year-olds get that excited about being allowed to write a program that will take up most of a week?" asked Diarmin.

"The same number as can take down a drug lord and his entire operation with a computer virus." She crossed her arms, not quite willing to let the subject go.

"Hey," Diarmin held his hands up. "You know how good our kids are at figuring out ways of keeping things from us, finding a way around the rules."

Her mind flashed on how Quinn's new disguise had deceived her so well. She pressed her lips tightly against a retort.

"Well, you taught them," she snapped irritably.

Diarmin shook his head. "Not that. I only taught the basics like any public school. When they developed their own interests, they learned those skills on their own." He waved his hand in the direction of Allison's terminal. "How many people, of any age, are as much of a genius at programming as she is already?"

"None." Lenore shook her head. "I only worry what will happen when she realizes that fact."

"Sell her services to the highest bidder? Come on, we raised her better than that." He pulled her into his arms.

Lenore leaned into him. "But what if she doesn't have a choice? What if something happens to us despite our careful selection of jobs? And then there's the reason we disappeared in the first place."

"Reason?"

"Okay, several reasons. Which reminds me, is the ship's identity scrambler turned on?"

"Of course. And Alli added two new ones."

"Good." Lenore pulled away. "Wait, why did she write new ones?" Her eyes narrowed. "The attack?"

"That, and the other thing I think you know." Diarmin tried to pull her back into an embrace, but she shook him off and took two steps back.

"How did you...oh, never mind." She put her fingers to her temples. "Damn that boy. He is so sneaky. Did you know that he was in the room when the shooter attacked?"

"He is worried about you. And don't change the subject. This is the third time this year you have let slip your connection to the Xa'ti'al. It's like you want them to find you."

"It's the quickest way to cut through the crap and get idiots to butt out."

"You always say that."

"It's true. You've seen the reactions. You had a similar one when we first met as I recall." She grinned at Diarmin.

"Flirting won't distract me either. If you keep this up, the kids will find out that the Xa'ti'al never voluntarily let anyone leave the order, and that they will stop at nothing to get you back into their ranks. Or punish you for deserting."

"Well, they haven't caught us yet, and I don't intend for them to." She twisted her hair back into a knot. "I was the best they had, and I know their limitations. Besides, with your inventions," she leaned in to give a peck on the cheek, "I know we can get out of anything they plan. Enough of this gloomy talk. Let's find something for dinner and talk about this job. It might pay for new gravitational plates, or at the very least, a meal that doesn't involve you cooking."

"Hey, I'm a better cook than you. It's one of the reasons you married me."

"Can't deny that."

Chapter Seven

The *Roberto del Esponja* yacht was docked at a platform in the largest city on the planet. The contact was unable to meet in a small out-of-the-way town like Lenore usually preferred. But this ship identification was one of Allison's new ones (where she got them, Lenore had no idea), so she felt as safe as possible in a major port.

As usual, Lenore had put a lot of thought into this meeting, thoroughly reading all the information Allison could find on the planet and the contact. Strangely, not much could be found about him, not even a last name, though the normal amount of data existed about the planet. She sat in the lounge with Diarmin, reader pads spread across the dining table.

"Language will most likely not be an issue," she said.

"How can you be sure? The planet has a native language, the population is mostly Earth-Hindi descent," he answered, tapping on the relevant pad.

"It says that children are taught Standard in the schools. Since Lavan's last message was in Standard, we know he's educated."

"Wait. Lavan? I thought his name was Beltan?" said Diarmin.

"That's the name he used, but since there was nothing in the database about any Beltan, Allison used his picture from the last message to cross reference and find his real identity. This." She held out a printed sheet of paper with a picture. "It was hard to find, but you know Alli, very in-depth searches. His name is Lavan, and we can see he is young boy, about sixteen or seventeen. But since the reward is substantial, he must have access to a great deal of money, and thus is not a person to inadvertently insult or cross. The big question is if I should take anyone with me."

"Well, even though the native people have mid-brown coloration nearest to Allison, she is the least comfortable with people and would not enjoy leaving her beloved computers," said Diarmin.

"You're nearly as bad with your 'beloved' machines to play with."

Diarmin grinned. "And I don't enjoy crowds. So that leaves Quinn. His ability to blend in and adapt to any situation would be very helpful."

"But he is still young and inexperienced." Lenore grimaced. "Not to mention his tendency lately to do his own thing regardless of the possibility of danger." She shoved the pads around, not really reading them but pondering the possibilities. Diarmin cleared his throat, and she knew she wouldn't like what he was going to say.

"If this contact is about Quinn's age, then a local boy about the same age might put him more at ease. Quinn could easily disguise—"

Lenore waved her hand to cut him off. "Lavan also could be either extremely intimidated or enamored of a mature woman, especially if I presented myself as an important figure. I think the Baroness persona would do fine." She began gathering up the pads.

"And Quinn? You know he has been asking to go with you to learn negotiating skills."

"I don't want to put him in danger. Stop," she said as Diarmin opened his mouth to argue further. "I'll give it serious thought."

***

That night, the night before the meeting, Diarmin turned to her in bed before they fell asleep.

"Look, if this is going to be the family business, we need to let *all* the family learn *all* parts of it. I don't like the idea of Quinn or Allison in a dangerous situation either, but how are they to judge what is safe and what isn't unless we give them a chance to learn? And to be honest, this seems like a standard missing person case with the victim most likely dead long ago. Minimum danger."

"The school was supposed to be minimum danger for Quinn, but he was there when the shooter showed up." She rolled away from Diarmin, not liking the idea at all. He rolled with her, snuggling his front along her back, draping an arm around her waist. He laid a chin on her shoulder to speak softly in her ear.

"You'd better start teaching him where you can keep an eye on him. He's bound to start trying more stuff on his own if you don't. Look how well he plants monitors and takes photos. He learned most of his skills by only observing you. Not to mention his uncanny ability at disguises."

The tension melted out of Lenore, and she rolled over to face Diarmin.

"How did you get to be so wise?" Her left hand cupped his face while the right one caressed the tight curls on his head.

"Tinkering with machines all day gives a person time to think," he replied. He buried his face in her hair. "And I know how boys think." He pressed soft, full lips on her shoulder.

"Hm, yes. I know what you are thinking." She reached lower. "I can feel it, too." Diarmin didn't answer except to cover her mouth with his, move his hands down her back and gently pull her against his body. Lenore responded with heightened excitement as she always did before missions.

Chapter Eight

Lavan fiddled nervously with his drinking glass trying not to look as out of place as he felt. He hardly ever left the palace, and, in fact, this was the only restaurant he knew of close enough to walk to. He tried not to stare at the other customers and wondered for the tenth time if he was doing the right thing. Nobody knew where he was or that he was meeting with strangers who might or might not find the missing princess. Would they be friendly? Rude? Dangerous? Would they even take him seriously? Was this a bad idea?

Lavan had arrived early and had been waiting for what he felt was suspiciously long, even though no one appeared to be paying any attention to him. He was dressed in clothes he had borrowed from the stable boy weeks ago in hopes of being able to meet someone who would take the job.

The place was growing crowded with adult clientele. The sun had set hours ago, and families were probably at home preparing for sleep. Some people at the tables were obvious romantic liaisons and other tables held groups of drinking friends or perhaps colleagues. Lavan felt singled out being a lone diner and hoped his contact would show soon.

A tall, elegant woman wearing a flowing, colorful dress entered the restaurant followed by a servant boy. The clothing and her pale coloring marked her as an offworlder, but visitors from other planets were common enough in this city due to the large spaceport. Lavan noticed the woman drew several glances, but only of appreciation of her exotic beauty, not for suspicion.

The servant boy looked like a native of the planet so was probably a local, hired as a guide. But as the lady's eyes met Lavan's, he knew this was who he was waiting for. The lady looked at her servant and nodded. A thin, tall man pushed in front of the maître d' to greet the duo. Lavan knew the man as the owner of the restaurant, but it was the boy, not the woman, who spoke with him, heads bowed in deep discussion. After only a moment or two, they shook hands. The owner bowed to the lady and led them both to a door beyond the kitchen.

Several minutes passed and Lavan thought perhaps he had misconstrued the situation, that they weren't the ones he was supposed to meet. He resumed his watch on the door. The sudden sound of a throat clearing immediately to his left made his heart jump.

"The Baroness Delilah requests your company in the private salon, sirrah Beltan." The offworlder's servant boy bowed respectfully.

Startled at the sudden appearance of the boy, Lavan momentarily forgot his false persona.

"Um, I need to pay..."

"Already taken care of, sirrah. This way, please." The boy's hand indicated the direction.

Lavan stood and made his way toward the back. He supposed he should be annoyed at their presumption, like the prince would have been, but instead he felt a sense of relief. These people seemed quite competent. He needed them to be if they were going to find the princess who had been missing for eighteen years.

As he entered the room, he noticed the lady was seated behind an empty table in a cushioned chair. She indicated a similar chair across the table, so Lavan sat in it. To his surprise, the servant boy pulled up one of three other hard-backed, cushionless chairs to sit at the table as well.

"I hope you aren't offended by my preference for privacy," she said. "I am Delilah, and this is my assistant, Hewel."

"Pleased to meet you, Baroness."

She laughed softly. "I am not a Baroness. When it is assumed one is rich and holds a position of power, people strive harder to please."

Lavan nodded, knowing that truth, having grown up in a palace.

"So, tell me, young sirrah, how may we help you?"

"It is very simple. I wish you to find the girl who went missing eighteen years ago."

"I have read the reports you sent. I also have read the original reports when she disappeared, as well as those of the various officials who looked for her in the past."

She paused, perhaps to see his reaction to the oblique admission that she had illegally obtained those documents. When Lavan merely nodded, she continued.

"What I need to know now is anything unofficial that you can tell me. Any information that you can give that might help after so long."

"What sort of information do you mean?"

The boy spoke for the first time. "Like why someone who wasn't even born when the girl disappeared wants to find her now."

Lavan jerked in his seat, not just because he had dismissed the boy as irrelevant, but he was also taken aback by the question. He felt his cheeks grow hot as he looked away. He had a story worked out that wouldn't reveal who he was, but he hadn't expected confrontation right away.

"How much do you know about our planetary politics?"

"I am familiar with how your system works but tell me your view."

He took a big breath and rapidly delivered his rehearsed speech. "The democratic council has the powers of the people, but the king, or queen when we have had one, has always had an important part. His opinion carries a lot of weight, and people tend to follow what he prefers. But the current king has become ill and, in truth, has not been a powerful force in the last years. Fortunately, the way the system was designed allows the king to be overruled or relegated to simply a figurehead when he is not an ideal ruler. The current king is much beloved by the people because he was a brilliant and capable man until his personal tragedies. You see, the missing girl was his daughter, and he never recovered from her disappearance. I think if his daughter could be found, the king would regain his health and be more like his old self again."

"That makes sense," said Delilah. "But I also know that most of the general populace have no knowledge of the king's weakness because the rest of the planetary leaders hide the fact. How is it that you know of this?"

"I...I work in the palace, so I see the king in his private time."

They both nodded, and Lavan relaxed since they appeared to accept this explanation. Until Hewel spoke again.

"But how does the current prince feel about finding his long-lost sister?"

This time Lavan felt he covered his response better, but he could feel his cheeks warm again as he answered. "I did this on my own. The prince does not know about reopening the investigation."

"Why not?" asked the boy again.

Delilah narrowed her eyes at Hewel, obviously annoyed with her assistant for speaking out of order. But he ignored her, keeping his eyes locked on Lavan's face.

"I, um, feel he would not appreciate a rival."

"How—" was all Hewel got out before Delilah cut him off rather forcefully.

"What my assistant is trying to ascertain is if the position held by a king is just a figurehead, why would it matter to the prince to have a rival?"

"All siblings have rivalries, don't they?"

"Do they?" she retorted.

Silence descended on the small group. Delilah tapped her fingers on the table and Hewel simply stared. Lavan knew they didn't quite believe him, but he kept his mouth shut, not wanting to go further. He was in enough danger as it was. Finally, the woman broke the silence.

"All of this is very interesting, but you haven't told me anything that I simply couldn't find out listening to local gossip or news feeds."

Hewel reached into a vest pocket and pulled out a paper, laying it open on the table between them.

Lavan saw a picture of the prince and himself standing behind the king at the opening of a new upper-level academy in the city.

All his ideas and attempts at intrigue came crashing down. *I should have known it wouldn't be like stories and entertainment shows.* Not knowing where to start, Lavan tried to calm his racing thoughts.

"If I am going to help at all, I need to know things that aren't public knowledge, things that can't be told to just anyone, and maybe even things that seem obvious to you but might be meaningless to others. For example," Delilah pointed at his right hand. "What is the significance of that tattoo on your wrist?"

Lavan simply stared, thoughts still jumbled, not sure how to respond. She gave him a gentle smile, most likely trying to put him at ease.

"Other people I have met in this city have tattoos, but yours has such exquisite detail. And there is a similar one on the hand of the prince. And, though it isn't easily seen, there is an intricate tattoo on the king as well, but of a different pattern. So, I am assuming you are closer to the prince and king than you let on."

Lavan's shoulders slumped and he looked down. He could no longer stay anonymous, but she didn't seem to be anxious to turn him in for blasphemy or reward. The fact of her skills only proved to him that if anyone could help him, she could. So, he would tell her everything.

"This," he held out his hand, palm up so that the tattoo on his wrist was visible, "is the mark of the Heir's Companion."

Chapter Nine

Delilah spoke in a whisper to Hewel who disappeared out the door. Before Lavan could settle his thoughts and emotions enough to figure out what to do and say next, Hewel was back with a tray carrying two glasses and a bottle. Delilah poured two glasses and pressed one on Lavan. He downed it in one gulp, recognizing an extremely expensive strong liqueur that the prince and his lackeys often drank. It burned all the way down his throat and lit a small fire in his stomach. Relaxation spread through his entire body, steadied his nerves, and, strangely enough, gave him courage. He could see why people got addicted to these sorts of beverages. He noticed Delilah merely sipped, but the smile she gave Lavan indicated she knew it was exactly what he had needed. She poured a little more in his glass and set the bottle in front of him.

"Now," she said. "Start from the beginning."

"When an heir is born, they are marked on the edge of the right palm with a special tattoo that is a royal identification. As I am sure your, um, assistant can tell you"—he waved a hand at Hewel—"within the first couple years, another child of the same age is chosen to become a lifelong companion. Then he or she is tattooed with the same symbol on their wrist so that when hand to wrist is grasped, the symbols align." He attempted to demonstrate this with his own hands, but it was awkward, so he just continued. "Private citizens get their own tattoos to mimic the royalty, but what is known to only a few is that there is more to the bond than just ink. Most believe the tattoo is simply tradition, but the fact is that the prince and I are linked in strange ways." He took a tiny sip of the liqueur and noted that it burned less. "I really don't know how it works or why, but when one of us is sad or sick, the other feels it as well. I know the prince can sense things in me like...like pain."

Lavan swallowed against the memories but continued. "I am supposed to be aware of these things too, but I only feel a whisper of a connection. I...my bond with the prince is different because..." his voice dropped to a whisper, "I do not like him. He lives to torture. He has never known pain or strife and enjoys hurting people."

Lavan looked earnestly at Delilah. "He must never become king, and the only way I can think of to prevent this is to find the first heir, the lost princess Maya."

"But, again, if a bad king is kept from power by the ruling council, why would it matter?" asked Hewel.

"Understand that I could be imprisoned, perhaps even executed, simply for talking to you about this. In fact, I think the only reason Prince Hahn has not gotten rid of me is because he does not know how the bond will resonate, perhaps even harm him. But he detests me as well, and I will tell you all since I have no one else to turn to. No one in the palace would dare speak out for fear of retaliation against their families. I have no family, and there is little worse the prince can do to me."

Lavan swallowed again, trying to drum up the courage to speak and fighting the urge to look over his shoulder for eavesdroppers. "The prince is very skilled at hiding his cruel side. I may be the only one who knows his true self."

He took a deep breath and finished the rest of the liqueur in his glass. "The prince is supposed to be officially confirmed as Heir when he turns eighteen next month, but he is not content with the title. The problem is that he plans to have more power in the ruling council, eventually doing away with them altogether, to be the sole voice of authority. At first, I thought the prince was merely being immature, saying such things to seem older and more important as young men do. But when he started to make the plans a reality, I began to take his rantings seriously. Now he has already got several 'strings' in place and controls more than a few of the current elected officials. I am not sure how far it has gone, and I cannot do anything against him. My role as Heir's Companion is supposed to be one of support and protection, so I am powerless to openly oppose him. If Maya returns, she is the only one who can challenge his right to rule."

"May I see the mark again?"

Lavan held his hand out to the woman, and she took it gently, lightly running her fingertip along the pattern. He wasn't sure, but he thought he felt a slight tingling where she touched. Her eyes flicked to Hewel who nodded very slightly.

"So, tell me," she said, still holding his hand. "Does—"

She was interrupted by three short, loud pings from Lavan's wristcomp. Lavan snatched his hand back and stood up abruptly.

"I have to go."

"But there's more to discuss."

"You don't understand. That signal was from the guard who is supposed to be keeping me under lock in my rooms. The prince is on his way back from his nighttime revels, and if he finds out I am gone..." Lavan shook his head, not even willing to imagine the consequences.

Hewel grabbed his arm. "Quickly then. The girl with the princess when she disappeared. Was that the princess' official companion? And was her tattoo the same as yours?"

Lavan stared. The story of the missing princess and her companion was a favorite tale told to little children at bedtime. How could a local boy not know of it? Hewel shook his arm slightly. "Her tattoo?"

"It was different, unique. And, yes, they were together at the time. Really, I have to go."

"Get us a picture of that tattoo." Hewel shoved a paper in the companion's other hand. "This is the new contact code." He released the prince and said in a whisper, "We will meet again. Soon."

Lavan fled.

Chapter Ten

"Pay the bill," Lenore told her son. He looked surprised at her gruff tone but went to pay the manager. While they had learned much from the young companion, Quinn's first contact had been less than exemplary.

As they left the restaurant and walked down the street, Lenore could tell by Quinn's nervous adjusting of his clothes that her silence was getting to him.

"Why are we going this way?" he leaned in close to ask.

"Because this is the way I am going, and you are to follow me." Lenore saw Quinn's face darken at the rebuke, but he didn't get the hint and kept on.

"Why did you interrupt me in there? I had, Beltan, or Lavan, whatever. I had him telling the truth. I could have gotten more..."

"First of all," Lenore said through gritted teeth, her voice low, "you were supposed to be observing, not participating, and second, I am discussing nothing further until we are home."

"But, why..."

"And you are not behaving like a proper servant boy."

"The job is over, we're heading home. Why do I still need to act?"

"Because we are being followed."

***

Outside of the eatery, a woman watched Lavan race out the door. She took only a moment to decide whether to follow him. The cowardly companion would run scared back to his hole. The elegantly clad offworlder and her young assistant were the ones to follow, so she pretended to enjoy her caf while engrossed in her personal tablet. Her features marked her as a native of the planet, almost too thin, which belied her strength. Scars, mostly unseen, spoke of a rough past, but she seemed more than capable of having earned them all.

She didn't have long to wait before the two came out

and left in the opposite direction than Lavan had. Also, a different direction than they had arrived from. Interesting, mused the woman. She stuffed her cheap, second-hand tablet in her ragged bag slung over her shoulder and tossed her cup in the trash. Keeping to the many night shadows, she tried to follow close enough to overhear them, but the noise of the city streets let her catch only a few raised words. Oddly enough, the woman got the impression that they were arguing, though their faces seemed calm and pleasant enough. And the way they interacted spoke to the woman that the two were far more familiar to each other than just a lady and a hired servant. It didn't make sense since she was clearly an offworlder and the boy a local.

While they argued, their erratic wandering made no sense. They weren't heading toward the spaceport as the woman thought, nor were they heading to the district that housed offworlders. They also didn't seem to be angling for transportation of any sort. In fact, if they kept going, they would shortly be in an area of the city that most visitors, especially the wealthy, studiously ignored and avoided. She knew it well. It had been her home for the past five years.

Wait, the lady was tapping something into her wrist comp. *Paging a ride? Sending a message?* The two stopped chatting, and the one trailing them was trying to think of a way that she could figure out why they had been meeting with the Prince's Companion. Talk to them? Pretend to be a reporter? A beeping from her bag interrupted her thoughts. She fumbled it out quickly since the sound was attracting attention from the two she was following. *Who would be calling her now?* She knew few people and not one of them knew she had a tablet, much less her contact information.

She yanked it out and flipped it open just as the sound stopped. A couple taps indicated a contact she didn't know, and no return message was attached. Couldn't be an ad. Probably a cross transmission, a simple mistake. Annoyed, she shoved it back in the bag and turned back.

But the two she had been following were gone.

Chapter Eleven

Lavan entered the palace grounds through the servant's entrance, breath coming fast since he had run most of the way home. Why was Hahn back so early? He usually stayed out until near sunrise, drinking and doing who knew what with his friends. The prince termed them his "council," but in reality, they were spoiled upper class boys all quite willing to follow the prince so that they would be in high favor with the royalty. Lavan stayed away from them as much as he could, but when he was forced to go along, he usually regretted it.

He started up the common stairs, but one of the sympathetic palace guards, old enough to be a grandfather, hissed and shook his head. The back way then. It meant Hahn was close to their adjoining rooms.

Or maybe already there.

Lavan ducked back into the servants' living quarters and ascended the narrow stairs to the third floor. The common balcony opened right under his bathroom window, and he had a few climbing spikes he had secretly placed there at the age of seven. He had broken his ankle by jumping out that window to escape one of the prince's fencing "lessons," Hahn's term for beating Lavan with a wooden practice sword. After that, he professed a fear of heights to allow himself an escape.

Lavan climbed easily, used to the holds, then scrambled through the window to hear a pounding on the bathroom door. He had locked it when he left in case of this exact situation.

"Hang on!" Lavan caught his breath and made sure there was nothing on his person that might give away where he had been. When he found the paper with the contact code, he quickly memorized it then tossed it into the toilet and flushed away. Stripping off his jacket and throwing it in a wad on the bathroom floor, he opened the door to a red-faced prince.

"Why didn't you answer?" He charged into the small room, looking wildly around.

"Did I really have to? Can't I even have some peace to do my business?" Lavan pushed past him, trying to seem self-assured and a little haughty. Bad idea since Hahn's red eyes said he had been drinking and most likely doing drugs. That combination led to anger and a lowering of inhibitions that caused the prince to assert his superiority in a more forceful or even violent manner than usual.

Lavan had experienced those consequences many times before, but he could tell it was worse than usual tonight, which was why he was probably home. Most of Hahn's lackeys were smart enough to keep him out of the public eye when he lost his wit and charm.

Unfortunately, Lavan typically had to deal with the fallout, and the prince was spoiling for a fight. Probably hoping to find Lavan with a girl or drinks of his own to have an excuse to punish him further. If there was nothing wrong, it didn't calm him but enraged him more. Lavan tried not to think of other ways the prince let off steam using the companion as an outlet for his anger. When they were young, it was childish but cruel things: snakes in the bed or itching powder in clothes. But the older they got, the more dangerous the pranks became. Like when Hahn put tiny slivers of metal in Lavan's lunch.

Fortunately, the palace had an excellent doctor always on call who rushed Lavan to the hospital as soon as he began to vomit blood. Hahn blamed the kitchen staff, and the head chef was fired. A few days later, however, Lavan had found a small box of metal bits in the prince's desk drawer. From that point on, he was more cautious and began to find interests that would keep him separate from the prince. Nevertheless, in the intervening years, Hahn found other ways of inflicting pain.

The prince grunted. "'Do your business,' huh. Being snooty again, aren't you? Just call it pissing and shitting like the rest of the normal people. And since I'm here..." Hahn strode to the toilet, clumsily dropped his pants and proceeded to urinate, occasionally missing on purpose. As Lavan walked out, Hahn laughed.

"Ha, so sloppy you are. No wonder the maids hate cleaning your rooms." He continued to chortle as Lavan sat down at his desk, a book laid out as if he had just put it down a moment ago. The prince swaggered out, still looking everywhere.

"You weren't sleeping, were you?"

"Of course not, just catching up on some history

lessons." Lavan had learned long ago to not sleep when Hahn was awake.

"Schooling, bah. When I am king I, won't need any more stupid lessons. That's what the council is for. And advisors. And all those other useless people around the court who need to be put to work."

Lavan ignored the rant, thinking the prince wouldn't have so many followers if they knew how he really felt about them. The prince pawed through the room, picking up and tossing aside Lavan's belongings, taking far longer than he usually would. Lavan felt sweat break out on his forehead.

Does he suspect me of something? What does he know? Lavan felt a shiver go down his spine as he imagined the prince's reaction if he ever found out that Lavan was behind the renewed search for Maya. The torture would be unbearable and no longer private since Hahn, and perhaps others, would see it as a betrayal.

He tried to focus on the history lesson.

Finally, Hahn seemed to tire of the useless activity and slumped down on Lavan's bed. The sigh that escaped his lips was so unlike his customary bravado that Lavan turned in surprise.

"I'm tired of all this, Lavan," he said quietly. "Tired of trying to seem confident and in charge when in fact I am nothing of the sort." He flopped on his back and flung his arm over his eyes.

Somehow Lavan kept his mouth from dropping open in shock. He had never heard the prince talk like this. He even looked sad. But...Lavan had been taken in before. The prince wasn't stupid, just cruel.

"What do you mean, Highness?" he asked.

"I see it in their eyes. They only put up with me because of my title. Most would rather have nothing to do with me." He sat up and held out his right hand to the companion, a gesture Lavan hadn't seen in years.

Lavan left his chair and went to the prince to clasp his wrist with his own right hand. The bond tattoos touched and Lavan felt a slight resonance. The prince smiled, though the feeling coming through the bond didn't feel happy. Lavan struggled not to show any of his own feelings, grateful that the bond wasn't sophisticated enough to allow thought.

"You are the only one I can trust, Lavan. We are bound, and I have no one else. My own father wants nothing to do with me, the child he didn't want. My so-called friends only want to touch my power and wealth. But this," he squeezed Lavan's wrist. "I am glad to have you as my companion."

For the first time ever, Lavan felt sorry for Hahn. Was this the true reason the prince was so awful? Did he feel abandoned and unloved? Had Lavan been so wrapped up in his own misery that he failed to see how unhappy the prince was? He was overcome with guilt and almost confessed his own transgressions over the past few days, but experience had taught him to be wary. Was Hahn using the bond to manipulate him or was he truly unhappy?

Lavan stared into the prince's face and tried to feel something positive through the bond. Something, *anything*, that might hint of good, buried deep inside the prince. Hahn's face showed a perfect sad smile, but all Lavan could feel was anger and self-righteousness.

I will watch him. Give him a chance. Maybe if I was a better friend, he would feel less alone.

So Lavan quashed all emotion of doubt and tried to radiate support, though he wasn't quite ready to abandon the search for Maya. He fell back on his usual safe defense.

"I will always be your companion, Your Highness."

Chapter Twelve

"The Redirection Program worked great, as usual. Thanks." Lenore planted a kiss on her husband's head after a quick change to her favorite one-piece ship suit.

"I guess that's your way of telling me you were followed, huh?" Diarmin looked up from his workbench, one of many in a cleared space of the cargo bay. He pulled off his magniglasses and smiled back. "Don't forget, the miniature mechanics are mine, but the latest program is Allison's."

"The false signal worked great for a distraction, although Quinn failed to pull a photo of her."

"Not my fault, Mom," said Quinn as he collapsed into a huge stuffed chair across from his father's workspace. It was worn and ugly but the most comfortable place in the entire ship. Quinn was fresh scrubbed from ditching his own disguise, and Lenore had to admit he had blended in with the locals extremely well.

"There was some sort of interference that scrambled the minicam. Probably recognize her if I saw her again, though. Looked like she knew her way around those questionable streets. Most likely one of the local toughs looking to steal from unwary offworlder prey." He grabbed a handful of snacks from the bowl Diarmin kept next to his chair for those times when he was so focused on tinkering that he forgot to eat. "Didn't seemed interested in the companion, which would have made more sense." He popped a few nuts into his mouth.

"Companion?" Diarmin carefully packed away his tools and covered his work area with a small plastic shield so the tiny pieces wouldn't shift. "Sounds like you got some interesting information. Let's head up to the lounge so that teenage bottomless pit won't eat all my treats." As he climbed the stairs he yelled, "Allison! Family meeting!"

***

"Well. That was definitely interesting," said Diarmin.

They had all gathered in the lounge on the middle deck, a common area in the center of the ship on the same level as the bedrooms. One side of the lounge held the galley where Quinn was currently fixing something more substantial to eat than a handful of snacks. The rest of the family were seated, not around the dining table, but in comfortable chairs and a couch that surrounded a group of small tables pushed together in the middle.

"From the picture, I knew this boy was probably important, but I really had no idea he was so close to the royalty. Which reminds me." Lenore peeled a thin strip from her fingertip and handed it to Diarmin on the couch. "Here is whatever data I could pull about the tattoo."

He deposited it in his shirt pocket.

"I'll put it in the scanner later."

The scanner was only one of his many machines in his workshop, but it would read every detail of information stored in the tiny fingertip sensor.

Lenore continued. "A bonded companion. Why didn't we catch that particular nugget of information? Sounds like it is a well-known fact."

Allison was tapping madly on her pad, but she answered quickly. "I remember lots of references to companions, but I thought they simply meant friends, so I ignored the term." She shook her head. "Sorry, should have caught that. Let me check my notes on local traditions."

"Not your fault, Alli. We all missed it. Too focused on the details instead of generalities." Lenore patted her daughter on the shoulder. "At least that news printing came in handy. How did you find his image in the first place?"

"I just activated the camera he had turned off when he answered our message, then used the photo I took to run a scan to find anything public," Allison answered absently without even looking up from her pad. "No...no...not that." Each of her negatives were punctuated with a swipe on the pad. "Boy, no wonder we didn't find anything. Lots of references to companions but nothing specific. Ah, finally. Looks like the word 'bonded' is necessary..." She trailed off as she began reading what she had found.

"Allison, hello, aloud please," said Diarmin.

Allison blinked and smiled. "Sorry. Lots of stuff if you input 'bonded companion,' so this one is a relevant article. 'A bonded companion is a lifelong friend and bodyguard to the heir. In the past, families proudly presented their children in hopes for a possible bonding even though the bonded ones rarely saw their families again. The past four Royal Companions, however, were taken from orphanages to become a member of the royal family when King Rhimen the Fourth decreed that no family should suffer such a loss.'"

She swiped some more, and a frown wrinkled her forehead. "Even with all this information, there is nothing really personal about Lavan, only public. And so very little. Someone that important should be everywhere. Same thing with the prince. Strange." She sat back in her chair, legs pulled up, chin to her chest in what Quinn called her "ponder position."

"Well, she's out of the conversation for a bit," said Quinn. He sat in another chair, pulling a low table next to him to deposit his food on. "How soon do you think we will hear from him?"

Lenore looked at her son. He seemed to have shed his anger at being cut off midsentence. Seemed as good a time as ever to discuss his performance.

"Soon enough, but let's continue our earlier conversation that was so rudely interrupted by the follower."

Quinn's face reddened slightly. Diarmin cleared his throat, evidently reading the disapproval from his wife.

"First of all, Quinn," she said, "never, and I mean *never*, break your role until you are in a safe place, preferably the ship."

"But I thought that was only for the public, not our contact. You know, blend in while anyone else might be looking but not when alone or private. You even told him you weren't a baroness, so I figured that was a sign to ease up on our cover."

"I told him that to make him feel more comfortable, the same reason I wanted Lavan to think you were a local boy. Also, a servant or even assistant tends to be ignored or dismissed as irrelevant. Which would have been perfect for what you were supposed to do, observe only."

Quinn's face took on a stubbornness that he rarely showed. "But I got him to talk, to tell us the truth."

"That wasn't your job!" She felt her husband's hand on her arm which helped to remind her that, for all his skills, Quinn was only fifteen. She cleared her face of what she was sure was a similar stubborn look and took a slow breath.

"We already knew he wasn't who he said he was," she

held up a hand to forestall another comment, "and there is a great deal to be learned from the stories that people make up to hide the truth."

Quinn closed his mouth on whatever he was going to say and blinked rapidly. He tilted his head slightly, evidently considering this new information. Lenore felt a squeeze on her arm and turned to smile at Diarmin. More proof of Quinn's intelligence that he paused to consider what was said.

"What sort of stuff can we learn from his storytelling?"

"Things like the way his mind works, how he feels, whether he can keep a story straight, his personality, and much more."

"But you probably got all that within five minutes of him speaking."

"Yes, but I have years of experience, observing and learning." *That should make the point.*

"Well, at least I got him to give up the information about the tattoo before he had to leave so suddenly."

Ok, so the point was only half made. "Yes." Lenore was reluctant to say so, but he was right. "You did help there, but next time, observe only. And stay in character."

"But..."

Allison suddenly leapt out of her chair in one fluid movement, ignoring her family's startled glances.

"I know why I haven't found anything. And now I know exactly where to start looking. But I have to have my computer." With no further explanation, she dashed out, and Lenore heard pounding feet on the ladder to the bridge.

***

As Lenore and Quinn followed Allison up the stairs at a more sedate pace, Diarmin headed back down to his workshop to activate his scanner and drop in the finger pad sensor. It clicked merrily away and indicated at least twenty minutes to complete the analysis. *Huh, must be some strange anomalies detected.* He linked his hand-held to the scanner and headed to the bridge.

Allison was furiously hitting keys and mumbling under her breath while Quinn sat next to her in the navigator seat and tried to follow what she was doing. Diarmin approached Lenore, who was leaning against the science console behind the command center. He placed the tablet between them on the console so that they could examine the data together.

"Scanner is going to take a while to process all the info on the tattoo. Wait, look at that."

"These are some strange readings for a tattoo," Lenore said. "You're the one who reads diagnostics, what do you think?"

"Well, this indicates ink and flesh molecules, normal for any tattoo but these—" He tapped his index finger on the screen. "These are some sort of, well, I would say microscopic machines but with organic components as well. Very odd. Not your basic, simple tattoo, I would say."

"Nothing about this case is simple. A princess, and her companion that nobody talks about, missing for over eighteen years, the companion of her replacement, perhaps rival, is risking serious repercussions to look for her, tattoos with tiny implants and strangers following us for no obvious reason." She looked at him. "Did I leave anything out?"

"Other than the fact that we are on solid ground and don't have to depend on faulty gravity plates? And while we are in dock, we aren't burning any fuel."

"But we are paying dock fees."

"Which will be reimbursed by our employer."

"If we find the girls, which seems less likely with each passing minute."

"We have our health."

Both burst out laughing, and Lenore put her hand on Diarmin's face. "You are such an optimist."

"And you are the family pessimist, my dear." He grabbed her hand and kissed it.

"Realist, not pessimist."

"Aha! Found it, or rather him," crowed Allison, breaking the moment. "Check it out."

She spun the computer terminal around to display a face that looked like any of the planet's native population. "This guy is responsible for the lack of any information on the royal family."

"It's a terrible picture," said Quinn.

Allison made a face. "Well, I just barely got it. He noticed my hack and deleted it in seconds, so we have to make do with this. Good thing I never leave a trail. This guy is good." She smirked. "But of course, I am better."

Diarmin shook his head. He worried what would happen when Allison finally met her match. *It would be, well, let's just say somewhere just below Armageddon.*

"How did you find him?" asked her mother.

"Well, I figured there were two possible reasons that there was very little information about people who are famous. One is that they never leave their home and avoid all public appearances. But the news article I found shows that really isn't true, and I also found several innocuous references that would indicate similar things. You know, vague descriptions that could be anyone, but in context must be the royalty. So, that leaves the fact that someone has been deleting everything about the prince, king, and companion."

"Deleting? Everything?" asked Diarmin. "Why?"

Allison shrugged. "No idea. Privacy, I'd guess, but look at these security images I pulled up." She tapped a few times and there was a video showing Lenore and Quinn leaving the restaurant where they had met the companion. "See, here you two are, and let me back it up so you can see...ah there. See that break?"

"Um, no," said Quinn, shifting restlessly on his chair.

Diarmin figured it was most likely because he realized here was another reason to stay in character.

Allison gave an exasperated sigh. "I'll go slower then." She reduced the speed of image, rewound and tracked the video, watching a variety of people come out. Then, right as the door was opening again, a line tracked down the middle, and the picture jumped ever so slightly.

"That just looks like static," said Quinn.

"Well, maybe to you, but it happens exactly when the companion was leaving, and the fact that there is no video of it proves something was cut."

"How do you know this wasn't a single glitch?" asked Lenore.

"Well, that cut has a certain...I don't know what you'd call it...imprint? Signature? Shape?" Allison waved her hands. "Anyway, I created a program to search for that particular flaw and found it throughout video feeds going back for years. Then I tracked them all back to the source, and there was the guy." She turned back to her computer and resumed her work. "Now I just need to figure out who he is." She bit her lip in concentration.

Chapter Thirteen

"Jonah Wilkerson!"

The man behind the computer terminal nearly jumped out of his skin. "You don't have to yell, Ginette," he said to the woman who was his replacement for the night shift. He quickly tapped the board to clear the video he had been looking at.

"Yes, I did, boss," she answered. "I called your name three times. What has you so enrapt that you were off in dreamland?" She bent over his terminal, peering at the screen, but he had already locked it up.

"Nothing," he said. "Just observing some random video feeds."

"Looked like a woman to me. A pretty good looking one too. Ha, look at you blush. Caught you," Ginette laughed heartily. "Oh, don't be embarrassed. She was a looker all right, though I prefer them with a bit more meat on their bones."

Jonah gathered his stuff and shoved it all in his bag. "Yeah, Ginette. It's common knowledge what kind of women you like."

She stuck her tongue out at him and took his seat. "Anything interesting happen with the royals today?"

"Nothing really," he replied, carefully looking down, pretending to rearrange things in his bag. He didn't know how she felt about the prince and didn't want to explain what had happened that day. "The boys are in their chambers and most likely will sleep the night away. The king is in the conference suite as usual. Alone."

"Wow, early for the prince, isn't it?" she said in a neutral voice. "Makes my job easier. Anything else I should know?"

"There has been some hacking again, probably from the local media like usual. Nothing important I'm sure, but let me know if it happens again so I can track down the source."

"Ok, will do." She logged on and waggled her fingers over her shoulder. "See you tomorrow, Master Voyeur."

He left before she saw his face redden again. Today

had been an odd day. First Companion Lavan met with strangers without the prince's knowledge. Then those strangers were followed by someone obviously from the poor side of the city. Jonah assumed it had to do with the ad to find the missing princess, which he should have deleted but couldn't bring himself to. He desperately wanted to find her as well. And maybe that's why his mind had tricked him into seeing something that wasn't there.

He shook his head and stuck his hand in his pocket to feel the portable data stick. It was illegal to take anything from the palace, but he had to know. Not only who the offworlders were, but also the identity of the woman who had been following them. He had to be sure.

"Hello."

He turned, startled again, and found himself face to face with the prince, or looking down at him since the prince was three inches shorter despite his seventeen years.

"Oh, um, hello, Your Highness." He began to bow to hide his red face, heart hammering even harder.

"Please, no formalities. I'm sorry, I forgot your name." Prince Hahn put a hand out to halt Jonah's bow. The hand on his shoulder did not comfort Jonah but did exactly the opposite.

"Chief Reviewer Wilkerson, Your Highness." He resisted the temptation to put his hand back in his pocket, acutely aware of the illegal data.

"I said no formalities. Prince Hahn will do." His steely tone belied his friendly words. Hahn smiled. "You seem surprised to see me, Reviewer. I thought you always had eyes on us."

"My shift is over, Your...er...Prince Hahn. I was on my way home." Jonah's mind raced. Though he saw the prince every day through the cameras, he had only met him twice at formal affairs, and the prince had never come down to the security areas ever that he knew of. Had he been caught? Was the prince about to accuse him of stealing data? "Reviewer Previn is on duty now if you need anything."

"No, no. It's you I'm looking for. Come. Walk with me." The prince put an arm around Jonah's shoulder, even though he was shorter and much younger.

"Wh—what can I do for you?"

"I am sure you are aware of most things that go on in the palace. How is my father? He rarely tells me anything, and I worry for his health."

"His Majesty is quite well and performing his duties with his usual excellent capabilities."

"Good, good." Hahn went on to ask several questions in that friendly/not friendly voice that Jonah recognized as an attempt to charm. Most people were taken in by the prince's smiles and personable attitude, but Jonah saw him every day and knew his true heart.

"How about my companion? He seems a bit unhappy lately, and I can't quite put my finger on why. I thought you might have some insight."

Jonah thought very carefully before answering. What did the prince know? Did he suspect Lavan was looking for the lost princess? Or even meeting with strangers?

"I do not know, Your Highness."

The prince halted, his arm also stopping Jonah before he removed it from Jonah's shoulders. The absence of the prince's arm caused Jonah to sigh in relief. Until the next words.

"Look at me, Reviewer Wilkerson." The prince stared back as Jonah raised his head to meet the prince's eyes. "You are loyal to the family, are you not?"

"The king has my absolute, unswerving loyalty." He realized his slip as he saw Hahn's eyes narrow. "And the family as well, of course." Jonah's eyes flicked around, looking for the nearest security cameras to capture the prince's threatening position. His anxiety rose another notch as he realized they had wandered the hallways to the gardens, one of the three places in the entire palace that had no security cameras.

The prince pursed his lips before he spoke, and Jonah knew he was in trouble. "And you have seen nothing odd or out of the ordinary concerning Lavan?"

"Well, I, uh, have also noticed he seems a bit down, but I am at a loss to know why, Your Highness. He seems to be staying in his rooms quite a bit and reading a lot. Perhaps he is simply lonely." Jonah wondered if that sounded as weak as it felt.

"Do you mean to say I have something to do with this?"

"No, no not at all." A drop of sweat trickled down his back despite the cool night air. "I was thinking lonely in the female sense of the word."

The prince's eyes opened wide, and he threw his head back laughing, a completely unexpected reaction.

"I hadn't considered that," he said, still chuckling. "I

shall have to see about correcting that for poor Lavan." A wave of relief swept over Jonah, but it was brief.

"But, if you see anything that is questionable, you come straight to me, understand?" The laughter was completely gone from his voice as he gripped Jonah's arm tightly. "No one else, not the king or security, no one. Understand?"

"Yes, Your Highness."

"You had better." The prince took a step closer, face within inches of Jonah's. "Because I know who you are and where you came from. My father won't be around to give you special treatment forever." He released his arm and spun away, hurrying out of the garden in the direction of his rooms.

It took much longer than that for Jonah to rein in his fear enough to move his feet in the direction of home.

Chapter Fourteen

"Mom, Dad?" A quiet tapping on the door woke them simultaneously. Lenore was out of the bed and halfway to the door before her eyes were open all the way. She pressed the button to open the door, but it was Diarmin that spoke.

"What is it, Alli? Shouldn't you be sleeping?"

"Aw, you know I don't need much sleep. Anyway, there's something I found that you will be very interested in." She pointed in the general direction of her room and disappeared down the hallway.

"Maybe her tattoo search program pulled something up," said Lenore already heading toward Allison's room as Diarmin stumbled along behind her.

"Couldn't it have waited until morning?" he grumbled, rubbing his eyes and looking quite grouchy. "This better be good," he said as they entered the bedroom.

"Oh, it is." Allison was at her personal computer, a homemade hodge-podge of scrap parts with a cord trailing to her hand-held. Lenore knew that it had indeed been a pile of discarded machinery until Allison reclaimed them and built a deceptively powerful device.

"Well, I was randomly searching the IGnet, looking for interesting stuff like, you know, those articles on code breaking."

"What?" asked Lenore.

"You know, the IGNet, the InterGalactic Net server that posts everyth—"

"We know what the IGNet is Allison. She means 'what' as in get to the reason why we are awake in the middle of the night," said her father.

"Oh, um, right. Well. Remember when the Frazion Freebies won the Worlds Series last year?"

Both parents blinked for several seconds before Lenore answered.

"Baseball?"

"Of course, Mom. What else has the Worlds Series? Anyway, Frazie, the planet, or its people or government or whatever, has decided to build them a brand-new stadium." She grinned as if she had single-handedly brought it about.

"What does baseball have to do with the case?" asked Diarmin.

"Nothing." It was Allison's turn to blink in confusion. "You asked me to locate grav plates and I have."

"That was two weeks ago and..."

Lenore put a hand on his arm. He was never at his best when awakened unexpectedly, but even she was having trouble following her daughter. "Allison, dear. We just woke up. Walk us through this please."

"Oh, sorry. Anyway, you know how any planet or system that has a Classic Baseball Team has to have a true Earth Grav field?" She didn't wait for a nod or shake of head but kept going. "Well Frazie, stupid name for a planet if you ask me, is no exception, and instead of building over the old stadium, they are auctioning off the parts to help pay for a top-of-the-line new stadium. And that means we can get cheap grav plates for the ship. Um, that is if we cover our bid in the next twenty minutes."

"Our bid? Exactly when did we bid on them?"

"Ten minutes ago." Allison's face fell when Lenore crossed her arms and Diarmin scrubbed at the side of his face. "I had to hurry. The time for new bids was closing and..." Her voice grew very quiet and she looked down. "We do have the option to drop the bid. And it will automatically if we don't respond."

Diarmin seemed a bit more alert now, most likely because this was something to do with his beloved ship. "Let's have a look then." He stood behind Allison to look over her shoulder. "Well, I have to say that is a terrific deal. Hm. And you are sure it will be compatible with a ship, being a planetary grid?"

"I figure you would know best, Papa."

Lenore hid a smile and didn't let her eyebrows rise. Was Allison purposely being the "adoring daughter," knowing that her father could never resist? Or was she truly sorry?

"And look." Allison was back to her bouncy self with her father's approval of the grids. "The system is only a few hours away. We can grab and install them quickly while Mom solves this case."

"It shouldn't take too long to adapt them to our systems, and we are not going to find a better price anywhere, though they are nowhere near top-of-the-line." Diarmin pursed his lips. "I can probably tinker a bit and improve them to near-new specs." He reached out to the computer.

"Now wait a minute, you two," said Lenore. Both looked up guiltily, and she knew they had forgotten she was there. They often did when in their own world of computers and machines. Lenore held up a finger. "First of all, there are a lot of issues with leaving in the middle of a case, even for a day or two. Second," now two fingers, "I don't want the ship torn up while working. What if we need to leave suddenly? And third, can we even afford it? I thought we needed this job before we could get grav plates."

Allison looked down again. "I did think things through like you taught me, Mom." She held up fingers, but Lenore wasn't sure if it was mockery or sincere helpfulness. "You and Quinn can stay onplanet while Dad and I go get the plates." Another finger. "You said this was a safe job, so there is really no danger in having a ship undergoing some repair. And three...I checked the account, and we can afford this, barely, with our savings. That's why it's such a good deal. So, when you solve this case, we will have more than double back in the savings account."

"It will cost for Quinn and me to stay onplanet, and there might be dangers other than this case. And what if we don't find the missing girls? Nearly all our money would be gone. Is not floating worth all that?" Privately, Lenore agreed with Allison's reasoning but felt she had to instill a little more reality into her plans. Life wasn't an easy computer game.

"Oh. I didn't think of all that." Her face fell again but not for long. "Well, that's what grown-ups are for, and why I woke you two up."

"Can't you ask the companion for an advance on the job? That should give us enough money for the basics," suggested Diarmin.

"This is a posted reward, not a job-for-hire," she answered. *He must really want these plates.* "What do you think, Diarmin? Can you make them work?"

He had been tapping on the keypad, bringing up what looked like specs. "Hm? Oh, yeah and the price is unbeatable. I think we should get them." He looked up as Lenore cleared her throat. "If we can swing the other stuff, that is." The look on his face was identical to Allison's, sorry/not sorry.

Lenore considered all aspects, not wanting to be the voice of negativity and dousing their spirits. But she was the realist, keeping the flighty family grounded.

"Five minutes, Mom."

Lenore looked at her daughter's sparkling eyes with a bit of the impish in them. She should have known Allison's spirit wouldn't be slowed by reason.

"Very well. Can't pass up a good deal, I suppose."

"Yes!" said Allison with a tiny fist pump. Lenore could tell that Diarmin very much wanted to do the same, but he only smiled at his wife. As Allison punched in the confirmation codes, he gave her their special wink that meant "We are a great team." Lenore rolled her eyes and sighed but smiled inwardly.

Chapter Fifteen

"Okay. You are set up in the district close to the restaurant where you met Lavan." Diarmin handed her an info stick. "Not too expensive, but not the poor side of the city."

Lenore tucked the stick in a pocket. "Don't you think I can take care of myself?"

"It's not you I'm worried about." His eyes flicked to their son, who was waiting impatiently by the airlock with his clothes duffel slung over his shoulder. On the floor near his right hand was his "tricks trunk," which is what he called the large suitcase that carried all his disguises.

"He blends in very well," said Lenore.

"Maybe too well. You know Allison dug up a lot of information on a local slave trade that appears to specialize in children," he sighed. "Nothing to incriminate anyone of course, just the fact that business is thriving." He lowered his voice some more. "Something is up with that boy. He should have argued harder about your earlier outing."

"Maybe. But maybe he is maturing and can take the criticism and learn from it."

Diarmin snorted. "Right." He pulled her in close and brushed her hair back with his hand. "Just be careful. Both of you."

"Don't worry, I'll keep an eye on him. See you in two or three days." She raised her voice to yell, "Bye, Allison."

"See ya," came the response down the stairs from the bridge.

***

"I've been in a lot worse," said Lenore as she unpacked toiletries from her bag on one of the hotel beds. "Look, there is even a table."

"You've been in a lot better rooms, too, Mom." Quinn negligently tossed his duffel on the other bed and gently set the suitcase down.

"Well, yes. But only as a cover for a job."

In no time, they were unpacked and had dinner from room service on the table.

"So," said Quinn. His pause to take a bite told Lenore that her son was about to bring up an uncomfortable topic. She continued eating and waited, knowing exactly what was coming.

"Have you thought about my suggestion?"

"Yes, I have." She deliberately took another bite of the delicate white fish. "It's too dangerous."

Quinn's eyes flashed as his jaw set. "You let me go into a school with the likelihood of a shooting attack but won't let me ask some simple questions?"

"I was in familiar territory, and you weren't even supposed to be in the cafeteria when it all went down. And I was right on site. I couldn't be with this new plan."

Quinn pushed some vegetables around his plate. "So, we'll scout first, get to know the area and the locals."

"Which will take time, too much. And it could tip our hand, alert whoever was involved with the missing girls. Might be kidnappers, or worse, the slaver organization, and any remaining clues or trails will instantly disappear."

"But that's why I would pose as a local, looking for his lost sister. Surely there has been a girl gone missing in the past month or so."

"You are not even close to being experienced enough to do that anywhere, much less here with no background information."

"How else am I supposed to *get* experience?"

"Not...This...Time." Lenore stared into her son's eyes as she emphasized each word.

Quinn pressed his lips together and dropped his eyes to his dinner. He acted like he wanted to push his plate away in his usual dramatic fashion, but teenage hunger won out. He settled on looking anywhere but her. Lenore sighed inwardly. She could handle four enemies at once while protecting innocents. She had faced down alien predators ten times her size while a building burned down around her. But raising a teenager was proving to be much more challenging. And teaching him was probably going to be even harder.

But could she teach him? She stared at her uneaten food as memory flooded back from her days with the Xa'ti'al.

"You cannot have another apprentice, Lenore." Daviss

was the top agent and had recruited Lenore personally. He was her last hope.

"Give me one good reason why not." She sat back and crossed her arms, letting him see her frustration as she would very few people.

"You are an incredibly gifted agent. Probably one of the best we have ever had. But just because you can do, doesn't mean you can teach."

"Bev screwed up, not me. If he had listened, he wouldn't have two artificial legs."

"Look, you just don't have the mentality we require for training."

"You mean I am not cruel enough like that tyrant, Jernal."

"Well, actually, yes."

Lenore uncrossed her arms and leaned forward to tap her forefinger on Daviss' desk for emphasis. "That is the stupidest thing I have ever heard. I believe that a person can learn better if he or she is shown that the instructor cares, wants them to do their best."

Daviss put a hand to his forehead. Lenore felt he was about to be condescending and leaned back with her arms crossed again, smoldering.

"Why do you think we recruit the way we do? Orphans and kids outside society, even some hiding from the law?"

Lenore ignored the jab. Daviss wasn't going to rattle her. "Because they have no one to miss them, no other options, already of a particular mind set," she said.

"Those are only the basic reasons, but we also take them away from everything they have known and train them in complete seclusion."

"Exactly!" Lenore pointed. "That isn't—"

"I wasn't finished." He didn't raise his voice, but Lenore could tell he was losing patience. She bit back a retort.

"You treat your apprentices like family. You love them too much."

Lenore blinked, not expecting that answer.

"In order to train someone to have the expected skills, a teacher has to be willing to hurt their student, force them to learn. The student needs to have that fear and isolation, that feeling of all or nothing, a complete surrender to the fight. A person who cares wants to protect them too much and has a very difficult time being tough enough to give them the hard knocks that are needed to hone their skills to the level we require." It was his turn to point at her. "That

is the reason Bev lost his legs."

Lenore fought against the flush, but she knew her face was red. From both embarrassment and anger. She still wasn't sure she agreed, but she had the good sense to know when to give in gracefully. She stood and nodded.

"I understand. No more apprentices," she said. Daviss looked oddly at her but said nothing as she turned and left.

Lenore eyed Quinn scooping up the remnants of his dinner. Could she find the balance between tough enough and love? *I hope so. For his sake.*

***

All night, Quinn was sulking and silent. He had studied what little information Allison had given them and sorted his tricks trunk until he crawled into his bed. As Lenore did the same, she realized she needed to make a solid plan for teaching. Reluctantly, she admitted that Quinn did need to get some experience. She would figure something small so that he could work up to something as big as his idea of poking around the edges of a slave trade to get information. First thing in the morning, she would tell him that they would begin a strict teaching regimen.

Chapter Sixteen

Quinn slung his pack over his shoulder and propped the note on the table. He didn't try to be quiet since he knew his mother would sleep through normal sounds but wake instantly if she sensed stealth of any kind.

As the door shut behind him, his stomach fluttered. Now was the time for his mother to chase after him. As he stood at the elevators, he kept glancing back at the door. The note he had left indicated he was going out to get some breakfast, but he had a different plan. In his pack was everything he would need to start looking for the slave trade, a good idea despite his mother's argument. He knew she was being too protective. He could pull this off.

The elevator arrived, and as he entered, he risked one more look. Their door was still closed, and he was in the clear. For now. Quinn drew a deep breath as the elevator doors closed and mentally prepared himself for the adventure.

Quinn's first stop was a restaurant right outside the hotel. If someone were watching, this would be the logical place to go. He had already noted it last night when they arrived. Not only did they box food to go, but they had public bathrooms and, most importantly, a back door that led to a different street. He ordered meat and egg sandwiches with a couple of protein juices. Some form of that breakfast food was, curiously enough, found on nearly every planet he had been on, probably because it was full of protein, easy to make and carry, and lasted for hours. He bought enough for himself and his mother, placed it all in his pack, and went into the restroom. Entering one of the stalls, he checked with his personal pad whether the room was monitored. It wasn't, so he quickly set about changing his appearance. In record time, his disguise was complete, so he emptied the pack completely, turned it inside out and repacked it. Now anyone looking for a person with a gray pack would see someone with a blue lap bag. He left the washroom and slipped out the back door, heading away from the street with the hotel. Nobody was following, and he was ready.

According to Allison's information, the rumors of the slave trade circled around the outskirts of the small sector where the city's poorest inhabitants lived. Quinn had heard his parents discussing this and agreed with their conclusion that the trade was more likely based in middle-class areas to throw off suspicion. He pulled out a printed picture of a girl who had gone missing a year ago but had doctored it to seem like another girl entirely. He was quite proud of the fact that the girl now actually resembled him quite a bit. It would make the "sister" story much more plausible.

He took public transportation to the shopping district. This city was like most on the planet, having a mixture of modern shops in high tech buildings as well as open-air vendors and markets that sold local produce and trinkets. These were his targets this morning. Quinn swallowed to still his pounding heart and approached a man selling tourist items. Holograms of the cityscape and guidebooks to the best vacation spots dominated the shelves.

"Hello, sirrah. I was wondering if you might have seen my sister." He held up the paper with the photo. "She—"

"No. Haven't seen her." The man barely even glanced at the picture.

"Please, sirrah, she has disappeared, and we just arrived in this city..."

"Look, kid. Buy something or scram."

"Okay. Sorry to have bothered you. May the skies aid your sales." He bowed and left as the man gave him a look mixed of annoyance and confusion. *Hm. Maybe the traditional sales blessing wasn't used here.* Quinn fought down his own annoyance. He didn't even get a chance to try out his story of his family arriving from off world a little over a year ago, recently moved to the city, how his sister never made it home from school two weeks ago, and so on.

He looked for another vendor and settled on an older woman selling local produce from an old wooden cart. As he approached, he noticed steel rivets on the cart and the telltale blinking of an anti-theft field around the cart which, despite its old appearance, looked to be in great shape. He hid a smile at the deception that was evidently working well since many offworlders were crowded around to get some "real food from the charming old-fashioned local." When the crowd dispersed with their "native" treats, he approached the woman and tried his story again.

"Ah, the poor thing," she cooed as she eyed the picture. Her accent was thick, but Quinn's trained ear could tell she was exaggerating. "I am sorry, lad, but I haven't seen her."

"Do you have any suggestions who else I might ask?" Quinn said, not wanting to give up such an empathetic audience. Maybe she would let drop some local rumor about disappearing children.

"Ah, no, sorry. Can't help you." Her attention was caught by approaching customers and Quinn was promptly forgotten. He sighed and continued on.

After two hours of fruitless questioning, Quinn found a public bench to eat his breakfast and ponder his next move. He had spoken with all the outdoor vendors and had even ventured into a few indoor shops. Absolutely nobody had any helpful information, and several wouldn't even acknowledge more than a grunt when it was clear he wasn't buying anything. He sighed as he popped the last of the egg sandwich in his mouth. Time for plan B.

Plan B involved bribes.

Quinn hopped onto a public transport to try another district on the other side of the city. No sense trying the same group with money. Perhaps even a slightly seedier part if that was possible. As he contemplated whether to change his story, his wristcomp vibrated. He pulled out his personal pad and hit a series of numbers that would scramble his personal security code so nobody could locate him. Not wanting his mother to track him down before he could find some useful information, he had first done it as he left the restaurant and would need to rescramble every few hours. He grinned. So far so good.

The next area looked as if it was going to yield even less than the first. All the bribes seem to do was give the person the right to ask questions. One vendor of electronic parts was particularly voluble.

"When did she disappear?" he asked first.

"About two weeks ago. She never came home from school." Quinn put on an appropriate sad face.

"Where are you from?"

"Transden. My parents work there."

The man eyed him. "Transden is one of those upscale neighborhoods. Surprised she didn't have a security chip."

"She did, but since we arrived onplanet, my parents hadn't had time to activate or register it. My dad said we were safe." *Did I say that sourly enough?*

"Hm. I thought Transden kids usually have fancy computers and do schooling at home. Why was she at a school? Didn't even think Transden had public schools."

He was definitely losing this guy. "On the planet we come from, Carmal, they have no home education, just public, and my sister was more comfortable with them." Quinn was quite proud of his quick thinking and using the planet of their previous mission. *Can't wait to tell that to Mom. Uh, oh.* The vendor was squinting at him and opening his mouth for another question. *Time to move on.*

"Thank you, sirrah, but I need to keep looking." He bowed and walked away, pretending not to hear the last question. The good thing about the street sellers was that they couldn't leave their stalls to follow him.

After another few more fruitless interrogations, Quinn sat again and told his stomach to be quiet. How could he be hungry already? And what had he accomplished? He had eaten both breakfasts, questioned way too many people with no results, and was running out of bribe money. Well, he couldn't give up now with nothing to show for it, so he would finish this street, perhaps asking more direct questions, even mentioning that he thought she may have been kidnapped. Should he hint at a slave business? Nobody had brought it up, not even obliquely. Most people were like that, Quinn knew. Not willing to admit there was a problem. As long as it didn't affect them, it didn't exist.

He sighed and stood up. Buying some food from the next merchant he questioned should hold him over for a little while longer. And maybe get some useful information for once. He entered the code on the pad again so that he wouldn't be bothered with the reminder while investigating.

"Last time for today," he muttered under his breath.

Chapter Seventeen

The sound of the door closing woke Lenore. She sat up suddenly. Her first instinct was to look for Quinn. When she saw the empty bed, she came fully awake and leapt out of bed. Her eye caught the note propped up in clear view on the table and she breathed easier.

"Mom. Went to get some breakfast. Quinn."

Lenore smiled. *How thoughtful. This must be his way of making up for his sulking last night.* And yet...

She glanced at his stuff piled around the bed. Yes, his tricks trunk and overnight bag were still there. She gritted her teeth. *I will trust him.*

That only lasted a minute or two. She had to know. She grabbed her pad and typed in his security locator code. It popped up at the store on the corner which she knew served breakfast pastries. Relieved, she got dressed and began to pore over the data that Allison had given them.

A while later, Lenore pushed away from the table in frustration. There was simply no pattern to disappearances on this planet that would point to any specific clues for the location of the slave trade. No area had more, or fewer, abductions than any other, and official reports were no help. About once a year, some authority reported finding a small slave ring and breaking it up, but there was absolutely no decrease in disappearances. Whoever ran this trade was extremely thorough at hiding their tracks. If there even was an actual organization. She shook her head. The fact that the statistics were so evenly distributed meant that there was some mind directing the child snatching.

The Xa'ti'al didn't give her a lot of experience in this area. She could only remember one mission the group had taken that involved slaves, and she, as a solo agent, hadn't been a part of it. It was rare that local authorities brought in any outsiders to deal with slave traders, especially outsiders as expensive as the Xa'ti'al. Unless there was someone very rich or important involved.

I wonder why they never hired the Xa'ti'al to find the princess. I should check into that.

Her ruminations were rudely interrupted by her rumbling stomach. Abruptly brought back to the present, she realized Quinn should have been back long before with food. She dialed his wristcomp but received no answer. She ran his security trace again and found nothing. A sudden burst of fear for Quinn caused a surge of adrenaline that would send most people into a panic. But, thanks to her training, that rush focused her into action instead.

Lenore dialed the ship as she searched through Quinn's belongings. As she suspected, the ship was out of contact, either in transspace or offline while installing the new grav plates. She left a message for Diarmin, then quickly made a mental list of all the contents of Quinn's luggage. Aha, his backpack was missing as were several items from his trunk. If memory served, and it always did, a change of clothing and some make up that would let him blend in. As well as all his money.

She gave a wry smile. Always leave some money so it is not obvious you have planned this. That would be the first lesson she would teach him.

If I get the chance to.

Lenore headed for her own gear to prepare. As she tucked her tiny stunner in its hiding place under her belt on the right side in back, her personal comp bleeped that a call was coming in. She answered it without looking at the sender, expecting it to be her husband.

"Yes?"

"Baroness Delilah, so glad you answered."

Hm. Lavan.

"I don't have much time to talk now," he said. "But I will have some free time shortly and wondered if we can meet again."

"Across the street from the previous restaurant in two hours. We will depart from there to a secure place."

"Two hours, yes, I can do that. Thank you, Bar— um Delilah."

She closed communication and shoved her comp in her bag. If she couldn't find her son in an hour, he was already in greater trouble than he had ever been.

Chapter Eighteen

"Well, that took longer than expected."

"Sorry, Dad," said Allison. "I have no idea how that ship tracked us. The new ID should be fine, and I have adjusted the drive specs so that they don't match the old ones. I really don't know what happened." She looked at her father who was prepping to return to normal space after three extra jumps through transspace to elude their pursuers. "It would help if I knew who they were?" The upward inflection indicated to Diarmin that she knew he wouldn't tell her but tried anyway.

He couldn't look at his daughter so instead busied himself at the console. "No idea." Which was technically true. Could have been one of several possibilities. Though, how they found the ship despite the out-of-the-way route they usually took...he would tackle that later. Now he had to distract Allison. "Probably from that criminal organization that was taken down in the last job."

"Not a chance," she replied. "They were scattered, most of them arrested, and that ship did not match any record I had of their fleet. And remember, I had all of their data."

"And nobody but you can alter an ID?" Diarmin instantly regretted his tone as Allison flushed and managed to look both angry and hurt. But he couldn't let her find out the truth. "Look, Alli. Just let it go. And use the downtime while installing the new plates to test some new specs, okay?"

"Sure, Dad. No problem."

She turned back to her console, but her flat tone told Diarmin she wasn't content with the dismissal of the conversation. *Someday she and Quinn can know the whole story.* For now, he hoped they could avoid any future encounters and simply be a family.

***

First stop was the shop where Quinn purchased breakfast. A few questions, a flash of credentials that were a perfect fake of local law enforcement, and a quick look at the shop's security cameras let her know that Quinn did indeed purchase breakfast. What she saw that the owner did not was his exit from the bathroom with a new persona. Now she knew which disguise he was in, and who and what to look for.

She retraced his steps with ease, knowing how Quinn's mind worked and what information he had read. Lenore smiled to herself, thinking he had the correct idea of getting on a transport right away, but his lack of experience made it easy for her to figure out exactly where he had gone. Mentally she added that to the list to teach him as well.

By the time she had found several people who remembered Quinn, her inner tension was rising rapidly. She concluded that he was either better than expected or incredibly lucky. If you can call locating the edges of the slave trade luck. And the fact that her hour was nearly up, and his trail went suddenly cold meant that he had most likely stumbled onto exactly what he wanted. And what she was afraid of. Lenore tried to ignore the knot in her belly as she questioned the man in front of her. He was obviously lying, as the woman before him had. Both had seen Quinn, and both knew what had happened to him.

She struggled to hide her own reaction as she realized that Quinn had been taken by the very people he had set out to find. If she continued, she would tip them off that she knew about them. And now she had to do the hardest thing she had ever done.

She had to stop looking.

Sighing heavily, she took back the picture of Quinn she had had the breakfast shop print for her, then handed the man a card.

"Thank you. If you hear anything more, please call me directly." Her wrist comp bleeped in a set pattern, and she walked away, pretending to answer to a superior. "No, nothing. This trail was a dead end. I am moving to the third district." Pause. "Yes, Commander, I will."

Lenore set her jaw and prepared to meet the companion. It felt like she was abandoning Quinn, but it had to be done. And maybe there was a chance Lavan could help. Somehow.

***

Lavan looked around nervously. He was early and

didn't know whether to wait for the Baroness or come back. As people walked around him, he felt like he stood out suspiciously. Voices and noises made him twitch unnecessarily. The prince was in a governing session with his father and the rest of the ruling body. Those usually lasted all day and into the night, so he figured he was safe for a while.

Where was she? He checked his wrist comp yet again. Still early. Maybe he would go get something to settle his stomach.

As he turned to head to the nearest drink shop, a hand brushed his sleeve. Reflexively he jerked his arm away, and his eye fell on a hunched-over person dressed in patched pants and threadbare shirt. A tattered hat with ear flaps tucked in tight hid most of the face. The hand remained outstretched in supplication. Lavan relaxed. Just an old beggar.

"Help out a fellow down on his luck?"

Lavan reached into his purse set under his jacket and grabbed two coins. "There you go. Hope things get better for you."

"So generous, thank you, kind sir. This will be more than enough for a hot meal. I know the perfect place two streets over that way. Perhaps you would like to join me?"

Before Lavan could stammer a polite refusal, the beggar tugged at the tattered hat, pulling the right ear flap a little. With a shock, he recognized his contact, Delilah. Trying to keep the surprise off his face, Lavan said. "I will personally buy you that meal. You keep the coins for future needs."

"Why you are most generous. This way." She left at a shambling walk, quick but with a pronounced limp. Lavan followed, face burning as he thought of how well this woman could fool him. He realized perhaps he could learn a thing or two and try a disguise next time he went out.

Two streets over was a shabby sandwich shop with few tables. Delilah held the door open and Lavan entered with doubt on his face. This place didn't seem very private.

"Perhaps you could get us a table?" she said as she followed him through the door, then stopped next to it as it closed. He nodded and threaded his way through the tables to find one by itself. He looked over his shoulder, but the woman hadn't followed. Instead, she had moved so that she would be hidden from anyone else coming in. The front door opened again, and a man entered and looked around, peering into the gloom. The baroness' left hand shot out and grabbed his arm. Lavan thought the man would pull away, but he became rigid and stared straight ahead.

With another shock, Lavan recognized him as Jonah, the Chief Reviewer. Before he could vouch for him, Delilah had spoken in Jonah's ear, and Lavan could see her hand squeeze harder. Jonah's eyes widened perceptibly, and he gave a minute nod that looked like he had to strain for even that little movement.

She called to Lavan. "Looks like we will need a bigger table, sirrah." She released Jonah's arm, stepped behind him and gave him a small push. He scowled and walked toward Lavan, rubbing his arm.

"This one should do." Lavan pointed at a square table with four chairs in a corner with no other patrons seated nearby. They all sat, and though it wasn't obvious, Delilah was guarding Jonah.

"Now," she said. "Tell us why you are following us."

Lavan's eyebrows shot up yet again, but surprise turned to fear when Jonah answered.

"I came to warn the companion."

Chapter Nineteen

Diarmin watched as the truck with the grav plates slowly made its way through the spaceport to their ship sitting on the pad.

"Finally, Alli," he said, grinning at her. "We won't have to float anymore. Shouldn't be too long to install."

"I'm glad they held it for us despite our late arrival," she answered without a return grin.

So, she's still not happy about being in the dark. Well, it couldn't be helped. She needed some more work to take her mind off the issue.

"Watch and make sure they deliver it to the correct spot for easy installation. I am going to check messages since we haven't had a chance yet."

"Because we had to rush to make the purchase, you mean."

Diarmin chose not to respond to the comment and climbed up the cargo ramp into the ship. The disadvantage to a cargo ship converted into a personal ship was that the primary hatch was on the middle level. The belly-down design meant that in a proper dock, the side hatch would debark on a middle level and the lower-level cargo hold door would open for easy loading. On an outdoor pad like this one, it was easier to climb up a shallow ramp into the hold than a ladder from ground to hatch.

On the bridge, Diarmin sat in the command chair and saw that there were five messages, all from Lenore. As he listened to them, he grew more and more tense, and the last one had him up out of the seat, down the ladders and running outside.

He ran toward the crane that was just beginning to unload the first grav plate.

"Not here. Please put them in the cargo hold. It's already open."

The operator began to grumble until Diarmin shoved a bunch of credit notes into his hand. The notes promptly disappeared into a pocket and the operator answered, "Whatever you say."

Diarmin rushed into the hold with a quick look around to make sure there was room for the plates. Allison came running up, dangerously close to the crane.

"What's going on, Dad? Why the cargo hold? Aren't we going to install them?"

"We need to get out of here now, Allison. Go start preflight and finish programming those new specs."

Allison's eyes widened. "But I haven't…"

"Do it now! Please. We have to get back to Sulous. Quinn is in trouble."

***

Allison dashed up to the bridge and straight to the control board. She input the sequence for preflight and double-checked her new specs. They were as best she could do without a few hours of testing, so she turned to go prepare the cabins for flight. Without gravity. Again.

She paused with her foot at the top step. She had never seen her father so rattled. Not even when being chased by strange ships. What kind of trouble could Quinn be in? Arrested? For what? Dressing up? She looked at the monitor of the cargo bay and saw that her father was supervising the storage of the grids. He would be occupied for several minutes.

Allison sat at the command console and brought up the messages. She had learned her father's security passwords long ago and accessed his secured profile in a heartbeat. There were a lot, all from her mother, sent at different times. To be sure, Allison played them all back.

"Checked into hotel. Hope the grid buying and installation go well."

"Quinn went out to get breakfast, and after we eat, we are going to start inquiries about the slave trade."

"Well, our son is not back with breakfast and since he has blanked his locator, I assume he has decided to try to find the criminals all by himself. He studied all the information that Allison dug up, so I have a good idea where he will look. Will give you an update soon."

"Diarmin, I don't like this. Quinn is either really good or really lucky. He has found the edges of these…these people and his locator still isn't working. Where are you? You should already be out of transspace and onplanet."

The final message was encrypted, but this gave Allison only a moment's hesitation. She had designed a special program that only took a few breaths to decrypt. But her moment of smugness at her success vanished as she heard the message.

"Quinn has been taken. By them. Get back here, Diarmin. I need help."

A chill overtook Allison. Never had she heard her mother ask for help. With anything. And the sound of her voice. Low, expressionless, stiff, like her teeth were clenched but not. Allison shivered. Her mother only sounded like that when getting ready for a dangerous mission. Quinn wasn't just in trouble; his life was in danger. She swallowed against a suddenly dry throat and went to finish prepping for departure.

Chapter Twenty

"Warn me about what, Jonah?"

Now I have a name to go with the face. She had recognized the man that Allison had discovered. He looked to be in his late twenties, probably educated and with a vital job. This was someone who could help her, not only with the case but with finding Quinn. If he was on the companion's side.

"The prince is getting suspicious."

Lavan shot to his feet, eyes wide.

Lenore hissed at him to sit down, but it was Jonah's hand on Lavan's arm that immediately calmed him.

"We are fine for the moment. I have bought some time, and you know they are in session for a few hours more. Let me explain."

The companion sat down as Lenore glanced surreptitiously around the room. Nothing seemed out of place, so she focused on the man, only to find him staring at her.

Jonah cleared his throat and glanced at Lavan, obviously uncomfortable with a stranger. Lavan seemed to guess the reason for Jonah's unease.

"This is the woman who is searching for Maya," he said. "You can trust her, and she needs to hear about the prince."

Jonah nodded, but his closed expression told Lenore that he didn't trust her. He turned to the companion, appearing to ignore her.

"Hahn came to me last night, asking about the health of his father and being quite friendly. At first." Jonah took a breath and continued. "It wasn't long before the prince started to ask about you. He wanted to know if there was anything wrong."

Lavan's eyes widened.

"I told him I thought you were fine, but suggested that if there was something wrong, it might be that you were a bit lonely for, um..." He glanced at Lenore, but went on. "Um, personal, female companionship."

Lavan burst out laughing, though Lenore could detect a nervous edge to it.

"Marvelous, Jonah. I couldn't think of a better thing to throw him off the track. Wish I had thought of that."

"But that won't last long so I came to warn you and maybe help if I can."

Lenore decided this was a good time to take back control of the conversation.

"Why would the prince come to you?" she asked.

Surprise filled Jonah's face, but he looked at Lavan instead of Lenore. At the companion's nod, for permission she assumed, Jonah turned to her and explained. "I am Jonah Wilkerson, Chief Reviewer of Royals, the person who keeps track of all of the royal family for security reasons."

"Young for that position, aren't you?"

Jonah colored slightly. "I have been at the palace longer than anyone else and have seniority." Lenore filed that information to inquire about later.

"So that's why the prince came to you specifically." She waved her hand to indicate Lavan. "You know him well, from seeing him all the time."

Jonah nodded, and Lenore turned to the companion.

"Are you aware that part of Jonah's job also entails erasing any camera recordings or other public views of you and the royalty?" Both started at this statement and spoke simultaneously.

"How?"

"What?"

Her hand stopped the questions.

"That is part of what I do. Now to business." She leaned back in her chair so that she could watch both closely. "What do you know about the slave trade in the city?"

This time their reactions couldn't have been more different. Lavan sported a confused look while Jonah's face tightened. The responses supported her speculation on who would be most useful.

"There's no slave trade in our city, or on the whole planet for that matter," said the companion. Jonah nodded stiffly, so Lavan was emboldened to continue. "It was investigated thoroughly years ago during the search for the princess. What little was found caused the organization to be wiped out."

"I see. Well, this is what is going to occur. Lavan, since you are under suspicion, I think you should stay inside the palace for now."

K.A. Bledsoe

"But I want to help."

"Of course, but I think we are lucky to have the assistance of Jonah, and he will be your go-between." They looked at the reviewer, and he nodded again.

"But..."

"Meanwhile, I need you to find whatever you can about the former slave trade. Any names or details would help me greatly. Can you do that?" Lenore smiled reassuringly.

"That's easy. Hahn always teases me about reading too much. I'll say it's a history project."

Her wristcomp vibrated against her wrist. "Excuse me for one moment." She stood. "Discuss how you will contact each other without the prince becoming aware of it."

As their heads bowed toward each other, Lenore took a few steps toward the back wall away from any other diners. She held the wristcomp to her ear so no one else could hear the message. It was from her husband and it was short.

"Message received. On our way."

Lenore breathed a little easier. With her worries about Quinn, she had pushed her concern about the delayed communication from Diarmin and Allison to the back of her mind. There were so many people looking for them... she shook her head slightly and berated herself. Time to focus on the present. Especially since her client and his friend looked like they were leaving. In two strides, she was back at the table.

"Done with your plans?" she asked. At the nods, she continued. "Before you go, did you bring me the information on the tattoos?" Though she was focused on the companion, she was aware of Jonah's sudden tension.

Lavan colored slightly. "Oh, yes. Jonah's arrival distracted me from the purpose of calling this meeting." He sighed heavily. "Unfortunately, I was unable to access the tattoo records. I couldn't even get into the secure room."

"Are you telling me the companion is not allowed in secure areas?" asked Lenore.

"Well, I could raise a fuss, but it would likely get back to the prince, and I don't want that."

"Of course not."

"I can do it," said Jonah quietly.

Lavan's look of relief added appeal to his young face. "Of course." He shook Jonah's hand and smiled. "Thank you so much. I owe you for your loyalty."

Jonah bowed, and Lavan checked his wristcomp.

"Now I should get back. Coming, Jonah?"

"If you don't mind," said Lenore. "I would like to keep talking with Jonah, since he will now be my contact." She flashed a smile at the companion and bowed low. "Thank you, sirrah, and the next time we meet, I hope to have a positive report."

Lavan smiled back and left. The remaining two sat down, and Lenore could tell Jonah was extremely nervous.

Good.

"Now, Jonah. Tell me the real reason you are here."

Chapter Twenty-One

Raahi swore silently. The berth that had held the ship belonging to the offworlders who had met with Companion Lavan was empty. She had paid dearly for the information and now it was useless. She was tempted to blame the man who sold it to her, but she'd had it two days ago. It had taken longer than she thought to scrounge up a uniform that would let her pass into the correct section of the spaceport. And then she had wasted a day looking in the expensive district, expecting the richly dressed visitors to be in the high-paying yacht berths. But the ship had been in a belly-down berth usually used for cargo ships.

Discreet questioning showed the workers to be surprisingly close-mouthed about the strangers. It meant that either they didn't know anything or the offworlders had already paid for their silence.

Raahi kicked at a trash receptacle in frustration. She would have sworn that those people had responded to the call to find the lost princess and her companion. A wry smile crossed her face. They must have realized that it was an impossible task and left the planet. Or maybe they had been here to receive cargo and she was looking in the wrong direction. Too bad. They might have been willing to pay well for any information, either cargo or lost princesses, and Raahi was the best in the city. But instead, she'd missed another chance to be out of the slums and on her way to a normal life.

Well, it wouldn't be the first time a plan had gone sour. She headed out of the spaceport and back toward her home. Ducking through alleys and back streets, she never took the same way twice. Despite her annoyance with her failure, she was quite aware that a gang of toughs were watching her as she passed by. She knew it wasn't to rob her. Her appearance did not suggest that she had anything worthwhile. Except that she was female and alone. The gang consisted of three men and a woman, all with ragged clothing like hers. Their faces read of desperation to find pleasure in anything, even if it was in hurting others. Her hunch was confirmed when they left the alleyway to follow her.

Raahi had only glanced at the group, but she knew exactly who to take out. As she turned a corner into another alley, the rush of footsteps told her where each person was. She waited for the exact moment when the footsteps were right behind her and paused. She ducked under the blow she knew was coming and spun in a crouch. She didn't go for the attacker but the person behind and slightly to the right that she knew was the leader.

In one swift move she had him in a headlock with her left arm, her right hand holding a tiny knife in front of his face at eye level.

"This might be a small knife, but it will go right through your eye to your brain if you don't tell them to back off."

She had hardly needed to say anything as the group stood with mouths open, staring at their prey turned violent. Nonetheless, the tough gurgled a command to back off. The girl was the only one to look angry instead of surprised, so Raahi accepted that information.

"Now, back off or someone will lose his pretty looks." *Hah, none of them are pretty. Not in facial features or disposition.* They shuffled backwards, and Raahi also backed herself and the leader away from them. When she felt it was far enough, she spoke into her captive's ear.

"Try it again and I won't stop at threats." She shoved him in the back forcefully enough for him to stumble and, for good measure, raked her knife along his shoulder to teach him a lesson. She spun and ran, taking a side bet with herself on who would follow.

She heard footsteps and glanced back. Yep, she was right. The girl was hot on her heels. Some people did not know when to give up. Raahi stopped suddenly and pivoted to face the girl. The girl hadn't anticipated Raahi's actions, so she backpedaled and tried to stop. As the girl collided with her, Raahi flexed her knees and used the force of the girl's charge to toss her to the ground. For good measure, she stomped on the girl's left knee, not quite breaking it but ensuring she would no longer follow.

"I said, 'Back off.' Next time you will know better." Another glance showed the rest of the gang watching their cohort being taken down. Raahi grinned at them, knowing she had to show a tough face, though she was a bit sickened at her own violence. A nod from the leader holding his bleeding shoulder indicated she had earned their respect and wouldn't be bothered anymore. Raahi continued to her home, reining in the shakes that always followed a fight. Her lips twisted. At least she had worked off her frustrations.

Only when she was sure that nobody was following her did she head to her tiny apartment. At the top of a four-story building with no elevator, the apartment was cheap. The room was barely larger than a shipboard cabin, with a bathroom so narrow that she could touch all four walls while standing in the center. The "kitchen" was a single heating unit in the middle of a board on top of a refrigerator that came up to her waist. The couch folded out into a bed and a single lamp shed the only light. No windows, but that was fine with her. She preferred the security from anyone trying to spy on her.

With a huge sigh, Raahi stripped and tossed her coveralls on the couch. She was tempted to sell them and at least make some of her money back, but they had been extremely useful and perhaps could come in handy again. She grabbed a drink from her refrigerator and sat on the couch, willing her pulse to return to normal. It didn't take long. This wasn't the first time she had to fight off a gang and it wouldn't be the last. She hated the necessity of the violence, but it was the only way she had survived this long. It was why she wanted out so desperately. She grabbed her tablet beside her on the couch and began to scan the local feeds.

Time for a new idea.

***

Lenore waited while Jonah attempted to answer her question.

"Like I said, I came to warn the companion." His eyes shifted and wouldn't meet hers.

"You could have easily met him at the palace. Why here? Why with me?" Her mind was screaming at her to hurry up and go find Quinn, but the logical part was saying this man needed to be cultivated. He could help. With the case and Quinn.

"I really can't at the palace. Too many ears. And I didn't know he was meeting with you."

"There are ears here," her wave indicated the security cameras, "And of course you knew he was meeting me."

Jonah's head snapped up, and now he looked her in

the eye. She pressed her advantage. "In fact, you were the one to allow the message through about the reward for the lost princess."

His eyebrows lifted, eyes slightly larger. "Who are you?"

"I am someone who is good at what I do. Now, please, answer my questions honestly. Why aren't you concerned about these cameras?" Several expressions crossed his face, and she held on to her patience as he shifted through doubt, then awe, perhaps some memories until he finally showed acceptance, not quite defeat but close.

"You know I am Chief Reviewer. I can erase any files."

"And?"

Jonah actually twitched. "I have a device that scrambles my identity for cameras and whatever it misses, I can erase later."

Lenore's mind flashed a picture of the girl who had followed them whose face had been blurred beyond recognition in the photo Quinn took. "Interesting, may I see the device?"

Jonah cleared his throat. "Um, no. It is an implant."

Only years of training kept her eyebrows from rising. Diarmin would love to get his hands on that tech. She would circle back to that gem of information.

"All right. Let's discuss the slave trade. Obviously, you know much more about it than the companion."

Jonah nodded slowly. "Yes, but not much, I'm afraid. Only that there is indeed a viable trade, and it was never shut down like most people believe."

"And where does your knowledge come from?"

"I was there when the search was conducted for the princess. A small organization was found, but it was a dead end, said to have nothing to do with the disappearance." The sour look on his face primed Lenore for his next words. "A few arrests were made, the organization disbanded, but nothing more could be found. With no further leads, investigations were stopped."

"Then how do you know about the current situation with the slavers?"

"I have kept up with my inquiries over the years but"— Jonah shook his head—"every time I get close, or think I do, the trail goes cold."

"Your inquiries? What about the local authorities?"

Jonah's eyes flashed angrily, and his face darkened as he looked down. For the first time, Lenore could sense a fighting spirit. "I am pretty sure they are being paid off.

They do nothing." His lips twisted like he wanted to spit but held back.

Lenore's estimate of the young man rose several more notches. The questions she wanted to ask kept piling up, but this particular mystery would have to wait.

"I need whatever data you have within the hour," she said.

"I can do it in maybe two as there are certain, um, precautions I need to take."

"Not good enough. They may already be suspicious of outside involvement." She reached into her right sleeve and pulled out a flimsy. She rarely used the thin information wafers, but this time speed was more essential than privacy. "This will allow you to download the files into my personal comp from any system but will only work once before it self-destructs and erases any traces."

Jonah took it carefully and placed it in his jacket pocket. He nodded and said, "I will do my best, but I need to ask something."

Lenore fought down her impatience but inclined her head.

"You're a Xa'ti'al, aren't you?"

Chapter Twenty-Two

Quinn came awake slowly, first aware of the bad taste in his mouth, then of unidentified tapping noises. Sounded like someone on a computer. Guess Dad and Allison got back early, was his groggy thought. He opened his eyes expecting to see the lounge on the ship, but the man seated on a stool in front of a table across the room was unfamiliar. As was the couch he found himself lying on. Coming fully awake with the surge of fear, Quinn tried to sit up but discovered that his hands were bound behind his back. A quick self-assessment showed his feet were tied together as well, and he was stretched out on his right side, helpless.

"Ah, the mysterious boy is awake." The man put down the tablet he had been fiddling with, and Quinn recognized it as his.

Quinn tried to ask where he was, but his throat was so dry only a croak came out. The man smiled and stood up, grabbing a glass before approaching Quinn.

"Thirsty?" He seized Quinn's left arm and wrenched his entire body upright.

The pain helped clear the last of the fog from Quinn's brain. The man held out the glass and placed a straw in it. Quinn regarded the glass warily though his body was screaming for the liquid.

"Don't worry. It's just water. See?" The man took a sip and offered it again to Quinn. "But now you might have to worry about germs." He chuckled, but it wasn't a nice laugh. "Come on, boy. It would be stupid to drug you again. You'd go back to sleep and we couldn't talk. Drink up or I will pour it down your throat."

Quinn sucked down all the water in the glass and cleared his throat experimentally.

"Better?"

He nodded, and the man returned to the stool. He refilled the water from a pitcher but placed the glass on the table, not offering more.

"Let's start with your name."

Quinn stuck to the story he had made up when pretending to look for the lost sister. "Isaac Demak. I am from—"

"Let me stop you right there. I know for a fact there is no Isaac Demak from Transden, recently arrived from Carmal with his parents and sister, so don't bother."

Quinn swallowed. Not only had they been watching him, but they had already checked out his false persona. He tried not to show his rising fear as his thoughts jumbled to form a story.

"Hm. Lost your voice?"

The man eyed him, probably gauging his reaction, and Quinn was not encouraged by the satisfaction he read on the face.

I can do this. I make up stuff on the spur of the moment all the time. It's part of a good disguise. And yet his hammering heart made it difficult to focus. *I just need a starting point.*

"Maybe a little encouragement." In one quick stride, the man was in front of Quinn. There was no time to brace himself before his captor's hand exploded across his face, knocking him back down on the couch.

"Hey, don't mark the merchandise," came a low voice.

Quinn hadn't even noticed there was another person in the room. The voice had a timbre that sounded like a woman, but it was rough, as if the person had a sore throat.

"I know my way around an interrogation," his captor snarled. "There's only a red mark. If I need to get tougher, it won't show." He tilted his head to look sideways at Quinn. "Talk before I actually get mad."

But the other person's comment had frozen Quinn's brain again. *Merchandise?* He had been captured by the slave ring, and they were planning on selling him. He had to stall. Say whatever. Surely, he had been here long enough for his locator to be no longer jammed. But his mind wouldn't work.

"M-my classmates—" he began and didn't finish from a blow to the back of his head that made his eyes swim.

"Liar," said the man. "You are not a native of this planet. Oh, the disguise is good, but from the makeup in your little pack, I can tell you are very good at hiding your true features, so let's try again and don't lie." His voice got quieter. "It will only serve to piss me off."

The mention of disguises gave Quinn his starting point,

and he thought quickly.

"It was a dare!" he yelled.

His captor had raised his hand again but lowered it at the shout. Quinn continued, slightly encouraged.

"It's true I am from off planet. I use the makeup to blend in. The boys are more accepting of me that way. There...there were these popular boys. They said I had to do this if I wanted to join their circle. Go to certain people, say certain things. Like a code." Quinn was pretty sure that hazing was common to all teenagers on any planet.

"Who are they?"

"If I tell, I won't get in. They made me swear I wouldn't tell." Quinn was doing his best to seem like a duped kid, unaware of where he was. He knew innocence was his best defense. It would keep him mostly healthy, yes, possibly prepared to be sold, but he knew his mother would find him before that happened. He continued blurting out anything that might help.

"I am not allowed to even say the school or town. I don't want them to get into trouble. I'm sorry, mister, please just let me go home. I won't tell anyone about this. They wouldn't believe me anyway and say that I just didn't have the guts to go through with it. Please..." he let his voice tremble and soften to a mumble.

The man stared at him. He thrust the picture of the girl in front of Quinn. "Who is this girl?"

The truth would serve here. "I don't know. Nobody I think. It was just a prop they gave me."

He shoved the picture back into a pocket and returned to the desk to hold up Quinn's pad. "And this? This is fairly high-tech stuff. Where'd you get that?"

"They gave me that, too, saying it would help, but I don't know how. I don't know where they got it, please. Can I just go home?" It wasn't very difficult to sound sincere about that and even a couple of tears managed to escape.

The man approached again and knelt so that his nose was an inch from Quinn's. "Hm. Some of that might actually be the truth. Stop whining kid." He shot a fist into Quinn's stomach, making him gasp for air, then walked away.

"Worthless brat."

"But loyal," came the rough voice. "I'll inform the boss. At least he'll bring a hefty sum." Quinn heard footsteps and a door slam. Soon his stomach pain eased and he could take a full breath, which sounded loud in the true silence. Never had he been so glad to be alone. Even if he knew time was running out.

***

In all her years with the Xa'ti'al and after she left the order, Lenore had never been asked that question. Told people, yes, but never asked. It was all she could do to keep her composure.

"What makes you think I am?" She figured that was a harmless enough response.

"Well, I have seen one before, long ago, and he was, um, I mean, well, you remind me of him."

Lenore allowed one eyebrow to rise but said nothing.

Jonah lifted his hands. "No, wait, he didn't look like you, completely different, in fact, but you both have the same manner and demeanor. Superior, but not in a rude way, like, well, like you have earned it. He was full of information and knew his way around people." He rubbed his arm absently where Lenore had grabbed him.

"Interesting. And where did you meet this Xa'ti'al?"

"I didn't personally meet him, but I was among the group that did. He came after the princess disappeared."

His eyes searched her face, but she tried to maintain inner calm, determined not to reveal any more than she supposedly already had. The mystery surrounding this man continued to grow.

"I had been wondering if the famous order had been called to assist in a search."

He looked away with a grimace. "Oh, they were called all right, but showed up apologizing profusely that they could do nothing."

"That does not sound like the Xa'ti'al we have all heard about."

"I remember thinking the same thing." He looked directly into her eyes. "You already seem much more competent and willing."

"Thank you." Lenore rose to leave. "The information as soon as possible please."

"Wait." Jonah reached for her arm as if to stop her but arrested his motion before touching her. "There is something I need you to do for me."

Much as she wanted to escape this enigmatic man's shrewd questions and get on with finding Quinn, she was intrigued.

She sat back down and lowered her eyelids a trifle. "And what do I need to do for you?"

Jonah blushed at her chiding tone but continued. "Someone has been shadowing the royal family, and I cannot seem to locate her."

Her? I wonder...

"From what little I have uncovered, I believe she is a local information broker, selling data, both fact and fiction, to whomever will pay." He held a data stick out and his voice dropped to a whisper. "If I am caught with that, not only will I lose my job but also be imprisoned for a long time. Those are directly from the palace files. I have erased the originals."

Lenore kept her hands clasped and Jonah deposited the stick on the table between them. "Why me? Why not palace security?"

Jonah shrugged. "You seem much more capable."

"Flattery is all well and good, Mr. Wilkerson, but why should I do this for you? Our time would be better spent on the original case, would it not?"

"I would think a local who deals in information would be of assistance to the case." He waited, but she didn't even blink. "And I will add my own payment on top of the already posted reward."

"How much?"

"I cannot pay you as much as the reward for the princess, but I can offer half that amount for this service."

For the third time in one hour, Lenore was surprised. The reward for the princess was quite a substantial one, and if this young man could come up with half, he had considerable resources of his own. When she didn't move, as if pondering the offer, Jonah's shoulders drooped.

"I need to find her. Please."

Lenore reached out and took the data stick, tucking it into the hidden pocket of her right sleeve. "I will assist you, but only if it does not interfere or detract from the first case."

Jonah nodded and, for the first time, smiled. "Understood. That would be wonderful." He stood. "I will collect that data for you and send it as soon as I can." He bowed and was out the door before she could admonish him about bowing to the street person she was pretending to be.

Lenore shook her head. This case was proving to have more mystery and surprises than the previous one involving a planetwide crime syndicate. But even that couldn't offer a respite from her concern for Quinn. She left the restaurant to return to the room. Diarmin and Allison would be here in a couple of hours, so she needed to have a plan ready to rescue her only son.

Chapter Twenty-Three

After struggling and squirming for a while, Quinn managed to push himself to a sitting position on the couch. Twisting his head as far as he could told him nothing. His bag was gone, most likely taken by Jerk Man, Quinn's nickname for his questioner. The only things left on the table were the glass of water and an empty pitcher. Both were plastic, and neither would make a good weapon, even if he managed to get free. His hands and feet were bound with a sort of plastic covered metal and hadn't loosened with all his exertions. Quinn eyed the water with longing, though perhaps he shouldn't as he was already feeling pressure on his bladder.

How long was I out? Did my comp pad reactivate my tracker? At what point would his mother realize he was missing and start to look? His last clear memory was of purchasing food for lunch.

That must have been how I was drugged. But that didn't make sense. He had moved to the next area and hadn't even started questioning anyone yet. The thought chilled him. It had to mean the organization was larger and more efficient than anyone had thought. What if it was too big for his family to take on? What would he do?

As he choked back the nauseating fear rising in his throat, he heard the slight whoosh of the door opening. He cranked his head around but couldn't turn far enough to see the entrance. The sounds of footsteps evolved quickly enough into Jerk Man and another man who looked like his sole purpose in life was to lift weights and be as scary as possible. *Time to act like the scared innocent.* Although, shrinking back against the couch didn't feel like acting.

From some inner pocket about chest level, Jerk Man produced a small stick with a rounded tip. He touched this to the bindings on Quinn's feet. Quinn felt them separate, though the cuffs were still around his ankles. He tried to indicate his hands behind his back, but Jerk Man only smiled. Muscles hauled Quinn up by the left arm and started dragging him toward the door. Quinn stumbled, his legs cramped from inactivity, proving that he had been unconscious far longer than he thought. He planted his feet, trying to appear stubborn, but really just waiting for circulation to return to his feet. He faced Jerk Man.

"Can I go home now?" He tried not to sound too whiny to avoid another punch. The rough chuckle from Muscles wasn't very reassuring.

"Well, there is a problem with that," said Jerk Man. "Evidently, your friends aren't as tight-lipped as you are, and someone is being nosy."

"What? What does that mean?" Quinn did his best to look confused, but his heart soared.

Mom.

A blow to the back of his head made his vision go dark for a heartbeat.

"Lesson number one, kid," said Muscles in a low voice.

Jerk Man leaned in close. "That's right. Don't speak unless spoken to." He spun Quinn around and pushed him and his guard toward the door. "Second, we have already taken care of the nosy person, so you are never going home."

Muscles ceased dragging Quinn so that he could turn him to look back, right into the horrible man's eyes.

"And third," Jerk Man paused to show a humorless smile, "there is no hope."

Chapter Twenty-Four

It took Lenore half an hour to make it back to the rented room, even though it was only a few blocks away. She used the extra time to make sure there was no one following, an almost subconscious ability by now, and the movement aided her thinking. She had to come up with a plan to find and rescue Quinn. If Jonah's information had any truth to it, the slave organization was incredibly large, with many officials in its pockets. And why had the Xa'ti'al refused to help? It should have been a perfect case, one that would gain the order some notoriety, not to mention quite a bit of money. Lenore shook her head. Illogical decisions and irrational choices were one of the main reasons she had left the order, but it still came as a surprise. She shoved the questions aside to focus on the task ahead.

Lenore entered the room and quickly packed, fighting a pang of worry and fear as she carefully stowed all of Quinn's belongings in their proper places. She was less careful with her own stuff, craving some action and anxious to get to the spaceport. She left to check out, letting the door slam behind her, determined to have a plan ready as soon as Diarmin landed.

I need to find a place to think and study those files the moment Jonah sends them.

It wouldn't be easy, but she would get Quinn back.

"Hang in there," she whispered to herself, wishing he could hear her and take comfort in knowing she was coming.

***

Quinn was struggling against panic as Muscles dragged him down the hall, Jerk slightly behind. *What did they do to Mom? What did they mean by "taken care of?" Is she...dead?* His knees buckled at the thought, and Muscles grunted as he pulled him back upright without missing a step.

No, they are lying to rattle me. But they know about

Mom. And what about Dad and Allison? He couldn't think straight.

No matter how much they know, it's up to me now. Quinn tried to focus on a plan but came up blank. He had learned a little self-defense from his mother, but in all the lessons he had the use of his arms. And if he got free, where would he go?

The three turned a corner. At the end of the hall, Quinn saw a sight that made his heart soar. A door with clear panels through which he could see daylight. He stumbled on purpose and pretended to go down to a knee, which succeeded in twisting out of Muscles' grasp. As the henchman grabbed for him, Quinn stood up quickly and rammed his head under the man's chin. Despite the exploding pain in his own head, Quinn kicked out at Jerk Man, aiming for the knee to disable him. He felt extreme satisfaction at Jerk's yell and turned to dash for the door to the outside.

A bit unbalanced with his hands still bound, Quinn reached the door quickly and twisted to allow his hands access to the pad that would open the door. It swooshed open, and Quinn dashed through, but only got one step before his legs locked together, pitching him forward onto the hard floor. He hunched up and took the fall on his left shoulder but was still stunned breathless by the impact. As he waited for his brains to stop rattling, two sets of feet approached his vision.

"Aw, isn't he cute," said Muscles in a fake high voice. He didn't appear at all affected by the blow under his chin. "Looks like we have an aspiring hero."

Jerk Man squatted down. "Didn't even break his nose, how about that? Kid's got some talent." He waved the small stick. "Handy thing, these magnetic cuffs. Snap! Feet are bound again." Both laughed.

Quinn was finally able to take a full breath. "Help!" he yelled as loud as possible. Surely someone outside would hear that and call the authorities. "Help me, I've been kidnapped."

They laughed harder. Quinn was momentarily shocked into silence, then opened his mouth to shout again. Jerk Man jabbed two fingers into Quinn's solar plexus, and he was robbed of breath again.

"Enough, little boy. I told you, there is no hope." He stood and waved his right hand over his head. The trees and sky disappeared, showing that they were only in a room. The outside had been nothing more than a hologram.

Muscles grabbed the back of Quinn's shirt, dragged him to the far wall and propped him upright. Jerk followed, uncoiling a long metal strip. Quinn started to sweat. It looked like a thick necklace with small, twinkling stones. He flinched as the man approached and crouched again, but instead of inflicting pain, Jerk gently attached the necklace around Quinn's neck. The fit was snug but not too tight and felt cool against his neck.

"Much better. And pretty enough as a bonus for potential buyers." He stood and backed away. "You are allowed the one rebellion, but that's all." He brandished the wand again and Quinn's hands and feet sprang apart. "But, defy us again and..." He twisted the back of the wand.

Pain shot through Quinn. He spasmed once on the floor, twitching as electricity sparked the necklace, sending a shock through his entire body. It only lasted a moment, but the relief when it ceased was intense. Tears flowed freely down Quinn's face.

"You will be good now, yes?"

Quinn nodded as well as he could, prone on the floor.

"Wonderful." They walked out, the door closing behind them with an audible click of a lock. A glance about the room showed a cot, wash bowl, and a toilet. Quinn realized he no longer needed to use the toilet, thanks to the electric shock.

As he slowly got to his feet to clean himself up as best he could, the realization hit him. The obvious cell, the fake hologram. It had been planned, staged. They wanted him to try to escape. To take hope away.

But that knowledge didn't send Quinn into despair. It strengthened his resolve. They could beat him and sell him, but he would survive so that one day he could escape and make them pay for whatever they did to him.

"And for Mom," he whispered.

***

Jonah had just finished erasing any incriminating files when a camera on the palace grounds caught his eye. The prince was staring at something outside the front gate, arms crossed and an angry look on his face.

He left the session early. Why?

The answer walked up the steps and Jonah's heart

stopped momentarily. *Lavan.* He should have been back already. What was he thinking? Jonah magnified the image and turned up the sound on the camera feed. Fortunately, this was one of the few palace cameras with audio capabilities.

"And where have you been, Companion?" The slur of the title fit Prince Hahn's sneer. The look on Lavan's face was of genuine surprise and perhaps a little fear.

"I thought you were in session," he replied.

"I got bored," said the prince, waving his hand in dismissal. "It was all about dull economics and the same old stuff." His eyes narrowed. "But you didn't answer my question."

"Uh, I'm sorry, Your Highness. I needed a walk." Lavan bowed his head with the correct amount of humility.

"And the extensive palace grounds aren't enough for you?"

"I, well, um..." Lavan put his hands behind his back and looked sheepish.

Please don't give it all away now. Jonah pulled out several personal data sticks, ready to pull as much information as he could before he had to run.

"It's kind of embarrassing, and I didn't want anyone to know," said Lavan. With the image enhanced Jonah could see the slight surprise on the prince's face and even a small malicious smile. Hahn loved to embarrass people, most of all Lavan.

"Do tell. You know I will find out anyway," the prince said, his voice a combination of silky and sharp.

"I went to one of those clubs that has, you know..." his voice dropped to a whisper. "Girls."

Hahn's laughter boomed out, but Jonah sighed in relief, wanting to cheer at Lavan's deception.

"Girls? You?"

Lavan winced at the derogatory tone. "Shhhh! I don't want anyone to know. I'm not good with girls like you are. I just wanted to get some ideas, or something, I don't know." His despondence seemed very real, and Jonah was impressed. He didn't think the companion had it in him.

The prince threw an arm about Lavan's shoulders and pulled him along toward their rooms. "Let's discuss this new side of you, shall we? I would be happy to help you all I can, Companion."

Jonah shuddered. He knew that "helpful" voice. Lavan was in for a rough night. Jonah reset the camera to normal operations and set about doing his part to help find the lost princess. Pulling his old files and sending them to the lady agent helped distract him. It wasn't long before the significantly large file about his investigations into the slave ring was downloaded into his personal reader and sent to the private number. Next would be whatever he could dig up on the tattoos and other data for the next time they met.

He tried to keep his spirits up, knowing the chances of finding any trace of the girls were extremely slim. And if a trail were found, the chances were even less that they would be alive and fit to return.

Jonah set his jaw with resolve. Anything was better than a future where Hahn was king.

Chapter Twenty-Five

The desk comp pinged, waking Allison from a fitful sleep. If all was well, they should land on Sulous within the next fifteen minutes. Her father had insisted they fly straight, something they had never done before. She rolled off her bunk and grabbed her personal pad. As she headed for the bridge, she checked her anomaly-detection program that she ran before she slept, but there was nothing new.

As she climbed the ladder, she could hear Diarmin mumbling to himself. He only did that when he was working on a very difficult machine or when tense. He didn't glance up from whatever he was reading on the screen when she saw him, but he stopped mumbling.

"Get any sleep?" he asked.

"A little. Did you?"

He nodded, but two empty caf cups on the console in front of him and his red eyes told another story.

"Buckle up, we are cleared to land."

Allison clambered into the navigator's seat and complied. Her pulse quickened, and she knew the next few hours would be particularly tough. It took a little longer than usual to dock due to a high volume of traffic. They usually landed at ports during slow times, late or very early hours when there weren't as many workers or other eyes and sometimes with only automated landing guides. But Diarmin hadn't wanted to wait, and the distraction of avoiding a collision in the crowded airspace helped to temporarily take Allison's mind off her worry for Quinn.

Right as the ship touched down, Diarmin said, "Power down" to her and leapt out of his seat and down the ladder. As Allison finished shut down procedures, a light flashed on the command board that indicated the main hatch being opened. Maybe her mother had already found Quinn. Maybe it was all a misunderstanding, and they would be there laughing, embarrassed that they had worried for nothing.

She hurried down the ladder and corridor and reached the hatch in time to see her mother closing it. Her father looked around a bit frantically, but there was no Quinn. His face seemed to crumple in on itself.

He had been hoping, too.

Her mother waved them to the lounge. As they filed through the door, she handed several data sticks to Allison.

"See what you make of this data, courtesy of a security guard within the palace, gathered over several years. I have organized and analyzed it, but I want your conclusions. A pattern analysis would be useful as well."

"Okay, Mom," replied Allison. Lenore gave her a peculiar look but said nothing. Allison immediately started working at the lounge computer as her parents sat on the other side of the room, heads together and voices low. Though the information kept her busy, Allison tried to catch part of the conversation, but they were being too quiet. She was a bit annoyed at being left out but let it go to focus on the huge amount of data. It wasn't long before she had a good idea and could even see a couple of patterns. She notated them on her pad and her idea sketchbook.

"Done."

They dragged chairs to the computer, each with their own pad.

"If this information is correct," she looked at her mother who nodded assurance. "We can see that every time a part of the slave trade is discovered, it vanishes."

"We already knew that from our own searches," Diarmin pointed out. "And then it resurfaces later, just as strong as ever."

"Right, but this information shows a lot more instances than we found, almost three times as many. It also confirms that when certain authorities are involved, the organization vanishes without any raids or arrests. Sometimes, like here and here"—Allison pointed out two instances on the screen—"the investigation was halted for unknown reasons."

"There is someone feeding the slavers information about the investigations," said Diarmin.

Lenore nodded and said, "Probably more than one inside informant."

"Four by my count," added Allison.

"Hm, I only found three, but let's assume four." Lenore tapped on her pad. "Have you narrowed down any likely prospects, Alli?"

Allison shook her head. "I know the most likely sectors but have to cross check individual records."

"How long will that take you?"

"Well, I need to run the analysis program and enter all known parameters then apply my own—" She stopped at Lenore's held-up hand.

"I don't need the details. How long?"

Allison clenched her jaw but understood her mother's impatience. "An hour, two at the most."

"Good, get started." Allison bristled against the demanding tone, but she knew this was how her mother dealt with stress, immediately taking control of the situation. Lenore asked her to do things all the time, just not in such a harsh manner like some flunky. She started the search immediately, and Lenore continued with her "orders."

"Diarmin, I will need at least ten subdermal monitors, undetectable as usual."

"Ten? I only have three."

"You'd better get to work then," said Lenore.

"I don't have enough micro parts for another seven, only four more..."

"Then cannibalize part of the ship. We aren't going anywhere, and I need those devices."

Allison heard her father's sudden intake of breath, and her surprise at her mother's severe tone was nothing compared to the anxiety on Diarmin's face. Allison saw muscles bunch along Lenore's jaw, and as her parents stared at each other, the tension in the lounge rose to a level Allison had never experienced before. Her parents argued like any couple, but this was different. She held her breath waiting for an explosion, but Diarmin merely nodded then spun about and headed for his workshop. Allison glanced back at her mother, but she had turned her face away.

"Let me know when you have names," she said, voice gruff. Without waiting for an answer, she grabbed her pad and walked out.

***

"And what was that all about?" asked Diarmin as he stepped onto the bridge.

Lenore's head shot up from her arms that were resting on the command console. *Had she been sleeping?*

"What are you talking about?" Lenore took her stylus and tapped at her comp pad with much more force than

100

necessary.

"This," Diarmin said as he gently plucked the stylus from her hand. "I'm worried about Quinn, too, but we'll get him back." He put his hand on Lenore's and knelt beside the chair. She turned to look at him, but he knew she was too much of a professional to become emotional.

"You've had missions that were a lot more dangerous than this. I am confident you can pull this one off," he said.

She looked away and spoke to the walls, as if it were easier to speak that way.

"This organization is huge, Diarmin. Much larger and more ordered than anything I have ever seen, even when I was with the Xa'ti'al. There is so much we don't know, and it's too massive for only one ex-agent and her husband to handle."

"Call in some help?"

"From who? I can't ask for help from the local authorities. We can guess but not be certain who is involved and can't take the chance of the slavers vanishing again. We know I burned my bridges with the order, and you certainly can't call upon your former colleagues."

"What about your informant at the palace?"

"He seems genuine, but there is also too much I don't know about him. And the more I talk to him, the more questions come up." She threw up her hands then let them fall to her sides. "One wrong step and they will probably kill Quinn rather than risk being exposed. It's going to be a fine line to tread."

"Then we will make the right steps." He stood and gently squeezed her shoulder. "We'll do it together, like we always have." Despite his words, Lenore stiffened against the offered comfort. He relaxed his hold and dropped his arm.

Sounds of Allison climbing the ladder forestalled any more discussion.

"Here." She thrust papers between Lenore and Diarmin. "There are five prospects in various departments, but I can't be sure of any of them. I pulled every last detail about them, so maybe you can find something I missed."

"Thank you, Allison," said Lenore. "This is a big help."

"So. What's the plan?" she asked as she settled herself in the navigation seat.

Diarmin peered at her and blinked, vaguely aware that his wife was doing the same thing.

"I need to know what more I can do."

"We will let you know, Alli," said Diarmin. "Why don't you get some sleep."

"No."

"What did you say?"

"I said, 'No,' because he is my brother and I am going to help."

"It's too dangerous, Allison," said Lenore. "We can't have you getting involved."

"Did I volunteer to run around getting shot at? Computers are my thing, and I want to do more," she said. She winced slightly, then set her chin, which told Diarmin that Allison knew she was pushing her luck, but was determined.

Allison crossed her arms. "At least let me know what you are doing so if I end up being an orphan, I can tell future generations why."

Lenore's face reddened, so Diarmin spoke up.

"You can stay, but no interruptions."

Chapter Twenty-Six

"Thank you, Officer Kibe." Lenore shook his hand, making sure to tap her forefinger on his wrist to implant the tracker.

"I am sorry that I cannot do more, Dama Gienne," said the officer.

"Here, please. Take my card and call me if you think or hear of anything." Lenore placed the card with her alias firmly in his hands, then grabbed them with her own hands. "Please, find my son." She gave her long, white-blond hair a toss for good measure.

"We will do all we can." He smiled and inclined his head.

Lenore showed a hesitant attempt at a smile but released his hands and hurried out the door. A block away, she tapped her ear implant to activate the transmitter. But before she could send a subvocal message to the ship, Allison's voice piped in.

"We've got movement!"

"Not so loud, Alli," Lenore subvocalized.

"Oh, Mom, hi. Didn't know you were back on yet. I was hollering at Dad."

"Reporting that the fifth and final mark is in place."

"Noted," cut in Diarmin, "but it looks like it might be superfluous."

"Agreed. Which one is moving, Allison?" Lenore knew from their previous discussion that "movement" meant one of her marks was being tracked outside of expected areas. "Number three. He left his office ten minutes ago, but he is not heading home or any of the other places on the 'approved' list that you left me. Hang on, looks like he is heading for a food cart. Little late for lunch, isn't it?"

Lenore imagined Allison tapping away at several computer stations as she mused out loud.

"Ha. There is a similar cart and a high-end restaurant much closer to his office and home. That's not suspicious at all."

"Maybe it has the best food," interjected Diarmin.

"Not according to the sales figures. Barely sells enough to even be considered a business."

"Ping that location for me, will you?" asked Lenore.

"Done, Mom," said Allison.

"Ha! The business card you gave him was just scanned," said Diarmin. "Looks like someone is concerned about a tracker or tap."

Lenore's wristcomp buzzed with the information Allison was sending, and she scanned it quickly as she walked.

"Might also be interesting to note that particular cart and vendor is *not* on the list of undercover agents or informers," added Allison.

Lenore shook her head, not even bothering to ask how Allison had gotten hold of those highly protected lists.

"Card destroyed along with its monitor," said Diarmin. "I think we have just confirmed our guy."

Lenore allowed herself a small smile as she glanced at her wrist comp again. The other tracker, the subdermal one she had planted on his wrist, was working just fine.

"Keep your eyes on the others. I'm sure there is more than one working for the slavers." She pulled out her personal comp pad as she switched direction. "Pull all the information on this one that you can, Allison, and send it to my pad. And I mean everything, down to his most recent bowel movements. I will study it while I wait for him to come home."

"Aren't you going to follow him?" her daughter asked.

"He won't be stupid enough to go anywhere near the organization today. That card is message enough."

Allison's absent-minded "uh-huh" showed that she was already deep into the computer system.

"Diarmin, give me a triple click when he is close."

"I will, Nora. Be careful."

Lenore fought down a surge of emotion. Nora was the name he had known her by for the first five years after they had met.

"I always am. Going dark." She tapped the implant off and, three deep breaths later, she had dredged the unhelpful emotions. Lenore went to find a place near the traitorous officer's home to study the loads of data that Allison had most likely already started sending.

***

A little more than three hours later, Lenore felt the

triple click on her wrist at the same time she spotted Lieutenant Harwick rounding the corner and heading for his residence. It hadn't taken long to sift through the data to find her leverage, despite the fact that Allison was extremely thorough, including detailed "urination records" that made Lenore roll her eyes.

As he approached her position, she pushed herself off the wall she had been leaning against and walked toward the lieutenant, timing her steps carefully. A few strides away, he looked up and gave an absent smile as people do when passing strangers on the street. He looked down, but his head jerked back up immediately, and she noted the recognition on his face. But by then she was already next to him.

Her gloved left hand shot out to grab his arm and triggered the semi-paralytic drug in the fourth finger, the same she had used to immobilize Reviewer Jonah. A quick yank of his arm pulled him off balance into the narrow space between two apartment buildings, out of sight from any other pedestrians. She gripped his right arm with her other hand and arranged herself behind him so that she could whisper in his ear.

"Don't say or try anything stupid. There are two trained snipers, one aiming at your heart, the other at your right eye." Details made lies more believable. Her voice lowered to a mere thread. "You are a liar and traitor to your department and fellow citizens."

"I don't know—"

Lenore pressed the first two fingers of her right glove together and into his flesh, delivering a not-so-mild shock. As his teeth clenched, a quick flick of her right wrist dropped a small blade into her palm, and she snaked her hand around to hold it at his jawline.

"Don't test my patience, Jon. I only want information and a small favor. If you comply, you and your family will walk away from all this."

He wisely said nothing.

"I want the boy back, and I know you have connections with the local slave trade that took him."

He opened his mouth but closed it as Lenore pricked his flesh next to the jugular.

"Good man," she said, voice still low. "You are going to give me the time and location of the next sale. I am going to get my hands on that wretched boy." Even she was surprised at the genuine anger in her words. "I figure purchasing him is the easiest way to keep all our limbs intact."

"They'll kill me," he croaked.

"I don't think so. No one will ever know we talked. I have a deflector that is hiding our conversation. I will simply show up, buy the boy, and leave. Everyone profits, and nobody gets hurt."

"Why do you want the boy?"

"That arrogant little bastard stole something worth a lot of money, and I want to know where he hid it." She chuckled nastily. "And, of course, to teach him a lesson. But that's none of your concern." Her left hand tightened even more on his arm. His twitch at the pain made her realize she needed to wrap this up quickly before the drug wore off.

"That daughter of yours, however, is your concern."

"Are you threatening my family?"

"Of course not. I'm really a non-violent soul. I simply mean that others might be interested to know that she wasn't adopted through regular channels. Perhaps even sold to you by this organization?" She watched his face closely and noticed the slight jaw clench. "Or even a gift to you and your wife in exchange for a little help now and again."

The fear in his eyes told Lenore she had him.

"What do you want to know?"

"I've already said, but I will repeat it because you are under such stress. I want the time of the next sale, where it is being held, and a way in. Shouldn't be too much for someone with your, um, standing in the organization."

"Anything," he said, and his shoulders slumped as she released the left grip slightly, allowing the paralytic to fade. "Just leave my family out of it."

"Good boy," she purred.

Chapter Twenty-Seven

Jonah was wrapping up his shift, reviewing video, his mind unbalanced as he reflected on the meeting yesterday. He trusted this Baroness and agreed that the slave trade was the place to start. But was she indeed a Xa'ti'al? It didn't make sense. Why would they send someone now, this late, when they wouldn't take the case when it was fresh? Late last night as he was trying to sleep, he came to the sudden realization that she had never answered his question.

But she seemed competent, almost frightfully so, he thought as he rubbed his arm. Somehow, she had immobilized him even though he was no slouch with defense, having learned many kinds of fighting, including hand-to-hand. She was an enigma, yet he felt she would be the one to find the princess if it was at all possible. She seemed to have the skills and resources, especially when it was likely that the princess and her companion had been taken off-planet by the slavers so long ago.

If not, simply finding that information broker would greatly help. That woman had information he could use, he was sure. Jonah scrolled absently through the videos, not really paying attention when one of his flagged posts caught his eye.

Ever since his own investigations into the missing girls, he had always tried to keep tabs on those he thought might have connections to the slave organization. This flagged security feed belonged to one of the command posts with local authorities. That blond...was that the Baroness? Wavy blond hair cascaded around her shoulders, framing a low-cut shirt with snug fitted pants. A huge difference from a street beggar, but he was good at discerning features from years of watching people. To verify, he input a facial recognition program and found her at two other similar facilities. Was she just following the information he had given her, or was she forming her own leads? And so quickly. Didn't she realize she was advertising herself to whomever was behind the kidnappings? He couldn't listen in on any possible conversations as the only audio he had was within the palace.

Not wanting to take any chances, he erased the feeds and video but realized, looking at the time stamps, that he might already be too late.

***

Raahi stared in disbelief at the ship. They came back? The name listed on the docking monitor was different and the berth was on the other side of the spaceport, but she knew it was the one with the offworlders who had met with the companion. What luck!

She shook her head, lip curled in disgust at herself for thinking that. She didn't believe in luck. She had learned the hard way that people made their own good fortune. Those who believed in luck were stupid, lazy folk who blamed others for their misfortune. It had been work and observation that led her back to the ship.

Using her new spaceport uniform, Raahi had wandered the docks, getting used to the surroundings and prowling for anything useful. She had almost passed the ship, but she knew belly-down freighters better than the average citizen, and this one had the same small dent above the tall hatch and scarring on the cargo doors. It had to be the same one, although there was some more carbon scoring along the right side.

In a fight in the two days since they left? No wonder the name was new. Well, time to see what else she could dig up on the people who were proving to be most interesting. She absently scratched her ribs, feeling the small lump that indicated hidden valuables. One of those items was a dearly paid-for tracking device. Should she use it on this ship or get more information first? It would be extremely useful if they switched berths again, but if they left, she would lose one of her most valuable assets.

She turned to walk away, but a strong instinct spun her back around. She headed toward the ship, looking around carefully for anybody watching. She shrugged. If they left, she could sell their information to cover the price of the tracker. Probably more so, since the name changes and carbon scoring indicated they had some enemies.

Raahi got within throwing distance but far enough away not to set off a proximity alert, then subtly extracted the tracker from the hidden packet. She activated it and felt an affirming ping from her wristcomp. She glanced around again and hesitated. Did she really want to do this? They had met in secret with the companion, which was why she figured they would be interested in what she had to sell. However, if she wasn't careful, she might come to the attention of the royal family, which is *not* where she wanted to be.

But her intuition told her that this ship and people inside it were her best way to make enough money to get her out of her current life and maybe even off the planet.

She threw the tracker.

***

"Tomorrow," said Lenore as the hatch closed behind her.

"That doesn't give us much time," Diarmin said as she handed him her gloves.

"It's enough." She stripped off her wig and headed down the corridor to their room. "Please restore the gloves. The paralytic is gone, and I am sure I used up the charge in the right."

"Wait, we need to talk about—"

"We'll talk when I solidify the plans," her voice echoed back down the hall.

Diarmin followed Lenore to their room. She was already undressing when he entered.

"No, we need to plan together." He tossed the gloves on the bed. "I am not some flunky who needs to be kept out of the way. You are going to need me. Quinn is my son, too."

Lenore never paused in changing and headed to the bathroom without comment. Diarmin wasn't giving up. He knew she was in mission mode, but he had to reach her somehow. He stood in the doorway for several breaths, organizing his thoughts while watching her remove her makeup.

"I do have the occasional good idea, you know."

Lenore placed her hands on the sink, leaning forward, head bowed as she sighed heavily. Diarmin knew that sigh. It wasn't one of defeat or sorrow. She was gearing up to tell him off and most likely insult him so that he would walk away and leave her alone. When she straightened up and started to speak, he beat her to it.

"Yes, you've worked alone and are good at it. I am not denying that." Her mouth closed with an audible snap, and her eyes began to smolder. He pressed on. "There is nothing wrong with help, a bit of back up, if you will. I won't hamper you in any way, and I might just be of some use. Either way, we need to plan together. We have done so in the past, why should this be any different?"

Lenore stared, face blank. Slowly her eyes lost the angry fire, but she still said nothing. He knew he should also be playing the silent game, waiting for her to speak, but he couldn't stop talking.

"I know you want to keep us safe, but that is not always only up to you." Her eyebrows raised slightly, but he ignored that. "We are a family, not a military squad that takes orders. We will watch out for each other, help each other and, when absolutely necessary, take risks together because that is what family is about."

He kept going, uncomfortable with her silent stare.

"We'll weigh the options and discuss—"

Quick as lightning, Lenore's hand flashed out to cover his mouth. "Shut up, will you? You've convinced me, you big lout. Sometimes I forget that I am part of a family. I'm glad you are here to remind me every now and then."

He smiled behind her fingers and felt the tension ease.

"But I have the final say," she added.

Before Diarmin could answer, they both heard pounding footsteps on the ladder and approaching their room. They headed for the door but stopped abruptly as Allison caught herself on the door frame and gasped out her message.

"There's a problem."

Chapter Twenty-Eight

"I count five in all," said Allison. They were in her bedroom, eyeing pictures of a blond Lenore on Allison's personal terminal. "I barely got copies before they were erased."

"Five images, pulled from a variety of cameras," said her father. "I don't understand. How is that a problem if you erased them?"

"But that's the problem. *I* didn't erase them. Someone *else* did, which means they were looking for Mom." Allison flicked her fingers at her console. "No others were erased that I can find."

"It could be the reviewer at the palace," said her mother. "Nobody else would have any reason to."

Allison closed her mouth, lips pressed together. "The deletion pattern is very similar to his previous deletions, but I would have to run detailed specs to be sure. But the point is, if he and I found the images, someone else could have as well, *before* they were erased."

Lenore reached out to pat her on the arm. "You were smart, Alli, to look for them."

Allison smiled, her mother's calm helping her feel a little better.

But not her father. "The fact still remains, however, that we have to assume that your cover is blown, Lenore. The slavers are most likely expecting you and know that you are not what you seem."

"Maybe, maybe not. We always knew that possibility existed. I can get around that."

"Right. Another disguise?" Diarmin shook his head. "These are not simple criminals. This is a highly ordered and lucrative business, well-protected and well established. They are sure to see through any disguise."

"I do have some that you have never seen. I haven't used them in a long time."

Diarmin didn't answer, just tilted his head and pursed his lips. Lenore looked away for several long moments. Allison and her father exchanged knowing glances.

"We'll stick with the plan. Diarmin, you and I will pose as buyers, nose around, find Quinn, get him and get out. Simple and quick."

"And me? Where am I during all this?" asked Allison. "Staying here won't do me, you two, or Quinn any good." She charged on before her parents could interrupt. "I am not stupid, Mom. I know this organization is massive and very good. And like I said, I would rather be far from any fight. But I've been thinking that they might find records of us and come after the ship and then where would I be? The safest place I could be is with you and..." She reached under her computer console and pulled out a bag. "You are going to need this."

"What is that?" asked Diarmin.

Allison emptied the bag onto her bed. Random junk scattered, a hand comp, small data files, what appeared to be a pocket light, and even a hand recorder.

"This," she said proudly, "is my secret project. These items may seem harmless but, when assembled correctly, they create a portable scanner, which you *are* going to need when inside. Chances are this is the same slave trade that existed when the princess and her companion went missing, so we might get some very useful information while inside searching for Quinn. And since they have a scattering field around the building, the scanner needs to be inside to work." She crossed her arms again. "So, I need to go, too."

Dad seemed to appreciate her logic, but Mom wasn't going to give in.

"Show us how to assemble and use that," said Lenore.

"It'll take too long," said Allison, "and it's very difficult to control or read unless—"

"I will think about bringing you because you would be safest with me. But"—Lenore held her finger up—"you can also be safe if you are offplanet when we hit the slave ring. So, while I am considering where you will be, teach your father how to use your scanner." She shot to her feet and paced the few steps to the door, stopped and pivoted back to look at the other two, face flushed and eyes just a bit wild.

"Let's brainstorm, everyone. This plan has to be perfect."

***

Quinn heard the click before the door opened and sat up on the edge of the bed to face his captors. He fought against the urge to scratch or tug at his collar and stared instead at the two men who came in, his old pals, Jerk Man and Muscles. Muscles carried a chair and set it down. Jerk Man sat, crossing his arms while Muscles took a menacing stance near the door. Quinn wondered if they were deliberately mimicking holo dramas, or if this was how criminals actually acted. Despite the irreverent thought, he kept his face expressionless.

"So, mystery boy. You are evidently much more than you appear," said Jerk Man. Quinn fought against showing a reaction, but his heart pounded a bit harder. He had already decided silence was his best option, so he simply waited for the man to continue.

"I am given to understand that you have obtained something of great value, and the owners are willing to pay very highly to have it back." He smiled slightly at Quinn's sudden intake of breath but had misread the reaction.

That must be the cover story Mom came up with. I have to play along. He smiled faintly. *It also must mean she's still alive.*

"Think you are clever, do you?" His eyes narrowed. "What did you take?"

Quinn didn't know what to say. What thing could a kid like himself have stolen that would be worth a lot. Jewelry? Art? Engine parts? His mind raced until the sudden pain around his neck jolted his thoughts. It only lasted a second, but it was enough to make his head swim and to grab involuntarily at the collar.

"I asked you a question, boy."

"I...I..." was all he got out before the electric surge again. This time was much longer, and when it stopped, he lay gasping on the bed. He vaguely heard footsteps and was jerked back to a sitting position by Muscles grasping the front of his shirt. Jerk Man's face leaned in close.

"Tell me, or I will activate this and walk away." He waved the wand.

"Please, no," whispered Quinn.

"Then tell me what you took." He turned it very slightly, slowly and deliberately. Quinn felt the growing tingle, and he blurted out before the shock became too painful.

"I don't know," *Oops.* He didn't mean for the truth to slip out, but he couldn't think. Couldn't invent a good lie or cover story. The answer was not what they wanted to hear, and the electricity kept getting stronger. What would be worth torturing and, more importantly, *not* killing for? *Think, Quinn.*

"Last chance." Jerk Man twisted a bit more. Quinn felt his muscles stiffening, and he forced words out before his jaws locked up with the increased voltage.

"I...don't...know...what it was that I took. Some...data stick or..." The sudden lack of pain caused him to gasp and go limp. He wasn't sure where the words were coming from, but he continued.

"I...I heard these guys talking about it. They said whatever was on it was worth a fortune, something about a lost princess, which I thought was a stupid story, but if it was worth that much, I'd risk it." He was babbling and knew it, but when Jerk Man's eyes widened with the mention of a princess, it gave Quinn more courage to continue embellishing. "I saw where they put it, came back at night when everyone was asleep, snatched it and ran. They ignored me, I was a nobody, just someone who was in the background." Quinn laughed a bit hysterically. "I guess now they know better."

Muscles gave a grunt that could have been a cut off chuckle, but he released Quinn who sagged down.

Jerk leaned back in his chair, a look of doubt on his face, but Quinn saw the relaxation in his posture and concluded that they bought his story. Jerk contemplated his fingernails for a minute, the very picture of nonchalance. He was a very good actor. But Quinn had seen his mother do better. Finally, he spoke the words that Quinn was expecting.

"So, where did you hide this data stick?"

"I can't tell you, not—" Quinn held up his hands to stop the angry looks forming on their faces. "Not that I don't want to, but I don't know the area very well and really don't know how to give directions. I can show you, though."

"A holomap?"

Quinn scrunched up his face, trying his best to look confused and doubtful. "Maybe. I'm not really sure. I could definitely lead somebody in person though. If I got back to someplace I recognized." He held his breath as Jerk crossed his arms. Was it convincing enough? Was he being too obvious that he needed to be kept alive if they wanted to find the alleged data stick? He couldn't help but jump a little when Jerk Man stood suddenly. The man's façade cracked slightly at Quinn's reaction, a small smirk at the corner of his mouth before he signaled Muscles to open the door. They both left, Muscles taking the chair with him.

Quinn let out his breath in a small explosion. They seemed to buy his story, but he couldn't look too satisfied since he knew there were probably cameras in the cell. He settled for curling back up on his cot, facing away from the door, knees brought up in an almost fetal position. He needed to gain some strength back, and all he could really do anyway was wait.

Chapter Twenty-Nine

Prince Hahn could barely keep a straight face. This was the best idea he'd had yet. He eyed Lavan sitting on a chair nervously picking at his shirt. All Hahn had told him was that he had a surprise for him. The worry was priceless, and Hahn could feel the delicious fear resonating through the bond, faint but undeniable.

"How long does it take to walk to the gates and back?" asked one of the two others on the couch. That was Rifkin, son of some duke or other. Hahn didn't really care how "well-bred" the idiot was, he was good at procuring illegal beverages and other entertainments. Despite being older than the prince, he deferred to Hahn and did whatever was asked of him. That kind of adoration was the only reason Hahn let him hang around. Rifkin thought he would be the right-hand man of the king when Hahn was crowned, but the prince laughed inwardly at the thought of the idiot in such a place.

Maybe I should bring back the position of court jester. Rifkin would be perfect for that. He suppressed a chuckle which quickly turned to a frown when Rifkin sloshed the expensive drink, dribbling on the couch.

"Sorry, Hahn," he mumbled, aware of the frown. A throat being cleared by his seatmate made him amend his words. "I mean, sorry, Your Highness."

Endon was the one who kept Rifkin in line, and he nodded at the prince as he reached for one of the plates of canapes. He was a bit thick around the middle, but Hahn knew his pleasant affability and slow demeanor masked a quick mind.

"Remember, Rifkin," said Endon. "It's not only the walk to and from the palace gates, but identities must be validated, and clearances obtained." He popped two snacks in his mouth while balancing four more on his lap.

With those brains, Endon would be a valuable ally or dangerous enemy. Hahn would have to make sure of his loyalty. But how? *Hm, he has a sister he dotes on...*

A quick rap on the door shook Hahn out of future

plans and back into the moment he had been anticipating all day.

"Come," he said, as regally as he could. Might as well practice talking down to subordinates. Everyone would be one soon. Another of his lackeys, Thom, opened the door a crack, mumbled to someone outside the door, slipped in, and nodded to Hahn with a sly quirk of his mouth. He enjoyed these "surprises" as much as Hahn and that was his value to the group.

"Now, Lavan." Hahn pulled up a chair and sat so that he could face his companion. "I have been giving much thought to you lately."

"You have?"

The spike of fear through the bond was more intoxicating than the liqueur.

"Of course. I only have your happiness in mind. You mentioned you were interested in girls, but we all know"—his hand waved at the others who snickered—"you are too shy to do anything about it, so that's what I am here for."

The fear was replaced by surprise, or at least that is what Hahn believed it was. The bond was the only time he truly felt strong emotions, and he was oddly grateful for it, but often the exact emotion eluded him.

"Wh—what did you have in mind? A movie?"

There was now wariness in Lavan's voice, and Hahn could sense a hint of determination. Well, that wouldn't do. He preferred the companion off balance.

"Well, a movie might be nice, but it won't teach you anything. You need experience, and I have thoughtfully provided it for you." The wariness kicked up a notch, which caused Hahn to smile as he gestured to Thom to open the door.

Thom obeyed, opened the door, then made a beckoning motion. A young girl edged in hesitantly, eyes downcast, not looking at anything but the floor. Thom put an arm around her shoulders and steered her toward Hahn and Lavan.

"This is Amala, Your Highness," said Thom.

At the honorific, the girl's head jerked up, mouth formed in a surprised "O." She dropped immediately to her knees and bowed her head.

"Your Highness, this is an honor," she said in a small, scared voice.

"Indeed, it is, young Amala," said Hahn. "But for more reasons than simply meeting me." He reached down to put his hand under her chin to tip her head up. He made no move to let her stop kneeling.

"This is my companion, Lavan." He gestured to Lavan and a glance showed his companion's face was bright red. The bond resonated with embarrassment. *Delicious, but let's see if we can up those emotions.* "He has need of some education and you will supply it for him."

"Your Highness, I...I'm not sure what you mean." Her voice quivered a little, causing the rest of the flunkies to titter. Her fearful glance at them showed she had an inkling where the conversation was going.

"Surely you do. A beautiful girl like you must have had several lovers by now," said Hahn, suppressing a grin at the girl's mortified reaction.

"Oh, not at all, Your Highness. You see—"

"Hahn, this is not necessary," said Lavan at the same time.

"Stop," ordered Hahn. *Arguing and disobedience has no place here. Time to remind everyone of that.* "You have said you are clueless with girls, and I have thoughtfully provided one for you to practice with." He stood and pulled his companion up as well, Lavan's face now red with anger. Amala still knelt, but she was covering her face with her hands. The other boys were watching with intense gazes, Thom's being the most avid of the lot.

"We will give you privacy and time," Hahn said and reached down to grasp Amala's arm roughly and haul her to her feet. Grabbing Lavan also by the arm, he steered both to Lavan's room. "Now, nobody comes out until the deed is done." He stared hard at Lavan. "Several times, if necessary, yes?" He gave Amala a brief shake. "Yes?" he repeated when she didn't answer.

When she nodded, he released her with a small shove toward Lavan. The companion caught her gently and stared at Hahn.

"Go ahead, get on with it," said Hahn. "And don't say I never gave you anything."

The comment set off another round of laughs and muttering, which Hahn ignored. With a look of resignation, Lavan took Amala into his room and closed the door.

Thom was at his side the instant the door closed.

"Do you think he'll have the guts to go through with it?" His smile was lecherous. "I told her she had to obey whatever you asked of her or else there would be dire consequences."

Hahn let the youth think he was successful at being menacing, then shooed him back to the couch with the others. Drink in hand, he lounged in his own chair, reveling in the confusion and anger resonating through the bond. It didn't matter if Lavan went through with it or not. The end would be the same, either way.

Chapter Thirty

Diarmin knocked on the door at the address that the detective had given them. He put his hand on his daughter's elbow as he waited for a response. The door opened, and he gave the bald man behind the door a folded piece of paper with one word written on it. With one hand, the man flipped it open then tossed it into a small flashtray where it incinerated instantly. The two were admitted and pointed toward an archway that Diarmin recognized as a weapons/tech scanner.

He and the hooded and cloaked girl beside him tossed their various accoutrements into a basket and stood under the arch, one at a time. Diarmin tried not to watch as another guard handled the various pads and trinkets that made up Allison's device. He stepped through and angled himself so that he could see the scan of Allison. He caught a glimpse at the screen and could make out the silhouette of his wife, complete with an outline of a wig and height measurements posted beside. He carefully hid his satisfaction that his special hologram device could fool their sensors so well. The device not only created a holographic image but sent false data to the machine, so it couldn't discern that it wasn't Lenore under the cloak, but Allison. He tried to show no emotion as the guard waved him to the basket of electronics that evidently passed inspection.

They were given a bidding wand and led through to the inner room, which already boasted a large crowd. They maneuvered to a table on the right not too close to the stage and were immediately handed drinks by a scantily dressed female. Probably a slave, mused Diarmin, and he let his gaze wander around the room, ignoring the pale hand that slipped from under the cloak to grab the data pad and various electronics. Slight movements under the cloak indicated Allison was assembling her scanner. He noted only one other exit, guarded by two toughs wearing dark glasses and belts with stun sticks and other possible weapons.

The crowd was an incredible mixture of all sorts. At the very front was an exceptionally dressed woman attended by at least two men and a third that roamed around the room. An Onarian, evident by the pale-blue tinged face and hands, was covered with voluminous wrappings that hid whether male or female. A few other tables had people ranging from a young man with a severe tremor, most likely a drug addict, to the elderly gentlemen in the farthest corner that would not be out of place in any position of power within a government or top business.

Not one of them seemed interested in Diarmin and Allison.

A tiny beep from under her cloak indicated the device was working. Allison nodded slightly, and he knew the scans had begun. After one final entry of a hugely fat man with pale, nearly translucent skin and several rings on his fingers, the room lights dimmed, and the stage lights brightened.

Looked like the sale was ready to begin.

Two young girls appeared on the stage, one about Allison's age and the other slightly younger. They stood holding hands and looked relatively healthy but scared. Their features hinted they were born on this planet, and Diarmin could see a strong resemblance as well. The tall, thin salesman with skin darker than Diarmin's began the pitch. His voice was deep and cultured, almost soothing in its timbre.

Perfect for selling live beings, thought Diarmin sourly.

"Strong and hardworking sisters," he said. "Their parents pawned them off to pay their gambling debts. Will do almost anything to keep from being separated."

Many in the crowd tittered at that, and Diarmin struggled to keep his face impassive. Whether that story was true or not, and he doubted it was, the suggestion that anything could be done with the children sickened him. He wished he had a hood to hide emotions, especially when the overweight man won the bid with a lecherous smile.

The second and third sales involved adults with specific abilities, one obviously for his muscle and the other, an offworlder with a green tinge to his skin, supposedly had excellent computer skills both legal and not. The strong one had sold to someone bidding off site and the other to the man in the suit. All of them had simply stood, staring, no fight at all, though the muscled one had a glower that deepened every time a bid was made, especially when the elegant woman requested he turn around.

A nudge at Diarmin's elbow caused him to put his ear close to the hood.

"They are all wearing the same necklaces," whispered Allison. Diarmin had noticed them but was hesitant to guess what they were for without his diagnostics kit. They looked like something to prettify the people for sale, but the makeshift scanner obviously detected more.

"Zzzzzt," was all she said but he knew what it meant. *Electrified to keep them docile.*

"Q?" he asked, but she shook her head.

Now they knew several things, but the most important question of Quinn's location still eluded them. In an attempt to distract himself from the next sales, more children, Diarmin cast glances around the audience. Lenore had told him that in addition to the obvious guards, there would be a disguised one, standard practice in these situations. He picked out two possibilities and was wondering if Allison's device could also take down the force screen surrounding the stage.

A sudden intake of breath from Allison snapped him back to attention.

Quinn was on the stage.

"This is a rare individual indeed. Excellent at thievery and disguise, he has already made a name for himself on the planet Carmal."

Well, they bought Lenore's story, and the talent at disguise was the truth.

"His parents died on the ship that brought him here, and we found him ragged and stealing food in order to survive. He is incredibly smart and docile and will make a terrific addition to any business or household. Opening bid will be at two thousand credits."

The fee brought murmurs from the crowd and Diarmin couldn't help his eyebrows raising. That was twice the beginning bid of anyone else. The Onarian was the first to signal, followed closely by the fat man, and then raised to three thousand by the man in the suit. Lenore had told Diarmin to wait to begin bidding, but the rapidity of the others forced his hand. He bid a hundred more, followed closely by the Onarian again.

Feeling a rising panic, Diarmin hissed, "Can you deactivate that shield?"

"It won't matter. He's not even there. It's a hologram,

projecting from somewhere else."

Diarmin's stomach dropped. The plan had been to take out the guards and snatch him from the stage but now what? He hurriedly placed another bid that was rapidly approaching the six thousand mark.

"What do you have?"

"I don't know. It needs to be analyzed."

"Do something quickly, or we will have to sell the ship."

The bid was up to eight thousand.

The heavyset man had dropped out of the bidding with a grunt, and the Onarian was hesitating after each raise, but now there was a bid off site that was competing with Diarmin and the man in the suit. The plan was to keep going, keep bidding, even if they couldn't afford it. But all the time in the world wasn't giving them the essential information of where Quinn was.

Ten thousand.

Jaw hurting from clenching, Diarmin raised yet again. They were already way over any money they could manage, but he couldn't let his son go to anyone else.

Suddenly the salesman threw up his arms to halt the bidding.

"We have been offered an exclusive. Bidding is closed." The stage went dark.

Diarmin's heart stopped for a moment only to beat faster and harder when the side door flew open and three armed men rushed in, heading straight for their table. Diarmin and Allison stood and edged backward so the table was between them and the guards.

"We have detected a prohibited scanner. Hand it over."

Diarmin tried to protest their innocence but only got one syllable out before the response.

"We will not hesitate to shoot and simply take it."

Movement under Allison's cloak caused all three weapons to be thrust forward menacingly. An open pale hand slowly appeared and drew aside the cloak, revealing the other hand holding the device.

As the man who spoke lowered his gun and reached out to take it, Diarmin noticed her thumb on the kill switch. Now the slavers would only find the device a slag of metal inside.

"Remove your hood."

The hands reached up slowly to fold back the hood, revealing a grim-faced Lenore. The slight recognition on the man's face told Diarmin they knew who she was and had probably been monitoring them since the first scan at the entrance.

"For violating the rules against prohibited equipment, you will be executed."

Chapter Thirty-One

Quinn's gut clenched, and he couldn't hold back a groan. It took all his will not to throw himself against the door in an attempt to get free. Jerk had told him to listen well. The slaves were required to hear their sale, each bid showing solid evidence of their captivity and helplessness. The monetary values meant nothing to him and lack of emotion had been easy until he heard his father's voice, bidding. He couldn't see the audience, but he knew that Diarmin hadn't won the bid. He groaned again and sunk to his knees, knowing he was giving himself away but unable to help it. He didn't care.

"Run. Just run, please. Don't try to rescue me," he murmured, tears now rolling down his cheeks. "I can't lose you all."

He knelt there, immobile. Until he heard footsteps outside his door, no doubt of those taking him to his new master.

***

Diarmin was frozen. Would they really shoot them, here? Now? As the man brought his gun back up, instincts kicked in, and Diarmin launched himself at the man.

"Run!" he yelled. Three bolts fired at him and sizzled harmlessly as he tackled the man.

"Personal shielding!"

"Get the other one!"

He tried to ignore the bolts firing at Allison's retreating back and instead activated the unique effect of his shielding. His specialized shields delivered a powerful stun to his opponent, giving him time to dash out the door behind Allison. As she slowed to look for him, he closed the distance, yelling, "Don't stop," and they continued outside, bolts firing ineffectually as they ran away.

As they turned the corner and headed toward a building, the bolts finally had an effect and the sparks and sizzles caused not only the shield to fail, but the hologram device as well. Lenore's face wavered and disappeared, replaced by Allison's. Diarmin snatched his shield off and attached it to Allison's hood as they ran. A few more shots came close, but they made it inside the building with no more hits. They entered an elevator where she removed her false boots that made her several inches taller.

"You know how hard it is to run in these things?"

"We aren't out of danger yet," Diarmin moved the shield generator from the hood to Allison's shirt.

"The shuttle is on the roof. I can handle that barefoot."

"I saw you activate the kill switch. Did you get the data sent off?"

"I...I think so. I know some did but not how much. I'm sorry."

"It's okay. We didn't have a lot of choice."

The elevator doors opened, and they dashed toward their shuttle. Within heartbeats, they were lifting and merging with the air traffic.

"It's all up to Mom, now," muttered Allison.

***

Lenore eased herself around the corner, gun leading the way, and dropped the guard before his weapon could sight on her. Sloppy. It should have been up already. Especially with the alarms. Maybe the best guards were out chasing the other mission operatives.

Her husband and daughter.

Lenore firmly turned her mind away from the emotions. It was easier to think of her family as operatives so that she could focus on her job. She checked her wristcomp for the data that Allison had sent her. It had cut off midstream, indicating the scanner was destroyed. She hoped it was only the scanner and not...

Don't think, just act, she told herself. Again.

If the data was correct, Quinn would be down one level and through a long corridor to the cells. She set her jaw and found the stairs.

Two guards later, she approached the door to the cell block. Her scatterer would mess up the cameras, but that alone would throw a beacon to whoever was watching them. It had only been a few minutes since the alarm, but she knew the area would be heavily guarded. They would be expecting someone being extra sneaky. So, she did the opposite.

In seconds, charges were set, and she blew the door and anyone within ten feet of it. Charging headlong through the smoke, she yelled at the top of her lungs, firing her weapon blindly, trusting the data that the cells were blast proof.

Groans and sharp yells indicated hits, and she crouched as low as she could while running, sliding along the left wall. Laser bolts and other projectiles shot over her head and down the center of the hall. One projectile hit her right shoulder, but she shut off the pain. These guys were good and in the next moment would start spreading the shots wide and low. If they all got out of this, she swore she would have her husband create more than two personal shields.

Operative, not husband.

Lenore reached the end of the smoke and quickly scanned the corridor for any residual barriers. One woman was on the ground with her weapon, leg smoking and useless. She sighted on Lenore as she emerged and got off only one shot before receiving a fatal one between the eyes. Lenore's left calf burned, and she batted at the hole in her pants to put out the resulting flame while assessing the wound.

Walkable, but not for long.

A quick survey revealed seven people on the floor, including one young man who was probably a slave. After reassuring herself it wasn't Quinn, Lenore felt a brief regret but searched the bodies for a key to open the cells, taking care to make sure the two guards still alive would never regain consciousness. She snatched up a set of electric keys and opened the first cell, revealing two young girls who shrank back in fear. Lenore turned to leave, then cursed silently. No matter how much she needed to find Quinn, she couldn't leave them.

"I'm here to rescue you," she said, voice rough from the smoke and her exertions. The looks of doubt on their faces were telling, but she couldn't deal with that now.

"Either follow, sticking close behind me, or stay. I am going." She turned away but was pleased when the older grabbed the younger's hand and dragged her out the door. The next two cells were empty, and the third held an unconscious man. She left him there, door open, ignoring the older girl's surprised gurgle. Lenore had no idea who he was or how he had become a slave, but his door was open now. He could help himself. Quinn was her priority.

As she continued to the next cell, a squeak from the smaller girl made her spin around. The older one pulled the small one down to the floor, and Lenore dropped the man coming after them with nothing but a force pike. Stupid. They must be low on soldiers. Her smile was grim as she spoke to the girls.

"Thanks for the warning."

Another cell held a small boy with a tear-streaked face, no more than a couple years old. The older girl ran to him and grabbed him up, staring defiantly at Lenore as if saying, "I'm not leaving this one." Lenore couldn't help but smile and nod in approval. She liked this girl's spunk.

Her heart drooped a bit upon seeing the last door. This had to be Quinn. She bit her lip. It HAD to.

She glanced at the three following her, now with trust in their eyes as they watched her key the lock.

She opened the door.

A soft "No" passed her lips on an exhalation.

The room was empty.

Chapter Thirty-Two

Quinn was hardly aware of his actions, but defiance flared up as he heard footsteps. He didn't want to be sold off, his previous vow of subservience for survival's sake gone out of his head completely. He grabbed the only possible weapon, a plastic cup, and flattened himself against the wall next to the door. He became aware of the alarms and realized they had been going off for several minutes. He heard the lock on the door click, so he raised the cup. As he prepared to swing at the height of a probable face, a soft "No," halted his movement.

"Mom?" Emotions swarmed him as he pivoted to face the door then stood there, gaping stupidly. Confusion, relief, happiness, and several other unnamed emotions swirled through him as he noticed his mother's weapon aimed at his heart. Reflexively he dropped the cup and raised his hands.

"Mom?" he said again, a waver in his voice.

Suddenly he was crushed in a hug that ended far too quickly.

"Let's go. Stay behind me. I'll lead all of you out."

His mother was gone, the Xa'ti'al replacing her. Quinn hesitated at the change for only a heartbeat, excitement at escape overcoming any uncertainty. He noticed the other children as they crowded together behind his mother. Instinctively, he brought up the rear, making sure none would be left behind.

Only ten steps toward freedom, he dropped to the floor, electric agony coursing through him. All he could think was that he should have known better than to hope.

***

"Uh oh," said Diarmin.

"What?" said Allison.

He looked at her, wanting to protect her from the truth, but the words slipped out anyway.

"Your mother's signal just went blank."

"What now?"
"I...I don't know."

***

Lenore turned as she heard the shrieks and sounds of bodies hitting the floor behind her. The sight of three children writhing in pain and the toddler staring in shock made her brain freeze in reflex. Only her past training made it possible to turn back and face the new threat pacing slowly down the corridor. The way out was blocked.

She didn't hesitate.

Lenore shot at the man only to have the bolt sizzle harmlessly a foot away from him. Not a simple personal shield but a force globe. Shields, no matter the strength, surrounded the body like a second skin and she could simply attack hand to hand. But with a globe, she couldn't get close, and she knew nothing from her arsenal could get through. The most she could do was physically push the globe, but her guess was that this was a top-of-the line force field and would most likely have electric shock defense.

His face lost its smile when she fired.

"That was rude." He flourished a wand and the cries of pain increased. "After all, I am only trying to prevent you from making off with my property."

Lenore rapidly assessed her options and didn't like any of them. The only way out was past the man, and unless she disabled that wand, the children would be helpless to follow. She slid a knife out of her left sleeve and backed toward Quinn, eyes never leaving the man.

"Ah, ah," he said. "Cutting through the collars will cause them to explode and neither one of us wants that, do we? Again, simply lower your weapon, and I will let you leave alone, unharmed. Nobody gets hurt."

Lenore again regretted the lack of Diarmin's personal shield with the stun effect but thinking about it gave her an idea. She nudged Quinn with her foot, shunting aside the stab of pain from her leg wound.

"This one owes me. Boss would kill me if I lost this investment. How about you keep the rest and I take only him." She pointed the weapon at the door behind her. "And I don't destroy an expensive cell."

He shrugged. "Things can be rebuilt, and *my* employer would kill me if I let such a valuable prize go. I am sorry, they all stay."

She appeared to consider it, allowing the point of her weapon to drop slightly and move closer to her body. "What guarantee do I have for my safety?"

He held his hands slightly away from his body. "I am unarmed. I will move out of the way and order my men to stand down." As if to prove his sincerity, he turned off the collars, causing the screams to drop to agonized whimpers.

"Order them now." She lowered the weapon more and took a few steps toward him.

"Power that down first."

She complied, making a show of activating the weapon's safety and reversing it so she couldn't shoot.

He lifted his wristcomp to his lips and began to order free passage for the "fighting woman."

As she drew close, their eyes locked, watching each other for the slightest betrayal, but she kept her weapon stomach level and pointed at the ground. He obligingly pressed himself as far as he could against the wall to give her enough room to pass his force globe. Lenore could see the man relax slightly, most likely because he knew that the only thing that could possibly take out a force globe bubble was an overload. Directly overloading her weapon would cause an explosion, a bit too much if she wanted to stay alive. But what few knew is that there was another way, especially if a weapon was designed for just such contingencies.

Using the knife she had drawn out of her boot earlier, she stabbed it directly into the control panel of her gun. Since the knife was solid metal, the controls began to short out, allowing a conduit for the overload. She threw herself with the sparking, electrified weapon at the man and his force globe, trying to ignore the shocks that were an unfortunate side effect. As the globe began to glow and flash in response to the overloading, she pressed her advantage and restrained the globe with all her strength so that the man couldn't get away.

"Run, Quinn!" she yelled through clenched teeth. "And get the others out!" She grunted as the man tried to push her back to win his freedom, but though this type of force field kept everything out, they also kept everything in. "Go! This only lasts a few seconds." At the edge of her awareness, she saw Quinn pick up the little boy and begin herding the girls in the correct direction.

Just a little longer, she told herself as she felt it begin to give way. As Quinn and the others passed her, he hesitated.

"Go!" she said. She risked a look at him to get her point across, but he wasn't looking at her. He was looking at the blaster the man had drawn.

Lenore's voice took on an icy calm. "I need you to get them safe. Out to the east. Two buildings to the east and three to the north. Take the elevator."

A look settled into Quinn's eyes as they met hers. The exchange was only a heartbeat, but Lenore knew he understood. The only way to free them from the collars was by shorting out the globe and grabbing the wand. But his blaster would take her down right after.

She was going to sacrifice herself for them all.

The weapon's electronics finished its death and the globe, though weak, was still intact.

I only need a few more seconds. The man inside the field had a smug smile on his face, and he taunted her by holding up the collar control stick. Quinn and the children had already disappeared around the corner, but she heard their yells as he activated the wand again.

In desperation, Lenore reached behind her back, under her shirt, for the small, powerful box that always nestled there. It was a specialized medical monitor that Xa'ti'al were fitted with when they were activated to full duty. A discharge from that would be even stronger than the weapon, as the monitor had the ability to deliver a resuscitating pulse to her heart. She didn't give a second thought about its loss as long as Quinn won free. With only a small wince for the implanted wires pulled out along with it, she cranked the voltage up and applied the device to the globe.

The man's smug look vanished, replaced by a look of fear. *He recognizes what this box is.* No time to think about that now as the globe began to flicker. She activated the pulse, which ruined the implant, but was worth it when the shield failed completely.

Lenore rushed the man, grabbing the wand as she braced herself for the blaster shot, and determined to take him down with her.

***

"I'm in," said Allison, voice calm despite the tension

Diarmin knew they were both feeling. In the minutes since they lost Lenore's signal, Allison had linked the shuttle's computer to both the ship and her personal comp. With help from the stolen data, she was now looking at the security feeds from the slave building. In a few more breaths, she had them under her control. He shook his head, more impressed than ever with his daughter.

"There they are," he said, pointing at the screen as she was cycling through the various feeds. "Looks like Quinn is getting some kids out while she holds the guy."

"Hang on." Allison's fingers flew over the computer pads and she reached over to snatch Diarmin's comp out of his hands. She flipped it open and the screen lit up with a map of the complex. Diarmin marveled anew.

"Can you help Quinn find the right way out?"

"That's the plan, wait," a few keystrokes. "There, those guys can't get to them and, oh crap."

"What?" asked Diarmin but didn't need an answer when he saw the children writhing on the floor with pain, jewels in their collars lit up. "Alli, can you block that signal to their collars?"

"Where's it coming from?" she asked, not looking up but fingers still flying.

"Looks like the man Lenore is after has a control stick of some kind. Probably that."

"I'll try but..." her brow furrowed as she cycled between cameras showing Quinn and the children and glancing at the map. "Gotta keep locking doors to keep the guards away from them."

He was thankful Allison had all her attention on her brother and not her mother. Diarmin had noticed the shield failing and the blaster coming to bear on Lenore. He had always known the chances were high that she would die before him, but he had foolishly allowed himself to hope. He didn't want to watch her death, yet he couldn't look away.

Lenore was on the man right as the shield failed, knocking away the wand.

"The collars' lights are off," said Allison. "Look, Quinn and the others are getting up and running again. I'll open the doors for them. Think I can clear a path..."

But Diarmin couldn't look away from his wife. He'd seen the flash that had to be a blaster discharge. If the video had sound, he would know for sure, but he was oddly relieved it was silent. He'd contemplate those feelings later, he thought as he watched Lenore tackle the man to the ground. Her back was to the camera, and Diarmin couldn't tell if she was injured. The man lay struggling flat on the ground with one of Lenore's knees on his chest, her arms still unseen to the camera. He managed to aim a fist at the side of her head, but Lenore twisted her neck, taking most of the blow to the back of her head. The man cried out as Diarmin noticed Lenore's shoulders flex, and he knew she had broken his wrist while disarming him of the blaster. She brought the blaster up under his chin, and his head snapped back to connect with the floor beneath him. He went completely still.

Lenore stood, blaster in hand, staring down at the man, breathing heavily. Diarmin saw blood dripping down Lenore's side and could tell she was favoring her left leg.

"Go," he whispered. "What are you waiting for?" He was answered by Lenore taking two steps beyond the man to pick up the wand. She turned and began to leave but stopped. She looked back at the man, raised the blaster and fired point blank into his face.

Then she followed the same way out that Quinn had gone.

"When Quinn is safe, show me how to erase these security recordings," Diarmin said.

"He just left. I can start erasing."

"No, I'll do it. You make sure Quinn and the others make it here safely. Reroute any law enforcement and do whatever needs to be done."

She raised an eyebrow at her father, but he was adamant. He did not want her to see her mother kill a man in cold blood.

Chapter Thirty-Three

Despite her injuries, Lenore caught up to the group of children before they entered the building where the family shuttle waited. She called to Quinn, who was carrying the boy. The look of relief on his face was brief as Lenore herded the lot inside with a quick glance behind to make sure there were no followers.

She kept an eye and her stolen blaster on the entrance as the slow elevator made its way to them at ground level. No one. How long could this luck hold?

"In. To the roof." She knew she was curt and demanding, but it worked as the oldest girl punched for the roof.

"Need me to take the boy?" she asked her son.

"I'm fine," he replied with a flicker of a smile. Privately, Lenore was glad. She knew she was coming close to the end of her reserves.

As the elevator pinged for the roof, Lenore felt a wave of dizziness but set her jaw. She never realized just how much she had depended on the implanted device for extra adrenaline and painkillers.

The doors opened, and the shuttle was in sight. They ran toward the ramp, Lenore right behind them, even though her injured leg made running difficult. Not needing Allison's urging, standing at the door beckoning them in, they clambered in quickly.

"Grab on to something," said Allison as the engines fired. "The authorities are on their way, and we want to be gone before they get here." She threw herself into the copilot's chair next to Diarmin.

Lenore took the nearest seat and held her arms out for the boy. Quinn deposited him on her lap, and she wrapped the strap around both her and the toddler. Quinn pushed the two girls onto the other chair, strapped them in, then tucked himself behind the chairs, holding on to the brackets.

Diarmin launched the shuttle and immediately banked hard east. He pushed the engines to the maximum, accelerating for several heartbeats before he yelled.

"Hang on."

The nose pointed straight up, and they headed for space, obviously intending to come back to the ship still at the spaceport from a roundabout way. Lenore glanced at the girls, but they were secure, pressed back into their seat and holding onto the arms of the chair as hard as they could. She craned her neck to check on Quinn, who was bracing himself with his legs to keep from sliding and gripping the brackets on the chairs. A wave of relief swept over her, and she felt dizzy again.

The shuttle leveled out, and Diarmin began the lazy turn to take them into the flow of other space vehicles heading to the port. Allison was punching keys on the comp, most likely erasing any video feeds of the shuttle.

In what seemed like no time at all, they were docking with the yacht, which awoke Lenore from a brief doze. Quinn stood up shakily and went to unstrap the girls, but the older one had already found the release. They all filed off the ship and into the cargo bay. Before the shuttle doors closed, Allison ran over to Quinn and enveloped him in a hug. She mumbled something, muffled by her face buried in his chest while a surprised Quinn hugged her back just as fiercely.

"I'm so glad you're okay, Quinn." She pulled away, tears running down her face. Diarmin joined in as well.

Lenore smiled. She had such a wonderful and talented family and had never been prouder. She gently set the boy down and started to limp toward her husband and children. She only had time for a couple steps before she pitched headlong to the floor and all went dark.

Chapter Thirty-Four

Lavan felt a smile cross his face and then realized it had been a long time since he had genuinely felt happy. Amala was coming to visit him shortly, and for the first time ever, he was grateful to Hahn.

Not that anything happened that first day. It had taken Lavan nearly half an hour to convince the poor girl that he had no desire to abuse her as the prince had demanded. He had sat her on the bed and took a chair across the room, trying to appear non-threatening. As he had talked about inconsequential things, she stopped trembling and began to realize he had no designs on her virginity. They had talked for over two hours and decided to pretend they had done what the prince wished to keep her from being punished.

To keep up the façade, Lavan had asked if she could be given a job in the palace so he could continue to see her. Thom made a rude comment about "use her, you mean," but the prince got her a job as a helper in the kitchen. Amala had visited Lavan every day since.

After reassuring her that there were no monitors in the room and no possible way Hahn could know the truth, she relaxed and became quite an enjoyable friend. She was as fascinated with history as Lavan, and their conversations often were stimulating debates over books they had both read.

Lavan quickly set up a strategy game that she said she loved to play. Hahn had never had patience for anything that wasn't physical, so Lavan was looking forward to playing it with Amala. A knock on the door made his heart lift, and he barely fought down the smile in case Hahn was watching.

He opened the door to a subdued Amala, head bowed, and hands clasped in front. A glance around the outer room showed Hahn glaring at them, arms crossed. Lavan motioned Amala to enter and nodded soberly to Hahn before he closed the door.

The change in Amala was instant. A smile lit up her

face, and Lavan returned the look with an even bigger grin.

"I am glad to see you," she said. She noticed the game board and clapped her hands. "Oh, you remembered!"

"Of course, I did," said Lavan, trying to ignore the squeeze of his heart at her delight. "Shall we play?"

An hour later, she had beaten him and began teasing about his lack of skill.

"Hey, I think I did fine, considering I have only ever played the game twice. Well, with another person, that is," he said.

For some reason she thought this was hilarious and broke out into laughter but covered her mouth when Lavan put his fingers to his lips.

"I wish we didn't have to be so careful," he said. "But it's better not to give Hahn any reason to think we aren't, well, you know."

"Yes. He scares me whenever he looks at me," said Amala. "I always feel that he is watching for any indication to accuse me of anything."

"He does that to everyone. I still find it hard to ignore." Lavan didn't like the serious mood and changed the subject. "So, you were going to tell me yesterday about your little brother."

She giggled, and her smile returned. "Georgie has this habit of dressing up like the heroes in whatever entertainment is popular. Usually the costumes look normal, like a detective or attorney. But last week he dressed up as a fictional character, cape and everything."

As she went on to describe his costume, Lavan was trying so hard to contain his laughter that he slid off the bed, cracking his head on the floor. Stunned, he focused his gaze on Amala leaning over him, a concerned look on her face.

"Are you okay?" she asked, brow furrowed with concern.

He sat up, his face coming within inches of hers. "It was worth it," he said softly. He so wanted to close the distance between them, but he had sworn she was safe from that kind of attention.

The point became moot when she leaned forward to kiss him. It wasn't very long but left Lavan breathless.

"I really like you, Lavan," she said, blushing.

"I like you, too," he replied and was bold enough to kiss her again.

Chapter Thirty-Five

Diarmin noticed Lenore's eyelids flutter, and he knew she would be waking up soon. He quickly detached all the IVs and backed away from the medbed. Sure enough, her eyes flew open, and she sat up instantly, hands coming up into a defensive position and body tensing. She did better than he thought, stopping herself before sliding off the bed into a fighting crouch. Or maybe she just felt the damage a bit more this time.

"Everything is fine," he said, knowing it would be the first question and then continued answering before she could ask. "Quinn is doing well, no injuries but a few bruises and a bit of dehydration from the electrical shocks. The collars, which we removed after finding the wand you picked up, targets the pain receptors so very little voltage actually runs through the wearer. It also sends drugs when turned off to counter any damage to the body. Rather ingenious, but Quinn would argue otherwise."

Lenore gave a humorless snort and shifted around. Diarmin grabbed an extra pillow to help her get comfortable, noting each grimace of pain.

"You, however, sustained quite a long list of problems. Not only severe electric shock but various wounds including a leg that needed extra bonding treatment, and a huge chunk taken out of your side that barely missed anything vital." He mimed with his thumb and forefinger just how close, trying to ignore his stomach clench as he remembered each injury and the fear he had felt when she passed out. He sat on the bed after arranging the pillow behind her back, wanting to hold her but just glad to be looking into her eyes. She smiled back.

"I didn't worry you, did I? I think that's the first time I have ever lost consciousness, well, since we've met."

"Losing this didn't help." He held up the blackened ruin of her Xa'ti'al medplant. "I don't know how you managed, but it was tucked into your belt along with the wand for the slave collars."

"Habit, I guess. I don't really remember after..." she

trailed off, a frown crossing her face.

Diarmin lowered his voice to barely above a whisper. "I saw."

Lenore's eyes widened slightly, then narrowed. "Saw?"

"Allison hacked into the security feeds after your signal went dark. They had blocked outgoing signals, but she had the codes from her downloads. We saw the fight and then she helped Quinn and the kids by locking doors, rerouting guards and traffic."

"I see." Lenore's eyes were unreadable. "I was wondering why nobody followed us."

"I erased the video since she was busy." He paused, not sure if he wanted to say out loud the chill he got when she shot the slaver. "I saw you pick up the wand, Allison didn't. Then it was over, and next thing I knew, you were coming out of the elevator."

"Okay," Lenore looked away.

They were both silent for several heartbeats. As the moments ticked by, Diarmin tried to think of something to say, but Lenore beat him to it.

"I had to. The man saw my face. He would never have given up looking. And..." she paused, still not looking at Diarmin. "He knew what the implant was. He knew it was a Xa'ti'al device. He could have turned me in to them."

Her wooden voice told Diarmin that she wasn't really trying to convince him. She was justifying her actions to herself. He knew she would be wrestling with that choice for a while, so he wisely let it drop without comment.

Wanting to lighten the mood, Diarmin cleared his throat and gave her a wink and grin. "Well, while you've been *snoozing*, Allison and I have been going over the downloads. She got quite a bit before they detected the scanner and so rudely threatened to execute us."

Lenore turned back, a small smile on her face, appearing grateful for the change of topic. "Mine cut off midstream, probably when they blocked the signal. Didn't look like we got that much."

"Ah, but remember, the download went to the shuttle first, then bounced to you. There is a significant amount of information, and Allison has also found some entries most likely pertaining to the princess's abduction."

"Already?" She correctly read his hesitation. "How long was I out?"

"A day and a half."

"What?! You let me sleep when—" she tried to stand,

and his hand on her chest was enough to keep her in place. More proof of her debility.

"I had no choice, you were...I don't know how you made it back." His panic at the memory surfaced again. "And without this"—he waved the medplant a bit wildly—"you are lucky to even be alive."

"Yes, well, I did, so let's move on." Her eyes looked at his restraining hand and back at him.

Diarmin gritted his teeth at her gruff tone but said nothing as he pulled back his hand. He knew she wouldn't talk about it. Lenore slowly swung her legs over the side, taking her time standing. He held out an arm, ready to steady her if needed.

"How is Quinn dealing with it all?" she asked softly as she grabbed the clothes Diarmin had brought earlier.

"Putting on a brave face, but"—Diarmin shook his head—"I can tell he is, well, not damaged, I don't think, but...changed." His voice caught as he spoke.

Lenore just nodded. "That kind of experience would affect anyone, especially a youngster." She shoved her arms and legs into the clothing so fiercely Diarmin was surprised it didn't tear.

"He'll get through it. He has you." The words seemed trite, but he knew Lenore blamed herself, and it was the only consolation he could offer.

She didn't meet his eyes, lips so tightly pressed together they were almost unseen. Diarmin felt the reaction was more than just guilt. Most likely something from her past. Again.

She pulled on soft ship shoes and headed for the door, slow but steady, her set jaw indicating discomfort.

"Let's see that data."

As they climbed the ladder to the bridge, Diarmin felt the vibrations of the ship's engines starting. He consulted his wristcomp. Yep, it was time. Lenore glanced down at him, eyebrow raised.

"Allison estimated that it would take the slavers around forty-eight hours to track us down, so I told her in thirty-six we would move." Lenore said nothing, so he continued. "She is prepping, and I will pop us out somewhere long enough for Alli to change our ID again and come back. Oh, I found a tracker." He reached into his pocket and tossed a small tracking device in the air. "It looks to have been placed before the rescue, so my guess is some local tagging ships."

Lenore sighed. "One in every port."

They reached the bridge and Lenore nodded at him. "Where's the data?"

"Mom!" The whirlwind that was Allison launched herself out of the command chair and in two bounds reached and flung her arms around Lenore. Diarmin could see Lenore wince slightly from pain, but she hugged Allison back just as hard.

"I was scared, you fainted, and Quinn was so tired, and they shot at me. Shot...at...me. But you're fine, Dad's fine, we're all fine, and I am keeping busy, you know 'cause that's the best way to get through, you always say, and I dug deep..."

Lenore smiled through the torrent of speech.

"Good job, little firecracker," said Lenore as she put her arm around her daughter and led her to the console.

"Now why don't you fill me in on what you found while Dad pilots the ship?"

Diarmin was quiet. They had safely made it out.

This time.

Chapter Thirty-Six

Jonah tossed and turned in bed. His mind kept returning to the main news story in all the feeds, a "terrorist attack on a local private dining club." It had appeared to be the usual drama that always occurred in any city on any planet, but something about the news reports kept nagging at him.

He glanced at the time and groaned. Still hours before he usually got up for work. This was the third time he had awakened from a fitful sleep. He mentally reviewed the stories, down to the last he saw, a thirty-second mention and reward for any information.

Jonah began to drift off again but suddenly sat bolt upright in bed as it struck him.

There were no recordings of the event. Somebody had been erasing the logs.

While this wasn't unheard of, it was rare enough that it stuck with him, causing him to get up, make some strong caf and leave for work long before his shift started. He sat in the corner, ignoring Ginette who was completely uninterested in what Jonah was looking for. Even with his access codes, supposedly the highest on the planet, he could find nothing specific on either the attack or the club itself. He leaned back, considering this, when the latest story came on the feed.

This time there was a video of the culprits racing away from the building. A concerned citizen had recorded them running on her personal comp, and the two figures were now wanted by the authorities. The picture wasn't perfect, but clear enough.

The cloaked figure was the woman the companion hired, the one who he believed to be a Xa'ti'al. Did that mean the club was part of the slave ring? He swore under his breath. They were good at removing all the security footage but, as he knew from long experience, there was very little anyone could do about personal comps. And now they were wanted fugitives, which would make meeting them that much harder.

Perhaps that was why he hadn't heard anything for three days. Maybe the search was right back in his lap as it had been for the past fifteen years. Grimly, he decided to begin by monitoring the club. The news said it was closed, and Jonah knew that if it had been a front for the slave ring, they had probably already moved on. Maybe he would get lucky, but so far, luck didn't seem to be on his side. With this lead gone, Jonah hoped the Xa'ti'al got what she needed, or this investigation into the lost princess was over. As he tapped into the public cameras, he set them to record and reached over to switch the monitor to the main board, now that Ginette was leaving. But his hand froze over the switch and he gaped in surprise.

Staring at the club was the information broker, the woman he had spent years trying to find.

***

Raahi couldn't believe it. She had seen the feed that morning, and the personal video they showed looked like the same woman who was meeting with the companion, though the man with her was not Lavan. Why had she been there? What happened? Raahi didn't believe in the terrorist story, but the coincidence that the people she was shadowing were here, messing with one of the buildings on her regular watch, made her very uncomfortable. Perhaps she should abandon her plans despite the time and resources already spent. She hadn't gotten this far without knowing the fine line between taking risks and being stupid.

She spun on her heel and headed home. This would require some serious thought.

***

Hahn paced back and forth. Thom should have been here by now. Lavan was in his room again with Amala. Yesterday, when she had left, a look passed between them that told Hahn it was time for the second part of his plan.

He looked at his watch, and his anger went up another notch as he realized this was the first time any of his lackeys had ever kept him waiting. He was about to snarl into his wrist comp to demand Thom's location, but there was a quick rap at the door followed by its opening.

Thom entered holding up a box about the size of his

head.

"I got it, Hahn."

"Who said you could enter?" Hahn demanded. "How dare you open the door without my permission. And how am I supposed to be addressed?"

Thom took a step back up against the door at Hahn's vehemence.

"I...I...apologize, Your Highness." He bowed low, but not before Hahn saw the fear in his eyes. "It will never happen again."

"See that it doesn't." Though it was satisfying to see the flinch at his intimidating tone, Hahn realized he shouldn't take out his anger on devoted followers. He reined in his temper. "So, you have what I required?"

Thom looked up, and Hahn was pleased to see subdued respect.

"Yes, Your Highness." He opened the box and produced a video camera. "Where shall I set it up?"

"On that table," Hahn said, pointing. "Are Endon and Rifkin coming?"

"They are awaiting a signal from me," replied Thom as he began to set up the camera.

"Signal them now. It's time."

Thom nodded, tapped his wrist comp, and only a few minutes later, the camera was ready. The other two lackeys were seated on the couch, anticipation easy to read on their faces.

Hahn lifted his chin and approached Lavan's door. He indicated with a wave of his hand that Thom was to start the recording. Hahn waited a heartbeat for dramatic effect then flung open the door to his companion's room.

The two were caught in a kiss. Not a very passionate one, but it made the prince sneer with satisfaction. *Perfect.*

"Well, this is nice," he commented as they sprang apart. "It appears I chose well for you, didn't I, Lavan?"

"Yes," said Lavan as he stepped in front of Amala.

This was just getting better and better.

"You have never thanked me, though, Companion," he said.

"I didn't?" Lavan looked confused but played it well. "I regret my omission. Please accept my gratitude at your generosity." He bowed slightly.

Amala stood peering around Lavan, looking frightened.

"You are welcome. Is she as talented as I thought she would be? I assume she has taught you a great deal and you her?"

"Of course, Prince Hahn," said Lavan.

"Good." He held out his hand. "Time for her to show how much she knows."

"What?"

The confusion on his companion's face was a delight.

"Thom wishes to learn as well. She needs to earn her position, you know." He beckoned with his outstretched hand. "Come, Amala."

A squeak from the girl only fired up Hahn's excitement. *Maybe I will have her as well.*

"You said she was for me. Nobody else can have her." Lavan was showing his anger openly for the first time ever. *That just won't do.*

"No, Companion. I said she would teach you. I never said she was only yours." Hahn took the few steps to the couple and roughly grabbed Amala's arm. Lavan actually shoved at Hahn to make him let go.

Expecting such a move, Hahn braced for the shove, then backhanded Lavan across the face as hard as he could. Lavan was flung back to sprawl on the floor. Hahn was impressed with his own strength and glanced at the camera to make sure it had all been recorded.

"I am the authority here, Lavan. Never, ever question that again." Still holding Amala's arm, he leaned over Lavan. "I gave her to you. I can take her away."

He dragged her out the door, ignoring her protests and struggles. Lavan scrambled to his feet and tried to stop them again. This time, Hahn slapped Amala, not as hard but enough to leave a mark. Everyone was stunned silent, including the watchers, though Thom had such a lascivious grin, it was humorous.

"No more protests. She is only going to show us why you have been with her every day. If she's that good, we all should experience it. If you try to interfere again, I won't stop with just a slap."

For the first time, Lavan looked as if he would stand up to Hahn. *Come on, do it.* Hahn was nearly disappointed when Amala shook her head at Lavan and the companion's face crumpled. *Cowards.*

"Please, Hahn. Let her go. For me." There were actually tears in Lavan's eyes. Hahn hoped Thom was getting a close-up.

"You've had your fun, now it's time for others to benefit from my generosity. You've ignored me for days and that is not how things are supposed to be, *Companion.* Remember that."

He shoved Amala at Thom, who quickly handed the camera to Rifkin. Thom grabbed the girl hard enough to bruise.

"Please, enjoy my room, Thom. No need to drag her all the way to your place."

His slow grin was all the answer they needed. Amala and Lavan kept their gazes locked on each other until the door closed, then Lavan dashed out of the suite, slamming the door behind him.

The perfect end to the perfect plan.

Hahn grabbed the camera and then dismissed the other two to go follow the companion so that he could watch the recording of Lavan's anguish in private.

Chapter Thirty-Seven

Diarmin looked up as he saw Quinn's head pop out of the stairwell. Quinn glanced toward Lenore and Allison, but they still had their heads together over the console. Diarmin wasn't sure how to interpret Quinn's completely blank expression.

"How are the youngsters?"

Quinn closed the distance and stood next to the command console.

"All asleep, finally. They're in the lounge because they threw a fit when I tried to get them into a guest room. Probably because it reminded them of the cell." A shadow of a frown flitted across Quinn's face, but Diarmin didn't interrupt.

"I think I finally convinced Surhi, the oldest girl, we would get her home, but that it was dangerous to return immediately." Quinn shook his head. "It would be easier if she spoke Standard fluently, but I think she's only had a year or two of instruction. The two little ones only speak the local language, and the translator has a glitch and isn't translating accurately."

"We'll have to have Allison look at that."

"Yeah, so I am pretty sure she understands we aren't just more kidnappers, and she told me where she lives, so I know we can find it later. Mom will know how long we have to wait." Quinn glanced at Lenore again, and Diarmin wanted to wince at the subdued tone. Quinn had learned a hard lesson, but Diarmin hoped it wouldn't crush his spirit.

"And when and if we can get a message to their family to leave for their own good," added Diarmin. Quinn nodded absently, deep in thought and still staring at his mother. Diarmin reached out and gripped Quinn's shoulder gently. "You did well, Quinn."

Quinn grimaced and looked down, clearly not agreeing with his father.

"Hey," he shook his son's shoulder a bit, causing him to look directly at him. "I mean it. You stayed alive and level-headed. You helped save those children and have since calmed and communicated with them when they would have nothing to do with us."

Quinn looked like he was going to dismiss his part, but Diarmin cut him off.

"It could have been a lot worse," he said. "A lot worse."

Quinn nodded and looked away. His lips tightened, and the fire in his eyes made Diarmin smile inwardly. *I will bet that Quinn has just decided that he would prepare so such a thing would never happen again.* It was good to know Quinn's spirit was still there.

He let go of his son's shoulder and tapped the board. "We will be here for several hours, but we'll get them home as soon as we can. Meanwhile, keep doing what you are doing."

"Okay. Thanks, Dad."

"Well, that's a good start," said Lenore. Diarmin thought she was talking to him and Quinn, but she was slowly standing up from the console and clearly looking at Allison. "I think this line will be the next to follow." She pointed at the screen, and Diarmin noticed a slight wince of pain. "It would go a lot faster if we could break the rest of the code."

"Well, the only reason I broke that one was because it was obvious that those were coordinates and dates," said Allison. "With words, it's a lot harder. First, what language, then what cipher, and so on."

Lenore smiled. "I'm not blaming you, Allie. You've done a great job. Let's let the programs chew on the code for a while. I'm hungry."

"And I need to alter the ship ID." Allison stood and headed for her station.

"Not so fast," said Diarmin. "You, young lady, need some rest."

"I'm fine, Dad."

"You haven't slept in two days, so get to your bunk."

"Let me just..."

"No." He strode to her station and turned it off, hand covering the switch so that she couldn't turn it back on.

"Hey!"

"Sleep. I am not risking your health on something that can be done later. And better with a rested mind."

Allison let out an exasperated sigh. "Fine." She stomped down the ladder to the rooms. Lenore looked on with a smile until her husband shook his finger at her.

"I'm tempted to send you back to bed. You are by no means recovered."

"I slept long enough, and food is more important than rest right now." Her gaze shifted to Quinn, and Diarmin could see a gauntlet of emotions flow briefly across her face.

"Good to see you up, Quinn. Hungry?"

He shrugged. "Sure, I can always eat."

"I will guard the bridge to make sure Allison doesn't sneak back up here," said Diarmin. "Catch her up on the kids, Quinn."

He nodded solemnly at his father, then followed Lenore down the ladder. Diarmin knew they needed the time alone together, but he had no idea what the outcome would be. Anger, tears, blame? He so wanted to be there, but he had to trust that Lenore wouldn't alienate their son.

***

Quinn and his mom were seated, each with a sandwich and drink, by the time Quinn finished reciting all that had happened with the children. They had gone below decks to the cargo bay so that they could talk without disturbing the sleeping children in the lounge. Perched on a stack of grav plates, Quinn searched for a way to begin what he knew was going to be an awkward conversation.

"Dad and I thought you would know best how and when to contact the girls' parents. Also, what we should do with the boy." His mother looked at him sharply but said nothing. He figured he wasn't doing the humble and contrite bit very well.

"I...I'm so sorry, Mom. You could have been killed and Dad and Alli. I should never have—"

"That's right, you shouldn't have."

Quinn hung his head.

"But..." Lenore cleared her throat. "But even though you did a lot wrong, there were a lot of things you did right." He looked up at her, but she turned her head away, as if she were searching for the right words. "You stayed healthy, you had the presence of mind to stick to your story and even changed it in a clever way when you heard what I had told them. They evidently believed you or you would've been sold or..." She swallowed but continued strongly, "or dead." She set her jaw and looked him straight in the eye. Quinn couldn't wrench his gaze from hers. "One wrong move, Quinn, just one, and that is exactly how it would have ended. In this case, I think your naivety served you well. It showed that you were not prepared or trained at all for espionage." Her rough assessment caused Quinn to flush, but he endured the rebuke. He deserved whatever punishment and admonishments he got.

"Your rashness forced us into a situation, and now we have angered one of the biggest, most organized slave trades I have ever seen. I am sure we are labeled as fugitives and that makes working the case we came here for even more difficult."

Now Quinn looked away, fighting tears at the knowledge of just how much he had screwed up.

"Fortunately, we salvaged something by downloading a lot of data from their files." Lenore gave a wry smile. "I am sure they are putting security in place to avoid just such an invasion in the future. Now, before I decide what to do with you, tell me what you have learned."

Quinn was confused at the quick change of subject. "Learned? I already told you how they reacted to me mentioning the princess. Do you mean about the slavers or about my actions?"

"Tell me what you have learned."

"I'm not sure..." He focused on his hands.

She interrupted his mumbling hesitations by grabbing his right shoulder, emphasizing each of her next words with a rough shake.

"What-have-you-learned?"

Not used to such harsh treatment from his mother, Quinn stared before answering.

"I learned that I wasn't ready for such an assignment," he said with a half-hearted attempt at humor. His mother simply dropped her hand from his shoulder, apparently still waiting. He looked around the cargo bay, focusing on nothing.

"I learned that the people who are part of this slave thing show no mercy and have no problem torturing children. I learned that they don't value anything but money. I learned that it hurts to be shocked. I learned that no matter what I did or said, they found an excuse to hurt me." He was nearly shouting now, though his eyes were leaking tears.

"I learned that everything they do is designed to humiliate and take away hope. I learned that I was nothing but an investment, and I knew if I wasn't worth keeping around, they would get rid of me. But mostly I learned," and here he choked, lowering his voice. "I learned that I knew nothing about what I was doing and was not prepared for...for that. And I learned that I was completely powerless and helpless for the first time in my life. And..." He broke off, not sure what else to say but feeling he wasn't finished.

"And you don't want to feel that powerless or helpless again. Ever." Lenore spoke in a whisper, but it cut straight through to his heart.

"Yes," he whispered back. Now his tears flowed freely, but it was a release. The weight that had been crushing his spirit seemed lighter.

"Then that is where we will start your training."

Quinn's head jerked up. "What?"

"You are right that you weren't ready at all. But now you know what it is like and why I didn't want you involved. Not like any entertainment program, but horrible and terrifying." Lenore sighed. "But if you truly want to do this, to learn what I know and do what I do, I will teach you."

Quinn couldn't believe his ears. He would have thought his mother would never let him off the ship again. He opened his mouth to answer but quickly closed it again.

"Don't answer now," she said. "Think about it as long as you want. Take time to recover from...that. Ask me whatever; talk to your father. You will know when and if you are ready." She reached over and embraced him. "I love you, no matter what you choose."

Before he could hug her back, she let go. "Now go get some rest. Sleep, if you can." She grinned. "You look as awful as I feel."

"But..." How could he tell her that his room felt too small? That he was afraid to sleep, worried in his gut that he would wind up back in his cell? That every time he closed his eyes, he could feel the collar back on his neck?

"I think you need to sleep in the lounge, in case the kids wake up." Lenore stood up. "I'll get some blankets and a pillow." She patted him on the shoulder on her way out.

He smiled, amazed at the huge sense of relief at her suggestion. Maybe she did understand. As he carried the dishes back up to the galley and lounge, he wondered how she knew exactly how he felt.

Chapter Thirty-Eight

Diarmin ran into Lenore coming out of the lounge.

"Allison is sleeping." He grinned. "I was ready to give her some sleeping meds, but it wasn't necessary."

"I just gave Quinn some blankets to bed down in the lounge with the kids," she replied, barely slowing down as she headed back to the bridge. "He might not sleep, but he's relaxed enough to get some rest, I think."

"Now that things are somewhat back to normal," muttered Diarmin as he followed his wife. Lenore glanced back at him but was quiet. She plopped herself in front of the display again and was immediately absorbed in the information they pulled from the slavers.

"You should get some more rest, too," said Diarmin.

"I'm fine," came an absent reply, causing Diarmin's brow to furrow slightly.

"Hey, we've got some breathing room and you need to recover—"

"Can you fix that medplant?" Lenore kept her eyes on the screen, making some notations on her comp pad.

Diarmin blinked at the sudden change in topic. "I haven't had time..."

"I need that implant. That's your priority while we are out here."

"We've got a breather, why don't..."

"No, we don't."

"What's going on, Lenore?"

"Nothing, just want to get the job done." She still wouldn't meet his eyes. He forcibly spun her chair so that she was facing him. He couldn't tell if the flash in her eyes was anger or fear, but it made his own anxiety soar.

"What is it?" he asked. Lenore pressed her lips together, and her face emptied of emotion.

"Hey, don't do that, not to me." He meant his tone to be gentle, but it came out terse. "I thought we were safe for the moment, relaxing before finishing this assignment, but you are acting as if, well, I don't really know. And when you go all emotionless, my gut says it's time to worry."

She sighed and gave a sad small smile that had no humor in it. "I am considering giving up on this case."

Diarmin felt his jaw drop and sat heavily in his chair. "Um...what?"

"It has already proved more dangerous than I thought. Especially," she gestured toward the display, "with all I found in here."

"Wait, so let me get this straight. You are thinking of leaving?" He put a hand to his forehead briefly, then dropped it back to his side. "You are aware that we have very little money, right? And let's not forget the fact that you, have never, never, walked away from any other job."

"Yes."

"Ok, you are going to have to explain that to me." Diarmin crossed his arms.

Lenore pursed her lips, oddly hesitant. He sat in the navigator seat, waiting expectantly, not willing to give an inch at this unusual attitude from his wife.

Finally, she tapped a few keys and brought up a screen, turning the display so he could see it.

"This."

Diarmin squinted at the screen, unable to read anything through the scrambled letters and symbols. "It's in code. I can't read it. What's it say?"

"I don't know yet."

"Well, if you don't know, then why—"

"Because I recognize the pattern as one of the codes used by the Xa'ti'al."

Diarmin didn't think he could be rendered speechless twice in one day much less in a few minutes. As his mouth opened and closed without sound, his wife continued.

"Somehow, the Xa'ti'al are connected, closely connected, with this illegal slave organization."

***

Lenore watched Diarmin pace back and forth, occasionally tossing glances down the stairwell, making sure nobody was on the way up. Usually, Lenore was the one unable to sit still, but he had insisted she stay put, citing the fact that she wasn't recovered yet from her injuries.

"Okay, to be clear, that code shows that your former colleagues are somehow working with these slavers," he said, continuing quickly as she nodded.

"If we follow this case, tracking the lost princess with the information we have from the same slave business, we might run across one of those we are trying to stay away from. But we are very low on money, spent the last of our savings on those grav plates. Our remaining fuel might not get us to another job."

He kept pacing, eyes on the floor. Lenore kept silent. She knew she was the strategist, but it came from logic and experience. When Diarmin was in one of his "focused inspiration" modes, usually dealing with inventing, but occasionally with situations, he often had leaps of brilliance that astounded her.

"Prince...companion...tattoos...slaves...grav plates... video feeds..." Diarmin's eyes took on a fire and Lenore paid close attention, knowing he was getting one of his gut feelings.

"This video guy, what's his name?"

"Jonah Wilkerson, and his title is 'Reviewer.'"

"Didn't you say he had a second job for us?" Diarmin sat down and absently grabbed some tools to fiddle with. He did think better when working with his hands. But now things were niggling at the back of Lenore's mind.

"Yes, finding some information broker." She stood up to pace now. "And the other inconsistencies around that man. The unusual tech, money, connections...wait." She halted and looked at Diarmin. "He had extensive knowledge of the slave trade, the inner workings of the palace and claimed to have met a Xa'ti'al before."

"Few people meet one Xa in their lifetime. I've never met anyone, myself excluded, that has met more than one," Diarmin said. "He is the center, the key." He rubbed the back of his neck, then threw up his hands. "Or not. Either way, maybe we can finish that job instead and at least get some money before we take off."

"We need to make arrangements for the children anyway, so investigating the possibility of finding the girl will be quick." Lenore sat again in front of the display, fingers typing away. "There, message sent. And while we wait for an answer, I will retrieve, well, you-know-what from you-know-where, to decode and see what the Xa'ti'al are saying to these slavers."

***

It took all of Jonah's self-control to keep from pacing

in the small office. The prince and companion hadn't left the palace grounds in days, so there was nothing for him to do. The king was ill, but it wasn't clear with what. The public story spoke of a virus, but rumors around the castle varied widely. He absently flicked through the screens, trying to look unconcerned but felt he was failing. The companion was spending most of his time with the king, offering what little comfort he could since the king's companion had died long ago, shortly after the queen. The prince, meanwhile, was sitting in place of the king as if he were already crowned.

From the public's point of view, the prince was stepping in, helping his father, but Jonah knew he was beginning his take-over. The princess needed to be found soon.

If that was even possible.

It had been four days, and he had heard nothing from the contact. Had they been arrested because of the break-in? Surely, if that were the case, he could have found out. Maybe they had taken off, run from the reprisals that the illegal organization was sure to mete out. That was the more likely scenario.

Jonah flicked through files again, trying to change his thoughts to curb his agitation. His last chance was that information broker he simply could not find. With the help of the contact, he felt sure he could find her, but now he had to proceed on his own.

He glanced around, making sure he was unobserved and reached into his pocket for the data stick that held all he knew about the girl. As his hand closed around the stick, his personal comp bleeped, causing him to give a massive twitch in surprise. Cursing at his nerves, he drew out the comp and checked the message. His emotions surged with both hope and fear when he recognized the contact code.

He glanced around, going so far as to lean outside the office to see if there was anyone near even though there was a security camera that showed the corridor. It looked clear, so he opened the message.

"Vital we meet. Pick a location as far from the palace as possible that you can reach in exactly thirty-six hours." A response code was given, along with a time limit of one hour before it was no longer valid.

His initial relief at hearing from the contact evaporated and anxiety returned twofold. The distance and exact time indicated trouble and perhaps even a bit of desperation.

Jonah shook his head and pulled up a map. He could make it nearly anywhere on the planet within that timeframe, but not without raising some suspicions. He picked a remote location that he had been to before while vacationing. If he left after his shift tomorrow, he could be there an hour before the specified thirty-six. He could even request a couple days leave, supporting the story of a small vacation. He hated to leave the companion alone with the prince, especially at this turbulent time, but Jonah could also use the time away to search surreptitiously for that information broker.

Wasting no time, he booked the vacation resort and sent off a quick message to the contact. A single beep acknowledged receipt and then the crackle before the link was broken, indicating the line no longer existed. Jonah put in the request for the days off, took a deep breath to settle his nerves, and began to cycle through the security feeds. He had to find a way to speak with Lavan to inform him of the plans and warn him that he would be on his own for a few days.

***

Jonah showed his credentials to the royal guards outside the king's private rooms. They both scanned the card and even scowled identically at him, but he knew they had no choice but to let him in.

As Jonah figured, the companion was there, sitting with the king. He was reading aloud in a soft voice from one of the planet's history books, but the king was faced away, eyes tightly shut. Jonah doubted he heard any of the words.

Lavan didn't notice Jonah's silent approach until he was within a foot of the chair. He gasped, dropped the book, and cringed. Jonah cursed under his breath, knowing Lavan was on edge. The new bruise on the side of his face tugged at Jonah's emotions. Had he been so wrapped up in himself that he missed what had happened? Unfortunately, he couldn't help Lavan now, he had to worry about finding the princess.

"How is he?" asked Jonah in a voice just above a whisper. The king's private room was not monitored, but he kept quiet anyway.

Lavan shook his head. "It's hard to tell. The doctors say his heart is strained, but he won't take any medication to help himself." He bit his lip. "I am afraid he is just giving up." He looked at the King. "He keeps asking for Maya, begging her to come home. I wish I had something to tell him." His head swerved toward Jonah, his voice ending on an upward inflection as if asking a question.

Jonah's heart went out to him. Lavan truly cared about the King and was worried. Jonah patted him awkwardly on the shoulder, feeling oddly paternal even though he was only fourteen years the elder. He reached down to pick up the book and, as he held it out, whispered to Lavan. "I have another meeting tomorrow evening and have requested two days off to investigate new information."

Hope sprung into Lavan's eyes as he took the book, but a small shake of Jonah's head kept him from asking questions. Jonah walked to the other side of the king's bed and knelt so that his face was even with the sick man's.

"Your Majesty? I have come to see how you are feeling." Jonah saw his eyelids twitch ever so slightly. Was he simply pretending to sleep so he didn't have to speak to anyone?

"Your Majesty," he lowered his voice so only the king could hear. "I have information about Maya."

The king's eyes flew open and immediately focused on Jonah.

"What did you say?" His eyes opened wide. "You! It's you, I remember, so long ago."

"Yes, it's me, Reviewer Jonah, remember? But you should rest, Your Majesty." Jonah reached out a hand to calm the man.

"What about Maya? You know something."

"I have some people working on finding her, but you must hang on. It will take time, but we are very encouraged."

"Tell me! Where is she?"

"Please, Majesty, you must keep quiet. I will let you know as soon as I hear. For now, however, you must stay healthy and keep this information between us. Nobody else is to know."

"Yes, yes," he said. "Always watching, always waiting. I will wait." He lay back on the bed and closed his eyes again, but there was color in his face now.

Jonah stood and returned to the companion.

"When he wakes, I believe he will take his medicine." He tried a smile. "Take care of him."

"Wait." The look on his face wrenched at Jonah's heart. "Do you have anything, truly?"

Jonah wanted to believe that the meeting would be good news, but he owed Lavan the truth. "I don't know. Maybe. Keep the king as healthy as you can. I will return in a couple of days."

"The King. He acted like he thought you were someone else. Like he knew you not as reviewer. Why? How?"

Jonah suppressed a smile. Despite his issues, Lavan was observant and quick. "He's probably delirious from the illness. No matter, whatever raises his spirits."

"You're right. Thank you, and"—his voice dropped to a whisper—"good luck."

Chapter Thirty-Nine

Lenore tensed slightly as she heard the lock disengage on the hotel room door. Jonah walked in and caught sight of her sitting on a chair in the corner as he let the door swing shut. She noted that though he jumped slightly, he didn't drop the bag or large box that he carried under his arm.

"How did you know which room?" he asked as he walked into the other room of the luxurious suite and deposited his burdens on the bed.

Lenore shrugged. "I told you before, I am good at what I do." She took her hand away from her hidden stunner, always prepared for a trap. She had felt it was safe, but now was not the time to be careless. She remained seated, back to the wall as he returned to the sitting room and pulled up the other chair to sit opposite her at the small table.

"This is quite far from the palace," said Lenore.

"That was the request, wasn't it?" came his terse retort.

Lenore merely raised her eyebrow, letting her lack of expression speak for her. She wasn't going to let this young man take charge of the conversation.

He colored slightly and dropped his eyes. "I have come here in the past on vacations, so I knew it wouldn't be suspicious."

She let her eyebrow drop and nodded, knowing continued silence was usually filled by the other party.

Jonah stood and walked to the other end of the room. He pulled back the curtain to reveal a transparent wall with a scenic forest view. From earlier inspection, Lenore knew it could be made translucent with the switch on the left wall and was also a door. Jonah stared out into the forest, hands behind his back. "I hope you have some good news. I have cleared a few days, though I should not have left. The king is doing very poorly."

"Really. All the public news feeds say he has a slight stomach ailment, and that he will be back in a day or two."

Jonah looked at her. "Of course, that's what the public

knows. In truth, he is pining for his daughter, and his heart is no longer strong. He is refusing to take any medication. I think he is giving up hope."

"That seems melodramatic."

Anger flashed across his face, so quickly hidden that had she not been looking for it, she might have missed it.

"He was very close to Maya."

"But not his son?"

The speed with which Jonah turned his face back to the window was interesting, but all he said was, "No."

"Well, it so happens I do have some news."

He looked back at her as if he wanted to speak but held his tongue.

She continued. "Our little raid, which I am sure you heard about in some way or another, obtained information for us that indicates the princess and her companion were indeed kidnapped and taken immediately off planet."

Jonah's shoulders slumped. "As I always suspected. That will make them nearly impossible to track."

"For you, perhaps." Lenore shifted slightly in her chair. "I have many contacts and resources that you do not. It will, I regret to inform you, require money to grease palms, open very tight lips, and so on."

"Lavan cannot—"

Lenore held up her hand to interrupt.

"I realize that. I am authorized to tell you that we will take your other job, finding the information broker, if you can come up with an advance. Half of what you offered should be enough to get us started on both cases."

He stared at her for a moment or two, then headed into the bedroom. Through the door, Lenore could see Jonah rummaging through his bag, fiddling with something, then grabbing the box. He returned to set the box on the table and hand her a credit flimsy.

"It's what I was hoping for, so I came prepared. That," he pointed to the flimsy, "is half, and this," he placed a palm on the box. "This is everything I have gathered through the years. I hope you can use it."

Lenore had suspected something of this nature might happen, which added to the interesting enigma of "Jonah." She stood and raised the lid of the box, peering inside. "Why store such important files on paper?"

"It's easy to incinerate if needed, and the printouts go back for years. There are some data sticks in there, but I prefer to hold things as I study."

"I see. You say you have two days?"

"Yes. Three, if necessary."

"I need to take this to my ship to do a proper search. Would you come?" She tried to look earnest and trustworthy but wasn't sure she was successful. This was a crucial point in her estimation of the man and his reactions would reveal much. Was he serious enough about these investigations to board a strange ship, maybe even leave the planet with someone he barely knew?

"Is it close by?" His eyelids lowered slightly, but his attempt at deception didn't fool her. He knew that it wasn't and was gauging her reactions.

The truth, she thought.

"There is no port here with facilities for my ship. I have a small shuttlepod hidden nearby. I believe that the research would go much faster if you were to talk to my computer expert in person." She held up a hand to stop his comment. "I will not take you far and you will be returned to this place before you are due to check out."

Jonah considered the offer and agreed, though he appeared reluctant. Yet he seemed to trust her. Lenore decided to push the edge of her investigation of the man. How far would he go? Would he resent her giving him commands?

"First, I need you to arrange things here. Order enough food for two days, to cover anyone who might be wondering why you don't leave your room to eat. Make sure some is covered in heating containers to eat later. And if you could, make some of that order local food that children will enjoy. We have some new guests."

He gave Lenore an odd look but went to the computer on the desk near the window. As he placed the order, she flipped through the files in the box, noting that there were papers from every year of the last fifteen. Hm.

He returned to the chair and plopped down with a sigh. "It shouldn't take too long. Most of what I ordered is packaged, and the kitchen won't need to prepare it." He grinned. "And it is what I usually get when I vacation here. I hinted that I wasn't alone and didn't want to be disturbed." He blushed and looked away again. "I hope you don't mind."

The blush threw Lenore temporarily. She had formed explanations on all the inconsistencies with this man but was still confused. Jonah appeared confident, knowledgeable, and experienced in many ways, but his complete lack of comfort at the mere suggestion of sex did not jibe with most of her conclusions. She needed answers.

"Who are you, really?"

Jonah's head snapped back to her. "What?"

"You say you've been at the palace a long time, evidently since you were about twelve or thirteen if you were there when the princess disappeared. You were close enough to follow the investigation and are somehow still involved because you will not let it go. You have implanted tech that is extremely rare, and no doubt expensive, that not even the prince and his companion have. You seem to be intimate with the king and yet have no influence on matters outside the palace despite the fact that you have extensive skills in certain areas, not to mention access to some serious funds. There is no such person as Jonah in the database near the time you were born and no records of you emigrating to this planet. And I am pretty sure that you have a tattoo, given your reaction to my earlier question to Lavan." Those last two were only a guess, but Lenore felt confident she was correct as she leaned back to await his answer. Her theory was a private agent planted by outside security or perhaps even the slave trade itself. A less likely scenario would be a distant relative or perhaps bastard child of the king. She watched him closely as he worked through her words.

"How..."

"Do I need to say yet again that I am good at what I do? Well?"

The look on his face turned to awe. "Is it safe to speak here?"

Strange that he is only asking this now and not when he first arrived, thought Lenore, but she affirmed a lack of surveillance.

Jonah strode to the window and hit the switch to make it translucent. He spun back quickly and reached inside his jacket.

Lenore drew her stunner before he could complete the motion and pointed it directly at Jonah. He froze.

"I need to show you something," he said.

"Slowly." Lenore was betting on identification for private security.

But instead of reaching into a pocket, Jonah undid the fastenings and let his jacket fall open. Slowly, he unbuttoned his shirt. About halfway down he pulled the shirt open to reveal a small tattoo over his heart.

"My real name is Sundeep Barad. I was the betrothed of Princess Maya."

Chapter Forty

"Curious....hm...don't like that...that doesn't make sense. What?"

"Mumbling to yourself again, Alli?" asked Diarmin from the command console.

"Huh?" She looked up from the screen she'd had her nose in from the moment Lenore had left to go meet the reviewer. She blinked distractedly at her father. "Was I mumbling again?"

"Yes, pet. A problem?"

"Well, yes and no, well...I don't know." Allison crashed a fist into the tabletop. Diarmin's attention was fully engaged now. A frustrated Allison was very rare.

"Try to explain, please, before I have to pound the dents out of my ship."

"These files that I hacked from the slavers. I was tossing and turning in my sleep, thinking I couldn't have been successful that easily."

Diarmin didn't say what he was thinking, that a full day of steady decrypting would probably not be considered easy to most. Allison went on.

"Reading more closely, they really don't make sense. These ship manifests, for example," she flicked her fingers at the screen. "They don't match up with any logged schedules from the time they were supposed to have happened."

Ignoring the fact that she had probably done some serious hacking just to obtain those, Diarmin ventured a suggestion. "Well, they were probably unscheduled, off the grid."

She looked away from the screen long enough to give him a disgusted look. "Obviously that was my first thought, but when I checked, I realized that several of these entries match up at a no-launch time, you know, gravity issues, one of the moons in the wrong position, that sort of thing. Nobody would launch at those times. Nobody *could*. And"—she began to twist a lock of her hair, another rarity that showed her confusion—"these kinds of places usually have at least some legitimate entries, you know, supplies, shipments, to make it seem nothing wrong is going on. But those don't even make sense."

"That is strange." He winced as he said his next words, but he had to say them. "Could you have mistaken the code break?"

"No, the decrypt is accurate but..." her voice trailed away, and it was a testament to her concentration that she didn't even take offense at her father's suggestion. "I am thinking this might be a Chanis cypher."

"As usual, I don't know what you are talking about."

Allison sighed, not stopping her continuous tapping at the keyboard. Her eyes didn't shift, but he knew she was going into "lecture to the ignorant" mode.

"A Chanis cypher is a cypher within a cypher. Most people stop at the first break, thinking they were successful and that's the end. BUT, a woman with the last name Chanis, nobody knows her first name, is rumored to have created a code that is either piggybacked within the first code or laid underneath it. A person needs both to read the original entries."

"Okay, so use that."

"I have never seen one, and there is no evidence that they even exist. It's just a rumor, but I have a sinking feeling that I am looking at my first one."

"So how do you crack it?"

Allison pushed away from the console, sliding her chair back with a very loud scraping sound. She bent over to put her chin in her hands, elbows on knees.

"The rumor, or theory, or whatever you call it, is that you need the code key. Undecipherable otherwise."

"I thought you always said nothing was unbreakable."

She rolled her eyes at him as she slapped her hands on her thighs. "I said this code was undecipherable, not unbreakable."

"Okaaaayyyy."

"What the key does is reword the already broken code into legible data. I could shift words and numbers around all day, but without the key, we don't know which are correct. There are billions of possibilities." She tapped her finger on her mouth for several seconds. "I suppose I could rig a program that might give me options, but it would take me at least a day to write and probably many, many more days to sort through the possibilities. *If* it's even possible." She grabbed her personal pad, drew her feet up on the chair to make a surface to set it on and began doodling. Diarmin knew he would hear nothing more from her for a while, so he went back to monitoring the surrounding space for any moving object. The shuttle was due soon, but he wasn't taking any chances after their dramatic escape from the slavers.

A red light flashed on the right side of the console and he grimaced. Another grav plate was failing. He quickly rerouted the other ones to compensate, but they were now down to seventy-five percent capacity. He knew his family had no problem with zero gee, but the young ones were another story. The last thing they needed was for little tummies to be upset and spewing; they were scared enough.

The light changed to green as the reroute finished. The only indication something had changed was a slight tremor that was barely noticeable. They needed to put the new ones in soon or there would be no gravity.

Diarmin spun the chair and half stood to go check on Quinn and the rescued children, but another light began blinking. He plopped back down to help guide the shuttle in.

***

The short trip in the shuttlepod fascinated Lenore. The way Jonah, Sundeep, gripped the arms of his seat, despite the double buckles, indicated his nervousness. The continual swallowing showed his nausea in zero gravity, indicating that he had never been offplanet. Yet he was still alert enough to ask questions.

He swallowed again before he spoke. "I noticed when you checked in, you called this ship a 'shuttlepod' and the man called it a 'shuttle.' Is there a difference?"

"A shuttlepod is a small ship-to-surface craft, whereas a shuttle usually has transwarp capabilities," answered Lenore as she maneuvered the pod onto the landing platform of their ship.

His relief as the pod shivered into the ship's grav field was palpable. Never having been offplanet would definitely have limited him in searching for his lost betrothed.

She unstrapped as the docking clamps took hold with a solid thunk and stood as her passenger did likewise. She grabbed some food packages and indicated he precede her through the door that was opening. He picked up his luggage and the remainder of the food, then stepped through the hatch cautiously, peering around at the empty corridor.

Betrothed fifteen years ago, at thirteen or fourteen if she was guessing accurately. How well would he even know the princess? It did explain why he was still at the palace and knew the king, though not why his identity was hidden. But was he looking for her out of loyalty to the king or a sense of duty? Well, that may not even be important, especially since his attention seemed to be on this information broker. Maybe Sundeep, (Jonah, she reminded herself since he had asked her not to tell anyone his true name) wanted to know the princess was never coming back so he could move on with his life.

Lenore squeezed past him and saw Diarmin exit the bridge and head down the corridor toward them, holding out hands to help with the packages. She passed them along as she tried to help Jonah with his food.

"I can manage," he said.

Is he being chivalrous? Lenore didn't know. Outdated manners were often seen on various worlds but unless they were necessary for a disguise, she didn't care for it.

"We need to drop the food off in the lounge, down that ladder. Holding that box will be awkward enough." She gave Jonah a small smile, intended to put him at ease.

He smiled weakly back and passed over all the food, keeping hold of the box of papers and bag over his shoulder that held his personal effects. They descended the ladder and Diarmin led them to the lounge/galley.

"This is Reviewer Jonah." She indicated the young man, then turned to him. "Jonah, this is my chief engineer, Diarmin." The words "husband" and "wife" rarely entered their discussions with outsiders. "How are our other guests?" she asked Diarmin.

"Still asleep," Diarmin held a finger to his lips as they entered, and he indicated the children sprawled in the far corner of the dark lounge. Quinn was also still asleep on the sofa. Jonah's eyes widened perceptibly, but he said nothing. Diarmin continued barely above a whisper. "I am sure they will be awake anytime now and probably hungry. I am assuming that's what these are for?" He held up the packages.

"Yes, and this—she tapped the box Jonah held—"is for Allison. The beginning of our new assignment."

"Ah, good. Shall we bring it to her now?"

"If she's not busy," said Lenore.

"Well, kind of, but she should start on this. It would do her good."

"Since we are on this level, I'll show Jonah the guest room first," said Lenore.

Diarmin's face looked like he was wincing inwardly. "I wasn't expecting a guest," he said.

Comprehension dawned as Lenore realized that the guest rooms were in no condition for anyone.

"He can use my room," came a whisper from the couch. Quinn hadn't moved an inch, but his eyes were open. "It's no problem. I will be in here with the children anyway." He rose slowly, his eyes on the little ones in their pile of blankets and pillows.

"Is that food?" he asked.

Diarmin nodded and jerked his head toward the galley. Quinn relieved Lenore of her bags with a tiny smile and followed his father.

Lenore led the way to Quinn's room where Jonah deposited his personal duffle on the bed. He followed her up the ladder to the bridge, eyes silently taking in everything and looking a bit more comfortable with climbing a ladder while carrying a large box. Lenore admired his adaptability. He was turning out to be a most extraordinary young man.

"Allison, meet Jonah," said Lenore before they were completely up the stairs, but to no effect. As they both finished the climb, Lenore noted her daughter sitting in her usual chair, intensely focused on her pad.

"Allison," she repeated. No response. Lenore grabbed her pad out of her lap.

"Hey," she said, hands reaching for her property, but she snatched them back and stood quickly as she caught sight of the stranger. "Who—"

"This is Reviewer Jonah, Allison. Jonah, our Computer Chief. Don't let her age fool you."

"Oh yeah. You're the guy I saw on the video feed before you cut me off."

Jonah's eyebrows shot up. "That was you?"

Allison shrugged. "Yeah. You blocked it quicker than the usual dopes who get hacked. Pretty slick."

"You're very good yourself," he replied with a small bow.

Allison flicked her fingers as if agreeing with him and the bow was her due. "Now, if you can tell me how to—"

"Allison," Lenore's warning only stopped the speech,

there was no regret in her eyes for asking someone to divulge trade secrets. "Jonah has brought his records on this person he wants us to find and some more about the missing girls."

"Sure. Let's work over here." She swept her pad and all her accoutrements into a bin kept next to the console for just that purpose. Diarmin, coming up the ladder, hissed softly at the mistreatment of machines. "Da— uh, Diarmin, if you could bring that chair for Jonah, we can get to work."

Clamping her lips shut on her imperious daughter, Lenore noticed Diarmin doing the same as he brought the chair. Jonah sat and began pulling files out, and soon the two were oblivious to all else. Diarmin caught Lenore's eye, then pointed down the stairs to indicate they should leave the two to work.

They glanced into the lounge and galley and saw Quinn sorting the various food parcels. Lenore thought Diarmin would go in to help, but instead he continued toward the ladder down to the cargo bay. Before either even sat, Lenore spoke.

"So, what did you want to talk about away from the bridge?" She took the comfortable chair, and Diarmin sat in his seat at his workbench.

"How did you know?"

"I know you very well by now, Mr. Kelton. If I can read a stranger, you are an open book. Something happened while I was gone that has you very concerned. Spill."

"Well, Allison was going over the files she decoded from the, um, the download."

Lenore suppressed a grin. Diarmin studiously avoided thinking of anything in terms of a raid or break-in.

"She has found some interesting discrepancies," he said.

"Such as?"

"Well, such as impossible launch schedules and messages that don't make sense. Bottom line is she thinks there is another layer of code."

"Huh." Lenore stopped her hand just short of pulling her lower lip. As she knew Diarmin, he also knew her, and that was her telltale sign of nervousness. She changed it to a chin scratch and tried to act nonchalant. "That would certainly explain what I got when I applied the Xa'ti'al code to what we found."

"When was that?"

"Late last night, when everyone was asleep." She looked directly at him. "I didn't want Allison or Quinn to see."

Diarmin looked at her strangely. He knew her enough not to push, but she could tell he was hurt that she had not included him.

"The messages I decoded also made no sense. Simple messages, refusing to have any dealings with the slavers. Seems very innocent and shows the Xa in a good light, but it felt wrong. What does Allison say about it?"

"She thinks it's something called a 'Chanis cypher,' a code within a code or something like that. Does that sound familiar at all?"

"No," she lied as her gut tightened. Luckily Diarmin had looked away at the sound of a giggle floating down into the cargo bay.

"Sounds like we got food at the perfect time. Let's go help Quinn." She bounced out of the chair and up the ladder so that Diarmin wouldn't have a chance to object.

"They're all awake now," said Quinn as they entered the lounge, nodding at the sleepy children watching a program on the large viewer. "I reheated enough for everyone." He indicated the pile of food, plates and utensils on the counter.

"Thanks, Quinn," said Diarmin. He started transporting the lot to the table as Lenore piled some selections onto a couple of plates.

"I will take these up to the other two. I am sure they won't interrupt research for such a basic thing as food." She exited the galley before Diarmin noticed her tension. As she slowly climbed the ladder balancing two plates, she thought about the revelation.

Yes, she had heard of the Chanis cypher. As far as she knew, it was only the highest ranks of the Xa'ti'al that ever used it. Did the slavers steal it, or were they working even closer with her ex-compatriots than she ever imagined?

Chapter Forty-One

"How is he, Lavan?" asked the prince as Lavan returned from the king's chambers.

"Getting better, Your Highness," he answered.

"Oh, that's good," though his tone belied the positive words.

Lavan grabbed one of his history books, but instead of going to his room, he stayed in the common area between their bedrooms. He tried to seem cheerful, but it was difficult, especially since...

Lavan swallowed, shoving the memory away. He had wanted to believe that the prince tried to do something about Lavan's supposed problem with girls, but what he did...Lavan swallowed again.

He has no kindness in his heart, nothing but malicious intent. He could have punished me merely by taking Amala away. When he gave her to Thom instead, I knew he would never be a good person. I just wish I had more courage.

He gently rubbed his cheek, the black faded to yellow, but still a painful reminder of what happened when he did stand up to Hahn. Lavan buried his nose in the book, but long habit kept the prince in the corner of his vision. He knew that Hahn didn't want the king to get well, but there was really nothing overt that the prince could do before he was confirmed. If he pushed too hard, the council could limit his powers. He had become very moody but left Lavan mostly alone, especially when he was with the king. The only drawback to the king's improved health was that Lavan had no more excuses to ditch Hahn to stay with the king.

"What do you see that could possibly be of any interest in those boring books?"

"Huh? They're not boring," replied Lavan, surprised at any comment about books from the prince.

"Tedious and dull recitations of the same facts over and over. How many ways can 'this happened' be told?"

"Well, yes, some are a bit dry, but some of these..." He reached for a couple books on the table to hold up.

"These are private histories from past royalty. It talks about personal experiences that aren't in history books. It's fascinating to see how they differ."

"In what way?"

Trying not to show suspicion at the prince's atypical curiosity, he tried to think of the most appealing subjects. "History books in the educational system tell of the planet's history and only briefly touch on the royalty, explaining that there has always been a monarchy since the first colony. Books about the monarchy are more specific, talking about stuff like how twice the ruling line was almost extinguished, but the public raised such an outcry that the queen or king was kept in place."

"Yes, yes. And how the council was formed to keep all the power out of a single person's hands." The prince waved his hand in dismissal. "I know all that. What do the personal histories tell you that is different?"

"Some are journals with only the thoughts of the author, but the most fascinating ones are the histories by people inside the court. They write about intrigues and power plays that the public never sees. Both the council and royalty felt that the public should have an image of a strong ruling body, so these struggles were kept quiet."

"Really?" The prince leaned forward, a bit of fire in his eyes. "Give me some good examples."

Now Lavan was curious. *Why is he so interested?*

"You would be surprised how many rulers who appeared strong had serious doubts about whether they could lead," said Lavan. "And others that were nearly unseated from the throne. Mostly by challenges to the right to rule. All fought within the court circles and carefully kept from the public."

"Unseated? By challenges? Like one of those stupid trials? Or real fights?" Hahn licked his lips as his eyes lit up at the possibility of fighting.

"Well, both actually," replied Lavan, a little unsettled at the avid look in Hahn's eyes. "Though it's been centuries since—"

"So, you're saying that just anyone off the street could challenge my rule?"

Despite his tone, Hahn's grin and calculating look showed that he would love the idea. Knowing how well the prince could fight, Lavan didn't doubt it.

"Not anyone. Only someone with a true claim to the throne and that would have to be—"

"Too bad. The public would enjoy such a spectacle. See their beloved prince emerge victorious from a fight to the death."

"Well, it's not exactly 'to the death,'" replied Lavan. "That barbarism never came to the planets with the first colonists."

"Well, that would be boring."

"Oh, no. Not at all. Usually, the council or current king establishes the winning decision beforehand—anywhere from first touch to near-death wounds. One of the more interesting was the duel between twins. The younger claimed it was ridiculous to choose the next ruler based on being born only an hour earlier. He wanted to be chosen on merit and, of course, the older refused to consider it. The younger found the obscure tradition of dueling and prepared carefully to challenge his brother. The older was caught unaware and lost the duel.

"But I'm going on and on," he said, realizing that the prince was already tuning out. He handed a book to Hahn. "Here, this is a good historical retelling, you should read it."

Hahn's eyes narrowed. "Why should I? You can tell me what I need to know. What else are you good for?" He threw the book down with disgust and stalked out of the room. The abrupt mood shifts might have surprised anyone else, but after all these years, Lavan was used to it. It still didn't make it less disappointing. He really thought he had been interested and, again, Hahn had managed to hide his true feelings from his companion.

The fact that he could hide it indicated that something was not quite right with the Companion's Bond. Despite all his reading, Lavan had found nothing to explain why only negative emotions seemed to resonate through his bond with Hahn. In fact, some stories were written about how the companion could cheer up their bondmate by being happy themselves. How they would laugh in tandem. Or how they were even unable to be apart for long. The Companion's Bond was considered to be the best stabilizing influence. Maybe the negativity was why the prince felt so isolated and alone. Despite his best efforts, Lavan found that Hahn never responded to him in any positive way. And every time he thought the prince might be turning around, Hahn said and did things to prove the complete opposite.

As usual, this brief interest had faded quickly, if it even

had been a true interest. Lavan knew now that Hahn liked to put on a show to hide his inner thoughts, but this time it was a token attempt. He shook his head. Perhaps the bond wasn't solid, but he knew that the prince was up to something far worse than his usual exploits. And he was no longer trying very hard to hide it.

***

"You sure have a lot of pictures of this girl," said Allison. "She an old girlfriend or something?"

Lenore sat quietly at the science console, trying to be inconspicuous. Her daughter and Jonah were at Allison's console next to the nav board, their backs to Lenore. Lenore had figured that the two would get along so that Allison could ask such a question, seeming innocent instead of invasive. Her patience was about to pay off.

Jonah blushed, again catching Lenore by surprise. He appeared to be very mature and knowledgeable and, as far as she could see, this planetary society had no stigma associated with casual relationships. But he was from royalty and, let's be honest, only such "traditionalists" stuck to outdated mores such as betrothals.

"I have never actually met her," he told Allison.

Hm, thought Lenore. *Maybe the blush was for that admission.*

"I thought she was someone from your past," said Allison.

"Well, in a way she is. I have been gathering information on the slave trade for years, and lately, she always seems to be nearby, interested in the same things."

"She could be working for the organization."

Also, my concern, thought Lenore.

"No, she has only gathered information, never sold any to them, well, that I know of anyway." A tiny line between his eyes showed briefly. "And a few things here and there have even been damaging, well, mostly just minor inconveniences, to the slavers."

"So...she's working for security? Undercover?"

"I don't think so. I believe she harbors a deep hatred of the slavers beyond the norm, perhaps even knew somebody who was taken by them. Maybe a former slave herself."

"Whoa," said Allison softly. "You don't think she could actually be the lost princess, do you?"

Jonah shrugged, a sheepish look on his face. "I admit I have had that thought, just a vain wish, but look." He pulled some clear pictures. "She wears gloves often, which gave me hope, but these clearly show bare hands." He pointed at a close-up of the right hand. "See? No tattoos."

"They could have been removed," said Allison.

Jonah shook his head.

"No, the tattoos are subdermal. To remove them, the entire hand would have to be rebuilt and there are no scars showing that. Also, if she were the princess, why wouldn't she simply go home? Why live in the poorest part of the city? No, she is just what she appears to be. A girl, scraping by on her wits, selling information to make enough money to live on, and with an odd obsession with the slave organization."

"Hm." To most people, Allison's noncommittal answer would be accepted, but Lenore knew her daughter. She had some ideas of her own. She just hoped she would keep it to herself and not tell Jonah.

The two continued to sort through the documents, occasionally pointing at information on a paper and Allison entering the data. Lenore assumed she was using one of her personal search programs, far beyond what Lenore was capable of. But she trusted her daughter to know what she was doing. She was also doing very well at eliciting exactly what Lenore needed to know.

"I guess I am wondering why you need us," said Allison. "With all your tech and skills, I would think you would have found her long ago. Your pictures are clearer than any we have taken of her."

Lenore hid her chuckle. There was only the one picture, but Allison was great at dissembling.

"She is exceptionally skilled at hiding, turning away from cameras, wearing hoods. Everything that I have gathered runs through the palace security programs, which are the best on the planet. The pictures are not only clearer, but extrapolation is possible as well. Yet, even though this data goes back five years, I only have a small amount of information that overlaps with my investigations into the slavers. And when I try to physically look for her, the trail goes cold."

"Even with all that tech?"

"Well, I have nearly found her several times. About a year ago, I located where she was living, but she never came back. Somehow, she knows when she is being tracked and keeps dropping out of sight. I don't know how she is doing it."

"Well, then, you were right to come to us," said Allison. "This kind of thing is what we do best. Now let's try my new program with this data."

Lenore smiled to herself and turned back to the science console, knowing they would tell her when they found something.

Chapter Forty-Two

Lenore sat in yet another disguise. Her fifth so far on this planet if she counted her battle outfit when she freed Quinn. She was pushing her luck with being found by authorities, or even worse, the slavers, but she didn't trust such a delicate mission to anyone else, even Diarmin.

She wore faded but clean coveralls, skin darkened enough to be a native of the planet.

Sunglasses and a wig with long black hair completed the outfit. Her obvious status was a person in the lower middle class, doing a job that required minimal education and earning just enough to allow her to stop for a drink once a week after work. She was alone, sitting at an outside table, pretending to read her pad as she watched for the woman that Allison had located.

Allison's program had searched for anyone with a scrambled identity. With the data that Jonah had provided, she had narrowed the search to a five-mile radius, though they had kept the exact distance and area from Jonah. Lenore had dropped him back at the hotel, reassuring him that they would be in touch when the girl was located. Meanwhile, he still had a day before he returned to work and would use that time to figure out what to do with the children. He'd spoken of two possible options, bring the children back and hide them, or get them and their families off planet safely. He had been very helpful and concerned after his initial shock at the story of their rescue, Lenore omitting the details about Quinn, of course.

After she had dropped him off, Lenore returned to the shuttle and flew it near the area where they expected to find the girl, then contacted Allison. Allison had put her "pattern-following cap" on and, using the past locations where the information broker had previously given Jonah the slip, estimated her next likely living area. This particular eatery, too nice to be a dive bar but not good enough to require human service and be designated a restaurant, had no cameras. None of the businesses on this street did. However, Allison was able to pinpoint some video from surrounding areas that led her to believe that the girl walked down this way every so often, apparently at random, but Allison intuited the patterns in her peculiar fashion and surmised that she would be along again soon.

Lenore had nursed three drinks for much too long and decided to pay her bill and head for her second stakeout at the clothing shop across the street. She could get away with another hour of window shopping along the shops and maybe another drink at the other end of the street. She dropped her credits in the slot and looked up to see someone rounding the corner wearing a light jacket with the hood partially obscuring the face. A breeze briefly lifted the hood for only a moment, but it was enough to show Lenore this was the woman she was waiting for.

Lenore stayed seated and angled her head down as if reading her pad but keeping her eyes, covered with the dark glasses, on the girl. The girl cast her gaze from side to side and started walking down the street. After only a few steps, however, she paused, and her gaze slowly tracked back to Lenore. *She can't possibly recognize me.* But when the look on her face went from wary to trapped, Lenore knew she had been identified. Lenore tensed in turn, ready to give chase if needed.

For several long moments, the two women stared at each other until the younger appeared to come to a decision. Her face blanked of all emotion, with the exception of tight lips. She slowly walked to where Lenore was sitting at the outside table and sat down across from her, hands still in her jacket pockets.

The plan had been to plant a subdermal tracker on her and then inform Jonah of their success, but apparently the woman had something else in mind.

"It's about time you got here," said Lenore, not exactly sure what was going through this girl's head but willing to play a role. "I was getting ready to leave. Can I get you something to drink?"

"A huffleberry, please."

Her voice was soft and melodic but with something missing, as if it were carefully cultivated but lacked depth. Lenore put the order in and added another herbal drink for herself.

"Is this going to be a long meeting? Should I run a tab?" asked Lenore, figuring it the best way to find out exactly what this woman wanted.

"That depends on if you are interested in what I have

for you," came the reply.

Now it was Lenore's turn to be wary, but she was too experienced to show it. Instead, she noted the girl's wiry strength, seen even through her jacket. More telling was the slight scar on the right side of her neck and a stiffness in her posture, as if she were ready to leap away at any provocation. Lenore deliberately leaned back, trying to look unconcerned. Perhaps this information broker was offering some information. To the very one that was looking for her. *Interesting. Not to mention bold.*

"I have some business connections that you might be interested in." She pulled her left hand out of her pocket slowly. "They are similar to the one you had dealings with a few days ago." She slid over a folded paper with her gloved hand. Lenore made no move to pick it up.

"Why come to me, Miss...."

"Raahi. And that paper will explain."

Lenore flipped the paper open and identified the address of the place where they had rescued Quinn. Quickly she crumpled it and stuffed it into her belt.

"Why should I be interested in more of the same, Miss Raahi? If you know about my previous business, then you should have guessed that we got what we wanted. What would more of the same offer us?" Apparently, Jonah had been correct about her interest in the local slave trade.

"It's just Raahi. And I figured you would want as wide a variety of options as possible. Especially if you are getting rid of your competition."

Was she thinking that Lenore's group was going to take down the entire organization? Or is she merely a plant to trap the one responsible for the damages to the sales venue?

"Addresses don't interest me. I am sure my associates already have the same in their books." Emotion flickered across Raahi's face, too quick for Lenore to analyze, but it seemed a bit like desperation.

"I have the security codes for some of the addresses."

"That is a bit more interesting, but we can get inside anytime, codes or not." In truth those might be worth purchasing, but Lenore could tell Raahi had more. She waited for another offer. But when the young woman bit her lower lip, Lenore knew she was contemplating running.

"Thank you for the drink." Raahi started to stand, but Lenore reached out a hand to keep her from leaving. Raahi snatched her hands back before Lenore could touch them, but she stayed seated. Lenore pulled her own hand back, not wanting to scare the girl into silence.

"Look, Miss Raahi. I do know someone who would be interested in what you are offering, and I would be happy to introduce you to him. However, I sense you have something bigger to offer that I might purchase." Lenore watched Raahi's eyes narrow, not in anger, but to hide the shot of fear. Was she afraid that Lenore guessed her intentions or of what she had to sell? She waited patiently.

"Please, just Raahi, no 'miss.' And, yes, I have more." She took a drink and swallowed, looking anywhere but at Lenore.

"I have the back-door security codes."

"I told you I have no need to break into more buildings."

"Not the buildings, the backdoor is for their core computer system."

Lenore's heart gave a few extra beats, and her eyebrows shot up as she thought of what Allison could do with those codes. Cursing herself silently for allowing a show of emotion, she quickly added to it to make it sincere.

"Really? That is big and definitely piques my interest." She tilted her head slightly. "With a gem like that, I am surprised you haven't used it yourself. Seems the ideal way to gather a goldmine of information to sell."

Raahi shook her head. "The core cannot be accessed on this planet. Where it can be accessed is extremely dangerous." Her eyes softened. "I lost a great deal acquiring those codes."

The tremor in her voice convinced Lenore that she did indeed lose much, personally, not monetarily. This girl was turning out to be as much a mystery as Jonah. No wonder he was interested in finding her.

"How much?"

"Excuse me?" The startled look showed that she thought Lenore was asking how much she had lost, which was why she had chosen those precise words.

"How much do you want for the information, Raahi?"

Raahi rattled off an exorbitant figure. Amazing how quickly she recovered, thought Lenore as she countered with a lower offer. Haggling was done in moments and Lenore was satisfied.

"I'd like to see it before I turn over any credits."

Raahi dipped her head in acknowledgment and for the first time, gave a slight smile. "Of course, but such sensitive information I keep in a safe place, not on my person."

"Of course."

"It will take me a day to retrieve it from its secure location. Shall we arrange a time and place to meet?"

"Yes, and I will bring my associate who will most likely wish to purchase that other information you offered."

The smile vanished, and wary tension returned. "That would be acceptable."

Lenore pulled out her own pen and paper, scribbled something and held it out to Raahi. "Will this place and time tomorrow be satisfactory?" Raahi bent to look at it and nodded but didn't take the paper. Surprised, Lenore folded it and placed it in front of the girl.

"Very well. Bring that other information as well. If you have what you say you have, I will be more likely to believe that the codes are also what you say they are."

"I understand your skepticism, but my information is accurate."

"I will see you tomorrow, then." They both stood, and Lenore offered her hand to shake. "May the skies aid your sales."

Raahi kept her hands clasped and bowed low, ignoring Lenore's outstretched hand. She departed abruptly, the paper still on the table. Lenore swore under her breath. The girl was uncanny at evading Lenore's attempt at planting a tracer. She snatched up the paper with the microtracker and went to her third option. She didn't like using it, but it was necessary. Retrieving her pen, which could also shoot tiny projectiles, she pulled out the mini dart and attached the other microtracker that had been in her fingertip. She had to hurry as Raahi was already disappearing around the corner.

With the girl's paranoia, Lenore knew she had to be extra clever. As soon as she approached the same corner, she had the pen aimed. She had only a moment to fire, but she saw Raahi's right shoulder twitch as the dart hit, causing her to look back. Lenore ducked around the building before she was seen and headed in the opposite direction, confident that the tracker was in. Even if Raahi removed the mini dart, the tracker would be imbedded beneath the skin just like the ones she had planted on the officers, was it only six days ago?

She headed back to the shuttle, satisfied with the mission.

***

"You have got to be kidding me."

"Nope," replied Diarmin. "The tracker isn't working." He was irritated, but clearly his wife was even more so.

"Damn! After all the trouble I went to? Nothing?" Lenore crossed her arms. "What do you think is the problem?"

"Honestly, I can't tell." He shook his head. "My best guess is that whatever tech scrambles her identity also scrambles the tracker. I did get a few brief pings, but each one bounced around for a radius of a hundred kilometers or so, not settling in place long enough to try to locate." Diarmin gave a little cough, halfway between a snort and a chuckle. "It looked rather like an insect flitting about on the display screen."

A stern look from Lenore sobered him up quickly.

"I'd give quite a bit to get my hands on that tech," he commented.

"Yes, Allison said the same thing," mused Lenore. "I suppose I should amend my communication to Jonah. If we can't give him a tracking signal, at least we have a meeting set up for tomorrow. He said he would be able to extend his 'vacation' by a day. I hope she is what he is looking for."

"And the rest of the money he has promised should go a long way to tracking the princess and her companion."

"Yes, especially if the information that Raahi has is what she says it is. That would be a huge advantage."

"But dangerous."

"Hmmm…" Lenore's attention was obviously elsewhere, and to Diarmin's annoyance, she changed the subject. "How's Allison's work on the Chanis cypher coming?"

"According to her, 'Not at all.'" He gave a wry grin. "She is not liking the fact that she isn't all-knowing."

"Typical youngster genius."

"And how would you know?" Diarmin put his arms around Lenore.

"I saw a lot of them when I was young," she said, then suddenly lost her distracted look and softened in his arms. She smiled at him. "Quinn busy too?"

"Last I saw, he was starting a quite intricate and involved game with the youngsters. Should be occupied sufficiently."

"Then let's make the most of this calm before the storm."

Ignoring the sense of unease those words brought on, Diarmin followed his wife to their cabin and locked the door.

Chapter Forty-Three

The time and place to meet Raahi was the diner at the other end of the street where they had met yesterday. This time, Lenore got a table far from the door but angled so both she and Raahi could see the exit. She figured this would allow for privacy and yet leave an escape to put the jumpy Raahi at ease. Jonah had reluctantly agreed to be in the next room, out of sight until called for. Lenore knew meeting Jonah would probably cause a scene and wanted to be prepared to deal with the girl.

Raahi entered in the same outfit she had worn yesterday. Her hands were in the jacket pockets, hood still close around her face. Lenore could see her eyes flicking around to the other patrons and tension easing slightly at the near empty restaurant. She sat across from Lenore, who suppressed a smile as the young woman turned her body slightly to have a clear view of the door.

"I took the liberty of ordering a huffleberry for you. If you'd like something else, just let me know."

"Thank you, but I would rather complete our business quickly if you don't mind." Raahi shifted in her seat, and Lenore could tell she had something under her jacket. While the girl didn't seem the type to carry and use a weapon on clients, Lenore's guard went up anyway.

"Where is your associate? I have his information as well."

"He will be along shortly, when I verify you have what we want. Both deals." She pushed forward her pad that had a readout of credits from an attached flimsy for Jonah's purchase. "His first."

Raahi nodded and pulled her right hand out of her jacket pocket to produce a data stick. Her left arm was still tight against her body, protective of whatever was under her jacket.

Lenore removed the credit flimsy and inserted the data stick. Sure enough, there were the codes and addresses of the various slave buildings that she had seen on the list that Jonah provided to verify accuracy, including some

Jonah had apparently missed.

These two will work well together. She sent the silent signal to Jonah.

"Excellent. My associate will be interested when he arrives." Lenore pulled out the stick and lay it in front of Raahi, leaving it for Jonah to complete the sale. "Let me see my intended purchase."

"Show me those credits." For the first time, Lenore heard some emotion in Raahi's voice. Excitement, perhaps.

Lenore took another credit flimsy out of the chest pocket of her coveralls and put it in the pad, showing the balance. Raahi's eyes widened with satisfaction, and she relaxed her left arm to let the jacket fall open.

Interesting, mused Lenore. She knows exactly how to not appear threatening, showing that she knew Lenore was aware of her bundle and letting her see it was harmless before reaching for it. Her estimation of the girl rose several notches. Too well trained to be a street urchin. *Undercover agent, possibly?*

Raahi pulled out a rolled bundle of cloth and placed it on the table. First to be unrolled was a scanner she used, after a questioning look to get Lenore's permission, to wave over the credit flimsies. A clear beep indicated, Lenore guessed, that there was no trickery involved like maybe a tracking device. She hid another smile when Raahi, in pulling away the device, managed to wave it in Lenore's general direction. The apparent random movement was no such thing, and she saw Raahi glance at the device before she thumbed it off.

Raahi unrolled the cloth more and revealed the next item in the bundle, a tiny, self-contained reader. These were private and allowed the reading of only one piece of data, usually extremely sensitive information. It reinforced the fact the girl did indeed have what she said she did.

Raahi picked up the reader and, hidden from Lenore, rapidly entered a code with her thumbs. She then laid it down for Lenore to look at but kept it close enough to prevent Lenore from grabbing it away. It was a series of symbols that could only be a security code.

"That looks like what you claim, but it is useless without knowing which computer to use it on," said Lenore, trying to sound haughty when she was instead gaining serious respect for this girl.

Raahi simply nodded, pulled the reader in close, and finished unrolling the bundle to reveal a pad of paper and pencil. She rapidly scribbled and turned the entire pad over to Lenore.

What she read there, left her speechless. The location of the computer was on one of the planets known to be home to some of the wealthiest people in the galaxy. Lenore even recognized the name of a retired business mogul who had built his fortune in several far-reaching businesses, including ship building and marketing new technologies.

"How did you get this?"

The slight excitement left Raahi's eyes. "You really don't want to know."

Lenore felt a tug at her emotions when Raahi's voice cracked slightly. "It is legitimate, I promise you." Here she lifted her chin, her attitude a commanding one. "I only ask one thing when you use this information, or I will refuse to sell."

Lenore could see most of her attitude was bravado. The girl was unsure whether her demand would be followed but hid it well. Raahi was bluffing and would probably sell anyway, but Lenore was curious about the demand.

"And that is?" she said.

"That you don't harm the man who holds this information."

Another surprise. The softening of Raahi's eyes showed real feelings. Of what, Lenore had no idea. She would have thought the request would be to kill the man since Raahi indicated she had lost so much. Annoyed that her heart again went out to the girl, Lenore hastened to reassure her.

"You have my word that neither I nor my colleagues will harm the man," she said, then slid over the correct credit flimsy. Raahi reluctantly let go of the reader, then scribbled the reader code on another paper. Lenore gathered the reader and papers and tucked them very carefully in a hidden pouch.

"Thank you, Raahi. Now you have enough credits to set yourself up in a very nice part of town for a long time." The girl's eyes narrowed, and Lenore read her quick glance to the other flimsy.

"My associate has authorized me to say that he will buy the other information but would like to offer you a temporary job as well." Lenore ignored the slight shake of Raahi's head and raised her arm to indicate Jonah as she sensed his arrival. He had been waiting for the exchange to distract Raahi enough for him to approach.

The girl's eyes widened as she caught sight of Jonah and the look of betrayal on her face nearly broke Lenore's heart.

"You!" she said as she stood, looking like a frightened animal ready to run for the door if Jonah hadn't been blocking the way.

"His name is Jonah, and he is no threat to you, Raahi," said Lenore quietly, in a calm voice. "Please sit."

"I truly wish only to speak with you about an opportunity for both of us." Jonah's voice was kind and cultured and would reassure even the most terrified person, but it didn't seem to ease Raahi's mind at all. It was obvious to Lenore that she was extremely shaken.

Lenore put some steel in her voice. "I will not let him injure or detain you in any way." She stood and gently pushed Jonah into the seat she had just vacated while positioning herself by Raahi's side. Lenore hoped she seemed protective instead of keeping her from fleeing. Raahi's slight relaxation showed the ploy worked. The girl slowly sat back down and, though Lenore was supposed to leave at this point, she felt responsible for the girl's safety, oddly enough.

"I know you," whispered Raahi, voice thick with emotion.

"Yes, I have been looking for you for quite a while, and you have been very adept at evading me." When she didn't answer, he went on, voice still radiating reassurance. "I know you must have seen me several times in the past year since I have also been investigating this vile slave trade, trying to find a way to shut it down once and for all."

"Yes, that must be it." Her demeanor changed to one of relief which puzzled Lenore. What else could it be? But the conversation was continuing, and she couldn't let herself be distracted.

"You seem to be quite good at gathering information," said Jonah. He slid the credit flimsy close to Raahi and waited politely for her to return the favor with the data stick. In one quick movement, she gave him the stick and retrieved the flimsy and scanner, jamming her hands in her pockets and leaving the roll of cloth on the table.

"Even information that is very difficult to come by." He tilted his head slightly and waited for a response.

Raahi said nothing but lifted her chin slightly.

Pride, thought Lenore. *Or defiance?*

"I think if you and I work together, we can bring down this organization."

Lenore had to fight back a snort of derision at Jonah's audacity. He had no idea of the size and scope of this business. She was startled to hear a similar snort emerge from Raahi, who evidently was also aware of the impossible task.

Jonah gave a slight, lopsided grin.

Quite charming, thought Lenore.

"Well," he said. "At least take it down a peg or two and maybe get many of them in custody or off the planet. Make it too costly to do business here. What do you say?" When she still hesitated, he continued. "You would be compensated for your time and efforts. And wouldn't it be worth it to finally bring them to justice?"

Raahi twitched at the comment. Lenore could see he wanted to say more but hoped he wouldn't. Though it was obvious to Lenore that Raahi had a past with this group, mentioning it would most likely scare her away. But what was said must have been sufficient since the girl spoke to him quietly.

"I believe we can do business, sirrah Jonah."

***

Lenore paced impatiently. She had left the two alone to work out the details and returned to Jonah's hotel room as planned. Nearly two hours had passed, and she was trying to offset her growing restlessness with thought. The mystery surrounding Jonah had been mitigated slightly with his revelation, but the secrets around this girl were even more strange. How did she know so much about the slavers? There was a lot more to her than simply an escaped slave. All that poise, culture, and training could be from whatever role she was expected to play as a slave, but that didn't quite fit.

And she seemed to recognize Jonah from elsewhere, not just as the man who had been following her. Could she be spying on the royal family as well and recognized Jonah from his position as Reviewer? What if she had seen him with the companion and realized they were working together to find the princess? Would she sell that information to the prince? She could make a true fortune and be in royal favor for a lifetime.

Lenore shook her head. It didn't feel like she would do

that, and yet the girl was good at manipulation. Nobody, except her children and husband, had ever aroused her protective instincts like she had. Lenore had the distinct feeling Raahi could take care of herself in any situation, so why had she felt the need to reassure the girl?

Lenore abruptly stopped pacing and let her hands fall to her sides. It wasn't her problem, it was Jonah's. If Raahi betrayed him for money to the prince or even the slavers, Lenore and her family would merely disappear, though she hated to leave a case unsolved. Especially since there was now a good chance that the codes she was in possession of would give her the answers they needed. She glanced at the timepiece on the wall and unconsciously started pacing again. Where was Jonah?

Footsteps outside the door indicated the return of the reviewer. Lenore sat at the desk and, as was her longtime habit of not letting anyone know her emotions, had completely schooled her expression by the time he had unlocked the door. Not that he noticed. He came in smiling and humming loudly.

"That took a while," she said.

"Yes, but absolutely worth the time." He tossed his jacket on the bed and sat on the edge. "She has some remarkable and extensive knowledge, and I am sure we can work together with success."

"Does she know you work at the palace?" The question slipped out, and Lenore was annoyed with herself.

Jonah looked at her in surprise. "Of course not. I let her think I was a security agent." He grinned again. "Not that she didn't try, the sly one, but I have had too many years of practice at keeping my identity secret." Here his smile vanished as if he didn't want to be reminded of his true name.

"Well, I hope it works for you." She stood. "As you know, we are leaving tomorrow to follow the leads, so I need to know if you have a plan for the children."

"Ah, yes. Please bring them here. I have found someone trustworthy to watch and care for them for a week since I must be back at work tomorrow. After that, I have also arranged for their parents to come, and that afternoon they will all be on a ship headed offplanet. There is a place ready for them with new identities that will hide them from possible followers."

"Impressive. How did you manage all that in a day?"

His mouth twisted, not quite a smile. "You forget, the

first half of my life, I was trained in extensive organization, leadership, and decision making. A perfect spouse to the potential ruler." He looked down. "It feels good to be able to use that training again, even if only for a little thing."

"Those families don't think it's a little thing, I am sure." *Damn! I'm doing it again, letting myself get emotionally involved.*

"I will have the children to you by the end of the day. But before I go, I also need to ask about the tattoos. Have you or the prince's companion had any luck in finding records of the patterns?"

"There is good and bad news with that. Unfortunately, those records are sealed and cannot be accessed by anyone except the king himself and the original tattooer."

"Yet you said you could help."

Jonah smiled a bit sheepishly. "I had intended to simply give you a drawing, but now that you know, you may photograph my tattoo." He began to unbutton his shirt. "It was made to mirror the princess's, as a symbol of the bonding."

Lenore's eyebrows rose at that. Interesting information. Would it have those microsensors that were noted in Lavan's tattoo? That would help although she didn't know if she could trace Jonah's tattoo on his chest with her finger without creating suspicion. A quick scan would have to do.

She pulled out her pad to take a photo and activated the scanner as well. It would probably also record some interesting information about his internal organs, but a directed scan would require extensive testing.

"Fascinating pattern. Do any of the designs have significance?"

"Well, the flower here is the royal symbol," said Jonah, pointing to the relevant parts. "And these lines are an ancient script of their family name. I don't know what the curves and loops are. Maybe just to connect the two with intricate marks."

"Why is it on your chest and not the wrist like Lavan?"

Jonah smiled. "The wrist is for companions, hand for born royalty, but for spouses..." he paused to put his right hand over the tattoo. "Hand to heart. The queen had one like me to match the king."

A beep from the scanner indicated completion. Lenore put it back in her bag and faced Jonah.

"Thank you. This should be very helpful. We could not

have done as well without your help." She headed toward the door, doing her best to ignore Jonah's grateful smile.

"It feels good to be able to talk about my true self with someone." He dashed in front of her to open the door.

"It has been an honor to work with you," he said as he bowed her out.

She clenched her teeth briefly but forced a smile. "It will only take an hour or two to bring the children. After that, we will be back within a week, two at the outside. And I hope to have some news." She refused to consider the possibility of finding the princess and her companion alive. As Jonah's face fell, she knew he was thinking the same.

"Any knowledge will be better than none. Good luck."

"And to you, Reviewer."

***

It was a quick trip back to the ship to get the children. After so many shuttle runs, the flight no longer required focused attention. But Lenore's thoughts were not on the upcoming mission as they should have been. Instead, she was distracted by her completely out-of-character emotions. She had always prided herself on staying detached from every situation and mission.

Why was this so different? The mysteries surrounding these people were interesting but no reason for her to be emotionally involved. What happened to Quinn was a legitimate reason to feel excessive emotion, but that came later, after he was safe back aboard the ship.

And it wasn't just big things. Lenore was even tired of the same routine trip between the ship and hotel room and was glad she only needed to do it once more. That made her consider the fact that something was seriously wrong with her and her emotions. She squashed it down for now. She could talk to Diarmin about it after the children were safe and the family yacht on the way to the planet that held the computer destined to be decoded.

***

In no time at all, the children were on the shuttle and heading back to the planet. Quinn was sitting in the copilot chair but kept sneaking glances back. They had been given nausea medication, and the littlest one sedated, to make the trip back easier. After they landed, Lenore got out to make sure they weren't being observed while Quinn administered the meds to revive them. Double clicking on the wrist comp told Quinn all was clear, and he exited the shuttle carrying the boy who was still a bit groggy. The girls followed close on Quinn's heels, and Lenore felt an odd satisfaction that they seemed so attached to her son.

Jonah answered the door to the hotel room, but his earlier friendly demeanor was gone. He quickly introduced the two women who would be caring for the children. The first had a kindly face that showed years of nurturing and the other's no-nonsense disposition said "bodyguard." Lenore felt that Jonah had chosen very well.

The children, however, were not trusting and refused to leave Quinn's side, the younger girl bursting into tears when he said he had to go. He knelt and embraced them all, murmuring something that Lenore couldn't quite hear. The bodyguard walked to the farthest corner of the room as the older woman slowly approached the group. She got down on her knees as well, radiating welcome and reassurance, and soon they were detaching themselves from Quinn and listening to the woman's quiet voice speaking their native language.

"Good, I am glad you were quick," Jonah whispered to Lenore, startling her out of her absorption of the emotional scene. "Lori," his head nodded toward the woman, "has told me of a developing situation back at the palace, and I need to return."

"Oh?"

"I cannot say anything else at this time, but suffice it to say, I hope you find something useful in your travels." He bent down to pick up two packed bags, and Lenore knew she would get nothing more.

By this time, Quinn had disentangled himself and was backing toward the door. The little boy was now in Lori's arms and all were waving.

"Goodbye. It was fun having you visit," he said with a smile. Lenore waved as well, and they headed back to the shuttle.

Quinn didn't say a word all the way back to the shuttle and remained silent after they took off. Lenore couldn't tell if the awkward silence was Quinn missing the children or just him deep in thought.

"I am sure they will be fine," she ventured.

He nodded.

"You did very well with them; they trusted you. I'm not sure I could have done that."

"It was my job. I did it, that's all."

His gruff tone was not what Lenore expected. *He must really miss them.* "I think you were better than that, a natural. Shows you will be a great father someday."

"No. I'm never having kids."

"Hey, now, don't be so quick—"

"No. Never." He crossed his arms on his chest, and his pinched, closed face showed his seriousness. Lenore dropped the subject, taken aback at his vehemence and unsure of what to say at this revelation.

They finished the trip back to the ship in silence.

Chapter Forty-Four

"I'm telling you Diarmin, Quinn was adamant."

The ship was on its way to the system given to them by Raahi. With plenty of downtime while in transit, Diarmin watched his wife pace back and forth in the space available in the workroom. Somehow, despite her agitation, she kept from knocking things off the tables and benches, though a few times he winced at near misses. He unobtrusively began moving things to the side, out of the direct path of any extreme motions. He had never seen Lenore so upset. Maybe when Quinn had been taken, but that had been a controlled fury. This was, well, different.

"Now, remember, you used to say the same things."

She halted and blinked at him for several seconds as if accessing those memories. She shook her head and resumed her strides.

"That was different. I was raised, well, taught, by the Xa that procreation was impossible. I have never given the kids that impression." She halted again, staring at Diarmin, eyes slightly haunted. "Have I?"

"Of course not. If anything, you have shown that despite all odds, they exist."

"Yes, yes, you're right." She didn't resume her pacing but sat, tapping her fingers on her knees. "Why does it bother me so? In fact"—she looked away, face reddening—"maybe you haven't noticed, but I have been so agitated, emotional, and I can't figure why."

"Oh, I've noticed."

Lenore's head whipped around, eyes sparking. "What's that supposed to mean?"

Diarmin sighed softly. *So much for trying humor.* "We've known each other for nineteen years. I can tell." He tried a small, wry grin.

Lenore relaxed in turn and chuckled. "I should have known." The smile faded. "Is it this case? Quinn being captured? But it's not just agitation. I feel for the clients, find myself wanting to help for no reason other than I sense they need it. What's wrong with me?"

Diarmin choked down another joke about her finally being human. "I have a suspicion, but you're not going to like it."

"I already don't like it but go ahead."

He leaned forward in his seat, elbows on knees and folded his hands. "The Xa didn't just train you to be emotionless," he took a deep breath. "I think that implant has been suppressing those feelings."

Her eyes snapped again, and she opened her mouth as if to reprimand him, but then she clamped it shut. He felt pride at her logical mind working it through, holding back what he was sure was the strongest feelings she had felt in years.

"How did you come to that conclusion?"

"I have been tinkering with the control box that you so conveniently destroyed. To help Quinn escape, of course," he added quickly at her sour look. "The electronics are very complex, and there are quite a few that I don't understand. Most of it biological, as we knew, raising adrenaline and suppressing pain when needed and so on. Those are the easily read programs. But there are more than a few that have bewildered me. And Allison too, before you ask. Some I cannot even open and download, but are, strangely enough, similar to those sensors found within the tattoos. One seems to deal with rapid cell growth, some with dispersion of drugs, but there was one that dealt with suppression of something I can't identify. Not pain, that program was easy. This was a constant suppression that dealt with a code of DNA that, I am not fond of admitting, left me completely flummoxed."

"Hm. Entirely possible." Lenore sat back in her chair, obviously thinking hard, but her lack of expression did not fool Diarmin.

"It's no use getting angry."

"Why not?" she asked. "The Xa'ti'al had no right to take away that fundamental—"

"Stop," he said. "There is nothing to be done now." She didn't speak, but he knew the fire wasn't out. "It's simply another reason to add to the ones that made you leave in the first place. Now you know. And now you can use that knowledge. To your advantage." He steeled himself for the reaction he knew was coming.

"Advantage?" She exploded out of her seat. "So far, these emotions have been distracting, confusing, and overall, a pain in the ass!"

"Then you agree with the Xa'ti'al?"

"I didn't say that." But she calmed quickly as her face became pensive again. "I have always said you and the kids seemed to have better instincts and gut feelings. Maybe I can learn to use them."

"Well," he hated to break her newfound calm, but he had to say it. "*If* I can fix the implant without that program. But I think we will need a specialist who deals with bioimplants. And that would mean…"

"Yes. It would be like sending a message to the Xa'ti'al. I am sure that implant is personally coded to me and that any qualified medical specialist would know what to look for. Or if not qualified, then it would reveal one of the Xa's well kept secrets."

Diarmin nodded but didn't know what else to say.

"Fix what you can. I will deal with the choices when they come."

"Choices?"

"Using a custom version of our own design," she waved her hand to include both of them, "using the original version they used on me, or…" her face was sober. "Doing without it altogether."

She abruptly turned and walked out of the room. Diarmin knew better than to follow. She needed time to consider everything. He knew Lenore thought she would be fine without the implant, but he worried. She had had it for over half her life, and he had no idea how much it helped when she went into action on a mission. Even her rapid emotional swings just now were a bit…unnerving.

Well, it wouldn't be fixed before the mission to break into the slave central computer, so she would be finding out soon enough.

***

Lenore wandered the ship, trying to reconcile this latest discovery, wanting to deny it. It was just like the Xa'ti'al to do such a thing. They were all about the mission, about creating the perfect soldier, never mind what it did to the human being. Their inflexibility to consider any other way was the biggest reason she left them.

How dare they? They took away her childhood, took away her freedom, took away any choices she might have made, and now she found they even took away feelings. It had been over fifteen years since she left the Xa'ti'al, and they were *still* interfering in her life.

She halted and clenched her fists. This wasn't helping. But it did make clearer why the Xa never let their soldiers go. Too much to hide, needing to keep it "in the family," as they would say. She felt her lip twist into a sneer. Huh, family. They had no idea what a real family was.

Lenore took a deep breath. Yes, family. That was what she would focus on. She couldn't do anything at this moment about the implant, so she would let the knowledge simmer quietly while she focused on other things. It would work out in her subconscious, or she would deal with it later.

She shoved the thoughts aside and noticed that her wandering feet brought her to the bridge ladder. She climbed it enough to glance at Allison typing madly away at her station, mumbling to herself, something about hiding, and making the program search for specific things. Lenore knew not to bother her daughter in the middle of such important work and left her to it.

She retreated down the ladder and wandered past her bedroom on the right and peered into the lounge on the left. Quinn, however, was nowhere to be seen, so she continued down the corridor toward his room. She passed Allison's room, glancing in only to shake her head at all the stuff scattered around. As she approached Quinn's cabin, she could see the door was open, but she was suddenly reluctant to enter. Would he want to see her? She hadn't had a chance to say more than a few words since the children had left. She had thought things were cleared up after their talk, but now she realized she had only scratched the surface. She approached his room slowly and saw him sitting on his bed, eyes closed, headphones completely covering his ears. Allison was usually the one to use them to shut out distractions. Quinn rarely used them to listen to music. He usually just blared music through the speakers, liking the freedom to move around while it played.

But, in watching him, Lenore had the feeling that, though music was probably playing, he wasn't really listening to it. She smiled to herself. *See? I can use these new emotions to "feel" things.* Then she mentally kicked herself. *No, I can tell because when he listens to music, he always keeps the beat somewhere on his body, with his fingers, feet or even head.* He wasn't moving at all, sitting there, back against the wall, eyes closed, and eyebrows drawn slightly together in a frown. It wasn't a gut feeling, it was simply good observation.

Lenore stood there, looking at her son, unsure of herself and him. She wanted to help but was afraid she would make things worse. After all, what did she know about being a parent? Diarmin was the one who had been there to kiss their boo boos, cook their meals, comfort them when they were sick. He understood them better emotionally, but even he admitted he didn't know how to help Quinn now.

Lenore struggled to get a rein on her emotions. There was one thing she knew she could give Quinn. Whether it would help or not she didn't know, but it was her strength. She slowly and silently entered the room, watching his reaction carefully. After only two steps, his eyes popped open, and she could see his sudden tension. Aware enough to sense another presence nearby. Lenore knew how to change that wariness into something useful.

"What's up, Mom?" he asked, brow still furrowed.

"It's time to start your training."

***

Since the cargo hold was still loaded with grav plates, the only place with room enough for physical activity was the lounge. Lenore recruited Diarmin and Allison to help clear away furniture and anything that might get in the way. When the room was as empty as it could be, they turned to go.

"Where are you two going?" asked Lenore.

"Back to my program."

"The workshop."

"You are going to learn this as well, Allison. And Diarmin, I need your assistance for demonstrations."

Lenore suppressed a grin at Diarmin's groan. She'd used him as a practice dummy many times in her workouts.

Allison whined. "Why do I have to learn how to fight? I'm not out there like Quinn."

"Oh, no? What about last week?"

"That was an unusual circumstance that will probably not have a recurrence."

Allison's pompous tone and big words told Lenore she was trying to sound more mature.

"You know I would much rather be safe on the ship."

"First of all, something of that nature might occur

again, and second"—Lenore put her hands on her hips—
"what if someone breaks into the ship?"

Allison's mouth opened and closed. She looked
pleadingly at her father, but he shrugged. "I agree with
your mother. Besides, physical activity helps the brain
work better, and you've been at that computer for days."

"Fine," said Allison as she threw her hands up. "I am
stuck on this program anyway, so a little distraction might
help."

Quinn had stood there during the entire exchange,
expressionless, unmoving, hands hanging loosely at
his sides. This rather unnerved Lenore, but she tried to
concentrate on the lessons. This would help him. It had
to.

"First thing you are going to learn, is how to break a
hold so that when someone grabs you, you can get free.
Diarmin?" She beckoned him over, ignoring his grumbling.
"Let's start at the easiest one and work our way up, shall
we?"

Two hours later, all were dripping with sweat and
very sore. Allison was even panting, and privately, Lenore
thought she needed to put her daughter on a training
regimen as well.

"Well done. Now, what would you do in a situation
where you can't break the hold?"

"I know this answer, so can I make lunch for all of us,
Instructor Lenore?" Diarmin said with a wink.

Lenore flicked her wrist toward the galley and focused
on the children.

"You just showed us how to break all holds," said Allison.
"Why would we be in a situation where we couldn't?"

Lenore opened her mouth to answer, but, surprisingly,
the answer came from Quinn, who had spoken very little
during the session.

"What if your ankle or wrist is broken? You couldn't get
the leverage needed to get free. What if they stunned you
and you haven't fully recovered use of limbs yet? What if
there are two of them waiting for you to try just that so
they can have an excuse to hurt you? What if—"

Allison put her hands up as if to fend off the tirade.
"Okay, okay I get it. So, Mom, what would we do?"

Lenore barely heard the question, having been
distracted by Quinn's outburst. Clearly these possibilities
had occurred to him, and she was not sure how she felt
about that. But she pressed on.

"Well, what you need to do is look as helpless as you can, even pretend to pass out or faint if possible. This works very well with one of the chokeholds. Show me your best faint Quinn." She opened her, arms and he let her put him in a hold, arm across his throat. Lenore gently applied pressure, not enough to hurt, just enough for him to imagine the possibility. She felt her gut tighten as she did, but she was determined to teach them.

"Now, you need to time it just right. Pass out too soon, and they know you are faking. Wait too long and you pass out for real. Let's pretend you have reached that phase where you need to faint. Show me your best acting skills."

Quinn went limp in her arms.

"No, too quick. It felt forced. Here, Allison, you try."

The three went through a variety of attempts with Diarmin shooting glances at them while cooking.

"NO! Still too fake, Quinn. Allison seems to grasp the idea, why can't you?" She ignored both kids' eyes widening at her loud voice. She grabbed Quinn in a hold.

"Again!" She could feel Quinn's tension, and she fought the urge to let him go. He needed to learn this. "Focus on your breathing. Don't make me teach you the way I learned." The words just slipped out. Diarmin had stopped cooking and was watching intently. She wouldn't look at him but began to speak directly into Quinn's ear.

"You can't breathe, you start gasping. Your legs go weak as your vision starts to blacken around the edges. Spots swim before your eyes and your heart is spasming wildly. Your muscles clench right before the end of all sight and sensation and suddenly they release." Quinn obligingly followed her directions, tensing and going limp as she talked him through it. Though it wasn't quite right, she knew it was time to quit.

"Much better, Quinn."

"Wow, I almost thought Mom had really choked you," said Diarmin with a chuckle. Lenore appreciated his attempt to alleviate the tension. It seemed to work as Allison laughed a little nervously, and even Quinn gave a wry grin as he stood up.

"So, lunch everyone?" she said, eager to put the awkward situation behind them.

"Wait, Mom." Quinn swallowed, and Lenore felt guilty. But his next words showed that the swallow was from uncertainty, not from her pressing too hard. His face showed doubt, and Allison's head was swiveling back and forth between the two of them, intent on their interaction.

"How did you know all that about passing out?"

"Yeah," Allison chimed in. "And what did you mean by 'learn the way I did'?"

The tension was back, but Lenore was sure most of it was hers. She didn't want to tell her kids, didn't want to face that memory. But they had asked. Could they handle the truth? She glanced at Diarmin, and his slight nod reassured her.

"I should have known my sharp kids wouldn't miss anything," she said and attempted a smile, but it didn't stay. She closed her eyes for a moment before she spoke. She took a deep breath, her eyes locked on the wall.

"In the Xa'ti'al, the recruits take turns choking each other until they pass out. We weren't allowed to fight it, and we had to both do it, and have it done to us. It was to teach us the feeling of losing consciousness as well as how to feel when someone is truly passing out or faking it. For a week, it was all we did, learning the limits of our endurance, figuring out that exact moment to pretend so that it was believable. If we didn't learn, we had to repeat the entire week. It gave us more incentive to learn quickly." Her eyes dropped to the floor, and she grimaced at the feelings the memory brought up.

Silence brought her gaze back up to her children, and her gut clenched as she noted the horror in their eyes. "I am sorry I said such a thing. I would never make you do that. Never."

"How old were you?" asked Quinn. Again, Lenore was surprised by his insight, then chided herself. He was extremely smart and intuitive; they both were.

"I was eleven."

Allison slowly closed the distance between them and gently took her hand.

"I'm sorry, Mom. That you went through that." The solemn look on her face tore at Lenore's heart.

Quinn lightly put a hand on her elbow. "I'm sorry, too."

Lenore hugged them as her eyes met Diarmin's. The look of love and understanding on his face along with the kids' demonstration made the effort to tell the story worthwhile.

"I have the best family in the universe. Let's eat and forget all about the horrible past, shall we?"

Chapter Forty-Five

The second day of training involved ways of incapacitating attackers long enough to get away. Quinn wasn't full grown, and Allison was even smaller, but Diarmin was well aware that Lenore knew many ways they could still escape.

"Anything, and yes, I mean anything, in this room can be used as a weapon. Be prepared to think on your feet and open to possibilities that might not normally occur to you."

"So that pillow on the couch can be used as a weapon?" asked Allison. The kids giggled, but Diarmin saw the glint in Lenore's eye and grinned.

Lenore picked up the pillow, contemplating it as if she had to admit she was wrong. "Well," she started, then flung the pillow at Allison's head. Allison blocked the pillow with a hand and ducked, nearly losing her balance.

"See? That pillow can cause a distraction long enough for you to get a good head start. It probably won't hurt anyone, but a good throw can make them lose their balance, block their vision, even." Here she hesitated but set her jaw and went on. "Even cause them to shoot the pillow if they are holding a weapon. A sudden discharge from a weapon distracts everyone, perhaps freezing them for a moment, allowing you to get away."

"You're teaching an awful lot about 'getting away,'" said Quinn a bit contemptuously. "When do we actually learn to fight?"

Lenore gave him a long look. Probably searching for the correct thing to say, Diarmin thought. But she stared long enough to make Quinn break eye contact and look down. After several extremely awkward moments, she spoke very quietly.

"I guess you haven't ever really seen me on many missions and are getting your ideas from holonovels and videos. The preference in any situation is to get out. The last option is to engage in a fight that keeps you from completing your task. Especially you two at this stage.

The main goal is to escape and get back to us."

"So the grown-ups can handle it?" Quinn sneered.

"Yes!" said Lenore.

Quinn's eyes widened, and he looked up sharply at her vehemence.

"Like it or not, you are children, and you should never, even when you are full-grown, maybe large and muscled, never look for a fight. Always avoid them."

She sighed, and Diarmin knew she saw as well as he did the flash of defiance in Quinn's eyes. "Look. I will teach you those skills that are needed when you can't evade a direct confrontation. But they take years to learn and, right now, I am concerned with keeping you alive, intact, and free long enough to learn them."

Quinn winced at the word "free," and Diarmin was sure Lenore deliberately used that term to make her point. He opened his mouth to try and break the tension, but Allison beat him to it.

"Well, I, for one, am not looking for any kind of fight. I am all for running and saving my skin. Besides, a fight might damage my hands and then how could I input code for my programming?" She inspected those hands carefully as the rest of the family chuckled.

"Wise lady," said Lenore. "Now, what, other than deadly pillows, can you use as a weapon?"

"How about that lamp?" offered Quinn. "I can try to trip you with it or just block an approach or—"

"Excellent, Quinn. Show us."

He grinned as he picked up the long, slender lamp. "Okay, but don't blame me if it gets broken."

***

The lamp didn't break, but a few other items did by the end of that session. Only two days, and Lenore felt a little better about her kids if they found themselves in a bad situation. Of course, she would do everything in her power to avoid that, but at least they were more prepared. Even Diarmin said he learned a few things. During the next two days, until they reached their destination, she would start them on the basics, focusing more on Quinn since he seemed the more likely one to be in a sticky situation in the future.

In between training sessions, each prepared for the mission. Lenore had studied the information until restlessness kicked in, and she did her usual walkabout on the ship. She found Diarmin tinkering at his workbench.

"Allison is at her terminal, staring at her hands and then typing madly." Lenore slumped down in the huge stuffed chair. "Do you think she is truly contemplating what would happen if she damaged her hands?"

Diarmin didn't even look up from his work to answer. "Not at all. Haven't you noticed the look on her face? She's very, hm, I would say 'triumphant.' I think we are going to find out very soon exactly what she has been working on so diligently."

Lenore was a bit miffed that she, in fact, did *not* notice that, but she let the irritation pass. "What are you working on? It looks like a personal shield, and you have already made enough for all of us."

Diarmin finally looked up with a grin. "Yes, it's a shield but with some special alterations. Watch." He attached the generator to his belt. It looked larger than the usual shield, about the size of a fist instead of a walnut. He pushed a tiny button, and it sprang into existence around him like a second skin, allowing the freedom of movement.

"So? It's exactly like any other shield I have seen, though a bit more cumbersome on your belt." Even she didn't like the slight whine of annoyance in her voice.

He didn't answer but took several steps away from his bench to a clear space. Lenore's curiosity spiked. He touched another button, and the shield fizzled out briefly to create a bubble.

Lenore abruptly sat up in the chair, gripping the arms. "A combined personal and area shield. Brilliant!" she said. "I wonder if we can patent it and sell it."

Diarmin chuckled briefly, but it sounded sad.

"What?" she asked.

"I am looking for better ways to protect you; all you see is a way to make money." His smile fell completely as the bubble fizzled out. "And that's the problem. Since they are connected, the bubble shield is not as strong as normal. If I make the personal shield stronger to compensate, it becomes too unwieldy, and I can't move easily or even toggle the switch to the bubble."

He snatched the device off his belt and returned to the workbench. Lenore approached and put her arms around him from behind.

"While I am trying to keep us from being broke, you are trying to keep us alive. Thank you, and..." She hugged him tighter and whispered, "I love you, Diarmin." He kissed her hands on his chest, and she could hear the smile back in his voice.

"It's why we fit together so well and why I love you, too."

Loud footsteps from above and heading down the ladder interrupted the tender moment. Allison leaped off the ladder when only halfway down and Lenore *tsked*.

"You'd better not get used to that when our grav plates are back to a hundred percent instead of forty."

"Actually, they are down around thirty-six percent now," added Diarmin.

"I know, I know," said Allison. "I need some gloves."

Lenore blinked at the abruptness, but obviously Diarmin was used to her blunt changing-of-topics. "Top drawer," he said, pointing to indicate.

Allison opened said drawer of the cabinet and rummaged around, occasionally lifting a glove or two. Finally, she held up a pair of white silk gloves that looked like they belonged at a royal reception rather than a workshop.

"Are these the thinnest you have?" she asked at the same time that Lenore asked, "What do you use those for?"

"First, Lenore, I use them while working on small electronics that have a toxic coating. The white makes a great background for better visual inspection. And Allison, I have a thinner pair that I use for the same thing, but they aren't cloth, they are like thin plastic."

"Better, where are they?"

"What do you need these for, Alli?" he asked as he headed to the other side of the workroom to fish around in his portable toolbox. He tossed her the gloves and waited for an answer.

"Better, but not quite what I need," she murmured as she tried to put the too large gloves on.

Diarmin repeated his question.

"Huh?" Allison blinked at her father, still absorbed in thought.

"Why thin gloves?" asked Lenore.

"Oh, well, I need a baseline for my glove flaw program."

It was Lenore's turn to blink confusedly and say "Huh?"

"As usual, Alli," said Diarmin, "you have leaped to the end without supplying us the story of how you got there. Please do so as it might help you find what you need."

"Oh, okay, well, as you know Jonah and I were looking at pictures of the girl he wanted to find. He pointed out that there were no tattoos in the few pictures we had of bare hands. Well, I noticed something that sort of looked like a wrinkle and I thought maybe she was wearing thin gloves to hide the tattoo. But they are not really gloves, more like a second skin. My program is designed to look for glove flaws in any video or still picture, but in order to be sure, I need a baseline. But these gloves are obvious that they are gloves and wouldn't help. I mean the program can still note them, but so can anyone with eyes. And then—"

"Wait!" Lenore held her hands up to stem the constant flow of Allison's explanation. If this was the way her brain worked, no wonder she muttered to herself and was always so distracted. "What you need are gloves that look like skin."

"Yes."

"I can probably help you, in fact, so can your brother."

Allison smacked her palm to her forehead. "Of course, stupid me. I should have thought of disguises. I didn't know you had gloves, but I should have figured it out."

"You've had other things on your mind, my genius daughter. Let's go see what Quinn and I have for you."

The rest of the day was taken up with Quinn and Lenore putting on their gloves and Allison photographing them, all the while mumbling things like, "Wow, that really looks real," and "totally changes the color of your skin, should have thought of that." She finished with a final comment of "Done," and turned to her terminal again, completely ignoring the other two.

"I'd be offended, but I know Allison enough by now to know it's not personal," said Quinn. He picked up his gloves and handed Lenore hers. "We'd better go put them back where they belong in case we need them in a couple of days?"

His upward inflection and eyebrows indicated he was asking a question. But Lenore wasn't sure if he was asking about details of the mission, or if he would be coming along. Maybe both. Lenore sighed inwardly. She absolutely did not want any of her family involved in a dangerous mission but was resigning herself to the fact that Quinn wanted more.

"Let's go to the lounge and go over the mission plans," she said. The smile on his face was answer enough. "After all, if I don't, you'll probably try it all by yourself anyway."

Quinn's first laugh in days was truly a joy to hear.

Chapter Forty-Six

Jonah stood awkwardly outside his apartment door. *Feels strange to be knocking on my own door.* But he didn't want to disturb Raahi. She refused to have Jonah rent another apartment or even get her a hotel room in either of their names. "Too easy to track," she'd said though would not elaborate on who would be looking. *Probably has her fair share of enemies that she sold information on.*

He had volunteered to sleep on the couch and give her his bedroom, but he could see that had made her extremely nervous. There were three tiny rooms at the palace that workers could use if they were on call or working very late hours. He had used them before, though not for an entire week. He told anyone who asked that he was having remodeling done on his apartment and wanted to stay out of the way. The look on Raahi's face when he presented her with this option had been complete relief and gratitude, so he was pleased with himself for the solution.

Now, however, he was left with the strange situation of asking to be let into his own place. As he reached to press the buzzer, the door slid open.

"I have told you that you may come in whenever you wish, Jonah," said Raahi. He entered, noticing she was wearing her usual comfortable clothing, work slacks and a plain long-sleeved gray top.

"I don't want to disturb you," he answered as he sat. Raahi gracefully sat on the couch as well, but he noticed at the farthest point from him.

"It is your place, you have more right to be here than me."

Again, that way of speaking, thought Jonah. Not at all how people on the back streets talk, not even the general working public. He desperately wanted to ask where she was from.

"And that doesn't look like the food you promised, either." Her hand indicated the papers he was holding.

He laughed.

"Is that all I am to you? A food delivery boy?"

"You've brought some fabulous meals, and I suppose I am getting a little spoiled. I haven't eaten this well, since... well, in a long time." Her eyes turned a little distant and sad.

Jonah was growing used to that look and knew she was reliving memories. She had done it most of the times she was recalling information to give him. He wanted to erase that haunting in her eyes.

"I can whip something up in the kitchen. While the food will not be as tasty, I promise the company will be entertaining."

"Entertaining as in conversation or will you perform?" The smile was back, and Jonah kept up the lighthearted mood.

He stood and swept a bow.

"Whatever you wish. I could use a night of fun."

Her light laughter unexpectedly lifted Jonah's heart, and he felt it give an extra thump.

"However, Jonah, you have done so much for me, I will prepare something for us." She stood and headed for the kitchen but looked over her shoulder at him with a smirk. "You may prepare your entertainment while you wait."

He laughed but followed her out of the room. "I don't need any preparation, but I think you might need help around my disorganized kitchen."

Jonah and Raahi worked flawlessly as a team and created a meal that they both admitted was quite good. Neither brought up the slave organization or any of the usual uncomfortable topics they had been discussing nonstop for the week they had been working so closely together. Jonah had never felt such contentment and realized he had never had any sort of normal life.

When Maya and her companion, Lara, first went missing, he stayed at the palace because everyone assumed they would be found soon. He had been kept busy with the investigations, and circumstances were never right for him to leave, even after the prince was born. The king didn't want him to return home for that would mean all hope of finding the princess was lost, so he found him a place in the palace. His name was changed so as not to publicly be viewed as a challenge to the new prince. Resolutely, Jonah shoved the memories away, determined to enjoy the present.

"And then I said, 'Back off. Next time you will know better.'" Raahi took a drink. "Sure enough, I never had a problem from them again."

"Wow, I guess I'd better stay on your good side," said Jonah. They were back on the couch, sipping wine after dinner. She was still opposite but slightly closer, and he was heartened by the development.

"Keep me plied with this fine wine, and you shall not worry."

She lifted her glass, and he did the same, wondering again at her demeanor. Despite her stories of being on the street, he knew that was not where she really came from. She looked back at him, a twinkle in her eye, and their glances held for a moment that seemed to stretch for way too long. She finally broke the silence by tearing her gaze from his and reaching for the papers he had placed on the table in front of the couch when he arrived.

"So, Jonah," she cleared her throat. "Have you found anything new today?"

Jonah looked away, embarrassed for staring, and chided himself for lack of manners.

"Um, well, hm. As you said, that liner is no longer in service. Are you sure it was smuggling slaves?"

"Yes. And I knew it was no longer active, but I was hoping you could get more of a background than I."

"Unfortunately, no. The records indicated it was destroyed in an accident only weeks after it left this planet."

"A ruse? To cover?" She handed him the pile so that he could locate the correct sheets.

"That was my thought as well but without outside help, I won't be able to run analyses of hull designs and similar craft."

"How about the names I found?"

"Nothing new. But these three," he shuffled the papers to find the ones he was talking about. "Are you sure about these? They are very high ranking, these two are close to the prince, which sort of makes sense, but are you sure this man is involved?" He looked directly at Raahi as he brandished the photo. "This is the Supreme Councilman and a close friend of the king for over thirty years."

Raahi looked away and shrugged. "It's what I heard."

"Who or what is your source? Maybe with proof or verification I might be able to investigate further but without that—"

Raahi stood, cutting off his sentence. "I told you, I can't reveal my sources. It would ruin my reputation, and then where would I be as an information broker? I cannot risk that loss when I leave."

"Are you truly leaving then?" Jonah couldn't believe how much he was dreading that time.

"I don't belong here." She began pacing from one side of the room to the other. To most people this might seem normal, but Jonah couldn't remember a time when she had turned her back to him. Maybe she was starting to trust him. Maybe now was the time for questions.

"Then why did you come here?"

She stopped and stared for a long moment. He thought she wouldn't answer, but she resumed pacing, crossing her arms, staring at the floor, and hunching her shoulders.

"I had no choice and I...I promised someone, but"—she pressed her lips together, then continued— "But it wasn't what I thought it was going to be."

"And what did you think?"

"It doesn't matter!" She chopped the air with her hands, then crossed her arms again. "I have to leave this planet. Soon."

"What if you were asked to stay?" Jonah asked softly. Raahi stopped again, arms still crossed, eyes unreadable.

"What do you mean?"

"I don't want you to go. Stay."

Her eyes widened, and her arms dropped to her sides. A small, sad smile flitted across her face. "Impossible."

Jonah was embarrassed again by his outburst. "I mean we work well together. I can get you a job in security at the palace and—"

"Absolutely not!"

Jonah stared, shocked at her vehemence, and now she looked embarrassed at her outburst. "I mean, I make my own way. I don't want charity. And I can't stay." She looked earnestly into his eyes. "Come with me."

For a wild and reckless moment, he considered it, but that little voice inside told him that even if he wanted to, he couldn't abandon the king and Lavan. His life and duties were here. Princess or not, his life was irrevocably tied to the palace.

"I cannot. I wish I could, but I have certain obligations that won't allow me...I can't go." For some reason, he glanced down at Raahi's hands hanging at her side. She had stopped wearing gloves in the apartment, a sign of trust. But there was not a sign of what he wished were there.

"There is one more piece of information I can obtain that

might help. I don't know if you can use it, though, since you didn't get far with the ship. Maybe your associates who bought my last piece of intelligence could find something."

"What is the information?" Jonah tried to focus on the job and not his unhappiness that the intimate moment had passed.

"I must retrieve it from a secure location tomorrow."

"I'll go with you," he said.

She held up her hand. "No, I must go alone. But thank you for the offer." She clasped her hands in front of her body and bowed slightly. "I will return the following day. I have appreciated your hospitality, especially the lovely dinner tonight. Good night, Jonah."

"Yes, it was a lovely dinner, wasn't it? Thank you, as well, and good night, Raahi."

As she disappeared into the bedroom, his feet took a couple steps to follow before he reined in his reaction and turned back to the paperwork with a sigh. Perhaps if he found something more, she might stick around longer.

***

"Ok, are we clear on the plan?" asked Lenore, as she secured her parachute pack firmly so as not to dislodge her other accoutrements.

The two children nodded, but Diarmin spoke. "Since we have gone over them fifty times and have affirmed thirteen, I think we are prepared."

Lenore either didn't hear the sarcasm or chose to ignore it. "After the drop, you will give me three hours to make it to the compound, another hour to be in and out, and then the other three to make it to the rendezvous."

"And I will be there to pick you up in six hours, just in case things go quicker than intended," said Diarmin.

"Remember, it can go faster if you disable the scatter field from inside so that I can access the computer from the ship," Allison added.

Lenore shook her head. "As I've said before, that would be like lighting a beacon to any planetary security. And also quite useless since this kind of code requires direct contact with the corresponding core. The upload signal, once I have the download, should beam up to the ship through the scattering field with no problem."

"I don't like being stuck up on the ship," said Quinn, very close to sulking like a toddler. "I can't do anything to help."

"Oh, so you're saying I was useless up here when you and Mom went on that school shooting mission?" said Allison testily.

"Of course not, but that's you. You know your way around the systems and how to work them. Dad, too, which is why it should be me, not him, at the rendezvous."

"Hey," Lenore cut into their argument. She was about to say something more, but Diarmin spoke hurriedly, knowing his expertise as the family glue was needed.

"Now, we know everyone is apprehensive, but facts are facts, Quinn. Two quick lessons do not make you qualified to fly the shuttle for either the drop or the pickup."

"Then let me go with you."

"And leave Allison alone?"

Quinn grumbled to himself. Diarmin figured it was probably something about "Allison will be fine," but Quinn knew better than to argue at this point.

"Good," said Lenore. "Both of you monitor me and the shuttle. I will transmit data as soon as I can, and someone needs to be here to receive it." She gave her kids a quick hug, cinched the parachute belt a little tighter, and stepped into the shuttle. "Let's go. Sooner started, sooner done."

Diarmin gave each a squeeze in turn, ignoring the sullen look on Quinn's face and Allison's worried one. "Take care of each other and keep your eyes open." They nodded, and he entered the pod and closed the door.

He initiated the launch sequence and waited for Quinn and Allison to seal the hatch. As the shuttlepod's engines came online, he glanced at Lenore sitting in the copilot's chair staring straight ahead.

"You hid it well," he said softly, wondering if he was doing the right thing in bringing it up.

"Hid what?" she snapped.

"The fact that you are extremely nervous and more apprehensive about both the mission and leaving them aboard by themselves than you have ever been."

"Who said I was nervous?"

"Come on, the jaw clenching, the way you bark orders. I can tell." The all-clear sounded and Diarmin launched the shuttle.

"You are right," said Lenore. "I keep waiting for the calm before the mission that I always get, but it simply won't come. Instead of focusing on what I need to do, I keep thinking about what could go wrong. I mean I'm always prepared for things to go wrong, but this time it seems to be getting in the way."

"Now you know how we feel when you go on these missions by yourself." The look of surprise she shot him encouraged Diarmin to say what he felt needed to be said. "We have never had the fortune to have a little box suppressing those emotions of fear." Her eyes sparked, and he hurried to get out what he needed to say before her retort. "And now you don't have it either."

"You're right. And I don't need it." She looked back out the window and placed her hands on the console.

He placed his right hand over her left and said, "No, you don't."

She said nothing, but her breathing became controlled, and she was no longer tensing her entire body. The board pinged but didn't break their concentration.

"Ten seconds to drop."

Lenore took the three steps necessary to reach the door, pulled down the cloth mask that covered all but her eyes against the cold of the drop and any security cameras.

"Remember, hard about after I jump. You don't want to be detected," came her muffled voice.

Diarmin declined to answer, knowing it was just his wife setting the plans in her head. Instead, he placed a finger over the switch to open the hatch.

The pressure popped, and the rush of air may have drowned out his "Good luck," but he continued in a shout. "Three...two...one...mark!"

And she was gone.

***

The rush of wind in her face as she fell calmed Lenore as she felt her training kick in. Through the darkness below she could make out two sets of lights. The largest cluster would be the city and the smaller, though still impressive in size, was the compound she was aiming for.

The count in her head was nearly to zero, so she grasped the handle to open the chute. Parachuting in the dead of night and approaching on foot was the best way to reach the compound unnoticed. Almost without thought, she pulled the cord and felt the familiar *whoosh* and tug of an opening chute. She knew she had a grin on her face, and the fierce pounding in her chest let her know her adrenaline was working just fine.

She glanced at the horizon as she maneuvered her way down. Good. No hint of light. Plenty of time to traverse the two miles overland to arrive before dawn when night guards were the sleepiest and the household not stirring yet. The toughest part now would be to see where she was going to land without any illumination to help her. She couldn't help but feel exhilarated. This is what she was good at. Not being a mother, not training youngsters, but missions. She shoved the thoughts away as she heard the rustle of leaves below.

Damn! Trees! Everything was pitch black, the moons of this world already set. Now she regretted not having night vision goggles, but she would not have been able to accurately judge the distance of the lights if she had worn them. She needed to speak to Diarmin about creating some night vision contacts controlled with a blink. *Later, Lenore. Focus.*

There. A slightly brighter spot to her left. Lenore hoped that indicated a clearing rather than a lake but had no time to worry as she felt her feet brush twigs. She curled up her legs and pulled hard to turn the chute toward the light spot. Despite the abrupt change, she still felt herself dropping into the foliage and scraping through nearly up to her neck before bursting into open air once again.

The clearing was very small, and she had to drop quickly. She sensed more than saw the trees on the other side, hoped she was close enough to the ground, and pulled the cord that folded the chute. Her gentle descent turned into a plummet, and she absorbed the impact with a roll that tangled her in the chute cords only slightly. Putting her hand out, she realized her excellent judgement as she felt a tree less than an arm's length from her face.

As she stood to disentangle herself from the chute, she felt it tug at her shoulders, and she realized that the canvas had been caught in a tree. When she was unsuccessful at dislodging the chute, she removed the entire pack instead and left it there, even though Diarmin would grumble about the expense needed to replace it. She would have liked to request he pick it up on his way to the rendezvous, but she wasn't supposed to contact the ship until the data was in hand. Her biggest concern was that once the sun was up, the parachute would be seen by anyone flying over it despite its dark color. Well, she would just have to be back on the shuttle before then, wouldn't she? She glanced at her wristcomp to see which direction the compound was in and started out in the ground-covering lope she had never liked but was good at. Putting most of her mind to dodging trees, she mentally rehearsed the mission while covering the two miles.

***

"How are you following her through the trees?" asked Quinn.

"She has a steady speed and direction. I put the camera on that trajectory, and I know I am on the right...see?" Allison pointed at the screen. "There she is, oops, gone again."

Their eyes were glued to the screen, hoping for a glimpse of their mother. Suddenly the picture went gray.

"What's happened? Why is the picture gone?"

"Calm down, silly," said Allison as she tapped on the keyboard. "Dad's shuttle just docked so the camera is now pointing at the hull. Hang on.... there. Now using the ship's cameras. Give me a second to find her."

"How can you do that?"

"By tracking along the last route and estimating how far." Allison shot a glance at her brother. "It's different being up here, isn't it?"

Quinn grimaced. "At least you have something to do. I'm just waiting and watching."

"Status, Allison?" said Diarmin as his head preceded his body onto the bridge.

"Same as when you left. Ah, there she is."

"Good, Allison. Now," he said behind the command console, "prepare to break orbit."

"What?" said both kids simultaneously.

"If we maintain this stationary orbit over the area of the compound, someone is bound to get curious. We will come back when it's time to pick her up."

"But we can't just leave her, Dad," said Quinn as Allison prepped her board to maintain visual as long as possible.

"Quinn." His father's voice was not loud but there was steel behind it. "We can't help her if we are discovered." His attention was taken up with flight.

As the ship pulled away, Quinn felt it in his stomach, and it wasn't simply the weak gravity. He knew this mission involved the slave organization, and anxiety knotted his insides. He wanted to protest more, worried that his father and sister didn't know how horrible these people could be, but he kept quiet.

"No farther, Dad," said Allison, eyes glued to her monitor. "We need to be able to receive her signal when it transmits."

Diarmin nodded, and Quinn left to go find something to do to distract himself from his worry.

Chapter Forty-Seven

It took Lenore twenty minutes to circle the compound, even climbing a tree to see inside the walls. Worth the time but perplexing. There only seemed to be two guards at the front gate. Granted, the fence was electrified and probably had sensor detection, but there should be at least one guard roaming the grounds and more at the doors to each building. Maybe they were all inside the main house. Partying in the guest house? Asleep in the garage perhaps. Some of these high-ranking criminals were paranoid, and there might be ten guards stationed in and outside of the bedroom. Well, her plans would take her nowhere near the bedroom. She quietly extricated herself from the tree and headed for the fence near the south of the compound so that the house was between her and the guards out front.

As she approached, she could see the outline of the electrical field on top. *Not a problem, but where are the...aha!* There was one sensor and the other should be about...there. She unrolled the thin mat that would prevent electric shock and inside were two long wires with small plates on either end. She carefully placed a plate on one sensor and tossed the wire over the fence. She did the same for the other and quickly placed the mat on the fence. Lenore had only sixty seconds to make it over the fence before the sensors registered the bypass as more than a temporary blip, usually shrugged off as a random insect. She quickly scrambled up, feeling the electric vibration in her hands through the mat, and was down on the ground in only a couple of breaths. She gave a quick yank to both wires and mat, and everything was rolled up and stowed in her pack.

On light feet, she approached the nearest door, which, according to her information, was the laundry. While many places had guards at the back, she had found that obscure places like the laundry or garages didn't. *Well, usually.* She grimaced at a memory of finding three guards in the garage of an eccentric who loved his vehicles more than his wife.

Lenore mentally shook her head. *Get your mind on the mission.* The door was locked, but her pad showed it wasn't attached to an alarm. It also indicated no live beings on the other side. Lenore was inside in a heartbeat. In no time at all she located the office, and she began to feel uneasy at the lack of obstacles.

The computer room was locked with a palm pad and security code, so that posed another barrier. While it would deter most petty thieves, she had dealt with this many times before. One of Diarmin's clever gadgets picked up residue from the pad and created a false palm reading. The security code was a simple one and she was through quickly. She headed for the main terminal and pulled out of her pack the special device of Allison's that would let her download the information at the fastest speed possible. The first button she pressed would transmit the data to the ship, and the second would wipe the memory. Lenore doubted the wipe would be necessary as she also brought out a tiny tube, smaller than her pinky finger, that she carefully set to the side.

Lenore's fingers danced on the keyboard, bringing up the screen demanding a code. She opened the tube to slip out a rolled-up paper. She carefully unrolled the inch-long paper and quickly typed in the code before the paper, exposed to the air, caught on fire and burned from the center to the edges, leaving no residue behind. Before the puff of smoke dissipated, Lenore was into the files and downloading. She listened carefully, but still heard nothing to indicate that getting out of the compound would be any more difficult than getting in.

Lenore's brow wrinkled as she thought again how incredibly easy this all had been. A man as powerful and high up as he was, not only in his various businesses but also a large player within the slave hierarchy, should have much more security to prevent exactly what she was doing. Maybe she was just so used to things going wrong that she got nervy when things went the way they planned.

The indicator showed the download was nearly complete, so she quickly checked her gear for the trip back out to the rendezvous. This time she would be going out the front gate, stunning the guards from behind. Coming in, it was important not to show anything wrong, but by the time anyone noticed the front guards were not checking in, she would be long gone. A small beep and she removed the device and began transmitting to the ship.

She made sure everything was exactly how she had found it and headed for the door.

Lights in the office snapped on, and she had no time to reach for a weapon as there was already one pointed at her by an old man sitting behind the desk. He hadn't been there when she passed through a few minutes ago. She must have tripped a silent alarm in the computer room.

"How interesting," said the man. "From that device in your hand I am assuming that you have gotten into my files and perhaps downloaded the lot."

Lenore silently cursed herself at her lapse. He was about ten feet away. Maybe she could toss the device to distract him and then disarm him before he got off a shot. Despite his age, his eyes were clear, and the hand holding the blaster did not waver in the least. She decided not to underestimate him. A glance down at the device showed it was still transmitting and she could do nothing, not even hit the kill switch until it finished. Stalling would be the plan.

"Lord Timatay, I assume," she said in a deep, rough voice, still muffled from the cloth covering.

"I should hope you know who you are stealing from, young...lady, despite your attempt to disguise your voice." He tilted his head and narrowed his eyes slightly. Lenore knew there had to be a button on his desk to call security and wondered why he didn't press it.

"Perhaps," she said, voice still rough. She knew her clothing hid any telltale feminine features, so she wouldn't let his guess goad her into revealing anything. The silence lengthened, and Lord Timatay finally toggled a switch. Lenore tensed, ready to take on however many guards came through the door. A flash of light drew her eye upward into the corner of the office. He had disabled the security camera.

"Tell me," he said in a soft voice. "Who was it? Which one got out and managed to get the code to you? Was it Evan? Miranda?"

Lenore could only blink.

"The twins. I bet it was the twins. Those girls were the scrappiest and most intelligent of the lot."

"Twins," Lenore confirmed, though she had no idea.

"Hah! Good. I am glad they are well." He pointed with his blaster. "I hope you paid them handsomely for that code. They deserve it after all they have been through." His voice was thick as if holding back emotion. He cleared his throat before continuing. "Now," he said as he rose from his desk and slowly approached Lenore. She prepared to duck, but before he got within her reach, he reversed the blaster and held it out to her.

"You must kill me."

Completely taken aback, Lenore figured it must be a trick. She froze, not reaching for the gun.

"Why?" she asked.

The old man quickly closed the last few steps, shoved the gun into her hands and retreated to his chair. With a huge sigh, he sat, placing his palms face down on his desk. "When the organization discovers that my files have been hacked, they will kill me, but not before they torture and interrogate me. I don't want them to find out that I had purposely arranged for those slaves to obtain the codes, and then allowed to escape so that someday," he clenched his fists, "someday that information could be used to take them down." Now his voice was lower, menacing. "All of them." Lenore could see the fire that had helped this man build up his fortune. And that explained the lack of security. He wanted that information to be stolen.

She slowly approached Lord Timatay, blaster pointed at him. She half expected him to close his eyes, but they never wavered from hers. It was his turn to be surprised when she placed the gun on his desk, safety engaged.

"I am sorry, Lord Timatay. I promised the young woman that sold me the information that I would not harm you."

His eyes softened, and his voice dropped to a whisper. "They did understand."

His expression hardened so quickly, Lenore thought she'd imagined moisture in those eyes.

"You must. If the organization finds out about them, they will never stop until they are dead."

"I gave my word. I will also give you my word that this information will be put to great use and..." Here she paused, not sure what Raahi would say but tried to offer this man what comfort she could. "I will pass along your greeting and regrets."

"Thank you, stranger. Goodbye."

Lenore nodded and exited the room, emotions conflicting within her. She should have killed him, for all the reasons he said, and mostly because he might be able to identify her. But she wouldn't break her promise to Raahi, and deep down she felt he was someone who was trying to do something good against all the bad he had done.

She knew how he felt.

The sound of a blaster shot coming from the computer room made her stumble a few steps before she recovered.

Forgetting stealth and knowing she was now under pressure, she exited through the laundry room door and ran for the front gate. She switched the transmitter to her left hand as she activated her personal shield and reached for her tiny gun that shot paralysis darts. She came around the corner of the garage and ran headlong into one guard on his way to the house. She brought up her fist holding the dart gun under his chin, continued the motion as he fell, bringing the darts to bear on the other guard and dropping him before he could unholster his own weapon.

Should have had it out of the holster when you heard the shot. She hit the buttons that opened the front gate and disarmed the security field. She grinned as she sprinted towards the tree line. Mission accomplished.

Or so she thought.

With no warning, something wrapped around her legs, and she crashed to the ground. Despite having the breath knocked out of her, she unbound the cords in a heartbeat, but not before they gave an electrical discharge to knock out her personal shields. Without looking, she stowed the transmitter in the pack and reached for her other weapon. Before she could stand up, however, she felt a dart on her neck. She tried for the adrenaline rush that would allow her to dissipate the drug, but it was no use without the bioimplant. She fell backwards, her own dart shooter still clenched in her hand.

Footsteps approached from both sides and five faces stared down at her.

"Well, well, well," said the only one not dressed in stealth gear. "Looks like Lord Timatay has had a visitor." He held up a stun gun, slowly, menacingly as if to taunt his captive. "Good thing we were watching for such a thing." He waved a hand toward the compound, eyes never leaving Lenore's. "Check out the grounds and house." He grinned and pressed the trigger.

Lenore had one last thought before unconsciousness overtook her.

I knew this had been too easy.

Chapter Forty-Eight

"Dad."

Diarmin paused, one foot inside the hatch to the shuttle, one out. He yelled back in the direction of the speaker Allison had just paged him on.

"Yes, Alli?"

"The transmission cut out."

"Another glitch? I thought moving closer would help?" He took the foot out of the shuttle and stood on the ramp.

"It did. I mean it's not transmitting at all now."

"Hold on, on my way up." He had prepped for the shuttle launch as soon as the transmission had begun, knowing Lenore was on her way back to the meeting point. Instead, he headed back to the bridge.

"Is it finished?" he asked as he took the steps two at time.

"I don't think so. While I can't read most of this yet without applying the decode sequence, I can recognize basic structure. It cut off in the middle of a data block."

"What's going on?" asked Quinn as he came up the ladder.

"Transmission cut out," said Allison.

Diarmin saw the look of anguish on his son's face. "Maybe it won't transmit through the trees," he said, more to reassure Quinn than believing that answer. Allison, however, was all about reality.

"C'mon Dad. It transmits through buildings, so trees aren't going to do anything."

Diarmin hesitated for only a second then punched in the code to Lenore's personal tracker. Quinn noticed and batted his father's hand away before he activated the program.

"What are you doing? You said to never do that. They could lock on to the signal and find both Mom and the ship."

"I was only going to activate it for a few seconds, to see if she is on her way back. Even if someone notices the pulse, they won't have time to trace it back any more than a general direction." He punched the button. "And I don't plan on staying here."

The two held their breath as the program searched. But it found nothing. Not even a stationary Lenore. Diarmin felt his gut clench, but Quinn's scared voice steadied him.

"What does that mean?"

"It only means that her signal is blocked, and that may be why the transmission cut off." He deactivated the trace and started the ship moving. "I think we need to risk a clear view for a picture."

"But—" started Quinn but Allison's gasp startled them both. They looked up at the main viewscreen and saw a picture of a group of men carrying a body toward the compound.

"How are you getting that picture?" asked Quinn.

"I am pulling a video feed off a satellite."

"Turn it off, now!" Diarmin yelled.

"Don't worry. I've masked our identification."

"That doesn't matter. If they know someone is tapping into their feed, they will come looking. Turn it off."

"Ok," said Allison meekly. "I did copy it though, pulling video from about an hour ago to what I just saw. Do you want to watch what I got?"

Diarmin tried to put aside his guilt at yelling, but the situation was getting serious. He nodded, and Allison set the video back ten minutes, shortly before the signal cut out. They saw a quiet compound, guards in usual formation, but the camera picked up a slight flash of light from one of the windows of the house. The guards reacted, but the feed zoomed in on a door that was opening. From the mission prep, they knew it was the door to the laundry room.

The figure coming out had to be Lenore. Quinn groaned, voicing what they were all thinking.

"They were expecting her."

They watched in silence as she took down the two guards and headed toward freedom. They continued watching, helpless, as she was tripped and paralyzed. Allison let out a tiny squeak when the man shot the gun.

"She's not dead. That was a stun gun," said Diarmin.

"How do you know?" Quinn asked, his voice completely devoid of emotion. Diarmin looked at his son's expressionless face and thought how much he was like his mother.

"Pause and magnify that, Allison. See the blue corona?

That shows a stun discharge. A laser or blaster would have a single shot line."

Diarmin sat at the command console and input commands that turned the ship around back the way they had come.

"What are you doing?" asked both children.

Quinn's face was angry. "We can't just leave her."

"Of course not, but we are going to hide behind the moon while we come up with a plan. Allison, shut off all external sources of power, and Quinn, I know you have been going over the map of the compound. Since we know they took her back there, that's our best chance to get her." He bit down on the comment that if she was taken elsewhere, she could be lost to them. "Allison, start going through the transmissions that we received from Lenore. Look for anything that might help."

Both children nodded and began their duties. Diarmin was proud of their focus despite their fear. He knew they felt it. He did too. He didn't tell them that in all the years he and Lenore had been together, this was the first time she had been taken.

For the first time, it was up to him to save her.

***

Lenore came awake slowly, which was unusual, probably due to the lack of the dratted implant, but it allowed her to sense her surroundings without moving. Twice before, when with the Xa'ti'al, she had been taken prisoner. She drew heavily on that experience and her training now.

The first order of business upon awakening was to assess. She was in a chair, upper body tied to it with thick black cord, her hands separately bound behind her back. Her head lolled forward. The fact that she could feel her hair swinging down in her face said that her mask was off. A small twitch indicated that her legs were also tied to the chair. Such thoroughness suggested she was completely disarmed and prepared for interrogation.

"Come now. I am aware that you are conscious. Let's not start this relationship with deception, shall we?"

The voice belonged to the man who had stunned her, so she lifted her head to stare at him, trying to appear groggy. He was sitting in another chair across from her. Laid out on the bed were all her accoutrements, lined up as if each had been inspected. They had been extremely diligent as she saw the knife from her boot and even the tiny electromagnetic generator she kept in her bra. She was impressed that she was still dressed though her gloves were laid out on the bed next to the mask. She tried not to look at the transmitting device. Did she hit the kill switch? She couldn't remember.

The man waited for her to speak. He was dressed in expensive, but not gaudy, clothes. He was obviously the man in charge of the commandos who had captured her. His awareness of her awakening also led her to conclude that he knew his way in an interrogation.

She knew exactly which persona to play here.

"I've no reason to lie. What d'ya wanna know?" she asked.

He smiled, looking relaxed, but she could tell it was an act.

"Why are you here?"

"I assume you've already figured that out as I'm sure you've taken a look around."

He nodded. "To kill Lord Timatay. You admit that?"

"Why not?" Lenore looked him up and down. "You're not the local law and ambushed me outside of the compound, so I assume you were also heading to do the same job I was hired for."

"Interesting conclusions. Who hired you?"

She shrugged. "Don't know. Never saw his face. With the amount he paid me, I figured it was better to not ask questions."

"Did he ask you to make it look like a suicide?"

She grinned. "Naw, that was all me. My own personal method so people are less likely to come lookin'."

"How did you get to this planet? Do you have a ship?"

"Bribed a cargo ship to bring me unregistered."

"So why the parachute?"

Damn, these guys are good. "Okay, so they didn't know they had a stowaway until an escape hatch malfunctioned on landing approach."

His eyes hardened perceptibly. "I thought you weren't going to lie to me."

Lenore shrugged again. "Force of habit." With each shrug she felt her bonds, but they were quite snug. It would take a serious distraction on his part for her to get out of them.

He stared at her for long moments. She stared back

the amount she figured a tough independent mercenary would, then averted her head and looked down slightly. Her body alternated between her extremities going numb and activating sweat glands. She mentally tried to bring her reactions under control but had no idea if she was succeeding. Another side effect of not having the implant.

"It appears that you are not an ordinary assassin-for-hire." She looked back at him, using all her will to keep her face expressionless as her gut clenched. Did he suspect her of being a Xa'ti'al? She raised her eyebrows slightly as if in inquiry.

"This is quite a range of equipment for one quick murder." His left hand indicated the bed and all her gear. "Especially this." His sweeping hand stopped at the data device and picked it up to inspect it. "Most unusual." He peered at her, pursing his lips. "What exactly is it for?"

He knows what it is for. Picking it up had been deliberate, though he made it look random. She again wished she remembered if she had hit the kill switch.

"I always carry one with me in case I get a chance to download anything." She attempted a gruff look, bold, she knew, but in her persona. "Be careful with that. Paid quite a lot for it, custom job. And it's delicate."

"What did you download?"

"Nothin'." She tried to sound disgusted. "Only got into the office. Couldn't get through the door to the mainframe room."

"Hm." He tossed the device back on the bed, and Lenore hissed and glowered at the man like she was expected to.

"Now, we know that you were out in the courtyard mere moments after you shot poor Lord Timatay. Not much time to try to pick a lock."

Double damn. They have really done their investigations. Her estimate of them rose another notch, and she began to worry. These were most likely people from the slave organization, not another mercenary group as she hinted at earlier.

"I had Timatay—"

"Lord Timatay."

Lenore filed that interesting correction for later reflection and continued. "I had Lord Timatay already paralyzed while I tried to break into the data room. Easier to kill, especially since he refused to give me the code for the door." A small tidbit to throw them off the trail of Timatay's betrayal.

He stared at her. "Either you are indeed telling the truth, or you are a very good liar."

"Again, I have no reason to lie." And here she took a shot, one that a mercenary would do. "Let me go and I will make it well worth your while. I'm quite well off or will be when I collect the other half of this reward."

The man laughed. "Oh my, you are a bold one." He stood and slowly walked toward her. "But this is not about money. You have killed one of our own and must answer for that." He held up a wand, and she couldn't help her eyes widening as she recognized the same slave device as they used on Quinn.

"Ah, I see you recognize this." He twisted the base of the wand, and her bonds shot voltage through her, lighting up every nerve in her body. Another twist and it stopped.

She grimaced. The pain was more intense than she had expected. Again, she missed that implant. But she acted tough for the persona. "One of your own? I thought you were here to kill him."

"If we were, it would have been our place to kill one of our own, not some random gutter trash."

They had already been suspicious of Lord Timatay. That told her volumes, but she reacted as expected. "Gutter trash! How dare you, you whore's son, mongrel—" She was cut short as her bonds were activated again for an even longer time.

"Please," she panted when he switched it off. "I'll pay a fortune. Please."

"I'll repeat, it's not about money." Another twist of the wand. She felt her teeth grind against each other in spasm, and she held on. Finally, the shocks stopped, and she was not acting when her head sagged down as her muscles went flaccid.

"So kill me then."

The man grasped her by the hair and yanked her head up. "That decision will be up to my boss. He may have something better in mind for you."

"I'll work for you. For free. Do anything you want."

"Yes, that is always an option." He reached into his pocket to pull out and then uncoil a long strip.

Are slave collars standard issue for lackeys? She knew her nerves were making her giddy, but the irreverent thought helped her focus on her next strategy.

She began to struggle wildly and said in horror, "No, please. You don't need that. I said I would work for free.

Not as a slave, please anything but that." He reached to place the collar on and quick as anything, she bit his hand.

He pulled back and stopped his hand short of reaching inside his jacket again. Now she knew where his weapon was.

"Kill me. Better than slavery."

His eyes hardened, and he smiled again with a sneer. He activated the bonds again and when the pain stopped, the collar was around her neck.

"Slavery it is."

Chapter Forty-Nine

"Psst, Jonah."

Jonah looked up from the terminal to see Lavan peering into the room from the doorway.

"Well, hello, Companion. How may I serve you?" He rose from his chair and indicated with a bow that Lavan was to take it.

"Shhhh! I am not supposed to be talking to you, Hahn would not like it." He sat in the chair, looking like a caged mouse, jittery and on edge, ready to run at the least provocation. Jonah took note of a new black eye and the fact that Lavan was thinner than ever. He closed the door.

"It is perfectly normal for the Companion to speak with the Chief Reviewer."

"No, no, no. You don't understand. The prince will make things very difficult if he knew I came to you."

"Like he hasn't been difficult?" Jonah pointed to the black eye. "And I know he has been limiting your food, after he laced that meal with berry seed, knowing full well you are allergic."

"He wanted me out of the way for a few days," said Lavan with a grimace. "You know how the king has improved quite a bit since you spoke with him? Well, his Majesty has now noticed that the prince is not the heir he thought he would be and has been moving to limit him from gathering any more power." He swallowed and winced as if his throat hurt.

Jonah reached for the small refrigerator next to his desk and pulled out one of his special bottles of energy drink. He held it out to Lavan who shrank back from it. That showed more than anything how the prince had been treating him, and his heart went out to him.

"This is easy on the stomach, and it looks like you need a little pick-me-up." He uncapped the bottle and again offered it to the companion. Lavan took the bottle and took a small sip. He smiled and took a longer swig.

"Sorry about that. Been a rough road." He drank again and started talking quickly.

"The prince wants me to procure a device that scrambles camera videos. Sound, too, although I know cameras outside of the palace usually don't have sound. He knows he is being closely watched by the few people still loyal to the king. He is not allowed to meet with anyone privately in his unmonitored rooms like he used to, and he is becoming frustrated that his run for power is slipping."

"Ah, I see why you would get in trouble for telling me that. I am the one that he wants to hide things from."

"Well, you and the other reviewers. Can you get one for me—hold on," he raised his hand to stop Jonah from speaking. "I don't want one that works, I want one that is faulty. One that appears to work, but he can still be filmed. I think..." Lavan drew a long breath as if it were a great effort to get that message out. "I think he is plotting not only to regain his power but also to kill the king."

"Wow." Jonah was both impressed and afraid. Impressed with Lavan that even through the subtle tortures he was put through, he was still managing to outthink and do whatever he could to stop the prince's plans. And afraid that the prince was thinking about a forcible takeover. Not good.

"Can you do that? I have to get him something, and I don't want one that works."

"I think I know someone who can procure a scrambler, and I can tinker with it. When I have it ready, I will have a messenger give you a name and place to meet so you don't have to visit me again. And I will make it so that it works for one or two uses because Hahn will surely test it."

"Good idea and thanks, Jonah." Lavan took a very long drink, draining the bottle, then rose, giving the empty bottle to Jonah. "I'm glad I can count you as a friend."

"Lavan," said Jonah, reaching a hand out but not quite touching the companion. "Why do you stay? Why not spend a few days in guest quarters or even outside the palace? No one should keep going through what you do."

Lavan slowly shook his head as he looked at the ground. He sighed and stood there for several heartbeats without speaking. As Jonah opened his mouth to speak again, Lavan lifted his head to look directly into his eyes.

"I can't leave. Right now, Hahn thinks I am a simpleton whose nose is always in books and completely unaware of what is going on. Things have to continue as usual or he will suspect something."

"Nobody deserves the treatment he has put you

through."

"You are right. Nobody does. Yet if I leave, not only will we lose the one person on the inside, he will need someone else to take his frustrations out on." Lavan lifted his chin. "I will not let him torture another."

The resolution in his voice and eyes stirred Jonah's admiration for the tough young man. Very few people would take on such burdens. He gave Lavan's shoulder a gentle squeeze.

"Hang in there, Lavan. It will get better."

The companion smiled sadly and headed for the door.

"Wait." Jonah pulled up the cameras, found the corridor deserted, then located the prince in the Council Hall. "It's clear."

Lavan nodded and left. Jonah switched the camera back on and thought about how he could help the companion. Raahi was supposed to meet him at the apartment today after work with her last piece of information. He smiled. Now he had another job for her which would keep her from leaving for a little longer. At least until the Baroness, or whoever the lady was, came back with useful information.

He set about clearing any videos that showed the companion coming to him and began counting the minutes to the end of his shift.

***

"Wow, you really have been thinking all this through, haven't you, Quinn?"

"Well, Alli, you were working on the computer, and Dad was doing ship stuff. I felt useless and went over this again. In case we needed it." Quinn frowned. "Though I didn't think we would."

"It's a good thing you did, now tell me your ideas," said Diarmin.

"I still don't know what good we can do," said Allison. "We are not even close to ready. All Mom taught us to do is run away."

"Hey, Dad's no slouch if his old stories are to be believed, and as for us"—Quinn smiled—"if running away is what we are good at then that is what we will do."

***

The interrogation had been finished for a while, but

Lenore was still tightly bound to the chair. After the shocks, the man had turned to well-placed knife cuts. Mostly stabbing in non-vital but extremely painful areas.

He does know his way around the human nervous system, thought Lenore in one of her brief moments of respite.

Her best estimate of time passed was that she had been unconscious about an hour, interrogated for nearly twice that long, and now, left alone again for nearly an hour. She had continually stuck with her story, this not being her first torture. Although she had to admit that he was one of the more talented tormentors, maximum pain with little damage showing, typical for slavers.

So, four hours. She had missed the rendezvous and hoped her family had not tried to pick up the parachute. There would most likely be guards watching the area. But surely she would have heard if there had been another capture. Her mouth twisted. They would tell her if only to add to the torture.

It wouldn't be much longer until this group finished tying up loose ends here and returned to wherever they had come from. It wouldn't have been the city, or they would have simply interrogated her there. No, they were most likely from offplanet, directly from the organization. Which made her anxious to find a way out before they wished to return to their ship. Once that happened, things would be significantly worse.

So far, she was confident that she had them believing she was in a fog of pain and very weak. Granted, she was indeed weaker than she should be, but she knew she could find the strength to fight if only given an inch.

Lenore heard footsteps. She kept her head hanging limply and eyes closed. She had passed out at the end of the last session but had regained consciousness quickly. However, she hadn't moved in order to maintain the illusion.

"Wake up." Something nudged her left calf, probably the toe of her tormentor's boot. Since it hit a previous nerve stab, it was enough to "wake" her as well as elicit a yelp of pain.

"I've thought of more questions." The man twirled the knife.

Lenore knew there were no more questions, he just enjoyed the torture.

"Please," she gasped, throat rough. "I've told you all I

know."

"Then let's see if there's some hidden nugget you didn't know that you knew."

She held her breath and shrank away as he approached, distracting herself with bets on where he would use the knife next. *Five credits says he goes for the ribs. No, ten that he will revisit the previous site near the ankle. Ah... eyes settling near right shoulder...fifty credits he goes for the bicep nerve.*

"Sir, I need to speak with you." One of the lackeys, now devoid of all stealth gear, entered the bedroom, pad in hand.

"You know I don't like being interrupted, Number Four."

"Yes, but you must see this."

The man sighed and took a step back, holding out his hand for the pad. Whatever he saw there caused a quick intake of breath and an incredulous look turned toward his lackey.

"Yes, thank you for bringing this to my attention, Four. Continue with the extraction and clean up."

"Yes, sir." The young man nodded and left. Lenore was grateful for the distraction as the man perused the pad. He even appeared to forget about her, and she turned her thoughts again to escape. She was brought back to the situation abruptly when he began to laugh.

"Well, well, well, my dear. Looks like I have stumbled upon a great treasure."

Oh, no. Did they find the information on the data device after all?

"And that treasure is now in my possession," he said.

Lenore groaned inwardly. They did. Things couldn't get any worse. The man turned the pad around to show her the display.

There was her picture in what was obviously a posted reward for her capture.

She was wrong. It was much, much worse.

***

Jonah almost didn't hear the knock, busy as he was preparing dinner. He had been listening because he knew she never used the ringer that recorded her voice to announce herself. He dropped the spoon and went to see if it was indeed a knock.

He opened the door to Raahi. Her hair was completely

hidden under a cap, and she was wearing a jacket with a scarf over the lower half of her face even though it was quite warm out.

"Hello, Raahi. Come in and make yourself comfortable. Dinner is almost ready."

She didn't remove her cap or unwind the scarf until the door was closed. "You shouldn't have."

"It is my honor and pleasure to cook for you," said Jonah, not understanding the uncomfortable look on her face.

"May I help?"

"Thank you, but it is just about finished." Jonah sensed an air of melancholy about her and wanted to erase the sadness from her eyes. "To be honest, it's one of those quick-heat meals that all I have to do is pop the seal, give it a stir and wait for it to warm up."

Raahi gave a tiny smile, but it didn't reach her eyes. Jonah went to get the food, worried. As he heaped it on plates, he wondered at her mood. Maybe she couldn't get the information she was going to give him and didn't want to disappoint. *No, there's more to it. But I will focus on making her forget about her troubles.*

"Here we go." He placed the dishes with a flourish and opened a bottle of wine. He held a glass up and looked at Raahi with his eyebrows raised in a wordless question. She nodded, and he poured a glass for each of them.

During dinner, he chatted about his day, leaving out his visit with Lavan of course. He had never explained exactly what his position was in the palace but had told her he often pulled security monitoring duties there.

She answered noncommittally in all the right places but added nothing of her own. He resorted to pulling out amusing stories about what people did when they didn't think anyone was watching. Usually, visitors to the palace didn't realize there were cameras everywhere. And the few palace cameras that included audio pickups gave him more humorous tales.

"I mean, even with the sound at normal volume I could hear the rumbling in her stomach. And the look of pain on her face as she sat in the waiting room chair." Jonah shook his head. "I was quite impressed that she made it through the entire audience with the council despite the digestion issues." Jonah laughed. "I kept expecting her to excuse herself, but she stoically presented her case." He took a drink of wine. "And then there was the delegate from the western province at the annual banquet two years ago who ate only the insides of the cheese rolls. I mean he unrolled the entire thing, scooped out the cheese, rolled the bread back up and returned it to the table. If he didn't want the bread he could have just thrown it away, but you know the westerners, 'waste no food.' Of course, I had to report it, and for the rest of the night, a servant quietly followed him unobtrusively picking out all the food he put back. It was worth the overtime I had to put in for that night."

Raahi pushed her plate away, having eaten very little. Jonah decided his joviality wasn't working but still was hesitant to pry into this very private woman's life.

"I am sorry. That story probably didn't make this cheap food any more appealing."

She looked up at him and back down at her plate. "No, it's not that. I am not very hungry. It's been a long day."

"And a difficult one?" he asked softly. "Would you like to talk about it?" The question just slipped out. The surprise on her face embarrassed him, and he berated himself for the slip.

"I apologize. I shouldn't have..." He stood and started to clear the table but stopped when she put her hand on his arm.

"No. I apologize. I have been a terrible guest. I am unused to people caring about how I am feeling."

Jonah was frozen, acutely aware of her hand. In the week they had worked together, it was the first time she had touched him. His gaze flicked to hers and locked there. He couldn't look away and hoped desperately that she couldn't see the turmoil raging within him.

For several long breaths they both stared. Then she looked down at her hand as if she hadn't realized that it was there, but, to his joy, she didn't remove it. Instead, she smiled the first genuine smile of the night and squeezed his arm gently.

"Thank you. For caring. And after I help you with the dishes, I will tell you about my long and difficult day."

Jonah didn't give a damn about the dishes, but it gave him time to cool off and bring his emotions under control. Stealing glances at Raahi every chance he got didn't help, but he could tell she was using the time to collect her thoughts.

When the dishes were clean and put away, they returned to the couch, wine glasses in hand. Raahi took a long swallow and held it out for a refill. As he filled it, she reached into her jacket to remove something. It wasn't in an inner jacket pocket but hidden on her person. It must be incredibly valuable, he thought.

"This is what I wanted to show you." She opened her hand and resting on her palm was a small, square chip about the size of a thumbnail. Jonah set the glass down on the table and reached for it.

"May I?"

She nodded, and he carefully took it from her hand. The top had what looked like embedded tiny electronics, and when he turned it over, he could barely make out markings. He would need a magnifier to read them, but he had the feeling they were manufacturing identification.

"What is this?"

She took it back from him with a sigh. Her jaw clenched briefly as if she didn't want to answer him.

"This is a chip implant that carries a tiny explosive. Don't worry it has been disabled." She took another deep breath. "It is usually implanted close to the heart of a slave to 'discourage' escape attempts."

"You were a slave, weren't you?"

"Yes."

"Was this yours?"

She shook her head, emotions flitting across her face. "It belonged to my twin sister." She reached into that hidden pocket again and pulled out a photo on permanent plexiplastic. It showed two women so alike that he couldn't tell which was Raahi. Both had long, flowing, black hair and looked to be only slightly younger than Raahi was now. Both were also way too thin but smiling with clear eyes and smooth dark skin.

"This was taken after we gained our freedom."

"Where is she now?" He suspected he knew the answer but couldn't hold back.

"She died." The set look on her face meant she wasn't going to give any more detail than that. "I had the chip removed after she died in case I ever had a chance to give it to someone who could use it against the slavers."

"But—"

"If you couldn't find out about the ship, you may not find out about this, but perhaps those friends of yours who are now offplanet could."

Jonah allowed the subject change even though he greatly wanted to keep the subject on Raahi and her past.

"Yes, if anyone can find out about them, it would probably be them. When they return, I will inquire. However, I have a favor to ask, a small job which I believe you are extremely suited for."

"What would that be?"

Her wariness was back. Jonah regretted the return of the distance between them.

"I need a device to scramble video signals, but it needs to fail after a couple of uses."

"That's an interesting twist." She cocked her head. "What is it for?"

He wagged his finger. "Ah, ah. Can't give that information away. Can you do it? You will be paid well."

"Certainly. That's easy, and I can have it for you tomorrow. Strange, though."

"What?"

"I would think you would have easy access to that sort of device yourself, seeing what you do. I am guessing that you even have one already."

"Well, yes, but I can't really use that." Without thinking, he touched his collar bone, where the implant that scrambled signals was placed.

Raahi suddenly rose, grabbed her cap and scarf and, not bothering to put either on, headed for the door.

"I shall have that for you tomorrow, Mr. Wilkerson."

"Wait, where are you going? We haven't—"

"Thank you for dinner. Have a good evening." And she was gone.

Jonah stared at the door, wondering what had happened.

Chapter Fifty

"And who are you that commands such a high price?"

"Wouldn't you like to know?" answered Lenore with a sneer. Experience and training kept her voice calm, though she was feeling the panic crawl up her throat.

"Yes, I would," said the man who approached her again with his knife and slave wand.

"I wouldn't if I were you," she warned, throwing the full weight of the Xa into her voice. "If that is who I think it is, they will want me in perfect health and would not appreciate what you have already done."

For the first time, he had a small look of doubt. It pleased her much more than it should have, considering she was still tied up and about to be delivered back to those she wanted to see even less than slavers.

The man muttered to himself and left the room. Lenore's heart raced when she heard him order someone right outside to call for a shuttle. Her escape had to be now. The next orders were to let no one in or out. That would make it harder but not impossible. There were no windows, this being a paranoid slave lord's bedroom, but if she could slip her bonds, getting out would be no problem, especially since they so kindly left all her equipment on the bed.

"First, the chair," she muttered and set about freeing herself.

***

"Ok...now," said Quinn into his wristcomp. Watching through the binoculars, he saw his father get Allison through security by simply tossing her over the fence. Quinn's "now" had been the signal that there was no one within hearing distance of her landing. He watched while Allison dashed toward the same back door as Lenore had used.

He stowed his binoculars, hefted his pack and headed for the wall nearest the garage. Allison's job was to take down whatever security she could, the wall being the most important, then get out of the compound, hide in the forest, and wait for the others. Quinn's job would be a bit more dramatic.

He aimed his detector at the wall and knew the instant it was down.

Way to go Alli. He clambered over the wall, landing in the narrow space between it and the garage. He hugged the outer wall of the garage and put his electronic eye around the corner, a tiny camera on a near invisible wire.

Nobody there.

He made a quick dash for the side garage door and cursed as he saw the security pad. But smiled an instant later when he read the words "security disengaged" and again sent favorable thoughts to his sister.

Inside were two large land vehicles that ran on anti-grav cushions, and two three-wheeled vehicles that held only one passenger which he knew could travel over any terrain much faster than anything else in the garage. Perfect.

First, he attached a tiny box under the dashboard of one of the tri-wheels. This would drain energy from the engine, slowing the vehicle. Quinn climbed aboard the other single-passenger vehicle and activated his personal shield and the other little surprise. He glanced at his hands that now looked very feminine, and he knew the overlay of his mother's hologram was working.

All set. He took a deep breath to settle his nerves and double-clicked his wrist comp. A triple-click back meant his father was ready.

Here we go.

Quinn started the engine and hit the center switch to open the large garage door. As it slowly rolled apart, he revved the tri-wheel and was through as soon as the opening was wide enough. He grinned as he nearly ran over a guard coming to check out the noise in the garage. He laughed in a high-pitched voice as the guard hit the ground. A quick look back showed the guard speaking into his own wrist comp as he scrambled up to head into the garage, presumably for another vehicle.

Straight for the exit now.

The two guards at the front gate were frantically pushing the security pad, obviously attempting to close the gate, but thanks to Allison, it was stuck open. He gunned the throttle and yelled as he went by.

"Your boss is not going to be happy!" He laughed again, adrenaline making it sound a little deranged but maybe they wouldn't notice. Sure enough, they ran back into the compound, and he was barely down the road before he saw the other tri-wheel and moments later, a car.

Three guards less at the compound. Quinn set his jaw and continued toward the city at maximum velocity.

***

Diarmin was in position, hidden only meters away from the front door. As he heard the first vehicle start, he could hear voices and, as expected, people rushed outside to see what was happening.

Quinn, as Lenore, was speeding across the yard toward the gate and his laughter was a good imitation of his mother.

"Impossible," said one of the men by the door. Diarmin took advantage of their distraction to hit them all with stun beams. Two guards dropped instantly but his third shot merely sizzled against a personal shield. *Damn!* Obviously, someone of more importance than mere guards. But the man was no slouch as he pulled his own blaster out and got off a shot of his own before Diarmin could dive out of the way. Heat bloomed on his leg as the blaster fizzled against his shield. Powerful gun. Diarmin rolled and switched from stun to blaster, shooting again, though he knew the first few wouldn't be enough to get through the shield. Only one hit as the man darted back inside the house. Diarmin slowly got up, keeping his blaster trained on the corner the man had ducked around. He shot as he saw the man's head peek outside but still the shield held. The head jerked back, and Diarmin dodged as a blaster snaked out and shot exactly where he had been standing.

This guy is good. Diarmin's move had taken him within view of the man, but before he could fire again, Diarmin saw a pensive look on the man's face right before he turned and dashed up the stairs.

Diarmin cursed as he realized the man had figured out the deception. *Why would I be trying to get in if Lenore had truly escaped?* Diarmin charged headlong into the house, trusting his shield to absorb any shots. One came right at his head and he managed to duck enough to take it on the shoulder. The shield wouldn't take much more, but he had to get to Lenore quickly.

***

Quinn reflexively jerked the tri-wheel as another bolt whizzed by his shoulder. They were pretty good shots considering he was quite far ahead. They had managed to land a couple shots on the vehicle and maybe on his shields as well, but it was too far to cause much heat. Another bolt hit and this time the engine began to sputter. Not that it mattered much. He had reached his destination.

City buildings surrounded him as Quinn took two quick turns to get out of sight of his followers. He braked hard in front of a large department store, then headed into a café across the street, which had been specifically selected. As he entered the first set of doors, he was relieved to note the vestibule was empty and promptly turned off the simulation of Lenore. He entered the café leisurely and took the first table he saw. He made a quick decision and, risky as it was, deactivated his personal shield as well.

Only a breath after he had sat down and picked up a menu, two of his followers came barreling in through the doors. They stopped and looked around, and Quinn, along with all the other diners, shouted in fear at the blasters sweeping the room.

"Not here. Check in the back," the first one ordered while scanning the room with a handheld device.

"All clear," said the man as he emerged from the kitchen.

"Nothing here," said the other, squinting at his scanner. "Must be the store after all."

With loud curses, they departed the café, and the diners breathed a collective sigh of relief, chattering a bit too loudly to one another. Quinn ordered a drink and sat drinking it slowly though every instinct was to flee. He wasn't sure what the scanner had been looking for but was glad he had listened to intuition and turned off his shields.

After he finished the drink, he placed money on the table and slowly walked out the front. The cars were still in the street, the searchers most likely still in the large store. He was tempted to disable the vehicles, but instead, shoved his hands in his pockets and walked toward the port where the shuttle was docked. Using his skills at blending in, he was sure he wasn't followed but took a roundabout way as a precaution. He made it to the port safely and settled in. He pinged the wristcomp twice and started the launch sequence, double-checking everything since this was only the second time he had piloted by himself. Anxiously he waited as time stretched. At last, just when his nerves were reaching the breaking point, he felt a triple pulse against his wrist.

Time to go.

***

As soon as her torturer left, Lenore began a certain "wiggle-flex" that allowed her to loosen the bonds around her chest and chair. Within moments the cords were loose enough that with a couple shrugs and ducking of her head, they were on the floor. Her hands, however, were still firmly held together behind her back. While she couldn't see them, she guessed they were probably magnetic cuffs like the ones that had been put on Quinn.

Noises from outside stole her attention for only a breath. Good. Her captors would be distracted from her next move which wasn't quiet. She eyed the bed, found the piece of equipment she wanted, and began the laborious process of scooting the chair within reach. Her bound legs wouldn't let her feet touch the ground, so she was left with gripping the seat behind her with her hands and "jumping" the chair.

It took longer than wriggling out of the chest bonds, but she finally got the chair where she wanted. Now this next part would be tricky. She had to lever herself onto the bed in exactly the correct place. With tremendous effort, she managed to stand straight up, her arms wrenching in their sockets as they pulled up from the back of the chair. Luckily her toes now touched the ground and she could balance a little, though her leg bonds were as tight as ever. She let herself fall forward and, even though she kept her bound hands between her and the chair, the chair fell with her and she received a dizzying blow to the back of her head.

Lenore shook off the pain quickly as she saw that the ploy had worked perfectly. She opened and closed her mouth on the exact tech she wanted, pulled her legs up slightly and abruptly sat back in the chair. Though she managed not to swallow what was in her mouth as she sat down hard, surprise almost made her do so as her torturer came running back in.

She was faced toward the door, and he inserted himself behind her, a knife appearing in his right hand. For a wild moment, she thought he was going to free her until he put the blade to her throat.

"Don't move," he breathed in her ear. Lenore did nothing and couldn't talk as she surreptitiously manipulated the tech with her tongue to try to find the correct button. A heartbeat later, Diarmin came into the room, blaster drawn. He froze at the door as he saw the situation.

"If you kill her, you are dead the next second," Diarmin said.

It had been a long time since Lenore had heard that specific tone.

"That's why we will all be reasonable here," said her torturer.

Lenore heard his left hand rustling, hidden behind the chair from Diarmin, and suspected he was preparing a knife to throw. She widened her eyes to warn Diarmin, but he must have already noticed since he extended his blaster arm and toggled a switch at his belt. The shield extended out to form a bubble with the tip of the blaster outside and able to fire.

"Don't even try," said Diarmin. "As you can see, nothing will get through now and you will be just as dead."

Lenore momentarily forgot all else as she realized Diarmin was taking a huge risk. She knew it was just a bluff, and that the shield would fail at any moment. But it was enough for the man to hesitate, and then it no longer mattered.

She had found the correct button.

Lenore closed her eyes as her tongue pressed. Even so, she could see the flash of the white light of the electromagnetic pulse through her eyelids. Both men gasped as they were temporarily blinded, and she felt the knife pull away from her throat at the same time her hands sprang apart. In one fluid movement, her right elbow came up and connected solidly under the man's chin. His head snapped back, and knives clattered to the floor as he sprawled in a heap, out cold.

Lenore spit out the EM generator into her hand and stuffed it back into her bra. Suddenly, Diarmin was there, hands on her face and kissing her.

"Are you okay?"

"Well, enough."

He paused only for a moment at her brusque tone but

then nodded. They weren't out of danger yet.

"Hurry, help me out of these." She began working at the leg cords and, with his help, was free in no time.

"Watch the door. Sorry your blaster is useless." She snatched up the knives and tossed them to him. "Use these if you have to."

Diarmin deftly caught both and angled himself to see down the hall. Lenore quickly put her gloves on and gathered her equipment. She stuffed most into the bag, not bothering to equip anything since the pulse had rendered most of them useless. It only took a couple moments to gather everything, but the man started groaning.

"A lot tougher than his rich clothes would suggest," she said. As he stirred, she reached down and gently placed her hand on his neck. The needle in the glove did its proper paralyzing trick. The fury in the man's eyes was truly a sight to behold.

"I should kill you, and indeed the thought has crossed my mind, but I think I can afford to be, *hm*, merciful today. Besides, I only kill those that I am paid to kill. Usually. I can always make an exception." She waved a knife in front of his eyes and was impressed that his expression didn't change a bit at the threat. "Well, not today. I hope you will appreciate me sparing your life and let me be. Next time, I won't be so accommodating. Now"—with her other hand she held up a dart—"this will keep you immobile for about thirty minutes so that you don't have to try to follow. We will be long gone by then." She jabbed it into his neck and removed her glove.

He managed a twitch, but the drug was quick. His eyes never left hers.

"Oh, and just to show you how agreeable I can be, I suggest you put your time to better use than following me. That pulse also deactivated any security on Timatay's safe, which, incidentally, is hidden there in his closet." She smiled as his eyes lost their anger and instead took on an avid look. She laughed. "Yes, remember my generosity. It should more than cover the reward for me."

Lenore turned to Diarmin who glanced back at her with raised eyebrows. She shrugged and hefted her pack.

"Let's get out of here."

They headed downstairs and out the front door where Diarmin paused to gather the blasters from the downed guards.

"You didn't..." asked Lenore, concerned.

"They're only stunned." He tossed a blaster to Lenore. "Quinn should be landed by now."

They rounded the corner and nearly ran headlong into the shuttle. The door hissed open and Allison's face peered out. As soon as it was wide enough, Lenore and Diarmin clambered in

Allison yelled, "Got 'em," then threw herself into a seat and grabbed the safety harness. Lenore had barely enough time to hold on securely as Quinn lifted the shuttle and shot away. As the pressure evened, Lenore made her way to the copilot's chair. Quinn started to relinquish control, but Lenore stopped him.

"It seems you are more of a pilot than we thought. You keep flying."

"You always say that desperation improves skill."

His grin was the best thing Lenore had seen in a long time.

"Let's go home."

***

"You were supposed to land outside the gates," said Diarmin angrily as they all disembarked the shuttle.

"I knew there was enough room and that I could do it."

"And he angled the door to the best spot, too," added Allison.

"What if you had crashed? Then how would we have gotten away?"

"I wouldn't have done it if I wasn't sure." Quinn's fists clenched, his voice rising with each word.

"Hey, hey, everyone. Take a breath." Lenore felt odd being the one to calm everyone down. That was usually Diarmin's job. But then, she was used to the excess adrenaline after a mission and especially after escaping a dangerous situation. It had been a very long time since her husband felt that.

"Diarmin, it worked, and we are back safe. Quinn, your father is working off his extra nervous energy." Diarmin opened his mouth, but Lenore held up a finger. "No more. I am sure everyone is exhausted and hungry. Allison, how are you doing?"

"I'm okay, Mom. Not hurt, but a bit shaky."

"Good. Will you go make us something high in protein and carbohydrates? We need to replenish. Quinn, secure the ship, and Diarmin will set our course back to Sulous."

With jobs to do, the family dropped their disagreements and left for their various assignments. Lenore headed to the cabin and took a very quick shower, changed and bandaged her various wounds. All of that only took a few minutes, but she knew everyone would be feeling the letdown about now.

Sure enough, Allison was drooping as she exited the kitchen with a platter of finger foods. Lenore took the platter and thrust a handful of the snacks and an electrolyte drink into her daughter's hands.

"I'll take it from here. You eat that and then go to bed."

"But—"

"Now, young miss. I am sure you have had very little sleep lately." She smiled. "And you did a very good job today."

Allison shoved a meat roll in her mouth and mumbled something but headed for her room. Lenore found Quinn on the bridge and did the exact same thing to him, squeezing his shoulder as he started down the ladder.

She brought the plate to Diarmin, noticing his sunken eyes. She held out a drink.

"Here. You look worse than the kids."

He merely grunted, eyes glued to the control board as he punched in the course. As Lenore devoured her own food, she watched him carefully. It was the first time in a very long time that he had been off the ship in an active role. She knew he was wrestling with inner turmoil and didn't want to interfere, but she had to know.

"How are you?"

"Fine."

"Really?" Lenore took a drink and handed him a tiny sandwich. He took it, still without looking at her.

"Yes."

"Do you want to talk about it?"

"No," he said, but his voice was a little softer. They ate for a while in silence and finally she could take it no longer.

"You said you didn't," she commented.

He hesitated before answering, which worried her considerably.

"But I could have," he finally said.

"But you didn't."

"But I could have, that's just as bad." He ran his left hand through his hair and stared at the drink as if it were the enemy.

She kept silent, knowing he needed to work it through.

"It's been years. Seventeen years, two months and three days, to be exact. I had thought that part of me, those...emotions were gone."

"They never leave, Diarmin. They only hide until something brings them out into the open. At least this time it was for the right reason."

"Maybe." But he didn't sound convinced.

"You're tired. I am sure you haven't slept since we started this mission and that was over a day ago. Get some rest." She knew better than to suggest he sleep. The nightmares would probably return.

"You need sleep, too."

"I had a good couple of hours more than you. It's amazing how restful being stunned can be."

Diarmin merely snorted, rejecting her attempt to lighten the mood. Fortunately, she knew how to manipulate people, especially her husband. She hardly ever did, but he needed to focus on something other than himself.

"Go. You know I won't sleep well for a few hours anyway."

He finally looked at her and the haunted look in his eyes receded a bit as concern replaced it. "I am sorry. I didn't think. Was it bad?" His fingers lightly brushed a bandage on her arm.

"I've had worse." She gave a little smile and patted his hand. "I know my brain is going to be rehashing events, figuring out what went wrong, and how I can plan better in the future. I might as well watch the bridge while my rescuers get some sleep."

Lenore could tell he really didn't want to relax, but she noticed his muscles go slack as the last of the adrenaline wore off.

"It wasn't your fault."

"I know. But at least now I know I can count on you and the kids when things don't go as planned." Immediately she regretted her words as he looked away again.

"Yes." He turned and left the bridge.

Lenore followed him long enough to make sure he went to their room. Despite her stealth, he turned and smiled at her before he entered.

"I'll be fine. Come get me when you need to sleep."

She smiled back. "I will." But she doubted if he was going to be fine for quite a while.

Chapter Fifty-One

A solid day of rest returned the family to normal. Or mostly anyway. There would be scars, physical and mental, but at least all were safe, and healing could begin. When Allison awoke, she went straight to her computer with the information they had downloaded. By the time Lenore woke up from a short nap, Alli had found and used the Chanis cypher code.

They had a trail to follow.

"I don't believe it," said Lenore as she deciphered where the slave records ended, and her search would start.

"What?" the other three said all at once.

"Remember how Timatay mentioned twins? That was the princess and her companion."

"They were surgically altered to look alike since they couldn't be separated," said Allison, who had found the original entries.

"Why couldn't they be separated?" asked Diarmin.

Allison scrolled through her data and stopped to read. "Says here, 'Sulous products both sickened when put in separate facilities. Subject A nearly died for unexplained reasons until the doctors gave in to her begging to be returned to Subject B. Health returned to both shortly after being reunited.'"

"Do you think that was the Companion's Bond?" asked Quinn.

"Probably, though Lavan never hinted at such a deep connection," said Lenore.

"Well, twins are easier to track, although it would go quicker with pictures. Strange that the organization never photographed them," said Quinn.

"Photos make it much easier to find a person," said Diarmin. "The organization wouldn't want that. Neither would the girls after they escaped."

Lenore was eager to move on. "Allison, pull up the roster of ships that left the planet soon after they escaped, or I should say, after Timatay let them escape. It won't be long now."

A couple more hours of hacking records brought an exclamation from Allison and Lenore simultaneously.

"No way."

"What's going on?" said Quinn as he entered the bridge, damp towel on his shoulder that he kept blotting his sweaty face with. Lenore was glad he was keeping up with the exercises she had shown them.

"We finally have a picture of the twins, well, pictures," said Lenore.

"After tracking them to three different planets," said Diarmin, shaking his head.

"But their fourth stop, Melanalerrie, weird name for a planet if you ask me," piped in Allison, who was printing something out, "they applied for ID cards, and a still photo was taken. On an old-fashioned camera because the new one wasn't working." She held up the paper with copies of the new IDs, and Quinn's mouth fell open as he saw the photos.

"No way."

***

All day, Jonah was distracted at work. He felt he should be able to guess why Raahi had run away like that. Something was worrying in the back of his brain, but it wouldn't come to the forefront. Absently, he scrolled through the few pictures he had of her on his personal data stick. Nothing new, although that one was quite blurred. Not as bad as the one from the Baroness' ship... wait. That was it. The images.

He pulled up several pictures of himself within the palace and noticed they were clear. Indeed, any coming through the palace computers were quite unscrambled. Yet he knew that cameras outside the palace couldn't unscramble his features; they didn't have the programming. He hadn't realized that his pictures of Raahi were being unscrambled since he only saw them from the palace. He was such a fool not to put the pieces together. The girl on the ship who was so good at computers even pointed it out, but Jonah had forgotten. The program to decode the scrambler would exist from those who had implanted it.

Jonah called his shift replacement and asked if she would come in early. He couldn't wait to return home to check on what he now suspected. Waiting for Ginette was the longest ten minutes of his life.

"What's wrong?" she asked as she walked in. "Couldn't hold on the last couple of hours?"

"I don't feel well. Need to go home."

She peered into his face as if she didn't believe him, but her brow furrowed. "You do look a bit pale. Are you sweating? I've never seen you sweat."

"Thank you, Ginette, for coming. I will see you tomorrow."

"Not if you are still sick. I don't want to catch it," she hollered as he left, her voice echoing down the hall after him.

Jonah rushed home, trying to look normal, but his heart was racing. He arrived and went straight to his personal terminal. He had barely pulled the data stick out of his pocket when there was a soft knock on the door.

Damn! He'd wanted to check his theory before Raahi came, but she must have been watching for him. He would have to improvise.

Jonah opened the door, and a gloved hand shot forward holding out a small box the size of his fist. Reflexively he took it.

"It is of medium quality and should fail after two uses." Raahi pivoted and walked away, catching Jonah completely off guard.

"Wait, your money," he said.

"Forget it," she called over her shoulder, not stopping. "Consider it a favor for all you have done for me." She was nearly to the corner, and Jonah hurried after her.

"Wait. Stop."

"I have to leave. Goodbye, Jonah."

"Nirav misses you."

She stopped so abruptly, he nearly ran into her. She slowly turned to him, her face completely devoid of expression, but the tightness around her eyes betrayed her tension to Jonah.

"What did you say?" she whispered. Her reaction gave Jonah all the confirmation he needed.

"I said, Nirav misses you. Or should I have said 'Your father, King Nirav, misses you?'"

"I don't know what you're talking about," said Raahi as she turned away and headed for the elevator.

Jonah grabbed her arm.

"Yes, you do. Your reaction told me that you recognized the name of the king. Very few know his personal name."

"And how would you know his name, a mere security

officer?"

Jonah felt a blush but held his head high. Nothing but honesty would work here. "I apologize for the deception, but I am not law enforcement. I work at the palace as the Chief Reviewer and have been close to the king for many years. Ever since Princess Maya, or I should say 'you,' disappeared."

"You're crazy," she said. With her next words, her voice dropped, and a smoldering anger suffused her eyes. "Let me go." The menace in her tone and tension in her stance made Jonah loosen his grip on her arm.

She wrenched herself out of his hold and stepped away, face unreadable.

"I am not who you think I am."

In the next breath, she was gone, down the stairs, not bothering with the elevator.

Jonah stared, unable to move, feeling as if she had punched him in the gut.

Chapter Fifty-Two

After another inattentive day at work, Jonah returned to the apartment with absolutely nothing any clearer in his head. He tried to keep himself busy by arranging an anonymous messenger to deliver the package containing the scrambler directly to Lavan. Though he took care to be sure it could not be traced back to him, oddly enough, he found he didn't particularly care. Without Maya to challenge the right of succession, the prince would have to do something truly horrific, such as killing someone, to be removed from the hierarchy. Bad as he was, Jonah didn't think he was a murderer.

Raahi had to be the missing princess, she had to be. He had been so sure. But the logical voice inside of him argued convincingly.

Why does she have to be? Is it only because you want her to be?

True, he was extremely attracted to her. He had been from the moment he first saw her on the video feeds. It could be the betrothal bonds.

Or simply an attractive woman.

The scrambling tech.

Just because she has the tech doesn't mean she is from the palace. The slave organization could implant similar tech, and the fact that the palace has a program to decode it is a coincidence. The people who did the original implants are no longer alive, which is the reason the prince and Lavan don't have it.

She knew Nirav's name.

Are you sure or are you just looking for any reaction?

Jonah slammed his fist into his palm. He had been going back and forth with himself all day, and it was getting him nowhere. He had come straight home, hoping to escape the questions and doubts. But if he were truly honest, he had hoped Raahi would be here, knocking on his door like every day for the past couple of weeks. He missed her.

Enough self-pity, he told himself as he launched to his

feet. He ordered more food to restock from all the dinners for two he had made recently. He organized his files, did his laundry, cleaned the apartment from front to back, and he still couldn't settle. After glancing at the door for the tenth time, he finally admitted that she wasn't going to come. Why would she? Especially after he had lied to her and accused her of being someone she wasn't? His heart clenched as he realized he would most likely never see her again, and he truly didn't know if the pain was because she wasn't the princess or because he had lost Raahi. Maybe he could find her and apologize. He shook his head. He should have gotten his facts straight before he jumped to conclusions and drove away the only woman he ever had feelings for.

He continued with similar regretful thoughts until he glanced at the time and realized with a shock that he had to be back at work in only six hours. He sighed and readied himself for bed, though he was probably too wound up to sleep. He poured himself a calming drink, but nearly dropped it when his terminal pinged. He leapt for it, ignoring the splash of liquid on his hand.

"Hello?"

"Sirrah Wilkerson. I apologize for the late hour."

When he recognized the face, Jonah was extremely disappointed that it was not Raahi.

"Oh, um, I wasn't expecting you, Baroness." He was vaguely aware that he had never given her his personal code for contact, but he was too tired to really care.

"Don't worry. This call is encrypted. I wanted to inform you of our progress."

To his complete chagrin, he realized he had completely forgotten about the search.

"We have discovered that your new friend has the information we are looking for."

Even with encryption, Delilah wasn't taking the chance on revealing anything. He wasn't quite clearheaded enough to completely catch her hints.

"Friend?" Did she mean Raahi knew about the princess?

"Yes, the young lady." The woman tilted her head at him as if considering her next words. "She is one of the two that were lost."

Jonah felt a surge of renewed hope. "I had thought that as well, but she denied it."

The Baroness' eyes narrowed. "You confronted her?" Jonah couldn't tell if she was angry or surprised.

"Yes." He felt his face redden. "Are you sure?"

She briefly held up a photograph identical to the one that Raahi had shown him of her and her twin sister. "Here they are. We are preparing to physically affirm the information."

"Do you..." Jonah swallowed and fought against rising emotions. "Do you know which one she is?"

"Not at this point, but I estimate we will in three, perhaps four days."

Jonah's thoughts tumbled over and about each other. He had never been so assaulted with mixed questions and emotions. How? Why?

The Baroness cleared her throat, bringing his attention back to the viewscreen.

"It would be helpful if you could keep an eye on her, maybe find out her story."

Jonah shook his head. "I don't know if that is possible. She hasn't returned after our last conversation." Again, his heart plummeted.

The Baroness gave an exasperated sigh, lips in a thin, disapproving line. "We will arrive as soon as we can to help find her."

Jonah opened his mouth to apologize, but she had broken the connection with the usual static. He sat there staring at the blank screen, questions flitting through his tired mind. Nothing made sense.

He downed what was left of his drink and went to his room to attempt to sleep.

***

Lenore nodded to Allison, who typed a few commands before nodding back, letting her know that the transmission records had been erased.

"Do we have to physically retrace the girls' entire trip after their escape?" asked Diarmin. "Seems like a waste of time and resources. Can't Allison hack into the databases like she usually does?"

Lenore tried not to show her concern about her husband suggesting their daughter do illegal activities, especially when he was usually the one to admonish her when she did. "We need to fill in the details, get verbal confirmation directly from people. Especially since Raahi denied her origins to Jonah. Also, since Raahi seems to be the only one who made it home, what happened to the other? When did their paths diverge? Let's start near the end of the trail and hope we find what we are looking for there."

"Melanalerrie?"

"I think so. Since they received new IDs, we can verify if both really did take a ship to Recavan," answered Lenore.

"I figured as much." Diarmin began to punch in codes on the command console.

Lenore turned back to the terminal that was working on decoding more information with the Chanis cypher.

"Course laid in. Should take a little over fourteen hours," said Diarmin.

"It's not direct, is it?" asked Lenore, a bit distracted with new information the cypher was displaying.

"Of course not," he answered, a slight edge in his voice. "Have I ever forgotten to program in changes to throw others off our own trail?"

The tension in his voice was enough to grab Lenore's attention.

"Sorry, force of habit." She looked at her husband and noticed the deep frown lines. He noticed her scrutiny, stood, and walked to the ladder.

"I'll be in my workshop. Plenty to fix." Without waiting for comment, he disappeared down the steps.

She was tempted to follow, but a ping from the computer meant another decoded section, so she was pulled back into processing data.

Chapter Fifty-Three

Melanalerrie proved quite useless with the few people who possibly remembered twins. The picture helped, but all anyone could tell them was confirmation of what they had already uncovered through the IGnet. Yes, they were here. Yes, they were quite similar, beautiful, couldn't tell them apart. No, they didn't talk to anyone else that they knew of. No, nobody else has asked about them. Yes, they got on the transport to Recavan.

"Well, at least we now know that nothing out of the ordinary happened here," Lenore said. "They weren't hurt or scared into leaving."

"And I got some experience," said Quinn as Lenore leaned back into the shuttle's copilot chair with a sigh.

"Yes, you did fairly well with the questions. Next time try a little less emotion."

"Okaaaaay."

The way he strung out the response was an interesting reply. She considered all the encounters and decided what he was thinking about. "Except with that young baggage handler who looked to be in his twenties, like the twins in the photo. Those emotions were perfect, commenting on how cute the girls were, playing on his obvious attraction to them. Very well done and something I couldn't do." She gave him a mock punch on the shoulder.

"Thanks," he said, but his lack of reaction made her realize that wasn't what he was thinking.

Everyone is still recovering from the stressful events over the last few days. He'll talk to me soon enough.

***

Two days later, they hit pay dirt on Recavan. Several remembered the girls, though neither was named Raahi. The most information they got was from a former employer where they worked for several months, a farm relatively close to the city with the largest spaceport. Lenore was solo on this trip.

"I told them I would rent them one of the cottages right outside the farm, but they insisted on the poorest section of the city. Needed to save money." The owner of the farm was a large, friendly woman with sunburned cheeks and comfortable, rough clothes that showed she dug in as much as her workers.

"Money for what?" asked Lenore.

"They said they were traveling the galaxy, nomads enjoying adventure, but I could tell they were pining to go somewhere in particular. Shame what happened."

"Oh?"

"The day after they booked passage, one of them got sick. I would have thought the one that worked in the fields would be more likely to catch the Lungus, not the one in the processing center."

"Lungus?"

"Oh, sorry. That's what we call the lung fungus that people catch. It's very rare nowadays. Only one or two cases a year at the most. And most usually survive. Not this girl." The farmer dabbed at her eyes.

"What happened?"

"The oddest thing. I happened to be there when she collapsed. I had just barely reached her side and had started to ask someone to find her sister when suddenly there she was. Her sister took her to the hospital, and I did check on them, only to find out that she had died. Never saw the sister again."

"Thank you. I appreciate your time."

"Pass along my greetings if you find her. They were so very close, I'm afraid she might have..." She couldn't finish her statement and dabbed her eyes again.

Lenore thanked her and returned to her rented vehicle. While driving back toward the city, she reported the conversation to Diarmin.

"So, what now?" he asked.

"I am heading for the hospital and then, well, I am going to need your help for something quite illegal. Well, more illegal than usual."

***

"When you said illegal, I thought you were joking," Diarmin said as they scaled the rather large wall with their usual stealth. Lenore was nothing but a shadow against the light-colored wall. The sliver of a moon did nothing to help their footing as they slowly made progress to their destination.

On the other side of the wall, Lenore pulled out her hand-held and her face was briefly visible when she opened the tiny map.

"This way," she said. She thumbed off the hand-held and they were again in darkness.

Maneuvering between headstones and other grave markers, Diarmin tried to keep his tension under control but was failing miserably.

"Couldn't we have done this in the daylight? Maybe even gone through proper channels?"

"Take too long," said Lenore. "Besides, the grave might be under surveillance by the very people we don't want to piss off."

"You mean 'piss off' any more than we already have?"

Her head turned and though he couldn't see her face in the dark, he could imagine the set lips and scolding eyes that meant "Really? Jokes now?" His attempt at humor was not helping him ignore the fact that his pulse had spiked at her comments.

He concentrated instead on not stumbling, and soon they were at their destination. The large structure had one hundred spaces for coffins, five high and twenty long. The one they were looking for was right in the middle at eye-level, marked with the last name of the alias the girls had been using.

"What kind of backward planet buries instead of cremates anymore?" grumbled Diarmin as he pulled out anti-grav devices while Lenore worked at opening the crypt.

"Most agricultural planets do, some close connection with the dirt or something." She grunted as she levered the thick door open. "Be grateful we didn't have to dig."

Diarmin helped pull the coffin out. "It still doesn't feel right."

"Don't start the argument again. We need this for all the reasons I pointed out last night, and my guess is that we will find even more reasons after we get this back to the ship. You're just displaying the usual nerves at being in a graveyard. Lots of people have that."

He didn't bother with a response but silently attached the anti-grav units and they began the trip back to the ship. *Maybe Lenore is right, and my nerves are not my old emotions stirring, but unease at stealing a body.*

He halted abruptly when an odd chirp came out of his pack.

"Was that what I think it was?" asked Lenore as she dropped into a defensive crouch. He reached into his pack to pull out another of his special devices.

"Yes. There is a dampening field that just activated." He tapped his wrist comp. "All communication with the ship has been cut off." His fingers brushed against the gun in his pack as he replaced the device, but he couldn't bring himself to wrap fingers around it. Sweat beaded on his forehead as he stood there, frozen.

"Movement, to the right," hissed Lenore. They ducked down on the other side of the coffin, trying to make out the shadow moving toward them. It stopped quite a distance away, and Diarmin could feel his wife tense. His heart rate increased, and his breath caught in his throat, making it impossible for the deep breathing required to settle his churning stomach.

"Hello out there. I mean you no harm, and I am not going to keep you from what you are doing." The voice was masculine, and the shadow clearly showed that his hands were extended away from his body. "If you have a light," the stranger continued, "You may shine it on me to confirm I am unarmed. Nobody is around to see."

"Can we trust him?"

"He's unarmed," she said.

Diarmin was startled when she snapped on a light and removed her night-vision goggles. He had been so distracted with his own inner turmoil that he hadn't noticed her don them. The small but bright light showed a thin man, rather tall, with short blond hair that stood on end as if he had seen his fair share of ghosts in this graveyard. Diarmin firmly told himself to get control of his emotions.

"What do you want?" she called back to the man who was blinking at the light in his face. Even though the man couldn't see their faces, he wasn't acting threatening or afraid.

"Only to give you a message."

"Well, what's the message?"

"It is a recorded message that you are to deliver to the relative of that package you have obtained."

Diarmin said nothing, letting Lenore take the lead. "How do you know the contents of our package?"

"There has been a constant watch on it for years

because I promised the person who recorded this message that it would be delivered. Please, I would like to know. Is she...your package...going home?" The sincerity in the voice strangely did more to calm Diarmin than anything else.

"Boy, these girls did inspire confidence in others," Lenore muttered. "Yes. She is going home. You may leave the message there, and we will make sure it is delivered to the correct person."

"Thank you." The man placed something on the headstone next to him and left in the direction he came. Lenore pulled out the scanner, and the strange chirp came again from the pack, indicating the drop of the dampening field. Almost instantly, Diarmin's wrist comp vibrated. He answered, hushing Allison's frantic warning about a third person in the graveyard.

He signed off as Lenore came back with a portable reader, data stick inserted.

"It's clear. Just what he said."

"Great," said Diarmin. "Another mystery. Let's get back to the ship."

***

"You're sure?" Lenore asked Diarmin. She had been on her way up to the bridge when he intercepted her, straight from the cargo hold and his work on the last piece of evidence.

"Yes. My tests were extensive. The tattoos hold the key."

"But Raahi must have removed her tattoos."

"It doesn't matter," said Diarmin. "There is subdermal activity with the tattoos. The ink is mostly design, basically hiding the real purpose of the tattoos. Brilliant, actually."

"And Raahi didn't remove her tattoos," said Allison as they came onto the bridge.

"You have very good ears, my daughter," said Diarmin.

"In fact, I do, but you were talking loud enough that it carried down the corridor and up here just fine."

"About the tattoos?" asked Lenore.

"I said she still has them." Allison brought up the file with the pictures that she and Jonah had gathered.

"How do you know?" Lenore pointed at the screen. "Look, that video shows bare hands and arms. Both."

"Yes, but she is wearing gloves." The grin on Allison's

face was very smug.

"Gloves? How can you tell?" asked Diarmin, leaning close to the screen.

"Well, you know I have been working on a program, in what little spare time I have had between kidnappings."

Diarmin sputtered, but Lenore ignored the jibe, knowing Allison's idea of a joke wasn't the same as everyone else's.

Allison went on. "It's a program to find what I call 'glove flaws.' Watch."

She opened a file and activated it. The picture of bare arms now showed two slight red marks near the wrist. "See those? Those are slight imperfections like a wrinkle or tear. Check this out." She pulled up another one that had a blue line circling her arm right below the elbow. "That is an edge of a glove, above the line is skin, below is glove. These are very good, but still gloves."

Allison turned to her parents with a triumphant smile. "See, so she still has her tattoos."

"This is a brilliant program, Alli," said Diarmin.

"It's what I'm paid to do. That is, if I got paid." Allison sighed dramatically, but her smile widened even more.

"All we really know is that she wears gloves," said Lenore, voice slightly above a murmur, deep in thought. "We really can't tell if she has her tattoos or not." Lenore was scrolling through the pictures, scrutinizing each and noting the different ways the program noted the flaws.

"Why else would she wear the gloves?" asked Allison.

"Maybe the removal scarred her, and she wants to cover up," she replied absently, still flicking through screens. "And she has gloves on both arms when we know that the tattoos are only on the right hand."

"I hadn't thought of that," said Allison.

Lenore looked up as Diarmin cleared his throat loudly. His lips were compressed in a thin line and he indicated Allison with a slight tip of his head. Guilt racked Lenore as she looked at her daughter now slumped down in her chair, a look of despondence on her face.

"But this is an incredibly amazing program, Allison. I am truly impressed."

"Really?"

"Absolutely. I knew you were smart, but this"—she waved her hand at the screen—"this shows true genius."

"Wow, thanks, Mom." The smile was back, and Lenore was about to go on but a slight pinch on the back of her arm from Diarmin was warning enough not to overdo it.

Damn, she still couldn't get the hang of these emotions.

"We need to discuss if we want to patent this or not," she said, going for the change in subject. "Like the upgraded shield that we talked about but never decided on."

"Why wouldn't we?" asked Diarmin. "They both could bring in a substantial fee."

"Several reasons." Lenore straightened, and both looked at her eagerly. "A patent is an easy way to track us, not a good thing. Also, to make money, we would have to divert significant time and resources. And"—she smiled at her daughter—"once a patent is accepted, the knowledge that such a program exists will be out there, and I would like us to be the only people who know about it."

Both smiled back, but it was Allison who responded.

"Yeah, money is nice, but I kinda like it being our own secret. Both ideas. Besides, we are due a payment for the success of this mission anyway."

"Well, about that," said Diarmin. "They may not want to pay since Raahi was there the whole time and technically Jonah did pay us to find her."

"Yes, I considered that, but now," Lenore looked him directly in the eyes, "thanks to your tests, we know something they don't. And have proof in the hold." Diarmin nodded.

"Something incredibly vital."

"And there is this." Lenore held up the data stick that had been given to them on the planet. "This is worth even more."

Chapter Fifty-Four

Jonah couldn't stop pacing. He wasn't sure if his frazzled nerves were because he hadn't heard from Raahi or from the events of the past days. After he had spoken to the Baroness, he had called Raahi but only got a message service. He stumbled through an apology, but the message recorder cut off midsentence, and now the contact number was no longer active.

The next two days had been a blur between Jonah frantically searching videos of the city to find her, discussions with himself about what could possibly be going through her mind, and dealing with events in the palace.

The prince had tested the scrambler, first in the conference rooms during a regular discussion of various committees. Jonah sent someone to inform him that the monitors had failed and needed to be replaced. The next day, it happened again in a public corridor, but the static cleared soon thereafter so the scrambler had failed. The conversation had been quite innocuous, only a discussion about the upcoming birthday and affirmation of the prince.

Having given this situation much thought, Jonah was prepared. He went directly to the council shortly after with all the members in attendance, including the prince and king.

He bowed low after being presented. "Your Majesty. I need to inform you that several monitors in the palace appear to have some kind of glitch. I cannot find the flaw, but I suspect that an electronic virus is sweeping through the system, affecting individual systems before moving on. There will most likely be the occasional failures until I can track down the problem."

The king nodded absently and thanked Jonah for his vigilance. A quick glance around as he bowed his way out let Jonah note the satisfied smirk of the prince, complete surprise on Lavan's face, and greatly varied levels of interest throughout the council members.

The trap had been set.

Which, unfortunately, left him too much time to obsess over Raahi.

If the Baroness was correct, Raahi was either the princess or her companion Lara. But if that were the case, why hadn't she come forward? If she was the princess, it was a simple matter of presenting herself to the palace staff and her father. Maybe she thought because the tattoos were removed she wouldn't be accepted. That didn't make sense. She was young when she left, but old enough to know that DNA could be checked. Unless she was afraid of the slave organization finding out her true identity. But she would have been protected in the palace.

Was she angry because the new prince replaced her as child and heir? Maybe, but he didn't think that would stop the rightful heir from stepping back in. He had never met the princess, but he felt like he knew her well. He had seen videos going back to the time she was a baby, and she was a sweet child, always accepting of her duty as the future queen.

No. If Raahi were the princess, she would have come forward. She must be the companion. But why did she stay hidden? She came all the way back to Sulous but wouldn't tell Nirav about his daughter. Was she afraid of how it would affect the king? Afraid of the slavers? Jonah shook his head. Raahi wasn't afraid of anything. She never showed the slightest fear of anything. In fact, the only emotion he'd ever seen was sadness when she told him about the death of her sister.

That memory wrenched at his gut. Of course. She didn't want the constant reminder of what she lost because he had no doubt that they were as close as sisters. To go through what they did would make anyone closer. They even looked identical. A stray thought niggled at the back of his brain again, but it wouldn't form into anything coherent.

Too many questions rolled around in his head. He needed to talk to Raahi, but it had been three days and nothing. Jonah brought his fists down on the console in frustration.

"Hey, boss. Take it easy." Ginette patted Jonah's shoulder. "You'll find something."

For a long moment he simply stared at her, wondering how she knew of his dilemmas.

Ginette leaned back against the wall and crossed her arms, squinting at Jonah.

"In fact, I think it's you that has the virus, not the system. You look awful. Have you eaten today?"

Jonah relaxed. She was talking about the supposed system glitch. "Well, I am a bit hungry. Maybe I'll get some lunch."

"Um, hello in there." Ginette rapped gently on Jonah's head. "It's past dinner. It's why I am here. I'm glad I came in early. You need to go home and get some rest. Food, then sleep."

He shook his head. "No, I have to find something. Soon."

"What in the world are you talking about, boss?"

His eyes widened. Perhaps he'd better get home. Fatigue was making him sloppy. He tried to backtrack. "Oh, um, I just meant that if I don't find the problem in a day or two, I need to scrap the whole system and start again."

"Well, you are not doing any good in this condition. Tell you what. Let's download all the feeds, and then you can take it home to look at." She sat at her own terminal and began to do just that. "And tomorrow is your day off so that will give you another day to recover."

"But..." he began. She tilted her head and gave a crooked grin.

"I won't tell anyone you took it. You can trust me. And..." she hit a few buttons and entered a code. "I have put the feed directly to your place, so you can watch from home." She put a finger on her lips. "Don't tell anyone."

"Why would you do that?" whispered Jonah.

"Because you won't get rest if you are here, and you won't leave unless you keep working. Besides," she grinned again. "It means I don't have to work. I can be lazy, and I like that, boss." She gathered the data sticks and shoved them in his bag. She stood and hauled Jonah to his feet as well, draping his bag on his shoulder. Turning to the door, she gave him a shove toward it. "Now, leave."

Despite his weariness, he laughed.

"Yes, doctor."

"And eat something!" she yelled after him as he left.

***

The first thing Jonah did was turn on his console and activate the feed. He wanted to make a program to intercept only video of the prince but as a wave of dizziness swept him, he knew food was the more important item.

He stood and headed for the kitchen when there came a soft knock on the door. All thoughts of food left his head as he ran to see Raahi. The incredibly intense feeling of joy as his eyes fell on her face surprised him.

"You are home early tonight," she said with a smile.

He could only stand there like an idiot with a dopey smile, thoughts and questions racing around but forming no coherent pattern.

"You called. Said you wanted to apologize." She looked down slightly. "I agree that we need to talk." She raised her eyes back to him, and he unfroze long enough to invite her in.

"How did you...never mind." Somehow the fact that she had been watching his apartment didn't bother him at all. In fact, the feeling of warmth from the knowledge relaxed him as he hadn't been for days.

"I was going to make some food. Are you hungry?"

She turned and scrutinized his face. "You look awful," she said. "Here." She pushed him to the couch. "You rest. I will bring you something." Without waiting for a response, she disappeared into the kitchen. He smiled at this second display of caring. He must really look terrible to have two separate individuals order him to rest.

He was glad for Raahi's diversion to the kitchen so that he could put his thoughts in order. He leaned back and closed his eyes, but his mind wouldn't quiet. How could he ask questions when he didn't know what to ask?

But he couldn't sit on the couch either. Maybe working would help him focus. If he got lucky, he would find the prince in a compromising situation and that would give him an opening for a conversation with Raahi.

He flipped through the feeds until he found the prince, then input his security code so that all the feeds of the prince would come straight to this console and not routed through the palace as Ginette had set up. Right now, the council sessions were wrapping up, so Jonah figured he could get a quick bite before it was over.

"He looks so old," came a soft voice at his ear, startling him out of his musings. At first, he thought Raahi was talking about the prince, but a quick glance at her face showed that her eyes were on the king sitting next to him. Jonah took control of the camera and zoomed in on the king. Yes, he did look old, worn down, but he was listening intently to the councilman who was currently speaking. Jonah risked a glance again to see Raahi's reaction, but she became aware of his inspection and straightened up, brandishing the tray she was holding.

"Protein and plenty of carbohydrates. Exactly what you need, I think." She turned away and headed for the couch, placing the tray on the table in front of her and filling a plate. Jonah readjusted the camera and went to sit beside her. She thrust the full plate into his hands and started on another for herself.

"Thank you," he said, and the smell of the food kept him from any other comments. He ate ravenously and soon reduced the huge tray to the inedible parts. Raahi had only sampled the food, and when he realized just how much he had eaten, he reluctantly admitted that he was pushing himself too hard. He smiled at Raahi.

"I really needed that, and I appreciate it."

She smiled back. "It feels nice to take care of somebody again." They locked eyes and Jonah felt the pull between them. But there was also a barrier that needed to be broached.

"I'm sorry I lied about working in the palace," said Jonah, not sure why exactly he started there, but it seemed to break the ice.

"It's okay. I understand why you did," she replied.

"No, I don't think you do." Without realizing quite what he was doing and why, he continued. "I don't want to scare you but..." he pulled back his shirt to show his bonding tattoo. "My true name is Sundeep Barad."

She looked away with a blush, and he knew she recognized it.

"I am sorry I kept that from you, too, but very few know. It wouldn't do to advertise who I was with a new heir around." He gave a laugh and surprised himself with how bitter he sounded. This situation was affecting him in many more ways than he realized.

"I suspected that's who you were. When you talked about scrambling tech and touched the implant," her own hand tapped her collar bone in a similar fashion. "I figured it out."

"Then why didn't you...why aren't...who..." He struggled with exactly what he wanted to ask but different words came out. "Why did you leave?"

She looked straight into his eyes, and Jonah again felt a connection, a pull. His heart began to have hope that their bond was reacting to each other's presence. She had to be the princess. But her next words dashed his hopes.

"I left because I am not who you want me to be. I am not the princess. Maya is dead."

Chapter Fifty-Five

The tenuous connection Jonah felt with Raahi wasn't quite broken, but it did lessen with her statement.

"But you are the companion."

Raahi's eyes flickered briefly with some emotion he couldn't read, but she nodded. "How did you know?"

"Well, it began with a feeling, then I noticed videos were distorted with every camera except the ones that went through the palace. I figured that had to be the same tech that I had, but the final proof..." Here he paused, but only briefly. "Again, something I didn't tell you, but I am promising that there will be no more deception." He took a deep breath. "That woman who found you, she and her crew have been investigating your disappearance. They confirmed my suspicions that you were one of the missing girls but didn't know which one." He smiled at her, grateful it was out in the open, but her reaction was not what he expected.

"I see." Then she looked away and began to gather the dishes, body stiff, the vague feelings between them gone.

"Wait," Jonah followed her into the kitchen and watched her toss the dishes into the sink. "I didn't mean to upset—"

"Thank you for telling me the truth," she said in a formal tone. "And now you know that the prize you sought is never to be found. You are left with the unneeded remnants. Sorry to disappoint you. You may inform those searching that they can stop." She pushed past him, but he put a hand on her shoulder to stop her.

"That's not it, I mean, you're not...I'm not..." He didn't know what to say. Was he disappointed? Yes, he felt that, but there was more. He couldn't focus. So much had happened. Now she was looking at his hand on her shoulder like she wanted to forcibly remove it.

He dropped his hand and said the first thing that came into his head.

"Please, don't go." Though she continued to stare, she didn't make a move to leave, and he could swear her eyes softened. He tried another tactic.

"Raahi, or should I call you Lara?"

Her eyes widened, and she looked away but didn't move.

"Raahi, please, Lara died when Maya did."

Jonah closed his eyes briefly at the pain in her voice. He wanted to reach out again but didn't dare. "At least come to the palace, tell Nirav what happened to his daughter."

Raahi's head whipped around and now her eyes, snapping with anger, bored into him.

"What good would that do? Tell the king how we were taken, altered, abused, trained, and sold. How I couldn't protect her from the horrible things done to us by our various owners. How, when we finally escaped, we couldn't send a message because we knew the slavers would be waiting for that and immediately find us. How we traveled to several planets, selling ourselves to make our way home. How, when we finally managed to scrape enough together to buy new identities and tickets home, a strange, untreatable fungal infection in her lungs caused her to gasp out her last breaths only two days before our flight. And how—" Her voice caught as Jonah stood transfixed, her face inches from his. "How I had to sell her ticket to bury her, not even able to afford the cost to bring her home." One tear from each eye slid down her cheek, but she ignored them as she crossed her arms, took a step back and lifted her chin again.

"So, tell me, Bethrothed. How would that help at all? It's better that Nirav believes his daughter to be alive somewhere, perhaps having an adventure, too busy to come home." Her voice and eyes became distant again.

Jonah stood there, aching to take her into his arms and tell her everything would be all right, but he knew she wouldn't accept the comfort. Because it wasn't all right. What could he say?

"Please," he said, voice rough with the attempt to suppress emotions. "I am truly sorry. I don't...I just...I'm sorry."

She softened again, but only slightly. "Thank you." She looked at him a moment longer, then turned toward the door again.

"Raahi, wait."

She paused back still to him.

"Stay. Please. We need to talk."

She turned back to face him but still said nothing. He

felt the tension rise and he hurried to get words out before she changed her mind.

"Ok, well, then I will talk. Bear with me as I am sure I am going to be unclear or say something wrong or..." He cut himself off as she crossed her arms again.

"Ugh! I know I am not making sense." He briefly put his fingertips to his temples, then riveted his gaze on the wall instead of Raahi.

"I am not disappointed that you are not the princess. Well, maybe a little, but not for me. When you two first went missing, I stayed at the palace to be there when you returned. As time went on and nothing was ever found, I should have left, but by then the king and I had grown close, especially after his companion died. Up until about ten years ago, I was his confidante, and I grew to love him for himself and as King."

Raahi shifted and he tried not to envision her face. He couldn't bring himself to look and hurried on.

"I am telling you this so that you understand that I wanted to find the princess for Nirav, but not only because he misses her. If there is one thing he loves almost as much as his daughter, it is this world and its people. I don't want to see that ruined, but if the prince is crowned, I am afraid everything will change for the worse. Now that there is no princess, that will be more difficult...but that isn't all I wanted to tell you." He took a deep breath and closed his eyes, determined to get the words out.

"When you showed up at my door today, the only thing I could think of was that I was happy that you were back. You, Raahi, not the princess or companion." A slight rustling caused him to open his eyes, and he saw she had uncrossed her arms, but he still kept his gaze averted.

"I know you are...were...the companion, and I understand why you didn't come forward. But we were great together, working to find information about the slave organization, and I am asking you to help continue with that. You are better at uncovering evidence than I am, much better. And maybe we can find something against the prince so that he will never rule."

He straightened and looked directly into her eyes, trying with all his will to show her his sincerity.

"Stay. As Raahi. That would mean more to me than anything else." He wanted to say more but forced his lips shut. The silence stretched on, but he ground his teeth together. He'd said enough.

Finally, she spoke.

"I will help to the best of my ability." She held up a finger. "With the slave ring."

The breath he had been holding exploded in relief.

She smiled in response.

"But it probably won't be enough," she said.

"That's okay," he replied. "I'll take it."

Chapter Fifty-Six

"So where do we start?"

Jonah smiled as he considered Raahi's question. The connection between them was fragile, but at least she wasn't angry anymore.

"I know you think I have a plan but—" he broke off as movement on his display screen caught his eye. The council session was over, and people were leaving the council room. He headed for the computer.

"I need to get back to work."

"In that case, I'll do the dishes. Until you come up with a plan." Raahi grinned as she gathered up the tray.

"Normally, I would not allow a friend to cook and clean for me, but in this case, I will make an exception." He gave her a small bow, then quickly turned back to the screens.

As he watched the prince head for his rooms, he kept being distracted by the sounds in the kitchen. That clunk would be the tray being washed in the sink. The swish was probably a cloth drying. His attention was quickly brought back to the screen, however, when the prince departed his chambers, having changed into soft loose pants and a lightweight shirt with a handsome embroidered half-sleeve jacket. A triple pulse against Jonah's wrist heightened his anxiety. Lavan had said if he knew Hahn was meeting someone, he would give Jonah a warning with three pings.

Prince Hahn headed down the corridors, finally ducking into a small conference room on the third floor. There was a man seated at a table who looked vaguely familiar. The prince sat in a chair across the table from him, pulling out some papers from inside his jacket. Jonah held his breath. This had to be it. He raised the volume to catch all the conversation, grateful the meeting was inside the palace where audio was available.

"These," Hahn flipped the top page to the man, "are all the guests invited to the celebration. And this," another paper, "is what I want the cake to look like. Now as for the menu, none of that fancy weird food that people only pretend to like. I want good stuff and lots of it so that everyone is satisfied."

"Damn!" Jonah tried hard to contain his disappointment, and he finally recognized the head cook in the palace. Without his apron and hair tied back, he looked quite different. A sudden burst of laughter behind him intruded upon his distress.

"Your dangerous prince might just get his way," she said, still chuckling. "Sounds like a huge conspiracy. Hope everyone can survive the birthday party."

Jonah felt a quick rush of annoyance, but just as quickly it disappeared. She was right. This was harmless.

"Maybe this time," he said. "But soon he'll do something that will make you believe me. Some of the things from his past are quite disturbing."

"How can someone that young be so conniving? Why would anyone on the council listen to him?"

Jonah looked at her, wondering if he could completely trust her, but a heartbeat later he realized he always had. He pushed his chair back and stood.

"I have some things you need to see. Not too long ago, the prince threatened me, so I felt compelled to hide certain information." He grunted as he pulled his desk away from the wall.

Raahi snorted. "I think you are overestimating a threat. A life in the palace is pretty sheltered, and I find it hard to believe that the prince even knows about the real world other than what he sees in entertainment vids."

"You weren't there." Trying not to feel slighted at her hint that he was just as sheltered as Hahn, Jonah told of the prince's interception in the hall and threat. He ran his hand along the blank wall until an open space appeared. "So, I felt it necessary to protect myself. It's a long story, and what I have will explain a lot."

Raahi leaned over to look in the hidden space.

"A safe? In your apartment?"

"Stand back, please. This is wired to destroy itself and anything inside if the wrong code is put in."

The look in her eyes was unfathomable, but she took several steps back.

"If your life is in danger, destroying evidence wouldn't help."

"These are copies. I have the originals stored elsewhere to be 'discovered' in case of my death."

Raahi didn't comment except to cross her arms and set her jaw. Jonah carefully input the code, breathing easier as he always did when it clicked open. He removed several data sticks with independent readers. He shuffled through them carefully, inserted them into their selected readers, and handed them to Raahi.

She uncrossed her arms as she took them and turned toward the couch.

"Just watch. I'm going back to my screens."

He kept one eye on the prince and one on Raahi. Far too quickly, she switched off the hand-held and tossed it aside with a disdainful snort.

"The prince can't be older than ten in these."

"Yes, but you can see his cruel nature…" began Jonah.

"All I see, all anyone will see, is a spoiled child. What youngster hasn't had moments of selfishness? His public face now is much improved. People will say he has grown up."

"But I am telling you, he is not improved. I think—"

"Look Jonah. I believe you. I do." She leaned forward on the couch, elbows on knees. "I am trying to show how he is viewed by the general public, and what they may say."

Jonah pursed his lips. "I understand. It's why I need proof. I know in my heart that Hahn is planning a grab for power and even getting rid of the council so that his voice will be the only authority on the entire planet. It's the only reason he would ask for the scrambler, so he can finalize his plans in private."

"Why would he ask you for a scrambler if he threatened you?"

"He didn't ask me, he asked his companion."

"And you thought of having it fail?"

"Actually, that was Lavan's idea."

"Really? I find it extremely hard to believe that a companion would turn on—"

"Their bond is not as strong as yo—the usual bonds." He had been trying to avoid any reference to Maya, but he knew he couldn't put it off. "There's one other recording I need to show you. It will explain—"

"No." She held her hand up to interrupt. "I can't watch any more."

"But…"

"Not now. Maybe later." She stood and walked to the other side of the room.

He slumped down into his chair, suddenly exhausted. He realized that though he had had so much upheaval and confusion, her emotional situation was probably ten times more painful.

"You're right. I'm sorry to push. I've been throwing all this at you, trying to be convincing with nothing but a gut feeling." He absently flicked through the screens again, watching Hahn return to his rooms to prepare for bed. So lost was he in despair and fatigue, he barely noticed a hand on his shoulder.

"Why do you care so much?" Raahi spoke softly, as if not wanting to intrude on his thoughts.

"He is not the person everyone thinks he is. He is very good at deception and I need to prove it."

"Are you sure?"

Jonah looked up at Raahi's sober face, trying hard not to focus on the touch of her hand.

She swept a hand toward the screen.

"What if he's only a young teenager who is used to getting what he wants?" Her face softened, and Jonah couldn't quite read her expression. "Maybe the reason you can't find anything is because there is nothing to find, and he is maturing beyond those boyish fantasies of power."

Jonah shook his head, understanding her logic but feeling that was not the case. He stood and took a step back, though he regretted the absence of her touch.

"I realize you have seen nothing that proves his ill intent, but I know that he would destroy all that is good in our government. Even more, his own companion feels this, and who would know better than he? Lavan has everything to lose, and yet he is still intent on keeping the prince from ruling."

She closed the distance again and gave him a penetrating look. "Even so, I will ask it again. Why do you care? What can one person do against such a plan of power if he indeed has the support of many others as you suggested? Why sacrifice yourself? Why not simply let others deal with it?"

He continued to stare, turning over her words, and trying to figure out exactly why he was putting so much effort into this.

"I love the peace we have, not everywhere, but we are mostly prosperous on our world. I love all the good that Nirav has done, and I don't want to see it destroyed by a greedy, power-hungry boy. But most of all, I love this city, the planet, and the people. And they don't deserve the chaos and deprivations that a ruler like Hahn would bring."

Raahi brought her hand to Jonah's cheek, cool upon his flushed face and the approval in her eyes was obvious. Jonah, reacting by instinct, leaned down to gently touch his lips to hers. The soft kiss turned into a lengthy one and her hand slid from his cheek to the back of his head. He pulled her close and all other thought was lost as he felt a warmth rush through him. He tried to pull away, not wanting to take advantage of someone who had been so abused in her life, but she held on to him, matching his passion.

"Raahi," he whispered, but she silenced him with her mouth on his and he gave in to his desire. Before he knew it, they were in his bed, clothes in various heaps around the apartment and he tried once more to stop, acutely aware of his inexperience. The thought that he might make a fool of himself disappeared when Raahi murmured encouragement, her breath warm in his ear. All doubts washed away as he abandoned himself to the moment.

***

Jonah awoke slowly with the awareness that he had slept deeply. As consciousness returned, so did memory, and he was intensely aware of the woman snuggled in the crook of his arm.

"Awake?" she said as she put her hand on his chest.

He returned her smile and gently took her hand in his. Strange how it was warm now when her touch had always been cool. The smile dropped from his face as he instantly sat up.

"What is it?" She peered at his face, brow furrowed.

He shifted and reached for her right hand as she sat up as well. She started to pull it out of his grip but then relaxed.

There were tattoos on her hand and wrist. Emotions hammered his brain and he tried to stammer out an apology.

"Sorry for what?" she said. "You were pretty good for it being your first time."

He felt his face burning hotter. "I had no right to...I am sorry...it's just that I forgot you were, I mean, not Raahi. It's not acceptable..."

"Stop," she said, but he continued to babble, leaping out of bed and grabbing whatever clothes came to hand.

He froze as her arms went around him from behind and her naked body pressed up against his. He trembled with the effort to not give in but, oh, how he wanted to.

"You have just given me the greatest compliment anyone ever has." She loosened her arms so that he could face her but wouldn't let him go.

"Compliment?" He felt stupid.

"You loved me as Raahi; saw only Raahi, not the companion or even a substitute princess. Not as a piece of property to entertain any fantasy but as a person, for who I am. That...that is a first for me." Now she looked down though her arms didn't let go.

Comprehension dawned, and awe swept over him as he realized all she was saying, and, more importantly, not saying. He could imagine that as a slave, she had felt like an object, used and sold from owner to owner. It never occurred to him that she may have thought of herself as nobody without the princess to be a companion to. He put his fingertips under her chin and lifted her head to meet her eyes.

"Yes, I love you. You, Raahi." He kissed her and dropped the clothes he had been holding, and they abandoned themselves to passion again.

***

Repeated faint buzzing woke Jonah from a slight doze. Absently he swatted at the air, his drowsy mind thinking it to be an insect. Next to him came a groan.

"Ugh. Turn off the alarm." Raahi pulled a pillow over her head.

Jonah chuckled as he snatched the pillow away. "I don't have that kind of alarm. Besides, no sleeping. It's already nearly lunchtime."

Raahi protested the pillow's absence, but her smile belied her irritation. She flipped over and sat up, modestly pulling the covers up over her breasts.

He smiled back and took notice for the first time of slight tracings of scars on her arms and shoulder. Briefly, he wondered what atrocities she had endured. Treatment to get rid of scars was commonplace, so her experiences had to have been horrible. He was about to comment, but her smile faltered when she saw what his eyes were following. Feeling she wouldn't want to talk about it, he instead gently took her right hand and turned it palm up to lightly trace the tattoos with his finger. She shivered, and the smile returned.

"These aren't true companion tattoos. There's more than there should be, like a mirror image."

"That's right. They were altered to match each other, more twin-like that way. But how do you know the pattern for me?"

He blushed. "Well, the princess's tattoo should match mine like it matches yours, I mean like hers matches yours. In my investigations, I looked up the pattern to be sure. Later, the records were sealed, so I couldn't make a copy to give to..." He watched her carefully to gauge her reaction. "To the Baroness, the one who introduced us."

Raahi didn't seem surprised. "I see."

"Companion Lavan was the first to contact her, but I took over due to his naivete and...Lavan!" Jonah scrambled out of bed and began digging through the pile of clothes on the floor.

"What's wrong?" asked Raahi as she knelt on the bed, brow furrowed.

"That buzzing, it might be Lavan trying to contact me.". He found the wrist comp and quickly scrolled through messages. "Damn! It was him. First the signal that Hahn might be meeting someone. He sent that twice, and when I didn't respond, he sent a quick text. Risky, Lavan." He pulled on a shirt and nearly tripped putting on shorts while heading to the computers.

As he scrolled back through the video feed to the time of the first signal, he was vaguely aware of the shower running. Why wasn't Raahi more concerned? Then he chided himself. He knew she had been avoiding anything to do with the palace, even trying to leave the planet. *She must have her reasons, but despite last night, I really don't know what she is thinking or feeling. Does she miss Maya so much she must turn her back on any reminders?*

Jonah had thought that if there was proof she would do something, but now he doubted it. Maybe he could convince her to simply speak out, bring a message from the princess to her people, something, anything.

His attention was brought back to the screen with Prince Hahn in the library with two, no three current council members and another man and woman that Jonah knew were personal assistants to two other members. That was half the council represented. Wait...he zoomed the camera to see them walking into a small annex of the library and turned up the volume.

"As you can see, I have decided on the proper ceremony for my coronation. As it is in a book that is quite old, I invited you to the library for viewing." They headed into a small conference room and Jonah's long familiarity to the monitoring system allowed him to quickly switch to the proper camera, though it was very small and had a terrible audio pickup. He turned it to maximum volume and input the command for the double recording system which made two copies. He strained his ears.

The group arrayed themselves around the circular conference table, and Hahn flipped open a book, probably a history of past coronations. Jonah groaned. More birthday plans. Maybe he really was imagining things, and Prince Hahn wasn't out to destroy the government.

Then he noticed Hahn's hand slip into his pocket. When he glanced at the camera with a grin that was rather frightening, Jonah's gut clenched.

"Gentlemen and ladies, my fellow supporters. The time has come." The youngster's façade was gone, and Hahn stood straight and tall, a quite regal bearing that left Jonah a bit daunted. "In twenty-four days, I will be confirmed as the official heir to the throne, and then it will be time for changes. Too long have we been forced to give our time and resources to help those who are too lazy to work. Too long have taxes taken your hard-earned credits. Too long have stupid regulations shackled certain improvements to our way of life." He nodded at individuals with each pronouncement. "Our king's health is failing. I have been assured that he will not survive more than thirty days following my coronation." His smile took on a decided edge. Jonah inhaled abruptly. He knew the king's doctors had said no such thing. He checked nearly every day. That meant someone else would ensure his death. Jonah fought against nausea but forced himself to keep watching.

"We are just the beginning. We can make these changes, but only if you act decisively. As you know, I am limited in my power because the royalty only serves in an advisory capacity, a voice of the people. If you and your constituents vote to give me true power in the council, I can push these advancements through fast, without the need for laborious committees and surveys." Hahn's hand swept over the book. "Back when kings had real power, things got done." He pounded his fist on the table.

"They weren't debated incessantly." The others nodded and murmured, caught up in the speech. Interesting how they all forgot that when the kings had that much power, eighty-five percent of the people lived in poverty, unable to even scrape up enough money to leave the planet in hopes of better lives. Now Hahn leaned forward, hands on the table, an earnest look on his face.

"The people love me. They would welcome me with the promises I have been feeding to them and give me that power willingly. Of course, once I have that power, you, my loyal comrades"—Hahn spread his hands to indicate those in front of him—"you will help me rule the way it should be, the power in the few strong people that will bring change to our world." Now he nodded to each person in turn. "Lower taxes for corporations and exports." Another nod. "Easement of manufacturing regulations. Pardons and expunged past records for those who have helped me." And now his smile turned grim. "And getting rid of those who might oppose us." A couple of the council members hissed agreements, and one man that Jonah didn't know smiled as he drew a finger across his throat. Jonah felt a shiver at the subtle threat. He'd thought that they only wanted more money and influence, not that they condoned violence.

"Good. Then I count on your support. My friends...to a new, more powerful monarchy!" He raised his fist and the others followed suit, eyes feverish and flushed. He then raised his chin and stretched out his hands, palm down and indicated that they should sit back down. Their immediate obedience shook Jonah to the core. The prince reached back into his pocket as he sat. When he pulled his hand out, the young boy was back, his voice higher, the mask back in place as he thought the cameras were back on.

"Does that sound like a good ceremony?" The others nodded, and Hahn marked the place in the book. "Very well. I shall pass along your advice to the planners. Good day, honored guests. Thank you for coming and for your valuable input." He shook their hands as they left and murmured something to each individual that the camera couldn't pick up, but Jonah could guess. Probably promises or something to appeal to each ego, making them seem special to the prince.

"Interesting."

Jonah spun his chair to see Raahi standing behind,

staring at the screen.

"Did you see?"

"I saw enough. Still proves nothing."

Jonah sputtered, and she pivoted abruptly and walked toward the kitchen. Without conscious thought, his feet followed. "You can't mean that."

"So, he wants power to make changes. Doesn't mean those changes will be bad." She began grabbing food and dishes to prepare a lunch, but the forceful way she was doing so indicated her mood. He pressed on.

"Did you hear the part where he assures the king will die?" Despite the fact that he knew she was purposely playing devil's advocate, Jonah was beginning to feel anger now.

"You told me yourself he was quite ill." She shrugged as she dumped food into pans to reheat, but she didn't look at him.

"I know the doctors intimately. They have made no such predictions. And now I am beginning to think there is more to his decline than simply grief. Don't you see?" Jonah grabbed her by the shoulders. "He is planning not only to grab power but kill the king!"

Despite the fact he hadn't been very rough, Raahi went absolutely rigid.

"Let me go," she said, voice low, eyes smoldering. Embarrassed by his angry outburst, Jonah snatched his hands behind his back. Raahi tossed the dishes to the stove with a clatter, stepped around Jonah out of the kitchen and grabbed her jacket.

"Don't go. Please, I'm sorry for my reaction. Please," Jonah said softly, feeling a tightness in his chest. She paused a few steps from the door, looked down, and sighed.

"I don't know what you expect of me. Maybe the prince is up to something, but there is nothing I can do."

Jonah's mind raced, grateful she had stopped, but her back was still to him and he struggled for something to keep her here.

"Maybe you can speak out, as the former companion, or..."

"No. Won't work."

"But with—"

She turned to face him, interrupting. "Not even with that video. It's not enough. They would say their words were misunderstood, probably decry the video as fake and maybe even get more people to his side in sympathy." She shook her head. "Face it, Jonah. I, we, are powerless here."

"Lavan..." he tried again.

"Is only a companion and fairly unknown to the public. Companions are only seen as friends of the ruler. Very little is known of the physical bond."

"The bond, that's it." The idea that had been teasing at the back of his mind burst into full flower.

"That picture, you both look like twins. You can become Princess Maya."

Chapter Fifty-Seven

"Impossible." Raahi stood frozen at Jonah's suggestion, fighting down memories and ghosts from the past.

"Not impossible. You have the tattoos, you look just like her, you know the palace and the king—"

"Stop!" Raahi tried to shut out Jonah's excitement and silence her own inner voices. "It won't work. When we were first taken..." She swallowed but continued, attempting to empty herself of emotions. "They surgically altered us to look like twins when they found out that we became very ill when we were separated. Any investigation would reveal that surgery and prove me a fake."

"Not necessarily. I know the person..."

"No, I won't do it." She turned away from him, eyeing the door, wanting to leave this situation, but her feet wouldn't move. Her right thumb rubbed a slight scar on her left palm as she searched for something to say. She settled for shifting the focus.

"Can't you just let it go?" she asked softly, not sure if she wanted to hear the answer.

"The prince isn't—"

She spun to face him, feeling anger now, which was preferable. "'The prince, the prince.' Is that all you can say? I see nothing to show a reason to change my entire self and live a lie. Perhaps you don't want to give up your position as the future spouse of the ruler."

It was Jonah's turn to be rendered speechless, and the hurt look on his face cooled Raahi's anger somewhat. Stubbornly she crossed her arms, not wanting to feel sorry for what she said.

"There might be some truth to what you say," he began, looking down. "But it would be worse to let Prince Hahn become king. I...I don't really know what else to say to convince you. But I know something you have to hear."

She let her arms drop with an exasperated huff. "Not another 'bad thing' the prince said?"

"No," he said as he rifled through the box that he had pulled out of the safe. "Something King Nirav said."

An icy chill ran down her spine.

Jonah pulled out a data stick and personal reader. He waved an arm at the couch and the serious, almost sad, look on his face impelled her to sit. He inserted the stick as he lowered himself to the couch as well. He began to speak, eyes distant.

"The night before the ceremony that officially named Hahn prince, the king called me into the gardens. By this time, I was a reviewer, junior grade, but I knew that there were no cameras there. Without conscious thought, because it was part of my training as a reviewer, I took my personal recorder, hidden in my pocket. I arrived at the garden, and the king was as far from the entrance as he could get. As I approached, I could smell liquor on him. I was shocked because I had never known him to drink. And then, well..." Jonah activated the playback. The king's sonorous voice tumbled out of the recorder and Raahi fought against the resurfacing memories.

King Nirav: "Ah, Barad, or I suppose I should say Jonah. How are you doing?"

Jonah: "Fine, your Majesty."

King: "Please, Nirav. If anyone deserves to call me by my given name, it's you." Sound of liquid swishing and swallowing.

Jonah: "I am honored, Nirav."

King: "After all, you were supposed to be my son-in-law. I don't suppose you will be now." Humorless laugh. "Tell me, what do you think of the prince-to-be?"

Jonah: "He is a well-grown eight-year-old, very handsome, lots of energy."

King: "Yes, well, you are very diplomatic. I suppose I should have taken more of an interest in the boy if he is going to be the next king."

Jonah: "Our planet is used to a monarch, even though they have voting rights. Your position is very influential."

King: "You are perceptive as well. And quite intelligent. I chose well for Maya." Pause, sigh. "Barad, do you have any hope that Maya is still alive somewhere?"

Jonah: "I always have hope."

King: "I should have abandoned everything here to look for her. I will always regret that."

Jonah: "Your duties here were too important. I...I'm aware that you were watched and even guarded against leaving. I promise you, I will redouble my efforts and investigations."

King: "Don't give up my boy." Another swig. "I am going to tell you why. And if the time comes, it may become necessary to find her." Long pause. "Hahn is not truly my son. A very small and quite secret group of people found a distant cousin of the queen who had just conceived a child. The cousin was all too willing to have her child become the next ruler and swore herself to secrecy. Passing her off as the nanny, she was left to the raising of the child which, as you may now see, was a mistake. He is spoiled and full of his own virtue and thinks all there is to being a king is getting his way. The only people aware of these facts were myself, the queen, my companion, Hahn's real mother, and two other men. The only one left alive is myself." Pause. "And now you. The prince himself doesn't even know. I never wanted it to happen, but I let myself be talked into it so there would be an heir. And without Maya, even if the truth were known, it wouldn't matter. The people need continuity. He is a relative, however distant." He sighed. "From this point on, I will take a hand in the young man's education. Maybe there is something left to salvage and become a proper king. If not, maybe you can find a way to remove him from the succession. I would rather the monarchy cease to exist than turn it over to a man less than worthy. The queen felt the same. She was the brave one. Took her own life rather than live a lie."

Jonah: "But Sire..."

King: "Take care, Jonah. We will never speak of this again. We will go about our duties as everyone expects us to. But we will always have this moment of honesty."

Jonah switched off the playback and waited for Raahi to speak.

"Why would this matter to me?" she asked.

"Even the king said he didn't think Hahn was a good fit for a future king."

"The prince was only eight at the time. Children grow up. And as he said, he started to take an interest in training him."

"But..."

Raahi sighed, "What do you want from me?"

"I want you to become Princess Maya. Like Nirav said, it's the only way to prevent the prince from inheriting. The public would never accept the end of the monarchy even though it is mostly symbolic."

Raahi looked at Jonah, trying not to be pulled in by those innocent, begging eyes. "Even if I wanted to, who is going to believe that miraculously the princess has been found only a month before the prince's eighteenth birthday, old enough to be confirmed king?"

"Okay, yes I suppose it does sound coincidental, but you—"

"Look, Jonah." She tried but couldn't quite keep pity out of her voice. "You have lived in the palace all your life, so I forgive your naivete." Jonah's face reddened, but she continued. "But I've been living among the people. I have seen all levels of prosperity and poverty, and they are all listening to this prince and his promises. His public face is very well known and liked, and few will believe that his true nature is different. And even then, I know some groups would prefer a new bloodline."

Jonah's face fell. "I understand."

Raahi's heart tugged again, and she wanted to convey how deeply she felt. Her thumb again rubbed the scar.

"Long ago, after we were first taken, M-Maya thought as you do." She held her left hand out to Jonah, showed him the scar. "Even swore a blood oath as sisters. She said that if anything happened to her, I should take her place if it was needed."

"See? That means—"

"No, Jonah." Raahi used the look of hope on his face to steel herself against the past. "She said, 'If it was needed.' So far, I don't see it is." She held up a hand when Jonah opened his mouth again. "You may not believe me, but I have given this a lot of thought and the main reason I won't do it is..." She looked down and clenched her fists. "It would be a great disrespect to my soul sister for me to think I can replace her. She was unique, and I could not hope to become anything like her." She looked up, closed the distance between them and put her hand on his cheek. "I am sorry, sweet Jonah. I simply cannot do this. In fact, I must leave. I've been putting it off, but I need to be away from here and the memories. I didn't come back voluntarily. There were some who thought it would be good for me, but..." she swallowed, "it wasn't. I...you...all this distracted me, but I have been trying to get away from this planet for years, and now I have the means to do so."

He brought his hand up to cover hers, and they were silent like that, eyes locked for several long moments.

"Then let me go with you."

She tried to ignore the extra jump of her heart. "You mean that? You'd leave everything you have here?"

"You are more important to me. I'm not saying it will be easy, but I don't want to be away from you, ever. And"—he swallowed—"and you are right. We don't have enough proof and maybe the prince won't be so bad." He sounded like he was convincing himself. She wanted to agree but wasn't sure if it was the right thing.

She brought her other hand to the opposite cheek and, as she opened her mouth to say something, a ping from the console startled them both.

Jonah turned back to answer. Raahi was flattered by his annoyed look at the interruption. He even mumbled something about getting rid of whoever was calling so that he and Raahi could "make plans."

The Baroness' face appeared, and as Jonah reached out a hand to dismiss it, Raahi stopped him.

"Let's listen."

"It is vital that we meet. New information concerning our search has come up. Bring our mutual friend. It concerns her as well." An address of a nearby park briefly scrolled across the screen with a time to meet in less than an hour. The screen abruptly cut out with the usual static sizzle.

"Why me?" asked Raahi.

"Remember, I told you they know who you are and have been tracking your path since you disappeared. They must have found something important."

She thought about what it might be, and her gut tightened, not liking any of the possibilities. Especially after the information she had given them.

"Shall we go then?" asked Jonah.

"A quick bite first. I'm hungry." Anything to delay what she knew would be a confrontation.

"You get started. I need a shower." His grin tugged at her emotions again and she smiled back, wanting to spend as much time with Jonah as she could before things changed. She knew that he probably wouldn't leave with her. He was too much a part of this world, had lived his entire life here. Most of her life had happened elsewhere. Grimly she suppressed the memories again. She needed to have a clear head when they met the Baroness.

Chapter Fifty-Eight

Lenore sat at one end of the large, circular bench and watched Jonah and Raahi approach. They weren't touching, but they kept glancing at each other with shy smiles, which gave her the feeling that they had been intimate. As they caught sight of her, Jonah's hand reached out slightly toward Raahi's, but he pulled it back and Lenore knew her instincts were correct.

She spread her hands to indicate they sit on the bench as well. Jonah took the middle and Raahi the opposite as Lenore expected. The curve of the bench allowed the women to be face to face. Perfect, thought Lenore. This message was primarily for her anyway. Jonah had been invited to put Raahi at ease, but he also needed to hear what Lenore had to say.

"Hello, Jonah, Raahi," she said, nodding at each.

"Good afternoon, Baroness," said Jonah while Raahi merely dipped her head slightly.

"Jonah, as we discussed previously, I know you are aware that this young lady here is one of the people I was hired to find."

"Yes. She confirmed it."

"Ah, good. Then you know that this is, in fact, Princess Maya, not the companion." Lenore watched the girl closely and, out of the corner of her eye, saw Jonah's jaw drop.

"Impossible," he said.

Raahi shook her head.

"I am sorry, Baroness. But your information is flawed. I am...was...Lara, the companion. You see I was surgically alt—"

"I know all that and please, call me Lenore," she said, trying to soften the abrupt interruption with her name to inspire trust. "I have detailed records. What you are perhaps unaware of is that in addition to physical appearance, they also altered both of your DNA. Some buyers need proof of close DNA typing before purchasing twins."

"Still, I know who I am."

"Ah, but I also know that the alterations had some interesting side effects."

Raahi visibly paled and her entire body gave a massive twitch, whether from being startled or not wanting to face this, Lenore wasn't sure.

"What side effects?" Jonah asked. Lenore ignored him, looking only at Raahi. This was a delicate situation.

"Raahi, I know the bond between you two was exceptionally tight. But after the surgery, it was even more so, not just with feelings but with thoughts and images. You two were telepathic."

Jonah's head swiveled toward Raahi. She nodded slowly.

"It wasn't complete telepathy, but we were always in each other's minds, always knew what the other was doing and thinking." She closed her eyes, obviously upset.

"When she died, it affected you profoundly."

Raahi's hand went to her chest as if in pain. She opened her eyes though they focused on nothing as she spoke. "When...when she died, I collapsed. I was delirious and couldn't move or speak. I wanted to die with her. And probably would have if the captain of the ship we were supposed to leave on hadn't intervened. He had taken a fancy to us and visited often. He found me there next to her and took charge, arranged for her burial by selling her ticket. When she was taken away, I fought them, kicking, screaming and cursing in my delirium, using up what little strength I had. The captain had to carry me, near unconscious and sobbing, to the ship." Raahi wrapped her arms around herself, unfocused eyes looking toward the ground. "I don't remember much after that, only vague dreams and images. The doctor on the ship said it was like a high fever, but there was nothing physically wrong. I stayed in the captain's cabin, and there was always someone to watch over me. He even arranged for someone to care for me when we reached the planet.

"It took weeks to regain my health. I didn't even realize where I was. When I finally could function again, I asked to be returned to her, but the man who was caring for me refused, knowing it would undo all the healing. I walked away without so much as a goodbye and vowed to find a way to return to her. As I came to realize that he and the captain saved my life, I tried to find them to thank them but have been unsuccessful."

Jonah had moved next to her but didn't embrace her

as Lenore thought he might. Instead, they sat, knees touching. She didn't react, continuing to stare at the ground, but Lenore had the feeling she was aware of the small contact.

"That delirium is what confused you. To be able to live with the loss of your...bondmate, you convinced yourself that you were her. In fact, became the companion instead of the princess so she would never be dead."

Raahi shook her head. "No, that is not possible."

"I have proof."

Raahi's head jerked up and her eyes narrowed. "How can you..."

"It is on my ship. You must see it."

"Very well." She swiped at her eyes though Lenore hadn't seen any tears, and she stood, all business. Jonah stood as well, but Lenore shook her head.

"Raahi only, Jonah. I'm sorry."

"No way. I am not letting her out of my sight." While his protectiveness didn't surprise Lenore, the intensity did.

Raahi put her hand on Jonah's arm. "I will be fine, Jonah."

"I'm going with you."

"I'll be fine." She looked like she was going to move her hand to his chest, but evidently thought better of it and gently squeezed his arm instead. "I can take care of myself, you know." He clearly didn't like it but relented.

"Let's go," said Lenore.

***

As they entered the ship, Raahi paused right inside the hatch and waited for it to close before she spoke.

"Ok, would you mind telling me what that was all about? Lenore, was it?" She crossed her arms and leaned against the hatch. She had a tight rein on her emotions, though with everything that had happened, the hold was fraying. More people urging that she become Maya, stirring up painful memories.

"About?" said Lenore.

"I may have been confused when Maya died, but not that much. If you have any sort of proof, you should know I am not the princess."

"Yes, I know."

Raahi's arms dropped, not expecting that answer. "Then, why?"

"There are things you need to see. Three things to be precise. They are for you and only you. It's why Jonah couldn't be here."

"Such as?"

Still she wouldn't budge. Lenore sighed.

"I was given a message to give to you, a data stick. Forgive me, but I watched it to make sure it was nothing harmful."

"Who gave it to you?"

"A man on Recavan. A tall, very thin man with short, spiky, blond, nearly white hair." She reached into her pocket, drew out the data stick and held it out to Raahi.

Raahi unclenched hands that had stiffened by her side at the mention of the planet.

"You were on Recavan?" she asked, voice hoarse and just above a whisper.

"Yes."

"Then one of the other things…"

"In our cargo hold."

"Take me to her."

Lenore opened her mouth but as she peered at Raahi, she simply nodded and said, "Follow me."

A man with incredibly dark skin who Lenore introduced as Diarmin was waiting in the hold. Lenore stepped aside to allow Raahi to go to the coffin containing Maya's body. She approached slowly and lightly touched the top, but didn't open it. Instead, she allowed herself to unleash some emotions.

"You had no right." Anger slurred her words. "She was my sister. It was my duty."

"We were hired to find the princess, and we did."

Raahi's head snapped around, her lip curled into a snarl.

"Before you judge us further," said Diarmin. "See what is on the data stick." He held out a reader.

Raahi took the reader and shoved the stick in. She was aware of Lenore's scrutiny as Diarmin put a chair close by.

"Hello my dear, Lara." Maya's face on the screen caused Raahi's hands to shake, and her legs gave way as she sat hard in the chair. Maya spoke softly, often pausing for slow, liquid breaths. Her ailment was quite evident, and the fact she was lying in a hospital bed only confirmed it.

"I have asked Menot to record this and give it to you after I die. Yes, I know I am dying, and I am never going to make it home. I also know how you are going to react, sister of my soul. You have protected me from the moment we met. And though I didn't know it at the time, I discovered you occasionally took my place when it was my turn to lie with those abominable men. Fought off those thugs on the cargo ship and other horrible foes when I hadn't the physical strength. You gained us our freedom, and I, in my weakness, couldn't even see it through to getting home. You have done everything for me, asking for nothing in return, and yet I have one more favor to ask of you. You have always been the strong one. Get home. And if...if it becomes necessary..." a deep breath and pause for several slow breaths. "As we swore all those years ago," she rubbed her scar with her thumb in a move identical to Raahi's. "Take my place. Become the princess. Protect the people. I know this is a burden, but I can go to my rest peacefully knowing that you will watch over our people and make sure they are well cared for as you have cared for me our entire lives. I love you, Lara and will always be in your heart and soul."

The tears she had been withholding for days finally broke free, running down her face unchecked. It was just like Maya, thinking of her duty and her people. She touched the image frozen on the screen, and her heart contracted. How very like Jonah she was, wanting nothing but the best for her planet. *Probably why I am so attracted to him. He reminds me of her.*

A throat clearing brought her out of her reverie, and she turned her attention back to the people who had brought this gift. She pulled the data stick out of the reader and wrapped her fingers tightly around it.

"You know, she said I was the strong one," Raahi spoke in a soft voice. Her eyes were still wet, but she smiled as she thought of her sister. "But in fact, she had an inner strength that was solid and unmoving. With all that happened to us, she never changed. Never lost that sweet spirit. I became cynical and tough, unwilling to trust in anyone. She always was a princess in her entire being. Had the strength to always be her true self."

She brought her fist to her chest, data stick still clutched tight. "Thank you for bringing this to me. And for bringing her home." She blotted at her eyes to give herself time to collect her thoughts, and her voice firmed. "But I don't know why you are pretending to Jonah that I am the princess. He knows I am not. And there is no way to prove such a claim. And no reason to do so."

"As for the proof, that will be no problem," said the woman. "My crew are quite skilled and can replicate the tattoos that are covered by your gloves." Before Raahi could protest, she went on. "Yes, we know there is more than ink to those tattoos, and that is the tech we can duplicate." Raahi snapped her mouth shut and tried not to show her surprise. Who were these people that could do this?

"And..." Lenore took the three steps needed to be closer without seeming threatening. "With those codes you gave me, we found the details of the alterations to your DNA so that it will explain why it does not match exactly. But there was also something else in the information we uncovered, which is the third thing that you need to see." She stepped aside and gestured at the ladder. "If you would follow me to the bridge and the secure terminal?"

As they climbed the ladder and headed down a corridor, Raahi's stomach tightened more and more. Was it fear? Repressing the wave of emotions that she was feeling from the video? Confusion over what they could have found that concerned her? Her mind searched for any distraction.

"Excuse me, Bar—um, Lenore? I have to ask. What about Lord Timatay?"

They took several more steps before Lenore answered. She paused at a ladder and seemed to be composing her thoughts.

Raahi felt a chill. "You...you didn't..."

"No, Raahi. I didn't kill him." But relief was short-lived. "He took his own life when I refused to."

Raahi was again swamped with emotion, wondering why she would be so moved at the death of one of her "owners."

Lenore touched her lightly on the arm. "He knew he would be tortured and punished because he had let you go. Because he had allowed you to escape with the codes that would help bring down the entire organization. It is... was...quite noble what he did." The look on Lenore's face was also emotional which, strangely, made her feel better.

They continued up the ladder to the bridge of the ship. Lenore indicated a chair at a terminal set aside from the flight console. Raahi sat, and Lenore turned the screen away, typed in what was surely a personal code, then turned the screen back around for Raahi to read.

At first, she didn't know what she was looking at. Lenore waited patiently for her to decipher what was exactly on the screen. Ok...they were messages...from who? Her gut clenched as she realized they were from very high ranked members of the slave organization. But when she saw who they were addressed to, a wave of nausea swamped her. She launched out of the chair and away from the console, barely stopping herself from climbing down the ladder and running away. She stood, breathing heavily for several moments and firmly drew on her well-honed discipline to bring the tumult under control. Finally, she turned back to Lenore, still shocked but able to speak.

"Those...those criminals. They are in collusion with Prince Hahn."

***

Lenore nodded, quite understanding the girl's reaction. She had felt much the same but now it was a slow, burning anger.

"From what we can tell," she spoke in a quiet, even voice that experience told her helped to calm others. "The organization has had its fingers in the workings of the government on your planet beginning right after you were abducted. They figured the best way to keep from being caught was to be on the inside. They quashed most investigations, bought off officials and kept their interests here quite unnoticed. Until you escaped from Timatay."

Raahi's eyes widened, then narrowed. She understands, thought Lenore.

"They were afraid you two would return here, so instead of secret manipulation, they openly approached the prince to help him consolidate his powers. They wanted him on the throne before the princess returned. When you didn't come back right away, their plans weren't as rushed, but the wheels are still in place. They have been giving the king, not poison, but a rare, relatively unknown drug that intensifies emotion. When the king had a recent upswing, they realized they needed to do more, and thus are planning his death when the prince is confirmed."

"Jonah was right. About everything."

"As you can see from the messages, the plan they have for the planet would devastate the economy and the people. The prince is too young to realize he will be, in fact already is, a puppet of this organization. All he wants is the power of a ruler, not caring how he gets it."

Raahi stared at her again. "Why do you care? What's

in it for you?"

Lenore smiled, having expected this question. "Money, of course." Then her lip twisted with her next words. "And the fact that we have our own score to settle with these slavers." She hadn't meant to add the last, but it seemed to resonate with the young lady.

"So? Will you become the princess and keep your planet intact?"

"I..." She opened her hand and looked at the data stick she was still holding. She stared for a long moment, then straightened, spine stiffening, and appearing to grow a couple of inches as she tucked the stick inside her jacket. The fire in her eyes told Lenore her decision. "Tell me about this proof with the tattoos."

"I will let Diarmin explain that. If you would follow me back down to the lounge?"

"And Jonah. What am I going to tell Jonah?"

"Nothing," Lenore replied, and she held up her hand to forestall the inevitable protest. "For what we plan to do, he must not appear to be involved. For his safety and yours."

Raahi shook her head. "I don't like it."

"Wait until you hear the plans. You will probably like those even less."

Chapter Fifty-Nine

Jonah slumped in his chair, eyes glued to the screen. He was so upset he couldn't muster up the energy for his usual anxious pacing. What was going on? Was Raahi really the princess? He shook his head. No. She wouldn't have stayed away. Would have sought her father out. But... he could only imagine the horrors she had gone through. Maybe she did block it out.

What if she really was the princess? Jonah jerked his head up then let it sag again. Would she even want him? Or be angry at him for taking advantage of her? They weren't married. Traditionally it was forbidden for royal betrothed to be together intimately before marriage, though it did happen occasionally.

He picked at his lower lip as he slumped farther. He would just have to wait until she returned to tell him what happened. They would figure it out then. Together. He glanced at his wristcomp. It had been over two hours. What could be taking so long?

The personal comp beeped, and he lunged toward it, chair tipping over in his eagerness. The relief he felt at seeing Raahi's face disappeared quickly when he realized it was a recorded message like the one Lenore had delivered. Had it only been that morning?

"Jonah, I am sorry for not coming to you in person, but the most wondrous things have happened." Her face was flushed, eyes bright. "I have remembered things, and I am now prepared for the next step. However"—her face dimmed a little and his stomach dropped—"I am sorry, Jonah, but we are going to have to cut all ties. Please destroy all evidence of us being together. Someone will come by soon and pick up all the other evidence that you have gathered over the years. I know you are going to argue, but I am asking you to trust me, and to know that this is all a part of the plan. It has to be this way if we are going to succeed." She smiled, but he felt his heart breaking. "Thank you for everything, Jonah." The screen cut out with the usual sign the recording was destroyed.

Jonah could only sit there in shock. She wasn't coming back? Break all ties? Only hours ago, they were planning on running away together, making a future. He had been ready to give up everything for her, and now she wouldn't even acknowledge him. He knew he should be crying, but all he felt was empty and numb. Now that he thought back, she had never actually said she would leave with him. Did she ever say that she loved him? He had to be brutally honest with himself. No, she never had.

When the doorbell rang, the numbness was replaced with anger. He flung the door open and stood facing Lenore and a young boy, probably in his teens.

"What did you do to her?" he yelled and reached toward her, but she shoved him off balance, and he stumbled back inside. They followed, closed the door, and Lenore pulled a small globe out of her pocket. Jonah vaguely recognized a dampening field generator, but he was too emotional to think. He quickly regained his balance, strode back toward her, fists clenched, single-mindedly ready to demand answers.

Suddenly he was on his back, staring up at the ceiling, unable to speak with the wind knocked out of him. He should have known better than to threaten a Xa'ti'al, but it was the boy who stood over him.

"Nice job, Quinn," said Lenore, who then came to look down at Jonah as well.

"Are you willing to calm down, or do you want to ruin everything with a barbaric display? I can always have Quinn tie you up if you can't control yourself." She brandished the globe. "And now your neighbors will hear nothing, well, except that first ridiculous outburst. Not very controlled behavior for someone who was supposed to marry into royalty."

Jonah realized his stupidity and simply lay there, trying to draw air into his lungs and clear his dazed brain. Lenore nodded at Quinn, and he disappeared from Jonah's vision. It sounded like he was getting a bag from the kitchen, and Jonah struggled to sit up. The woman crouched down to help pull him to a sitting position, but he could tell she was ready for any reaction.

"I apologize for my behavior. It will not happen again," he said then slowly got to his feet. The anger still burned, but he had himself under control. "What did you do to her? She's not Raahi anymore."

"Indeed, she is not." The answer shocked him into

silence again. "And for this to succeed, Raahi must cease to exist, must be as if she never existed."

The realization sank in and his heart filled with bitterness. "You just want your money."

She looked at him for several moments before answering.

"Yes, I do. But isn't this also what you wanted? To find the princess? Put her on the throne and depose the prince?"

Jonah's eyes dropped, and all the fight drained away, leaving him hollow and feeling as if he'd aged years. "You are right." He put a hand to his forehead. "I don't know what has gotten into me. I have no idea why I am so...so volatile. I assure you, I am not usually this emotional."

Lenore's eyes narrowed as she peered into his face. He was still sitting on the floor and felt uneasy with her scrutiny.

"More emotional than usual? This is a recent thing?"

"Well, I suppose." He didn't want to admit that it started shortly after Raahi came into his life.

Lenore rummaged in a small pouch on her belt and pulled out a syringe.

"Do you mind if I take a sample of blood?" she asked.

"What? Why?" Confusion momentarily broke through his thoughts of Raahi, but he held his wrist out.

She pressed the syringe to the vein and within seconds it filled. The device beeped, and he felt the usual tingle of the small puncture being sealed. She tucked the syringe in a jacket pocket.

"What is that all about?" Jonah gestured to the pocket.

"This"—Lenore patted the pocket—"may contain proof of a drug that amplifies emotions to an unhealthy level. If it has been given to you, which sounds very likely, we can synthesize an antidote for...well...others who may have been given the same drug."

"How? I haven't been to the palace for days."

"Withdrawal symptoms include extreme mood swings. Had any of those?"

Jonah nodded reluctantly, though he still thought it was from his newfound feelings for another woman, not a drug.

"We will take care of that. Don't eat any of the palace food. If you receive a package from someone named Delilah, it means the test was positive and will contain everything you need to counter the effects safely. Understand?"

Jonah nodded again, unsure at how he felt with an outsider taking control of his life.

"Good. Now give Quinn all your records, erase anything having to do with Raahi and"—she stepped close to him, so he would look her in the eye—"go to the palace. Tell them that you need to take all the cameras offline to purge the system of the virus, and that it will take a day, maybe two. Dismiss any reviewers and monitor everything yourself. The prince is going to feel threatened when the princess returns and may become reckless, an opportunity to catch him in an unsavory act."

"But Raahi..."

Lenore lightly gripped his arm. "Jonah, if you truly wish her to be happy, this must be done. She, and you, have a duty to your people." He stared. She pressed on. "Your primary responsibility now is to return to your job as Chief Reviewer. Watch everything you can. Sleep in there if necessary. If you see anything at all that might threaten the princess, you must let me know immediately." She held out a private communicator.

Jonah lifted his chin. He would do everything he could to protect Ra—no, it's Maya now. Even if it meant letting her go. He reached out and gripped the communicator tightly.

"You can count on me."

Moments later, they had all they needed except one final, important piece of information.

"Jonah," she asked. "Who is completely trustworthy at the palace?"

He considered for several breaths and came to a grim conclusion. "I'm sorry to say that the only one I can completely trust is the king. And Lavan, but he has no power. I know my second in command Ginette would support me over anyone else, but I have no idea of how much she would trust a stranger."

"Thank you," she said. "I am sorry how it all turned out, but it's for the best. Our plan will be set in motion first thing in the morning, so you need to be in place long before then."

"I understand." They left, taking everything he had of the only woman he had ever loved. He'd go to the palace soon. But for now, he began to make his own plans to help Raahi any way he could. Even if he might never see her again.

Chapter Sixty

"We will speak only to the King," said Diarmin. He was sitting in an office within the palace, a disguised Raahi in a chair next to him saying nothing. Her hands, pale from skin-changing gloves, shifted on her lap, and she kept tossing her blond hair. The security guard sat at his desk across from them, shifting paper around. He kept glancing at the young woman, but it was obvious he was attracted to her, not because he suspected her identity. Diarmin knew they would have no chance getting through with a hologram, so they gave Raahi a wig and makeup so that she looked nearly as pale as Lenore, especially next to Diarmin's dark skin.

Raahi had practice at hiding so nobody suspected the demure, self-effacing woman was the princess. Or the companion pretending to be the princess. He resisted a groan. One could go crazy with all the deception. He supposed he should think of her as Maya, but she was still Raahi to his mind, and he decided he would stick with that.

"An audience with the king must be scheduled in advance, and there is no possibility of a private audience..." the man was saying for the third time.

"Look, we know there is a private chamber, with absolute protection for the king. It is extremely urgent—"

"Do you have a piece of paper?" asked Raahi in a voice that somehow perfectly mixed innocence and seduction. Diarmin glanced back at her, eyebrows raised and hoped he appeared surprised.

"Oh, um well..." The security guard rummaged around in a desk drawer, and Diarmin suppressed a chuckle. She had obviously used that throaty voice in the past given how well it flustered the young man. He handed her the paper with a silly smile on his face.

"And a pen, please?"

"Yes, yes, my apologies." He fumbled a pen from another drawer, and then she scrawled a quick note. She folded it once and carefully placed it in the hand the guard held out. She used her other hand to gently close his fingers around the paper. His face reddened as she lightly touched his arm.

"It is urgent the king reads that as soon as possible. I know you must have the ability to accomplish that and if you do, both the king and I would be very grateful."

The man's chest puffed out. "I can do that. I swear it will be done." He left as fast as politely possible.

"Nice," murmured Diarmin. She shrugged, and he got the feeling that though she might be good at getting what she wanted, she didn't like doing it. Diarmin didn't know what she had written, but she had assured him earlier that it would spur the king to meet them.

Slightly less than an hour later, they were ensconced in the private audience chambers. Feeling naked without any defensive devices, Diarmin focused on the room. They were seated in two hard wooden chairs. Two similar chairs say in opposite corners, with one very large, cushioned chair with wide arms on the other side of the room. Between them, dividing the room from top to bottom, was a force field that Diarmin looked upon with envy. It was obviously top-notch and would allow absolutely nothing through. Not even sound, he guessed, eyeing the speakers near the ceiling on both sides of the field.

A door on the other side of the room opened, and the same security guard entered, then held it open for someone else. The guard looked directly at Raahi, clearly wanting her to know that he had done exactly what she had asked. She smiled at the guard, but then Diarmin heard her catch her breath as the king entered. The security guard bowed himself out as the king slowly made his way to the chair. He simply stared for a long moment, brows lowered, mouth in a grim line. Finally, he pressed a button on the arm of the chair, and the speakers crackled to life.

"So. I am here. You will tell me the meaning of that message before I have you imprisoned for your actions."

Diarmin was stunned at his angry reaction and, not knowing what had been written, went ahead with the plan.

"Your Majesty. I come to you with great news, but I had to speak only to you because there is also a dire threat. I have located something that you very much would like to have. The problem is that others are also searching, and it is not safe to reveal without being assured of protection."

The king's impassive face revealed nothing of his feelings. "Well?" He flicked his fingers in an impatient gesture.

Diarmin glanced at Raahi. She removed her wig and gloves and quickly cleaned the makeup off her face with a cloth she'd kept in her pocket. The king's reaction was instant as he bounced to his feet with indrawn breath almost exactly like hers had been when he came in.

"Hello, Father. I've finally managed to return home."

***

"Sit down, Mom," said Quinn as he sat on the hotel bed, legs stretched out, reading a book. "The maids will clean the room, and you're making me jumpy."

"It should have been me, not Diarmin." She continued making her own bed and started on the dishes left from their breakfast.

"Like Dad said, your face is too well known thanks to that spectacular rescue and subsequent posted reward," said Allison, eyes never leaving the screen of her own personal computer at the desk. "Besides, Dad signaled that everything is fine, going as planned." She kept clicking and peering intensely.

"Yes, and we all know what happens when it's too easy," Lenore replied sourly, more than a little annoyed that her children were acting calmer than she was. But she wasn't used to being the one who stayed put while others did the dangerous work.

"What could happen inside a palace?" He turned a page. "They are probably doing better than we are. Better food, better beds."

"Inside a palace where who knows how many people are working for the prince or the slave organization." She deposited the dishes outside the door and looked around for something else to occupy her time.

"Aha! There it is." Allison chuckled, and Lenore came to stand behind her. "It's amazing how accurate this 'rumor' of the lost princess coming home is."

Quinn snorted. "Yes, amazing when you are the one who 'leaked' the rumor, Allison."

"What bothers me is that none of the information we 'leaked' about the prince has been reported. On any of the news feeds," added Lenore.

"Well, maybe they have a silly superstition about defamation of their rulers or something," said Allison.

"More likely the information is being covered up."

Lenore frowned. "At least the princess is less likely to conveniently disappear now that the public knows she has returned. The only problem is that the organization's contact at the palace is aware of what is being attempted."

"Don't worry, Mom. Jonah's watching and will let us know. And Dad can take care of himself."

"I still think I should be there."

"Mom?"

"Yes, Quinn?"

"Can I ask you something?"

"Of course."

Quinn closed his book and swung his legs down, so he was sitting on the edge of the bed. Sensing the seriousness, Lenore sat on the other bed, facing him, waiting patiently as he gathered his thoughts.

"It's about Dad."

Allison turned in her chair to face them.

"What about him?"

"Well," said Quinn. "He's been different since...after... after we got back from...Lord Timatay's house." Now Allison slipped off her chair and climbed to sit cross-legged on the bed next to Quinn. This action showed Lenore that the two had discussed this and were worried.

Lenore knew what they were getting at but tried deferring. "That was a very trying day. He is probably still feeling the effects of the stress."

"But you went through even more, torture and stuff," added Allison. "And you haven't acted differently."

"And...back on the ship," Quinn bit his lip but continued. "I accidentally overheard you and Dad talking. Dad said, 'Seventeen years, two months and three days, to be exact.' What was he talking about?"

"I think that's something you should ask him," said Lenore.

"From what little I heard, I feel that it would upset him if I did."

"It would," said Lenore, more to give herself time to think. Should she tell them? Could they handle it? Would it change their opinion of their father? If she did tell them, it wouldn't alleviate the worry; it might make it worse.

"Please, Mom," said Quinn. "We need to know."

Allison nodded.

Lenore knew she should discuss it with Diarmin first, but this couldn't wait. After all they had been through these past weeks, she felt that they might be able to handle it. And if she didn't tell them, they would likely try to find out on their own and that would be disastrous. Hoping she wouldn't regret it, she spoke.

"That time that your father was talking about seventeen years ago. It was the last time that he killed someone."

***

Diarmin was restless and beginning to feel trapped. The tests on the tattoos were successful. The implants he had so carefully inserted within the ink were another item of proof. It should mean that he was free to go, but they kept finding reasons to keep him there. They wouldn't even let him retrieve the body of the companion from the city where he had hidden it. Instead, they had insisted that he tell them where, and they should be on their way back now to conduct more tests. He knew any test they could do would pass, but even if it didn't, Diarmin was sure it wouldn't matter. The king was convinced she was his daughter, even becoming angry at the people who questioned the story of her capture and sale. Diarmin's interview had been more of an interrogation, and they kept asking the same questions over and over as if to catch him in a lie.

Well, he was lying of course, but he was an old hand at fabrication, so he stuck with his story. Yes, he, and fourteen others, had been hired by a security agency to assist in the rescue of slaves. No, he hadn't known of the reward, but it wasn't uncommon with rescued slaves. It was part of the agreement with the law officers of the agency that the hired men get any rewards when they returned the freed slaves. Yes, he had done so on several planets. No, he hadn't wanted to retrieve the body of the companion, but Maya insisted and promised more money if he did. And so on and so on.

In between questions and testing, Diarmin was kept in a very comfortable sitting room with food and beverages whenever he wanted, entertainment available, reading, video, whatever. It was quite luxurious, and there were a woman and man by the door "for his protection." He knew they were watching him and not going to let him leave.

He tried to distract himself with various entertainment cubes since Maya was off with the king again, but he couldn't shake the feeling that something was very wrong. He wandered over to the food selection again, not hungry just bored.

"If I'm here much longer, I'm going to get fat," he said to the guards, but they didn't move a muscle. "Maybe I should get a workout. Got a gym anywhere nearby?" Again, silence. "Never mind, I'll find it." Diarmin walked toward the door, and they moved to stand in front of it.

For a wild moment he considered taking them both down just to show them he could and wipe the superior looks off their faces. But that would not be wise, so he took a step back, grinning as charmingly as he could.

"I suppose I can do sit-ups right here." He grabbed the fancy rug from under the table and dragged it toward a clear spot, trying hard not to think about his reaction to two guards just doing their job. He didn't "take down" people anymore and hadn't felt the desire to in a long time. It helped that Lenore had done nearly all the ass-kicking for years. He focused on the exercise to purge some adrenaline.

He had only got to thirty-two sit-ups when the door opened, and Maya came in.

"We have a gym, you know," she said with a light laugh. Diarmin got to his feet, appreciative of the outfit she was wearing, a soft, pale blouse with flowing sleeves and matching loose pants. They had only been here a few hours and already she looked regal.

"My faithful friends thought it better for me to exercise here," he said, waving his hand to indicate the guards.

Maya looked at them and frowned. "Wait outside, please."

Now there was a reaction. "Uh, Your Highness," said the woman. "We are supposed to…"

"You can guard as well on the other side of the door. I don't want strangers staring at me while I eat."

"But—"

"I think I am safe with the man who rescued me and brought me home," she retorted, deliberately misunderstanding. She lifted her chin. "Out!"

They both bowed and left. When the door closed, Diarmin chuckled.

"You didn't take any time fitting in, did you?"

She snorted and waved the sleeves a little. "I am very unused to this type of outfit. It even reminds me of certain clothes I was forced to wear…"

Diarmin knew what she meant, but she shook it off quickly.

"We need to talk."

"Oh?" he asked, eyes flicking up toward the camera.

"We'll take the chance." She lowered her voice and indicated the couch. They both sat, heads close.

"The king is so overjoyed at my return that he will not listen to my warnings. He speaks of keeping Hahn as the heir even after I am confirmed and crowned, at least until I produce offspring."

She grimaced slightly, but Diarmin wasn't sure if it was the idea of the prince still being heir or having children.

She continued with a slight frown. "He ignores the information we have uncovered, even concerning the drugs he has been given, and I don't know what to do. It almost seems as if he's losing his mind, but he is still logical, just dismissive."

"Remember that the drugs amplify emotion. Right now, he is happy you are home, and that emotion dominates all others, including self-preservation." Diarmin lowered his voice to a whisper. "He could also be concerned about spies and not tipping his hand. We need to act faster. By now, some of the details of the prince's collusion should be hitting the presses." He picked up the control for the entertainment system and spoke in a normal voice. "Shall we watch some news while we eat?"

But what they saw took away their appetite.

***

The children sat on the bed, saying nothing concerning their father. Lenore could tell they had thought such a thing but hoped she would reassure them it wasn't. They were thinking hard, and she let them process it all.

"So, when you mean kill, it was self-defense, right?" asked Allison. Her pleading eyes made Lenore glad she could confirm that it had been self-defense. The actual story was much more complicated.

"But you said, 'the last time.' There were other times?" asked Quinn.

I was hoping he wouldn't catch that.

"Look, kids. Your father was a very different man when I met him. He had a dangerous job and, well, the truth is that he didn't like who he was and what he did, so he changed, became the wonderful man he is today."

"What was his job?" asked Quinn.

"We don't have time to discuss this now, we are in the

middle of an assignment. The only reason I told you is that I can see it was bothering you, and you wouldn't stop until you got answers. I have confidence that you can handle what I told you, but you also need to understand that it is difficult for your father to face his past. When we have the time, we will all discuss it together, as a family. But for now, you have to let the matter drop."

"But—" they said simultaneously.

"I said, drop it. Don't make me regret trusting you with this private information. And remember, that is *not* who your father is anymore. At all." That seemed to work but distraction was in order. "Ok, back to the newsfeeds."

Reluctantly Allison returned to her computer, but Quinn had another question.

"Have you ever killed anyone, Mom?"

She should have known he wouldn't let it go. "You know what I used to be."

"I know," he answered. "But after you left the Xa'ti'al?"

"I'm sure it was self-defense, too," said Allison with certainty in her voice.

Lenore's mind flashed back to Quinn's rescue and all that had happened. She didn't want to lie to her children, but she also didn't want to take away Allison's youthful idealism. She compromised.

"Self-defense, yes. No more discussion now. Minds back on our mission."

Quinn took his computer out of the bag and returned to his position on the bed. Lenore did her best to follow her own orders and shoved away the memories of the bodies lying on the floor, especially the one that had had the shield bubble.

She turned on the public viewscreen in the room. The broadcasts were all about the return of the princess and how she was providing proof. Her story of being captured and sold into slavery was quite the tale. Speculations abounded, and Allison commented with a giggle that soon there would probably be dozens of stories in books and videos, people putting their own fictitious spin on such a tale.

Lenore was about to switch away from a program of a man and woman intently discussing how the fashion industry would be affected by the princess' return when a strange sound came from her pocket. It was a high-pitched whine that ended in a squeal that rather hurt the ears.

"What in the world was that?" asked Quinn, sticking a

finger in his ear.

"I'm not sure." Lenore reached into her coverall pocket and pulled out a private commlink.

"That's linked to Jonah's," said Allison. "Is he trying to contact you?"

"No, that would be a beep and flashing light. This light is solid. I think that indicates that the commlink has been destroyed. That has never happened before."

"Uh, oh. I think I know why," said Allison. She pointed to a live newsfeed that said it was coming directly from the palace.

Lenore and Quinn gasped and commented simultaneously.

"Uh-oh."

***

Jonah tossed another empty energy drink container into the recycler and absently watched the flash as it was reduced to molecules. His tired mind tried to think of how they would be reassembled with some sort of replicator, but he gave up. He'd been watching the prince for hours, but nothing happened at all. He accidentally fell asleep for a while early that morning, but rewinding the tape showed Hahn still in bed at the time.

Shortly after that, a package had arrived from "Delilah" that contained several energy drinks and a note to enjoy them in the order in which they were numbered. The first one he drank slowly, waiting for any negative effects but when it was done, his mind was more focused than it had been for days, despite his fatigue.

He reached for drink number three and glanced at a different screen. There was Diarmin and Raahi, the palace programs descrambling her appearance. Their heads were together on the couch, and they appeared to be talking intently. Jonah had been sneaking glances of her whenever he could despite the pang every time he did. He turned up the feed to listen, but only caught the trend of the conversation. The king didn't believe her that the prince was up to no good. Quickly Jonah erased the evidence and cut the line to the sitting room they were in. Now no one else could listen in. He'd heard all he needed to.

He sat back in his chair, staring at the camera that was outside the door to the room Raahi was in so that he would know when she left.

I have to do something. More than just erasing video. Maybe I can think of other ways to help now that my mind is clearer.

Three pulses against his wrist was his only warning. He looked at another screen and saw the prince approaching the Reviewing Room with a huge mass of people behind him, filling the corridor. Jonah pulled out the private commlink, but then realized he wouldn't have time for a message. Instead, he tossed it into the recycler. The reassuring flash came at the same time the door was flung open.

"Good afternoon, Your Highness. What can I do for you?" He bowed low, hoping he looked surprised and harmless.

Prince Hahn snapped his fingers at two burly men beside him and pointed to Jonah. In one fluid movement, they grabbed Jonah and had his arms restrained behind him. As they shoved him toward the door, he felt binders tighten on his wrists.

The prince exited, and Jonah was pushed out right behind him. His shock was compounded by the flashes of light in his eyes that could only be from news crews.

The prince turned back to him, his eyes triumphant and bearing regal as he said, "Jonah Wilkerson, you are hereby arrested and charged with treason."

"Wha—?" he began, but a jab to his solar plexus by one of the guards robbed him of breath.

"Quiet, traitor," he growled in his ear.

The prince turned to address the crowd.

"This man is responsible for many crimes against the government. He has conspired to have an innocent girl impersonate the princess and has been leaking false information about me and other key people in the government." He held up a large viewer that the crowd could see. "I can prove the videos given to the media were falsified so that I appeared to be unfit to take my place within the council." He turned back to Jonah. "As Reviewer, you were in the perfect position to create these lies and find an imposter."

"I have no idea—" Jonah began, but a shake from the guards silenced him. Clever, clever prince, to find a scapegoat. Jonah decided nothing he could say at this point would help.

"No idea? What about this?" The prince angled the screen he held so that he and the press could see it. It was a very poor picture, obviously off a distant camera, probably private security. Despite the poor quality, it appeared to be himself entering a restaurant. He suppressed a groan when the prince hit a button that now showed Raahi's entrance. He knew it was a fake because a real video would have been scrambled. But the false video was excellent, and there was nothing he could say without revealing the highly-specialized scrambling tech. The prince continued his accusation.

"You were seen going into this place and shortly after, so did the woman who is claiming to be Princess Maya. While you didn't leave together, there were only five minutes between departures. Going separate ways fools nobody."

Jonah couldn't believe it. That small video would ruin everything, especially when the looks on the newspeople's faces showed they believed the prince. He had to do what he could to convince them otherwise.

"A coincidence." He lifted his chin and tried to look perplexed.

"Oh?" taunted the prince. "How about this?" He zoomed in on the picture of the false Raahi, settling on her right hand. "No tattoos." He turned to the crowd. "I have the statement of a local tattoo artist admitting he was paid an enormous sum to ink the false tattoos."

"That's not true!" Jonah struggled, but the guards held fast. He felt a stirring of hope when a woman in the crowd spoke up.

"What reason would he have to do such a thing?" she asked.

But Jonah's hopes were dashed when the prince looked back at him with a triumphant smile. "Jonah didn't want to give up his position."

"But he could have a job anywhere with his security experience."

The prince looked at the man who had commented, then nodded at the guards. Their grip on Jonah tightened, and Hahn tore open Jonah's shirt to reveal his tattoo.

"He didn't want to give up his position as the Betrothed of the Princess."

Pictures clicked and flashed, the reporter's eyes shocked and angry. Jonah knew he was doomed. The prince knew exactly what he was doing.

"Take him away."

The worst part was that he knew he had failed Raahi.

Chapter Sixty-One

Diarmin watched Raahi out of the corner of his eye during the live newscast. Her face was completely devoid of emotion, but her hands, partially hidden by her flowing sleeves, gradually clenched into fists.

As they watched him being led away, Diarmin switched off the video.

"We need to leave, now."

That got a reaction as she leaped up out of her chair, fists still clenched at her side.

"I can't just abandon—"

"There's nothing you can do for him now. You will be the next target, and we don't know who to trust." His eyes flicked to the cameras to show that now they had no idea who was manning the security.

She calmed down, and Diarmin envied her well-controlled emotions, trying to ignore the fact that his own adrenaline was firing up.

"Very well," she said. "What do we do?"

"I think it's time for plan C."

Raahi's eyes widened and nostrils flared slightly but she nodded. "Fine. But first I need to see the king."

"That's not—" A beep interrupted them. Had to be Lenore. The only reason she would risk a transmission is if she saw the broadcast. "Hold that thought." He thumbed the receiver. "You saw?"

"Plan C?" Lenore's voice had the calm-tension that meant she was worried.

"Yes. Heading out now." He thumbed it off, but not before he could hear Allison's voice faintly in the background.

"Plan C? Isn't that the dangerous one?"

The communication ended before he heard his wife's response, and he turned back to Raahi. She was ready with the argument he had put on hold.

"I know that's not part of the plan, but he can help."

"I don't think..."

"Look, it's my life that will be in the most danger with this plan, and I am going to do it my way."

Diarmin knew it would be useless to argue, and if she had an idea of something that would make it less dangerous, he was all for it. He nodded, and they left.

As soon as the door opened, the guards snapped to attention. Diarmin tensed, but she was faster.

"Accompany us to my father." Without waiting to see if they followed, she began walking with Diarmin right behind her. Fortunately, the guards hadn't been in the room to hear the broadcast, so they didn't doubt her authority. The halls, this far from the security wing, were quiet.

As they reached the king's rooms, she turned to the guards. "Wait out here."

"But, Your Highness," began the woman who was evidently the higher-ranked, ignoring Raahi's eye roll and sigh. "It is against policy to allow a non-approved..."

"I think my father's personal guards will be able to deal with anything."

"I am sorry, but I cannot allow..."

"Fine," she cut her off.

Diarmin was sure that Raahi, like himself, was becoming aware of a distant commotion and had to hurry.

"You, come in," she said, pointing to the fellow who hadn't spoken. "I have reason to believe the king's life is in danger, so Lieutenant, you must guard this door and not let anybody in. Understand? Not a soul. That's not a request, it's a command."

"Yes, Your Highness," she said, snapping to attention yet again.

Diarmin admired Raahi's quick thinking as they entered the outer room of the king. As soon as the door closed, she locked it and turned to the other young guard.

"I am sorry, Louis. I'll explain later." With a quick motion, she struck a nerve point on the man's neck, and he fell to the floor unconscious. Diarmin reached for the stun stick still clutched in the guard's hands and tested his pulse to make sure he was fine. As he hid the stick under his jacket, Raahi continued to the bedroom and entered with no hesitation.

Both of the king's personal security guards brought their weapons to bear, actual guns, not the stun sticks that the rest of the palace security had. But they lowered them when they recognized her. The king was seated at his desk, working on a pile of papers and data pads.

"My dear Maya, what are you doing here?" he said.

She ignored him, approaching the guards instead. "Ila, something is wrong with Louis. Please check on him." She locked the door after he left.

Ok, getting rid of another guard is good, but now we are trapped behind two locked doors, so how are we going to get out of the palace to initiate plan C?

She turned to the older guard, slightly gray around the temples but still in prime condition. "Jagjit. As a child, I watched you personally risk your life twice to save the king. Once, taking on the wild rhino on safari and second, charging toward that crazed citizen who attacked him and earning a severe wound to your leg. I know I can trust you to protect the king, no matter what happens."

The man nodded, but the king had his own comments. "Now, Maya. Don't let your imagination..."

"Father, I am not imagining anything, and you will soon see what I am talking about. My life is also in immediate danger, and I need to leave." She had to raise her voice over his protestations. "Only for a short while. This man and his companions have initiated a brilliant strategy that will ensure my safety, but I need your help."

"I don't think..."

"Father." She put a hand on his arm. "Please. I know what I am doing and am not a child anymore. But"—and here she grasped his right hand in hers, lining up the tattoos in that extremely intimate bond—"if this works, in only a day or two I will be back forever. You can sing me the old lullabies like you used to every night, and we will remember the days when life was simpler."

The king folded her hand to his chest. "Very well, dear. What do you need?"

"First, you will listen to this plan and what you need to do. Second, Jagjit needs to move the bed so my friend and I can use that private passage behind it to escape."

***

Lenore sat at a table in an open spaceport cafe, slowly sipping her drink. Her arm was slung casually on the chair back, which allowed her line of sight to be directly on the stairs that led up to the second floor. The large bag next to her feet looked like simple luggage but instead contained everything they needed for Plan C. She had just retrieved it from a storage locker, stashed earlier in case it was needed in a hurry. But they'd had plenty of warning from that broadcast by the idiotic prince. The children were safely back on the ship, and she was relieved to have made it to the rendezvous before Diarmin and Raahi. Just as she began to worry, she saw a familiar blond wig rising up the escalator. They were arm-in-arm, as if a couple, and she was surprised at the strange pang of jealousy at seeing the two laughing together.

When they reached the table, Lenore showed them the globe that disrupted any electronics. Immediately, their arms disconnected, and the jealousy vanished as the façade dropped. Lenore was mightily impressed with the girl's ability at disguise. She'd had Lenore's instincts convinced they were a couple. She would have made a good Xa'ti'al, she thought, then instantly regretted it.

"So, what took you so long?" she asked as they seated themselves.

"I had to change. My outfit would have been easily tracked. The hair was a risk, but we hadn't much choice. Speed is necessary."

"Don't dismiss your actions so quickly," said Diarmin. "Lenore, you should have seen her. On the fly, she created stories and excuses for downed guards, established herself yet further as the princess, gaining not only her father's conviction, but his primary bodyguard's trust as well. And, to top it all off, led us out a secret passage to escape the palace without being seen."

The jealousy returned a little with Diarmin's obvious admiration of the girl. But a closer look showed his slightly flushed face and fevered eyes. *He has been fighting adrenaline again.*

Raahi waved her hands, distracting Lenore from her sudden surge of concern for him.

"Stop. It was nothing and certainly not 'on the fly.' I always have an escape route planned. Time is short. Let's get this in motion."

Despite her pesky emotions, Lenore herself felt more admiration for this tough girl. She was glad they were all on the same side.

"Okay then, let's get to the room and dig in." She stood, hefting the bag on her shoulder and placing the globe back in her pocket. Raahi's arm curled around Diarmin's again and this time, the silly, simpering look she gave him didn't spark a reaction in Lenore. She knew that the girl was all business and quite clever.

This might just work out, she thought, and headed

down the escalator behind the two.

***

The next morning, the city was all abuzz with the announcement of a press conference by the king and council. It was to be in the amphitheater just outside the palace where such public conferences were usually held. Even though the occurrence would be transmitted globally, crowds had already filled the seats and plenty more were standing, flooding out into the halls. Extra security was brought in to maintain order, but there were no disturbances at all. The people were eager to finally hear confirmation or denial of all the abounding rumors. Conversation and gossip were wild. A common field worker, scarf covering mouth and nose against the press of people, wended his way through the crowd, listening to the wide variety of speculations.

"I heard the princess was found near death on a planet which had no technology."

"I heard the so-called princess disappeared after the arrest."

"Well, my brother does the laundry for the head gardener, and he said that she was arrested and thrown into the dungeon."

"Don't be ridiculous. There aren't dungeons anymore."

"If she was caught, why would the prince be so furious? Didn't you see that last 'cast offering a reward for information to her whereabouts?"

"That's just a cover-up."

"I think the whole thing is nonsense, all created to hide the facts that nothing in our government ever gets done."

"Hush your usual rantings. There's the king!"

Any further conversation was drowned out by the cheering of the people. No matter what individual opinion was, they all loved the charismatic king. He smiled at the crowd and cameras, but his entire demeanor was melancholy. His loyal bodyguard, face, but not name, known to the public, walked directly behind him, eyes scanning the audience. The rest of the council filed in, and they all took their seats. Prince Hahn took his usual seat at the end of the table, his companion next to him.

"Turn the volume down, Quinn. That cheering is too loud. It's messing with the recordings."

"Hush, Allison," he whispered, trusting the noise of the

crowd would hide the communication. Perhaps he needed a subvocalizer like his mother. But it would be difficult for him to mention it to her since he wasn't really supposed to be here. "We will need the sound when they start speaking. They are quieting, no more contact from you, please."

"Well, watch your scarf. It keeps drifting in front of the camera."

Quinn shook his head. Allison always needed to get the last word in. But he tucked the offending scarf firmly behind his ear where the camera was set, looking like a simple old-fashioned, and quite cheap, communications device.

After all were seated, the king stood and held his hands up for silence. The fact that quiet was instant showed their respect for the monarch. He spoke clearly, his voice reaching all in the audience and the cameras that broadcast to the entire planet.

"I apologize for the unexpected conference, but I felt it was necessary to fill you in on the facts. It is true that yesterday a young woman was brought to me who seemed to be the long-lost Princess Maya. However"—he paused and briefly closed his eyes as if in pain—"even though the proof had convinced me, late last night Prince Hahn showed me all the information he discovered in the possession of the traitor, my Chief Reviewer. Yes, it is true he was formerly the betrothed, and he cruelly used his insider information so that the woman appeared to have personal knowledge of me and the palace." He shook his head sadly, and sympathetic murmurs ran through the crowd. "I was wrong to place my trust in them, and I'm embarrassed to admit I was duped completely. But the fact that she ran away the moment this was all uncovered only confirmed suspicions."

The volume of the crowd rose intensely as the king appeared to deflate.

"That's not true!"

The young woman who cried out was shoving people aside to reach the side platform where citizens usually addressed the council. It looked like someone else was helping her clear the way, and she climbed the few steps to the microphone.

"I ran because I feared for my life, Father," she said. The crowd gasped.

"Arrest her!" yelled Prince Hahn.

"I invoke the right to a public trial," she said loudly

into the microphone. It was enough to halt security and silence the crowd.

"Don't be ridiculous. Traitors don't deserve a trial," said the prince.

The crowd gasped again, and this time a couple of the councilors followed suit, staring at the prince. One councilor was brave enough to speak up.

"But, Your Highness, that is one of our most treasured laws. Anyone may ask for a public hearing, although it has been over a hundred years since the last time anyone has done so."

Indeed, everyone in the crowd was now talking about how nearly all the trials end in a guilty verdict. Quinn tried not to think about that dire possibility and instead concentrated on making his way to the edge where the microphone wouldn't pick up such minor chatter.

"Well, of course Councilor Behm. I only meant that it would take time to prepare, we can't do it on a whim."

"I am ready," Raahi said, her mouth firm and head held high. "I am perfectly willing to have these councilors as jury and these fine people to bear witness." Her hands spread wide to indicate the crowd. She bowed slightly to them, then turned her gaze upon the king. The murmurs now took on an admiring tone.

"If she's not the princess, she sure is brave like one."

"So very noble. And she does look like Queen Savitri."

The king sighed. "Very well, whoever you are. You have done your research well."

"I am Maya, but I knew that when I presented myself, I would be in danger from those who had taken me." There was a brief flash of light surrounding her, making her flinch slightly. She turned to address the audience, eyes sweeping the crowd.

"You see"—she flinched again as there was another flash and her eyes settled upon a disturbance—"to discourage runaways, every slave is implanted with a tiny explosive near their heart that can be activated at any time. I am fortunate that the people who rescued me gave me a dampening field to block the signal." The disturbance coalesced into two men dragging another toward the princess. "That sparkle was such a signal attempting to kill me by this person. Holding him are local security people who traced that signal when it was used on me."

One of the men holding the captive gave the device to the princess. She held it aloft. "This, with the implant, will prove my story. About the tattoos. Since it was another easy way to identify me, I was very careful about covering them up. Look!" She flung her right hand out, no tattoos showing. But then she pulled off a glove so snug that it seemed to be skin, and the crowd gasped as the tattoos were revealed. "I also have other proofs that show I have had these most of my life, and that"—here her eyes saddened—"I am sorry to say, that Prince Hahn was lied to. There was no local tattoo artist. The recordings he was given are also falsified."

The crowd's murmur increased, and a glance at the prince showed his face clouded with anger. Princess Maya held up her hands, and the crowd quieted instantly as they did for the king. She held up data sticks and readers.

"I can show you the proofs now, Honored Councilors, or display it publicly. In addition"—sadness crossed her face—"I also have proof of certain people inside the court who are working against the current government."

The crowd began another gasp but was interrupted by exploding laughter from the prince. "I have been given false recordings? Who's to say those you are holding are not also false, mocked up?"

The murmurs of the crowd were mixed. Some agreed, and most didn't know who to believe. The woman faced the prince.

"The recordings can be examined closely to determine if they are legitimate and..."

"But the specialists who do that might not be genuine or have their own agendas. Face it, imposter, it's your word against mine."

The crowd seemed to hold its breath, and there was an eerily timed swivel of heads to look back at the woman. She raised her chin, eyes locked with Prince Hahn's.

"I am willing to risk it."

"But I am not willing to trade my rightful rule to an ex-slave." His eyes quickly raked over the audience, and a slight smile creased the corner of his mouth.

"I challenge you to a duel."

The heartbeat length of silence was enough for all to hear the soft answer.

"I accept."

The tumult of noise was not quite enough to drown out Allison's comment in Quinn's ear.

"Was that part of the plan?"

Chapter Sixty-Two

It took several moments to quiet the crowd. Companion Lavan ran to whisper in Hahn's ear, but the prince pushed him away. The king spoke to his guard who immediately started speaking to all on the stage and into a private communicator.

All the while, the princess and the prince kept their gazes locked.

Quinn tried hard to sort out all the reactions, but he couldn't discern individual conversations. Some were shocked, some outraged, and some oddly supportive or even excited. He tried not to shake his head. No matter how civilized the society, there were always those wanting a fight.

"Quinn? Are you okay?" Allison sounded a bit panicked.

"Yes," he hissed. "Trying to listen to people's responses." But Allison didn't get the hint and kept talking.

"What about Mom and Dad?"

Quinn angled himself to see the two security guards still holding the man who tried to detonate Raahi's chip.

"They are just standing there, but I can't see their faces clearly to know what they are thinking."

"But what do we do?"

"Not much we can do, is there?"

"But—"

"Quiet, Allison. The king is going to speak."

After several attempts by officials to calm the amphitheater, the king stood up. When his outstretched hands did nothing to stem the flow of noise, his face reddened.

"Silence!" he bellowed. The hush was instant.

Quinn wasn't sure if it was the word or the fact that it was the first time that the king had to raise his voice that worked.

"I forbid the duel."

"You cannot, Your Majesty," said Companion Lavan. Quinn could hear the regret in his voice. "There are precedents, and the challenge supersedes the trial since it is directly related to accusations made during that trial."

Several councilors nodded, and Hahn's grin widened, eyes still never leaving Raahi's.

"One week. With swords." He tossed his head, eyes sparking.

"Your pardon, Prince Hahn." Raahi's voice was quiet but firm. Quinn admired her calm, knowing that if he were in her place, his heart would be racing.

"Since you issued the duel, I, as the one being challenged, have the right to choose the weapons."

The prince's smile vanished, and he turned to look at his companion. When Lavan nodded, he turned back to Raahi. "Very well. What do you choose?"

"Daggers."

Somehow, though the prince's expression didn't change, Quinn could tell he wasn't pleased. But he nodded anyway as if his agreement was necessary. "That will be acceptable. But still one week."

It was Raahi's turn to nod, and Quinn could sense satisfaction. "That is the tradition," she said.

Now Hahn's annoyance was obvious, and he simply sneered as he stalked out. The council, Raahi, the king, and everyone else on the platform followed suit. Quinn left quickly before the stunned crowd kept him from getting back to the ship before his parents.

Chapter Sixty-Three

Back on the ship, Quinn waited with Allison. He slicked back his wet hair and hoped he'd gotten all the dye out. As they came through the hatch. Diarmin smiled grimly at his children as he stripped off his jacket and gloves.

"Hey, Dad. Great job," said Allison. He bowed, but his expression didn't change as he went to fetch the bag that stored gear. She turned to the other who was taking off gloves and hat. "Hey, Mom. You sure make a good man."

Quinn admired her attempts to lighten the mood.

"Thank you, I think," their mother answered. "Good thing we deactivated that implant and gave her the personal shield to detect that attempt to detonate it. We captured the man who tried." She began loosening the body armor that the local security used.

"I know," said Allison. "Pow! Nice blow to the kidneys." She mimed the action.

"Excuse me?" Lenore's voice was muffled as she pulled the armor over her head, so fortunately she didn't see Quinn elbow his sister.

"Oh, um. It was on all the news channels. From every angle. We both watched." She shot a quick glance of apology to Quinn.

Quinn really had to struggle not to roll his eyes.

"I see," said Lenore.

Quinn noticed her eyes take in his wet hair. He decided on diversion tactics.

"What can we do now? The duel was not part of the plan, was it?"

Diarmin came back up the ladder and held the bag open for Lenore's gear.

Lenore eyed Quinn for a second longer, then apparently decided to drop the subject. She stowed her gear. "No. But it seems to be out of our hands now. Raahi will be protected until the duel, so her safety is assured. After that," she shook her head. "She is tough, but he is young and built to fight. Although..."

"What?" asked Quinn and Allison at the same time.

"The prince doesn't strike me as someone who would take the responsibility and actually face an enemy. I expected him to run like a coward or try to arrest her like Jonah or...something else."

"Doesn't matter." Diarmin sealed the gear bag. "Time to get our money and move on."

"No!" Allison said.

Quinn noticed his parents looked as surprised as he felt at Allison's outburst.

"We can't just leave," she said.

"What do you want to do, Alli?" asked Diarmin.

"I don't know. I...it just doesn't feel right...can't we help?"

"This is an internal matter now. We can't interfere," said Lenore.

"I know that, Mom, but..."

Quinn couldn't quite bring himself to understand how she felt. The job was done. They should start looking for the next. It's what they did. He was feeling the itch to be busy and maybe she was too. But the problem was that this job didn't quite feel finished. He shook himself mentally and quenched the doubts.

Emotions are not for the job, logic only. But there is one concern.

"How are we going to get paid if she loses?" he asked. "From what I understand, if she loses, that is proof that she isn't who she says she is and thus, no reward."

Diarmin and Allison stared as if the thought hadn't occurred to them, but the look on his mother's face before she turned away told him she had given due consideration to all the possibilities. It oddly pleased him that he was thinking professionally, like his mother.

"We should convince the king that no matter how it turns out, we found his daughter, provided proof, and deserve the reward despite an archaic ritual. There was no mention of any contingencies to the posted reward. We get paid and then go find another job."

Allison's mouth opened and closed a few times before she abruptly turned and stalked off to her room.

"She'll learn that life is not a fairy tale," said Diarmin gruffly, and he also left down the ladder, probably heading to his workshop.

Quinn looked at Lenore, a bit confused to see sadness in her eyes. She shook her head.

"Nothing we can do. What does Alli think? That we can

help her during the duel? Help her cheat? No, she is on her own."

Lenore's voice was steady, but Quinn knew his mother well enough to see she didn't like leaving it like this. He didn't answer, so she shrugged and turned. He was about to return to his room when she turned back to him.

"We'll talk later." And the way she eyed him, Quinn knew he was in trouble.

Chapter Sixty-Four

Prince Hahn couldn't sit. He paced, clenching and unclenching fists. His lackeys had followed him back to his rooms after the public assembly and pushed their way in, all babbling, varying from excitement to confusion depending on their intelligence level. Apparently, they didn't know that future duelists were supposed to be secluded. When Lavan tried to tell Hahn he shouldn't let anyone in, Hahn summarily dismissed him to his room. Now he needed to plan quickly, and while these followers had been useful in the past, they were being excessively annoying. The prince needed others.

"How exciting," said Rifkin. "A great boost to your popularity. You'll have countless admirers by the end of the day. The challenge was the noble thing to do. Very royal."

"A perfect way to make her pay. Suffer," added Thom. "How much damage are you allowed to do?"

"The council will determine the level needed for me to win," the prince said, growing impatient with their babble. "Look, I need you to—"

"What if she wins?" asked Endon softly. All three heads had snapped around at the comment. Endon looked startled but set his chin. Hahn knew he had to say it, but it still stung.

"That skinny bitch? I don't think so, Endon." He was satisfied at the wariness in Endon's eyes. He had rarely ever yelled at his followers but now was not the time for niceties. "Anyway, it doesn't matter, because I don't intend on going through with the duel. I am accelerating our plans. There won't be anyone left to care about a stupid duel. We are going to take over before then."

All eyes widened at that, Rifkin's mouth wide open and Endon's snapping shut. The gleam in Thom's eyes helped the prince decide who to trust with the next message.

"Thom. Fetch me Guard Alex Mannon. Nobody else. Inform him he is to be my attendant. Also..." Hahn strode to the armoire that contained his clothes. Rummaging behind the hanging formal wear, he came out with several data sticks. He returned to Thom.

"These are to be given directly to the person marked on each stick. Directly and to absolutely nobody else. As soon as possible." He looked Thom directly in the eye and gripped his arm hard enough to leave a bruise. "Understand? If you fail..."

Thom hesitated for only a moment. "I will do as you ask, Your Highness." He bowed low, and Hahn couldn't help but revel in the adrenaline rush.

"Tell them the messages are to be destroyed the instant after viewing, and that the timetable has been moved up."

Rifkin and Endon stared as Thom's feet hastened out the door. The prince turned to them, adrenaline still coursing through him. "It comes to this. You must go, but stay available. I may need you. You have been my allies, and I will not forget. Now, leave me."

They turned and left, Rifkin still looking confused and Endon thoughtful. Maybe they won't be as useful as I thought, the prince told himself. Doesn't matter. Child promises meant nothing to the successful leader of a coup. He could get rid of them without a second thought.

***

Raahi was trying very hard not to pace in the spacious guest suite, keeping a tight grip on her emotions. She had been led here right after everyone had left the amphitheater. Hours had passed, and she didn't bother trying the doors. They would be locked or there would be guards outside. She knew the rules of dueling well. Maya had loved the historical stories and, back then, when she had been Lara, she studied true accounts to keep Maya from running amok with her romantic notions. Raahi closed her eyes against the memories of her bondmate. Maya had been such a dreamer, always wanting to live the adventures she watched and read. Well, she got one.

Raahi tried to suppress the memories but being back at the palace made it harder. As she focused and regulated her breathing, she knew in her heart that Maya would be proud of her and would have enjoyed the idea of a duel. Raahi felt a small smile and tears threaten. She could almost hear Maya's encouragement and laughter.

A knock on the door yanked her out of the reminiscing. Chiding herself for her lack of discipline, she spoke.

"Come in."

The king's personal bodyguard entered and before he closed the door, Raahi could see two guards outside. She didn't feel any satisfaction at being right.

"Jagjit. To what do I owe the pleasure?" She smiled and bowed slightly.

"As you know, you are not allowed visitors except one attendant."

"Yes, of course. How did you get stuck with the job?"

"I volunteered."

Raahi felt her knees go weak at his simple words.

"I am honored."

"I did not do it for you," his voice kind, despite the gruff words. "The king wanted me to bring you a message and this was the only way to assure that you would receive it." He held out his hand with a personal reader. Despite the commonality of such an item, Raahi felt a pang. The last one she had seen had been Maya's.

"Thank you." She took it and Jagjit made as if to leave, but she stopped him. "If you are to be my attendant, you need to know everything, even personal messages."

His expression was unreadable as she played the message.

"My dear Maya. I am begging you, do not do this. Hahn is a talented fighter and though the duel will be closely monitored so no deaths occur, I fear he can severely injure you. As difficult as it would be to lose you again, I would rather you left so that I know you will be safe. Jagjit will see to it. I release him into your command, though I wish you still had your dear Companion Lara. She was like a second child to me, and I never got the chance to mourn her with you. Goodbye, my dear daughter, and know my heart has been with you since the day you came into our lives and always will be."

Raahi removed the stick and clutched it in her palm like she had with Maya's. She brought her fist to her chest, eyes closed. Did the king know she was really Lara? Was that why he mentioned the companion? A heartbeat later she realized it didn't matter. As a child, she had felt the love and knew she had been like another child to Nirav and his queen. It only made her course clearer, and she wondered how she could have stayed away for so long. All her previous anger and denial of who she was seemed quite distant now.

"Thank you for the message, Jagjit. Will you take one

back to my father?"

The guard nodded and pulled out another data stick, but she shook her head. "You can tell him personally. Tell him that I have been away from my duties long enough and will not abandon this one, him or our people, no matter the outcome or cost."

Jagjit's face didn't change a muscle, but his eyes showed a subtle shift. He bowed low to her, the first time ever.

"He said you might say that, and I am pleased his reading of you was accurate." He straightened. "I am to inform you that the council is deliberating the terms of the duel and what constitutes a win. You will have access to the gym only when empty and must be accompanied by me. You may request anything from the kitchens or library but no access to public broadcasts."

"I understand, and...thank you, Jagjit."

"Is there anything you would like, Your Highness?"

She laughed lightly. "I'm not the heir yet. Not until I win the duel and earn the right to claim it."

"To me you are unquestionably the heir, Your Highness."

She again fought back tears but for an entirely different reason, so she attempted to defuse the emotion.

"If I am going to be here for a few days, I will need a change of clothes. Or two."

He bowed again and left, and she felt a true smile pull her lips. She was amazed that only days before she was to duel for the future of herself and her planet, her heart felt lighter than it had in a very long time. But her smile faded as she thought about the one person who should be here. One who cared about the planet even more than she.

***

Lavan wandered the halls. Hahn had made it clear he wanted nothing to do with his companion, even as his attendant for the duel. Lavan felt he should have known that would be Hahn's response, but it hurt, nonetheless.

I tried to be there for him. I really did, but he must have known my true feelings. He also felt adrift and forgotten because the Baroness never even let him know that Maya had been found. *I started the entire process, and nobody remembers me despite all the horrible stuff I have gone through.* Lavan knew he was wallowing in self-pity, but he didn't care.

He looked up suddenly, realizing his inner turmoil had moved his feet to the one place he had felt even a little safe. He turned the handle and welcomed the sight of many screens. He was entirely surprised to see a woman leap out of the seat and berated himself for forgetting about Jonah's arrest.

"Companion Lavan? What, why..." She tried to bow but looked quite out of sorts.

"Relax. Just wandering the halls. You must be the new Chief Reviewer. Ginette, is it?"

"No, I mean, yes, Ginette, but not Chief Reviewer. I never wanted the job and responsibility, and I feel—" She abruptly cut herself off.

Lavan chuckled with little humor. "I understand, Ginette. Not easy to be thrown into the middle of a crazy situation unprepared."

The relief on her face was nearly comical. "Exactly."

Now she blushed, and Lavan realized she was probably closer to his age than to Jonah's.

"I am a bit desperate for help and thought just looking at my boss would help." She swept her hand to a monitor in the corner.

Lavan caught his breath to see Jonah.

"How did you do that?"

"I just tapped into the prison's monitors." Now she looked guilty. "It wasn't hard. They don't have a very secure system to keep out external monitoring, and the palace has clearance anyway."

"How is he?" Lavan moved closer to the screen. Ginette appeared to take his interest as oblique permission and began to talk rapidly.

"He seems to be okay. You know they take good care of people in custody, but I think he must be extremely bored. As you can see," she pointed at the screen. "He has access to public viewing, so he must know what is going on, but all he seems to do is to read the same book over and over." She shook her head. "He glances up at the monitor a lot. Probably because he has been a reviewer for so long, but I kinda feel like he is giving me encouragement. Stupid, I know."

Lavan felt a quickening of his pulse. Maybe he was trying to send a message. But how to find out without arousing Ginette's suspicions? He smiled at her.

"He might be doing just that. What book is he reading?"

"Some history. I can zoom in." She did so, and he

recognized it as a boring historical concerning past monarchies. There was a paper, like a bookmark, sticking out of the pages with handwriting on the front.

"What is that?"

"Oh, it looks like a scrap note to himself. I took a picture and enlarged it to read." She blushed again. "I am out of my league here, and I thought it was a test, but"—she handed him a picture sheet—"it wasn't anything in particular."

"May I have this?" Lavan asked. "It is a very good picture, and I know that kind of clarity with zoom is not easy." It was good enough to show what was written as well as the title spine of the book. The note read, "Remind the Baroness to read pages 34, 118, 27 and especially 58," but the last number was written in an odd block style with perfectly straight lines, no curves.

Ginette smiled shyly. "Of course, Companion."

He thanked her, but as he turned to go, she grasped gently at his sleeve.

"Companion. Can you do anything for Jonah? He is not guilty of what he is accused of. I mean maybe he is the betrothed, but I know he would never do anything to hurt the king. He loves him like a father."

"I believe you, Reviewer, but unfortunately I have no power in this situation."

Her face fell, and he was truly sorry he couldn't tell her that the picture may hold some answers if he could only figure out what it meant. "I will let you know if I hear anything."

"Thank you. I would be happy to help if you ever need something. *You* only. For Jonah."

Lavan was a bit taken aback by the emphasis. Did she know about his association with the Chief Reviewer? Or just not want to have anything to do with Hahn? Probably the latter. He smiled and nodded, then escaped out the door. He needed to get a copy of the book to see what Jonah wanted him, or the Baroness, to know.

Chapter Sixty-Five

Hours after everyone had returned to the ship, Quinn sat alone in the lounge, composing his thoughts and trying to compose his emotions as well. Allison was checking the ship's status and was supposed to join him before Mom came in.

Footsteps in the hall caught his attention and the light tread indicated his sister. She rounded the corner, eyes wide. Quinn wondered why only for a moment until he saw his mother come in a few steps after.

They sat, and as usual Lenore got right to the point. "Tell me what you two were doing there instead of on the ship like you were supposed to be."

Allison didn't speak, probably still angry about their earlier conversation. Quinn wasn't sure where to start, but he knew it would be worse to delay.

"To be honest—" he began.

"I wasn't there," said Allison.

Figures she would save herself, thought Quinn.

"Now don't lie..."

"She's not lying, Mom. She was on the ship. I was there," he said. As her head turned slightly to look at him, he set his jaw. He knew her silence and eyebrow lift were ploys to get him to talk. He was mature enough to admit it still worked. He took a breath to settle his stomach.

"I, we, didn't want to sit helpless here. I felt I needed to be there. Allison wanted to come too, but I knew she couldn't disguise herself as well." He ignored her tongue sticking out and continued. "So, I wore a transmitter that allowed her to see and hear what I did. I disguised myself as a local field worker, not even the same as earlier. I padded to look heavier, had putty for a large nose, and even grayed my hair."

"It's true. I was actually startled when I saw him," offered Allison.

"You were given strict instructions—"

"I know but hear me out. After these past few weeks, I don't think any of us can afford to stay at home. I truly felt that I had to be there, and that Allison needed to watch and be ready at the ship in case we were needed. Thankfully, nothing came of it. All the same," he squared his shoulders. "I would do it again. Better to be prepared to help and not be needed than...well...you know."

Allison was nodding vigorously, and Lenore sighed. "Apparently, you two think you can do what you want, no matter what we say. However..." She sighed again and seemed to be deciding what to say next.

"You are my children, the most important thing to me. When I knew you were safe, I could focus completely on my missions, no matter how dangerous they were for me. Now..." She took a long, slow breath. "Now I understand the stress of those who are left behind and how difficult it is to watch loved ones go into danger and being unable to participate." She looked at them with a sad smile.

Quinn was quite unnerved to see such emotion in his mother. He had known she was scared for them but had never made the leap that the fear would be a distraction. He had thought she merely wanted them out of her way, that she could do better by herself. This mission had changed her.

Lenore looked at her children, and Quinn couldn't decipher her expression. She pointed a finger at them. "Here is how it is going to be. In the future, you will be much more involved on missions, if..." Her look turned serious. "If you obey me as a mission leader, learn more defense techniques, and discuss with me beforehand what you'd like to do. The next time you pull something like you did today, acting without permission, you will be excused from missions. No exceptions."

They agreed, and she slapped her thighs. "Good. That's settled. Now, about getting in touch with the palace about our money. Ah, good timing, Diarmin," she said as their father walked in. "Your father will don his earlier persona of the rescuer and request an audience with the king. That shouldn't be—"

A beep from the lounge's console indicated someone was trying to communicate with the ship. Lenore opened a channel, routing the message from the bridge to the lounge. When Lavan's face appeared on the screen, Quinn could see everyone was as surprised as he. They had nearly forgotten about him.

"Baroness, I have a message for you from Jonah. Unfortunately, I don't understand it but perhaps you might."

"Wait, Lavan..." began Lenore, but his face was replaced with a photo. Allison hurried to the console to make her own copy while Lavan's voice continued.

"The new reviewer says Jonah keeps reading this and glancing at the camera, but I have looked at those pages and cannot figure out what he is trying to say. I am forwarding you a digital copy of the book with pages numbered exactly like his. I cannot stay on this line and will most likely not be able to contact you again. I hope you can use this information."

"We are not going to do any—" said Lenore, but Lavan had already broken the connection.

"How dare he?" said Lenore. "What gives him the right to order us around as if we were servants?" Diarmin looked like he wanted to put a hand on her shoulder, but he pulled back. Quinn was a bit frozen at his mother's outburst, but Allison didn't hesitate.

"You were saying there was nothing more we could do. Well, here it is."

"Read through an obscure book trying to figure out a specific code. And for what? What more do we get out of it?"

"We don't need—"

"Forget it, Allison. This is a business decision."

"But Jonah needs our help."

"That is the last time I wish to discuss this."

Allison's face took on a stubborn look, but she said nothing as she left the lounge. Quinn wondered if he was the only one to notice that she took the copy of the photo with her.

Chapter Sixty-Six

Hahn had already been awake for an hour and was picking at the remains of his breakfast in the suite when his attendant knocked on the door.

"Enter," he called, and then went to lock the door to Lavan's room. Right now would be the worst time for him to come in unexpectedly.

Guard Mannon, now his official attendant, entered and closed the outer door at Hahn's signal. He strode toward the prince and went down to one knee, technically a greeting only for a confirmed prince or king, but Hahn appreciated the loyal declaration.

"Your Ma—Highness," he stated. Perhaps the slip was another deliberate sop to his ego, but he didn't care. He would be called Majesty soon enough.

"You may rise," he intoned. "Inform me of your progress."

"All of the messages have been delivered successfully; all are ready to carry out your wishes at the appointed time. The package for the king has been arranged and will be delivered at your command."

With Mannon's careful wording, Hahn's eyes glanced up at the monitors in the outer suite and considered whether to take the conversation into his unmonitored bedroom.

No. Time for me to take a stand on my invasion of privacy.

"Very good, Attendant. Here are my instructions for today." He lowered his voice and turned away from the monitor, palming his scrambler on. "Fire the remaining reviewers and close down the security system. Blame the virus that Jonah never eliminated and let everyone know we will be hiring an entirely new staff soon."

The man nodded. "It will be done."

"Next, find Endon. He disappeared late yesterday afternoon, and he knows too much to be allowed out of reach. If he doesn't return, you know what to do."

The guard nodded again without hesitation.

"One last thing." Despite the jammer and low tones, he was taking no chances with this request. He pulled a paper out of his desk drawer, scrawled something quickly and folded it to give to his attendant.

"On this paper there is a name, an address, and an item I need you to procure."

The guard opened the paper and for the first time showed a bit of reluctance. "I—are you certain of this, Your Highness?"

"Absolutely, Mannon. Do as I command. In a few days, I will be the one with all the power and that item will not matter."

The other's face blanked of all expression before he bowed low. "Your will shall be carried out as you command."

A knock at the door from Lavan's bedroom interrupted the heady rush of power Hahn was beginning to feel. With annoyance he spoke to Mannon.

"Return as soon as you have completed the tasks, especially that last." The guard rose and was out the door.

"Hahn, what's up? I'm hungry." Knocking harder.

Hahn made sure to slowly turn off the scrambler, straighten his desk and tunic until Lavan knocked twice more. That will teach him to interrupt me, thought Hahn as he sauntered over to unlock the door.

***

"Dad?"

Diarmin was concentrating so fiercely on trying to fix Lenore's implant, he barely heard the soft address. He looked up, blinking through his magniglasses at the blur of wild hair he knew was Allison.

"Yes?" he asked as he took off his glasses.

"Can I show you something?" She eased into the workshop with her special hand comp clutched to her chest, her demeanor strangely subdued.

"What is it, little bug?"

The endearment usually made her smile, but not this time. He didn't like her closed expression.

"I found something. It's very important. Can you look at it?"

"Of course." He held his hand out for the pad. Instead of handing it over, she sat next to him on the workbench and began scrolling through images and documents. As the contents of the data began to sink in, he felt an unusual bewilderment.

"How did you get this Allison? And why did you come to me instead of your mother?"

"Well, Mom said the discussion was closed. She wouldn't even let me say that I had already figured out what Jonah was telling us."

"You did? You cracked the code that quickly? Without even reading the book?"

"Of course. It had nothing to do with the book. I think that was for Lavan's sake. The numbers were just his personal access codes. I knew it immediately because the last two numbers, written in block form weren't numbers at all. They were letters, his initials to be exact. Well not his initials as Jonah, but his real name. You know, SB for Sundeep Barad. The 'S' is the five and—"

"I get it, Alli. To the data."

"Ok, well, that code not only gave me access to his personal accounts, but I was also able to hack into the palace security cameras."

Diarmin opened his mouth to comment, but she was back to her old animated self and in her "explanation" mode.

"At first, I thought whoever replaced Jonah was terrible at the job. She only blocked me once, but I found another way around. Maybe she thought it was Jonah because she stopped trying. But then I saw this." She tapped and swiped at her comp until the camera showed someone coming in, forcing a woman to gather her stuff and leave. The last image was of someone reaching behind the screen and everything going dark.

"It's a good thing I saw it coming because I managed to insert a hook that helped me reactivate the system after it was completely shut down. These images," she indicated a data file on the computer, "are things that I picked up from old files and new. Now, if I'm right, it looks like we need to find someone important to tell. Maybe even the king. When you go see him."

"Is that the reason you came to me?"

"Partly. But I didn't want her to yell at me for doing something she told me not to."

"Since when has that ever stopped you?" He grabbed a twisty curl and gave it a gentle yank. "Let's tell her together then."

"Good. She won't yell at you."

Diarmin chuckled. "Oh, you'd be surprised."

***

Lenore didn't yell, but the thin-lipped disapproval was just as difficult for Allison to face. She squirmed slightly in her chair on the bridge, watching her mother scroll through all the information. She knew she had done the right thing, but she hadn't known how to convince her mother. And especially Quinn who, up until these past weeks, usually agreed with his sister on the subject. Allison concentrated on mentally urging the disapproval off her mother's face.

Lenore's lips began to return to normal, her eyebrows raising so slowly that if Allison hadn't been observing closely, it would not have been evident.

"You. Found all this."

"Yes, Mom."

"Decided which was relevant and put it in order."

"Yes."

"Despite my express wishes for you not to."

Allison looked away and resisted the urge to hang her head. "I thought I should at least try."

Her mother sighed, but Allison couldn't quite look back. Her father had said nothing. She thought he would have taken her side against Mom. Her shoulders drooped.

"Once again, one of my children has outmaneuvered me and shown me up."

Allison looked back at her mother, not quite sure what she was getting at.

"Diarmin. You have done way too good of a job of teaching our children to be highly independent and willful."

"No. I merely started them on the path. They get their stubbornness and determination from you." They both laughed, and Allison felt a huge weight lift.

"Do you know what you have uncovered my brilliant daughter?"

"It looks like a takeover plan."

"That's it exactly. Now the problem is we have to figure out who would be best to inform to keep this from happening." Lenore smiled despite the grim subject.

"We're going to help?" Allison jumped up and hugged her parents. "Thanks, Mom, Dad."

"No, I should thank you Allison, for showing me that there is more to life than money."

"But if the king and everyone around him is killed or

removed from power, we wouldn't get paid anyway," said Diarmin. Both Allison and Lenore gave him a mock punch.

"Enough," he said with a chuckle, but then his face sobered.

Allison could feel the tension rise in the room.

"How do we know who to trust with this evidence? Someone who can also help to stop it?" he asked.

"I've sort of researched that as well," said Allison as she snatched her computer back from her mother and perched it next to her station. "Jonah's records are quite extensive and if we work with his data, he has names which are listed as involved, innocent, and questionable. If we correlate that data with the most recent findings..." she began tapping and the rest of the room was forgotten as she navigated the world of computers where she was most at home.

***

"Hey, anyone else hungry?" asked Quinn as he climbed the ladder to the bridge. "Shall I fix something for dinner?"

"Dinner? How long have we been at this?" asked Diarmin, straightening up and arching his back, trying to stretch it after leaning over Allison's shoulder.

Lenore shrugged, and Allison kept tapping away, most likely not even hearing the question. Diarmin envied their ability to focus so completely.

"At what?" asked Quinn.

"Oh. Right. Sorry. We got really distracted, but I'll fill you in on what Allison found," he said.

Diarmin quickly summed up the plans of the prince and his followers. "And it has apparently taken the rest of the day to figure out which people to approach. A few trusted people in law enforcement, and less than half the councilors are a sure thing, but we can watch the questionable ones to see which side they might tend toward."

Quinn said nothing but stood with his arms crossed.

"Hey, it's not like we left you out on purpose," said Diarmin. "We just got swept up to the exclusion of everything else. Including food."

"Yes, thank you, Quinn, for the reminder to eat," said Lenore. She turned off her computer and reached over to turn off Allison's as well. Allison looked as if she were going to swat her mother's hand away but evidently thought better of it.

"Might as well eat," she said. "Ferreting out all the guilty parties is gonna take an entire day of working together with the proper authorities that we have already identified."

"And did we ever get a response regarding our message?" asked Quinn.

Diarmin wasn't sure if he was entirely mollified.

"Uh," he tapped on the console, embarrassed that he had forgotten about that. "Not yet."

"Don't you need to talk to the king even more now, because of this coup?"

"Yes," said Lenore and Allison.

Quinn rolled his eyes. "If you had involved me, I would have helped. My suggestion is for Allison to do one more hack."

***

Raahi swept her hair back out of her face. A long shower would feel wonderful. She felt awkward working out under the eyes of the guard, but it was the only way out of her room. The last few days had felt more like when she was a slave rather than a princess-to-be. Nice clothes, good food and always someone watching. The only difference was nobody was trying to...she shunted the memory aside. Memories were useless here. She needed to concentrate on the duel.

She began to strip off her clothing to let the water wash away the past, but a bleep from the communicator startled her. Jagjit had just brought her back from the gym. What could he need already?

"Yes, Jagjit?"

"I am sorry, but this is not Jagjit."

The low voice was obviously female and held a bit of humor. Raahi knew it belonged to the woman from the ship.

"Ah, hello. Didn't expect to hear from you again. Figured you would have left by now. Or are you calling from somewhere else?"

"No. We are still here. Having trouble getting in touch with the king for an audience. Is there any way you can help with that?"

What more could they want? *Probably something about money.* "I am allowed contact with only my attendant, but he can get a message to the king. I will pass along the message that you need to speak with him."

"Is he someone you trust? I mean, truly trust. We have some sensitive information that the king needs to see, and we know of no one who is trustworthy enough to make sure he gets it."

Raahi blinked a few times, confused. "What information?"

"It's better if I do not say anything over the communicator. Again, do you trust this attendant?"

"The only person I completely trust is in jail," she said, the words coming out a lot more bitter than she meant them to. "But I would say, next to the king, this Jagjit is honorable and completely dedicated to Nirav."

"Good. Please tell him to reply as soon as possible to the message from the man who rescued you. Within the hour if possible. If he needs persuasion, tell him his life depends on it."

"Does it?" Raahi wasn't prepared for the jolt of fear that last sentence induced. She'd gone soft and was annoyed at herself. "You need to tell me. I should know."

"Again, not over the line. And you have something very important coming up. You cannot get distracted. Know that if we can speak with the king, all will be fine. If you arrange that, you can rest easier."

Easier? But not completely. But what could she do? The powerless feeling simply amplified her past again. "I will pass it along. Be prepared for a contact, probably from Jagjit himself."

"Thank you, Maya. We won't contact you again, so we wish you luck in five days. I don't know the prince, but I know you and, if I were a betting person, I'd lay odds on your success."

"That means a great deal, coming from you. Take care of my father." She reached over and closed the connection. It took a few moments to compose herself before she contacted Jagjit. She was quite touched at Lenore's confidence in her. The last time she'd felt support like that was from Maya.

***

"Good job, Allison," said Lenore. "I think we should be expecting a message soon. How about erasing any evidence of the communication?"

"Already done, Mom," said Allison who hadn't looked up from her station for hours.

"Then what are you doing now?"

"One more thing I should have done days ago."

Chapter Sixty-Seven

The duel was only two days away, and the prince looked like he was ready to tear out the walls. He prowled around the suite from sunrise to sunset, stopping only to eat and talk to his attendant. He had insisted Lavan stay and help him prepare for the duel by looking up all the accounts of former such contests, so Lavan was feeling a bit stir crazy as well.

"Nervous?" he asked the prince.

Hahn paused midstride to whip his head around. "What?" His eyebrows were pulled into frown lines with his lips pressed thin.

"About the duel. I know I would be."

The prince gave one humorless laugh. "Of course you would. You can't fight at all."

He continued to the other wall and abruptly turned. "Where is my attendant? He should have been here hours ago."

"He was already here twice today. What else could you possibly need him for?"

"None of your business."

Lavan turned back to his book at Hahn's snarl. He had been going to offer to go find him, but instead buried his nose inside his book. Both needed to get out. Lavan knew the prince would start taking out his frustrations soon, and he was the only target.

"You could call him. Ask to go work out, practice." Lavan held his breath, unsure of the reaction. The prince was not skilled with daggers and if he wanted to win, he should go to the gym.

"Good idea," the prince said gruffly. "Surprised you came up with it." He stomped to the communicator and barked into it that he needed to see his attendant to take him to the gym.

Maybe now Lavan could get out for at least an hour or so. He hadn't been out since he saw the new reviewer and was glad he managed to sneak the communication to the Baroness. He hoped she figured it out but, unless he could be alone, he would never know.

One knock was all that was heard before the prince yanked it open. Someone Lavan didn't know was standing there, arm still raised.

"Your Highness." He bowed low. "Extreme apologies, but your previous attendant has become very ill and had to be hospitalized last night. I am Van Hart and will be your attendant until the duel." His eyes stayed on the ground obviously expecting a reaction.

Lavan looked at the prince whose face was flushed, hands fisted.

"Very well then. I wish to go to the gym for a workout."

"Again, apologies, but it is currently occupied by your opponent. We will have to wait until she is finished with the facility."

Hahn's face purpled, fists shaking, and a strange gurgle came from his throat. Lavan stood, afraid the prince might actually strike the attendant.

"Prince Hahn, I have found another interesting situation in the book about a previous duel that might be helpful." He had found it earlier and didn't say anything, but now seemed the right time. Lavan took a deep breath and held it.

"Go away!" the prince yelled at the man. "I will not require your services." He slammed the door, and Lavan released his breath as quietly as possible. It took several moments for the prince to regain his composure. He finally turned to the companion.

"Well? I hope it's better than the last useless thing you found."

"Here," he opened the book to the proper page and began to explain the odd precedent that was presented. Was it his imagination or was there fear in Hahn's eyes?

***

The meeting with the king had gone very well, and though he was upset that he had been caught unaware, he didn't seem too sad or shocked. With the weight of the monarchy, everyone involved in the coup had been quietly taken into custody, including those outside of the palace. Some were even working with and within the slave trade, and authorities were confident that interrogations would reveal more criminal activity. And yet, it wasn't over. The king was arguing with the remaining councilors, reduced to about half its former size.

"I don't see why this duel cannot be called off as well. The prince's guilt is obvious, and we have the evidence to prove it." King Nirav was still feeling the effects of detoxification of the long-term drug but was nearly restored to his robust self of twenty years ago.

"Your Majesty. So far, the public appears to remain ignorant of the arrests, focusing completely on the duel. If we cancel it, they will question why, and the coup will likely be discovered. That would be damaging for our government. And the monarchy. If the weakness were revealed, the next election would call for everyone's replacement and then where would we be?"

The king glared at the council leader but said nothing. He was astute enough to pay attention to Loyoa's advice, even if he didn't like it. It was fortunate that the leader was on his side. If he hadn't been, the coup might just have succeeded. Another chimed in.

"Also, the duel was a challenge against evidence in the first place. Traditionally, it could be argued that no matter if there is more evidence, the accusation results from the same source, the one who rescued the princess, and so the duel must still be fought."

"I am beginning to dislike the word 'tradition,'" grumbled the King.

"Nevertheless, the duel must be allowed to happen. Every precaution will be taken to ensure the princess's safety."

"I don't like the idea of hiding the truth from the people, but I agree that they are shaken and divided enough." The king felt a wave of sadness at the situation, but he was also determined to take back the control he had let slip away. "The duel will be the distraction, and the truth can be shared later when we can say we were successful in stopping a massive coup, and measures were put into place so that it can never happen again."

There were nods from nearly all the councilors.

"But what if the prince wins anyway?" asked a very junior member. "Doesn't that mean he is proven right and all charges are dropped?" He wilted under the glares of the rest of the council, but the king held up a hand to forestall any discussion.

"You are correct to bring that up, Councilor Tam. We will figure out what to do if the time comes. I have faith in justice and my daughter."

The king knew that the duel was only a face-saving way to preserve the monarchy's reputation. The prince had used it only to delay the acceptance of Maya as heir in order to instigate his coup. But the unaware public would see it as more important than it really was. In the old days, duels proved a future ruler's strength and will, and people hadn't lost that basic instinct. A public duel would appeal to the primitive inside them all and sway the populace, the same argument that kept a monarchy on a space-faring planet.

But not everyone knows the details about the tattoos, and those proofs will make sure that the prince, even if he manages to win, will never rule. It will be much more difficult, but I will make certain of that.

***

The day of the duel dawned bright and clear. Lines of people had begun forming outside the arena the day before and now stretched on. Such a spectacle hadn't been seen by anyone living on the planet. Many businesses were closed and the airports, trains, and any other stations with travel had been swamped with people wanting to see it live. Each person was patient with the extensive personal security searches, knowing they would be witnesses to a historical moment. The rest of the world who weren't so lucky could view it on any station due to over a hundred cameras already in place.

The Kelton family was not bothering to try to watch in person. They were seated in the lounge on the ship, watching the large screen. Allison had several feeds from news centers and also a private feed from the palace where the action was truly going to take place.

Diarmin, following Lenore's advice, had counseled the king to not hold the event in a public place, to pipe it in holographically if possible. Fortunately, one of only three venues that could accommodate the holographs was close to the palace. Only people sitting in the first few rows might be able to tell it wasn't truly live.

The family idly watched various news stories on different broadcasts, but their primary attention was taken up with the feed from the palace. The courtyard had been set up with a ring for the duelists and chairs on the side for the few who were allowed close. If Lenore guessed correctly, the large chair in the center would be for the king. The two chairs at either end would be for the prince and Raahi and their attendants. But there were only four others, two on either side of the large chair. Too few for councilors so it would be interesting who sat in those.

"How soon?" asked Quinn. He looked the most relaxed, and Lenore was concerned at his lack of interest.

Allison couldn't sit still and piped up from her seat at the console. "They are all still in their rooms. It's supposed to start in a half hour. The king is talking with his bodyguard, the prince is knocking stuff around, and Raahi is sitting with her eyes closed. There are a few people gathering outside the courtyard who look like councilors and maybe broadcasters, but that's all I can see."

"Why haven't you cut your hack into the palace's security?" asked Diarmin seconds before Lenore was going to.

"They still don't have anyone in there and therefore nobody to track me down," said Allison. "Anyway, if they did, I would know and be off in a nanosecond. I already have a kill command in place." She sounded smug, and Lenore just shook her head.

"Fine. Keep an eye on it, although if there hasn't been an intrusion yet there probably won't be now," said her father.

Quinn pulled out his personal comp pad and began to fiddle with it. Lenore opened her mouth to say something to him but thought better of it and turned back to the multiple screens. A hand on her knee made her realize she was jiggling it. She smiled at her husband.

"Don't know why I am nervous. It's not me dueling."

"That's probably why. It is harder to watch someone else do all the action," he said. Lenore looked sharply at him, knowing he wasn't only talking about the duel. "And worse when you are unable to help in any way."

She narrowed her eyes and nodded. "Exactly. I keep thinking the prince is going to find some way to hurt Raahi, er, Maya. Daggers require a closeness that will give him an excuse to grapple and use his strength."

"There will be doctors. They can treat nearly any kind of dagger wound quickly, even a heart stab."

"I know, I know," she said, not mentioning that she knew several ways to kill a person with a knife despite the best medical expertise available. She crossed her arms. "I don't like being a spectator."

Diarmin gave a snort and turned his attention back

to the screen. *At least he seems to have settled. No more twitching at every small suggestion or hint of violence.*

"Here they go," said Allison and there was no more conversation.

Chapter Sixty-Eight

Raahi followed behind Jagjit, breathing slowly. Oddly, her stomach was not in knots like she had thought it would be. She knew it was because she was finally doing something, not dependent on technology or other people for her future. This was it. This was for Maya, and she wouldn't fail. Briefly she wished for that dagger which had been given to her on her eighth birthday. The dagger had not only been to help with her bodyguard duties toward the princess, but had symbolized her Companion's Bond. But that weapon had disappeared when they were taken.

It won't be long now, soul sister. This will be all over, and you will be at rest.

Either way.

They entered the courtyard which was set up as an arena. Strange, no audience, only a multitude of equipment and cameras on all sides, and a single row of chairs. Jagjit led her to one of two chairs on an end of the oval denoted for the fight, but she was surprised when he didn't sit in the other.

Raahi let her gaze drift. Jagjit was meeting the king who entered with four others, two men and two women. She recognized one as the Council Leader, but the others were unknown. As the king sat in the largest chair with Jagjit standing behind him, she noticed guards at both entrances to the courtyard. Her gaze continued until her eyes came to rest on the prince and his companion taking their seats directly across.

He looks annoyed. Nervous, arrogant, excited, any of those I would expect, but not irritation.

The king stood as everyone sat.

"Before this foolish tradition begins, we have a new attendant for Maya." He lifted his hand toward the entrance, and Raahi's heart gave an extra beat when Jonah walked in.

"The Chief Reviewer's innocence was proven conclusively, and charges dropped. As soon as he returned, he asked for the honor of being attendant during the duel.

Jagjit will graciously resign his position if Maya agrees."
He faced Raahi. "Is this acceptable?"

Not trusting herself to speak, she nodded and was surprised to feel joy as he came to sit in the chair beside her. Her hand ached to reach out and hold his, to tell him how sorry she was for all he had endured, but she knew now was not the time. She settled for a direct look into his eyes. Dark circles shadowed under them, but the slight curve of his lips and nod of his head reassured her.

She looked back as the Council Leader stood. Time to clear her mind for only the task ahead.

The man looked sad but straightened his shoulders and addressed the equipment as if speaking to an audience. She was glad there wasn't a crowd. It made it easier to concentrate.

"The rules have been decided on. The bout will be won when a, erm, contestant reaches fifteen points. Points will be awarded according to the severity of"—he swallowed, obviously uncomfortable with the idea—"of wound. Touch landed, one point, blood drawn two points, and so on. The judges"—he indicated the men and women to the left and right of the king—"will determine the points as the bout progresses."

The Council Leader held out his hands, one to the prince and one to her. They both stood and approached the center, stopping to face each other about six feet apart.

"Under no circumstances is there to be an attempt to permanently maim or"—he swallowed again—"kill. Is this understood?"

Raahi nodded, but the prince was looking around, the annoyed look sliding into anger. *What or who was he looking for? An audience? Has he no idea of the hologram equipment?*

For the first time she was seeing him up close, and it hit her how young he truly was. Not even eighteen.

"Prince Hahn?"

The prince looked at the councilor. "What?"

"Do you understand the rules?"

He waved his hand as if dismissing the man. "Yes, of course." His eyes locked on Raahi and a chill ran through her. This was no youngster in front of her. The glint in his eyes and twist of his lips let her know he would not hold back at all. She faced him squarely, refusing to be intimidated. He might be physically stronger, but she had faced much worse and survived. She would now.

The prince's eyes narrowed, evidently taken aback. *Probably not used to anyone standing up to his bullying ways.*

"Select your instruments," the Council Leader said with a wave of his hands sending them back to their seats. "When you are ready, the bout will begin."

Raahi took three steps backwards, not looking away from Hahn, before she turned to go back to her chair. While she had been facing the prince, a table had been placed at each end with beverages and various things a duelist might need. Three boxes lay in front, lids lifted and displaying several daggers in each.

"Your 'instruments' Ma—, um, Milady," said Jonah. She smiled at him, forgiving him the near slip with her personal name.

"Don't know why he couldn't say what they are. Weapons."

Jonah's face went blank, and she could see the tension around his eyes. "Be careful. I know he is ruthless."

"I can see that. Worry not, all will be well." Maya had always said those formal words like a chant. They gave her strength now. She turned to the boxes. They were allowed to pick two, so she hefted each to get the feel and weight. Some were balanced poorly, and some appeared to be merely decorative. Only one box held daggers that were any good, and she suspected Jagjit had a hand in their selection. Finally, she selected two that fit her hand with a good balance for wielding and throwing.

She turned back to indicate she was ready, and her eyes lit on the prince lounging as if bored. Raahi knew she hadn't taken that long. It was just a calculated affectation on his part. She shut any reaction down.

The councilor walked to the center and motioned them in. They stopped the same distance apart.

"The bell will sound to begin the match. When it sounds again, the fight must cease. There will be breaks, or you may call for a halt up to three times." He placed his right palm down between them and asked if they were ready. They both nodded, and he lifted his hand as he spoke.

"Begin."

***

Hahn immediately rushed to close with the imposter. He wanted to get this show over with as soon as possible so that he could find and punish those who had failed him. He'd show the cowards how to take charge. He let his anger give him momentum.

The woman only raised her dagger and stupidly faced him. This would be quick. Too bad he couldn't end it sooner with a dagger in her chest. At the last moment, she brought the dagger in her right hand toward his face. As he ducked and lunged, she pivoted backward to her right behind the outthrust hand and brought her left around to score a scratch on his arm as he surged past her.

"One point, Maya." Even the announcer's voice was irritating, thought Hahn, annoyed that he had allowed her the first touch. As soon as he turned he moved to close again. The bitch wouldn't get another one like that by him.

He closed in only two steps and as she held her dagger out again, he feinted and ducked under her guard for a direct thrust. A wound to the stomach wasn't fatal and should score several points as well as weaken, even if she would be patched up. But he was shocked to feel his dagger slammed to the side and another score on his shoulder.

"One point, Maya."

Damn. He'd thought his loose clothing might hide some of the touches, but evidently the judges were quite observant. Now he pulled back to circle and evaluate. He eyed her up and down, which usually worked to make others nervous. He noticed her snug clothes, close to her body but not constricting, hair bound up on her head out of the way. She'd boldly removed her gloves to show her tattoos. Ha. That wouldn't give him pause at all. If anything, it energized him. She met his circling with mirroring strides, knives moving in patterns. As he noticed her graceful movements, he suddenly realized that she would be a tougher opponent than he believed.

So, he would take it up a notch.

He drove in again with both daggers extended, weight forward on his toes. As she brought her daggers up to defend, he kicked out with his leg and connected with her knee. She staggered, and he turned her own trick on her by bringing his right dagger toward her face and scoring a deep stab on her hip with his left. He had been aiming for her stomach but despite her knee, she'd managed to twist away.

"Three points, Hahn."

He smirked. *That'll show her.* He didn't bother to wipe the blade but circled again, waiting for another opening.

This time, when she rushed him, he was ready. He knew his height gave him the reach so, as she aimed low, he backed up, then stretched to block the blade and use his greater weight to pull her to the ground delivering another stab to her shoulder.

"Three points, Hahn."

A voice, not Maya's, cried "Halt," and the bell sounded. He strutted to his seat where Lavan waited with a drink. What weakness to call for a break with a couple of stabs. He had this wrapped up.

***

Raahi strode to her seat, eyeing Jonah angrily.

"Why did you call for a halt?"

His eyes widened. "You need those wounds looked to. And a drink."

"I'm fine, and I only get three halts. You wasted one."

"My apologies. It won't happen again." He avoided her gaze and handed her an electrolyte mixture designed to replenish and energize. She didn't need the extra boost; her adrenaline was already maxed. She ignored Jonah as he slapped self-adhering bandages on her shoulder and hip. She was angry at herself. She had thought the prince would stick to the formal knife dueling like she started with. But he scored with hand-to-hand techniques, not dagger fighting exactly, but not illegal either. Adding the dirty fighting like the kick to the knee was the last straw.

He had made a serious mistake. And she would show him exactly why.

***

Lenore watched, unable to look away, even during the break. She had always hated knife fights. Calling it a "duel with daggers" may sound noble but, as the prince showed, it was barely a step up from street fighting. She hated this helpless feeling and would rather be the attendant whispering advice in Raahi's ear.

"I'm glad Jonah is there for her," she said softly.

"You're welcome," said Allison. "I knew the evidence would exonerate him. And with the king's influence, he was sure to be released quickly. So..." She waved at the screen. "Yay."

"Yes, well done as usual Alli," said Lenore, trying to

forget how much her family had interfered in the planetary politics already. "It's my fault he was arrested in the first place. If we had let him in on the plan, he might have been more prepared."

"Too late for that now," said Diarmin. "Remember that for next time."

Lenore's eyes narrowed at her husband, wondering what he was thinking, but his gaze was on the screen. Allison was oblivious to anything other than the duel.

"So why isn't she winning? I thought she would be tons better than the pampered prince."

"I don't think she was quite prepared for the prince's underhanded methods," replied Lenore.

"She is now," said Diarmin.

Startled, Lenore glanced at him. "Why do you say that?"

"It's in her eyes. I know that look."

Lenore peered at a monitor on the right that showed a close-up of Raahi. Sure enough, Lenore recognized the fire and determination that was also tightly controlled insanity. She'd seen that look before. When she had first known Diarmin. Before they were married.

"It's starting again," said Quinn.

Lenore turned her thoughts away from the past and back into the present.

"Come on, Raahi."

***

"Come on, Raahi," Jonah whispered. He had seen the scars and knew she was capable of winning, but the fear gripping his heart made it difficult to breathe. Most of the fear was for her, but some of it was because she had closed herself off. From him. Their first tentative greeting had vanished in a heartbeat. He was afraid that no matter the outcome, she might never be open with him again.

The two circled and traded feints without closing. Hahn was becoming more conservative, inviting Raahi to engage, but she was too clever to take the bait. She kept just out of reach, not closing at all. The growing impatience on the prince's face showed her tactic was working, and he abandoned his defensive posturing. Instead of parrying the blow, she grabbed his wrist and twisted it and herself to push him past her. She slammed her elbow into the back of his head, showing she wasn't ignorant of or afraid to use the same sneaky moves the prince had. Before she released his wrist, she scored a small stab and then a deliberate deep scratch down the entire length of his shoulder blade.

Hahn cried out in pain, and Jonah realized it was the first time either duelist had made a sound other than the grunts and exhalations of any type of exertion. It was several moments before the announcement. "One point, Maya. Four points, Maya."

"Four?" snarled the prince. He looked like he was going to challenge the judges but evidently thought better of it. The score was now seven to six, Maya's favor.

Hahn faced her again, the blow to his head obviously bothering him as he started to reach up to touch it but pulled back quickly as she took advantage of the distraction to charge. They came together with a frightening flurry of blows and metal scrapings of multiple attacks and parries. Suddenly, with another grab and twist, Raahi unbalanced Hahn and he fell hard onto his back, breath rushing out with an 'oof.' His left dagger went flying and Raahi managed another stab to his thigh before he rolled out of her reach.

"Three points, Maya."

Ten to six.

She moved to score more before he could get up, but he had another idea.

"Halt!"

Raahi's dagger stopped midswing as the bell chimed.

Jonah marveled at her restraint. Since Hahn had called the halt, if she had continued the attack and scored, the points would have gone to him instead. She straightened, took one step back, then deliberately turned her back on Hahn as if she no longer feared him.

Jonah could see the anger rise in the prince's face, but it was overshadowed with a hint of fear. The emotion was plain to read. For the first time, the prince thought he might lose.

As Raahi approached, he looked at her. There was no anger or a suggestion of any emotion on her face. He gave her a towel to wipe away sweat and realized where he had seen that look on her face before. Whenever she remembered her past. What the memories were didn't matter. She knew she had to go back to that unhappy place in her head in order to win. His heart clenched again as he realized yet another sacrifice she was making. For her sister, Maya. Raahi was a true companion to her in every sense of the word, and he fell in love with her all over again.

***

As Lavan approached him with a towel and drink, Hahn snatched it without comment. He needed to rein in his anger but was finding it difficult. At least Lavan had the sense to keep his mouth closed as he slapped bandages on Hahn's wounds. His business-like attitude as he served helped to center Hahn. *It's my turn to put her off balance.* He could play just as dirty as she could.

"Places." The Council Leader came to the center again, palm down. He looked at one then the other and Hahn swore the look favored Maya.

How dare he!

His gaze swept over the few people watching. *They are all on her side, rooting for her.* This is why they had kept it from being fought with a live audience, so he would be cut off from his admirers.

He'd show them. He could not be replaced, and they would all see.

"Resume." The Council Leader barely had time to back away before the prince leaped to tackle his opponent. They went down hard in a tangle of limbs and Hahn struggled to get a touch, but she managed to block each strike, roll away, then leap to her feet.

"Two points, Maya."

What? Where? How? Hahn had felt nothing and was about to accuse the judges of cheating when pain blossomed on his cheek. He swiped it with the back of his hand which came away bloody. He snarled.

"How dare you!"

With no warning, he flung the knife straight at her chest. Hahn took sadistic pleasure in the gasps from the watchers and listened for the delicious thunk of the blade hitting home. But amazingly, Maya managed to twist fluidly so that it didn't even leave a scratch. Hahn froze in disbelief only for a heartbeat, but it was enough for Maya to close the distance. He brought his left hand up in defense, but a snap of her right leg connected her foot with his hand and sent the dagger flying. As her leg came down, the left one rose, her foot catching him directly in his chest. He crashed hard, head hitting the ground with enough force to daze him.

He blinked twice and fought to stand but couldn't move. It took a moment to realize she was straddling him with her knees on his arms, pinning him. Only three points, one large wound would do it. She raised the knife high and, for a moment, he thought she was going to deliver a heart stab. He might die, but at least he would win.

Only a hair from his chest she stopped. Her grin was wild and triumphant. She pricked him three times on his arm.

"Point, point, point, Maya. Total fifteen."

The prince had lost.

***

Noises of celebration came through all the monitors, but none were heard since the Keltons were cheering just as loud. Even Quinn had a smile on his face as he watched his sister jump up and down with glee.

"I knew it! I knew she could do it. The good guys always win!" Her face was flushed as she flopped back down on the couch. "And justice is served."

Lenore chuckled, but Diarmin turned back to the screen.

"Something's happening."

"Turn the sound up on the feed from the palace, Allison. The highest gain."

She complied, and they could see people beginning to congratulate Raahi. First, Jonah gave her a towel and water. Then the judges and councilman shook her hand.

The prince was still sitting on the floor, staring, apparently having not yet processed the fact that he had lost. Lavan was trying to console him, hand on his shoulder and urging him to drink something.

Lenore happened to be watching the prince's face as the king approached and embraced Maya. Suddenly Hahn yelled, the sound tortured and insane. He scrambled to his feet then reached behind his back and pulled out something hidden there underneath his clothing. Allison let out a small scream as Hahn pulled out a needle gun. Highly illegal and extremely rare, the weapon was designed to shoot a projectile that would penetrate any shield including some of those designed for ships. He fired at the princess, but all the guards were too far away to do anything, and those surrounding her had frozen in shock at the prince's cry.

One person, however, was quick enough to throw himself in front of the gun as it was fired. With an anguished cry, he crumpled as the guards reached the prince and disarmed him. But the weapon had done its damage.

"No," whispered the prince as he stared at his companion lying before him, gasping for breath. "You were supposed to be my friend," he said as tears began. The guards bound the prince's hands behind his back, but he didn't resist as they led him away. Jonah scrambled to Lavan's side and tried to stem the flow of blood.

"Hang in there, Lavan. You'll be fine." He yelled toward the others staring in shock, "I need a doctor!"

"No, Jonah. I don't want to...betrayed the bond."

"No, Lavan, you saved the Princess. And the king. You're a hero."

Lavan coughed and the blood ran faster, pooling around the kneeling Jonah. "Take care of the princess."

"No, Lavan!" Jonah gathered him up in his arms, but the boy went still. "You're the bravest of us all. Don't go. It's okay now, you're free."

Jonah held him in his arms, urging him to stay. Lavan tried to speak once more, then his body went limp. The doctors that had been on call gently took him from Jonah. They ran instruments over Lavan as Jonah watched, still kneeling, his entire body radiating helplessness and sorrow.

"I'm sorry," said the medic.

Jonah bowed his head, not bothering to stem the flow of tears. A hand on his shoulder shifted his blurred gaze upward. Princess Maya was looking down on him, tears also in her eyes.

"He will be honored," said Maya. Standing behind her, the king nodded in agreement.

"All will know of his loyalty to the government and the people." He raised his voice to the shocked crowd. "Know this. Lavan gave his life selflessly to save Maya. We shall never forget his sacrifice." The king knelt to honor the boy one last time, not even flinching when his knees sank into the pool of blood.

The Keltons watched, horribly saddened but deeply moved that people on every monitor and screen around the watching planet knelt as well.

Chapter Sixty-Nine

"Hey, Alli." Quinn tentatively stuck his head in his sister's room. "Can I come in?"

Allison shrugged, sitting on her bed with arms wrapped around legs pulled up to her chest.

Since that was a huge improvement on "Go away!" Quinn felt encouraged.

"How are you doing?" he asked. He pulled her computer chair close to the bed. Her terminal was turned off and that bothered him even more.

"How do you think?"

"Do you want to talk about it?"

"What's to say?" Her eyes were glued on an imaginary spot on the wall.

"Okay." They both sat, not talking, but somehow it wasn't uncomfortable. The minutes ticked by, then suddenly words slipped out of Quinn's lips.

"That was the first time," he said quietly.

"What?" she said.

"The first time I saw someone die."

Her head turned toward Quinn, but her eyes didn't quite focus on him. He continued, trying to reach his sister.

"In the school on the previous mission, I was checking the data I had pulled from the fake janitor when he was shot. I didn't see it happen."

"What about when you were, you know, when Mom rescued you?"

"I didn't see anything. When I..." He swallowed, surprised he was still shaken at the experience. "When Mom got me out, I saw some people on the floor, but it didn't sink in that they might be dead. They might not have been, just injured. I was focusing on getting the kids out, so the images were pushed back into my brain until...until we saw Lavan." Quinn's voice cracked, and he couldn't finish.

"I know." Tears began to drip from the corners of Allison's eyes.

"I'm just glad we weren't there."

"How can you say that?" Allison uncoiled herself from the bed.

"At least watching it on the screen made it seem, well, detached. Had we seen it in person..." Quinn shook his head.

"But we might have done something. Might have stopped it."

"Allison," Quinn spoke softly, wanting to get through to his sister without hurting her more. "There were guards and lots of people in that room. There was nothing we could have done had we been there."

It was Allison's turn to shake her head, tears flowing freely. She tried to talk between sobs. "Mom might have. Or...I should have watched...security cameras closer... how did he..."

"Don't you think I have been torturing myself with the same things?" Despite wanting to be kind to his sister, Quinn's voice was rising along with a fire in his chest. "You never met him, Alli. I spoke with him, sat next to him, as close as I am sitting to you now. He's close to my age, or...was..." His voice broke, and he put his head in his hands. Allison crawled to the edge of the bed and put her hand on his knee.

"Mom told me she looked at the previous recordings and saw nothing. Nothing, Alli. Where, when, and how he got the weapon is a mystery. She also said it happened so fast that even she couldn't have done anything. It was amazing that Lavan managed to stop Hahn from killing Raahi." Quinn swallowed, fighting back the memory again. "Lavan is being honored even more by the king, did you know?"

Allison sniffed. "Really?"

"Yes. There's talk of a memorial day in his name, a statue in the courtyard where it occurred and stuff like that."

"That would be nice."

They sat in silence for several moments.

"But it's still not fair," she said softly.

"No. It's not." Quinn stood and shoved the chair back toward the computer table, wishing he could shove away thoughts as easily. Allison seemed better, but now horrible memories that he had suppressed because they had a job to do were resurfacing.

"Thanks, Quinn."

He attempted a smile. After all, he was the big brother and should appear strong. "Anytime, Alli." He held up a hand for a high five, but somehow it turned into a brief squeeze. As he left, he saw her heading for the computer. Yes, she would be fine.

Outside her door, Quinn nearly cried out in surprise when he saw his mother on the other side, hidden from anyone in the room. The anger he felt at the invasion of privacy lessened when his mother silently mouthed the words, "Thank you."

The anger lessened, but it didn't vanish.

Chapter Seventy

Jonah entered the garden, his feet unerringly carrying him toward the far corner to where the newly-confirmed princess sat. Her hands were constantly clasping and unclasping on her lap. She caught sight of him and immediately stood. He took three strides toward her, then dropped to one knee.

"Your Highness, you summoned me?"

"Stop it. Stand up. You don't ever need to..." She pulled at his arm to emphasize her words. He stood and let his eyes drink in the sight of her.

"Sit, please." She sat back down and indicated the bench to her right.

He sat, watching her constantly moving hands and waited for her to speak.

"I'm not used to bare hands." She looked out at the gardens and gave a humorless laugh. "Seems I am more at home in the slums fighting off thieves than here all dolled up." Her voice dropped, and she looked back down at her hands. "We are out of range of cameras here, yes?"

"Yes," he said.

"I wanted to apologize to you, Jonah. Or should I call you Sundeep?"

"You don't—"

"Arrg. Don't tell me I don't have to, you idiot. I want to."

She looked at him with the old fire in her eyes, and he felt his heart lift. He knew Raahi was still in there somewhere.

"Everything happened so quickly. There was no time for us to talk, and I regret that. You need to know exactly what happened and why. You said there will be no more secrets between us." She smiled. "I completely agree."

Hope suddenly flared within him, but he blocked it, not wanting to risk another break.

"I am not really Princess Maya."

He smiled gently. "I know."

She stammered. "How did...I mean...I thought..."

He took her right hand in his and lightly traced the

tattoos. "These."

She closed her eyes briefly at his caress but didn't pull away.

"People tend to forget about these bonds. And very few even know about mine." He touched his loose shirt over his heart, not quite bold enough to show it. "When we were...intimate...it didn't resonate with yours as it would if you were the princess. It was designed to match hers very closely. I was only very briefly aware of that as my mind was on other things." He smiled at her blush. "And to be honest, I had put it out of my mind until much later. When I had time to think about it." He released her hand, suddenly aware that it wasn't appropriate.

"I am sorry for not including you. We thought it would protect you. Cutting all ties would hide your involvement." She shook her head. "Guess that didn't work."

He shrugged. "It turned out well. Mostly." An image of Lavan popped into his head and he felt the grief again.

It was her turn to take his hand and squeeze it briefly. She released it to take something from a bag next to the bench that he hadn't been aware of.

"Here." She shoved a personal viewer into his hands. "This is why I had to do what I did."

When he made no move to activate it, she did it for him.

He did a double-take when he saw her face. But...wait. The halting breaths and slightly higher voice showed it was Maya.

"I have asked Menot to record this and give it to you after I die." He watched the rest of it without comment and looked at the woman next to him when it was over. Tears were running down her face, ruining the perfect make-up she had had for her confirmation.

"It's ridiculous. I have cried more this week than I have in years."

Jonah wanted to envelop her in his arms but held back.

"You see why I had to become Maya?"

He nodded, feeling her slip away again. He looked down at the ground, fighting back his own tears. Damn, he thought he was getting over her.

"She always thought of her planet, her people. You are just like her. I should never have excluded you from our plans. You almost had me convinced, before I saw her message. It's why..." She stopped, grabbed his chin firmly and made him look her in the eyes. "It's probably the main reason why I love you."

His heart skipped a beat and the words seemed to roar in his ears.

"What?" escaped from his lips, and he berated himself for his complete lack of dignity.

She laughed, and the light sound lifted his heart. "I love you, you idiot. You are the only person besides Maya I have said it to. I loved you as Jonah and, if you agree, I will love you as my husband."

He couldn't respond. He was immobile with the emotions flooding up from the soles of his feet and threatening to burst out of his chest.

"Aren't I supposed to ask you?" he stammered.

She laughed again, and this time he joined in.

"Too late. So, give me an answer. Will you come with me and help me take care of our planet and people?"

He stood, taking her with him, and swung her around in a circle, kissing her as passionately as he could. As he released her, he whispered in her ear.

"Yes, my princess."

Chapter Seventy-One

"So, as you saw, Raahi, or we should say Princess Maya, was confirmed this afternoon and renamed the heir."

The family was gathered in the lounge for the first relaxed evening in days. Lenore went on. "The council is mostly replaced with trustworthy candidates, and I do believe there is a wedding in the future."

Allison smiled, and Lenore felt her heart lighten at that expression on her daughter's face. "Yay, for Jonah," she said. "I liked him. What about the prince?"

"Prince Hahn is to be stripped of his title and imprisoned, though he is in shock at the death of his bonded. Doctors are concerned for his sanity, but the bond didn't seem as strong as the girls', so he will recover. And they are no longer going to have those tattoos. The king himself said it was an outdated tradition that only led to heartache."

"Did we get paid?" Quinn asked suddenly.

Lenore figured Allison's surprised look must mirror her own face.

He cleared his throat and looked like he hadn't really meant to say that out loud. "Well, that's why we took this mission, isn't it?"

"That is why we took the mission," she reluctantly admitted. "However, there's a slight snag."

"What snag?" asked Diarmin as he came in, wearing fresh, clean overalls, an oddity since he always seemed to have grease somewhere. He plopped down on the couch and looked around, either unaware of the sudden tension or trying to defuse it.

"The snag is, we didn't exactly get what the reward posted."

"But..."

"How could—"

Both Quinn and Allison started their protests, but Diarmin was the one who interrupted them before Lenore could.

"The royal assets were frozen," he said. "Pending a

lengthy investigation into who might be corrupt and who might not be. Sensible, but not beneficial to us. And technically, it was Lavan who posted the latest reward so there are arguments against any obligations of others. However, we did get quite a lot in, I guess you can say 'goods and services.'" You know this past week the ship was serviced by the king's personal mechanics to install our grav plates, and just this morning we received free refueling and supplies. Plus"—Diarmin held up his forefinger—"and this is the bonus. Raahi, or I should say Princess Maya, has given us the specs on the program that deciphers the scrambling tech they have."

"Nice," said Allison. "That could be very useful."

"You mean we don't get money?" asked Quinn.

"Well," answered Lenore, "we have the rest of the money given to us by Jonah that will go a lot further now that we don't have to pay for resupply. When the assets are unfrozen, we can come back to collect, although that might be quite some time from now. And don't forget, we have the eternal gratitude of a planetary royalty. No small thing."

"That's it? After we risked our lives, got captured, stole the dead body of a princess, faked the identity of another princess, and affected the politics of an entire planet?"

"Quinn..." began his father, but it was Allison who answered.

"What we did was the right thing to do. Taking down the bad guys, it's what we do."

"No, it's not. We took the job to find the princess, and now we don't even get paid for that. It's not fair," Quinn said and stormed out, not even waiting for a response.

Allison sputtered, face turning red.

"Now, Allison, calm down. Quinn has a point."

"Huh?" asked Allison.

Lenore tried to defuse the tension with a smile.

"We did break a lot of laws and bent a few morals."

"But all in the cause of good."

"Of course, Alli. Quinn is just feeling the let down at the end of a mission. You know how tense I get after a dangerous assignment."

Allison's lips lifted in a half smile. "Yeah. We don't usually say anything, but you do get a bit snippy. Can I look at that new descrambler program, Dad?"

He held up a finger. "As long as you find another job first."

"That will take all of two minutes."

Diarmin rolled his eyes and told her the name the program was logged under, and she was off, a kid with a new toy.

"I envy how quickly she can focus on the good and put the bad out of her head," said Lenore.

"Yes. Her romantic notions won't last much longer, though. She's growing up," said Diarmin. "Now, Quinn. What's up with him?"

"I am not sure, but I think he is still trying to suppress his traumatic experience by focusing only on the business side. You know, being professional to hide emotions."

"Sounds like someone I know." He playfully waggled his eyebrows at her.

She pretended not to notice.

"He will probably be worse when he realizes that, in addition to all that happened to us, we now have an extremely powerful slave organization with a personal vendetta against us."

"Nothing that we haven't dealt with before." He gave her a quick hug.

"Yes. But I have a feeling that things will be different from now on."

"Different, same. Won't matter as long as we are a family." Diarmin bounced to his feet and headed out of the lounge.

Most likely to his workbench. Lenore tried to be comforted with their usual routine, but now that the mission was completed, she had time to worry about the other things she had shoved to the side.

Like...how big was this slave organization and how badly would they want the Keltons? And, even worse, the hints that the Xa'ti'al were involved with them. Lenore shuddered. She wanted to know the details. Were they working together? Was it only a few Xa or the entire group? Was it recent or had the contacts been established for years, maybe decades or more? While her first thought was to delve further into the mystery, her newfound emotions were telling her to get her family as far away from both as quickly as possible.

"Found one," came the shout from the direction of Allison's room.

Lenore shoved her worries to the side to see what the next job had in store.

Acknowledgments

There are always so many people involved in the process of bringing a book into the world. First thanks go to my writing buddies, Shonna Slayton and Sarah Chanis, who stuck with me from beginning to end, not to mention constantly encouraging me and editing more than I could ever ask for. And a shout out goes to all the AZ Dreamweavers. Simply being around these fabulous writers energizes my determination to keep writing.

A huge thank you goes out to Christian Bentulan for the awesome cover.

Also, many thanks to my wonderful friends who gave me the emotional support needed to write a book.

And, finally, a simple "thank you" is not enough for my family. They are my inspiration and motivation. My Mom for always believing in me, and especially my kids who shoved me back on track when life tried to drag me away.

Be on the lookout for the Kelton's second adventure in book two:

The Case of the Dead Priest

Photo Credit:

About the Author

K. A. Bledsoe's writing journey began at the age of six with a story about kids growing up on a space station. Even through other jobs like scooping ice cream, shoe salesman, pharmacy tech, band director and parenting, writing has been a constant.

The author currently resides in Arizona and continues to pen stories in all genres despite the distraction of two cats underfoot and the occasional bobcat or roadrunner strolling through the backyard.